THE

GEOFFREY DAVID WEST

Text copyright © 2024 Geoffrey David West

All Rights Reserved

For Olga with love

This novel is entirely a work of fiction. Real events are referred to. but related matters described here that are not in the public domain are completely fictitious and bear no relation to anything that has actually happened and are not in any way intended to suggest that the facts known about the real events are incorrect in any way whatsoever. Likewise, real people are referred to in passing, but no fictional character is intended to bear any resemblance to anyone, living or dead, and if there are any accidental similarities these are entirely coincidental.

ALSO BY GEOFFREY DAVID WEST

Sean Delaney Mystery Series:

Black Ice
The Irish Goodbye

The Jack Lockwood Mystery Series:

Rock 'n' Roll Suicide
Doppellganger
Sheer Fear

And regular free short stories/podcasts at:

www.geoffreydavidwest.com

ONE

Top-floor corridor, Albany Court Apartment Block, Bradford, Yorkshire

A rainy night in January

The burglar's fist smashed into my mouth. There was that buzzed-out muzz I remembered from my days as a bare-knuckle boxer. The ring-ting-zing in your head, the second's headache and blackness. The taste of blood.

I got a right swing at his face which mashed his nose and knocked him backwards. But the corridor was in darkness, causing my grand kick to his balls to go awry, simply launching him into a stagger across the floor to pick up the hefty length of four-by-two timber that had been leaning against the wall amidst the decorators' detritus. I couldn't back away fast enough as he swung it at me viciously, hard enough to kill.

The whack to my guts almost knocked me off my feet, and as I retched, feeling my spine smash against the wall, the lights came on and I got a grandstand view of his deadly backswing, saw a nightmare close-up of swirling timber grain, leering as it came to pulverise my face.

Suddenly there was an echoing *boom* in the corridor behind him.

Time stood still.

There was a shower like rain behind his head, anointing his sparse grey hair and balding pate with an oozing liquid that was as red as a haemorrhage.

At last he collapsed to his knees, stunned, still grasping the timber. Coughing and choking, I managed to lean down, grabbed the other end of the beam and battering-rammed it into his chest, hoping to snap a rib or two. The impact knocked him over, so that he fell, sprawling backwards, down the stairs. Tumbling and crashing and smashing all the way down to the landing below, a disparate jumble of legs and arms and agony.

The corridor lights went out again. When they came on, I saw a little old man in front of me, clutching the jagged remains of a broken bottle in his right fist, staring down to the stairs below, where our would-be burglar was limping and stumbling down to the lower floors and Albany Court's entrance vestibule. Then we heard the door slam after he rolled out into the freedom of the cold dark night.

"Are you okay?" the small man asked me when he came closer, dropping the broken bottle, his hand on my arm, concern in his eyes as he looked at my bloodied face and helped me to my feet.

"Yes, thanks," I told him, spattering blood and wiping the redness from my numb split lip with the back of my hand as I trod into the shards of broken glass, almost sliding on the sea of red wine. I ran an exploratory tongue around my teeth, relieved to feel nothing loose. "That was a mighty fine way to use a bottle of wine."

"Well, happen it slowed him down a bit." The little fellow smiled, revealing a single front tooth in a bright-eyed face where a beard lurked like a silver surprise around his chin. All he needed was a Father Christmas-style hat and he'd be a dead ringer for one of the Seven Dwarves. "The bugger still got away though, didn't he? Come on, mate, let's get you downstairs to my flat. You can clean yourself up while I call the coppers."

"I'll not say no. That fella had a right hook to die for. You've got a rare chunk of courage to tackle him."

"Nay, lad, Bradford's pretty dull of a Saturday night, reckon you've given us a bit of excitement." He gave a short laugh. The timed corridor lights went out, and he nipped up to the wall and pressed the switch to turn them on again. My good-natured pal looked to be a nimble-footed man in his fifties, dressed in a mismatched blue track suit and trainers covered in mud stains that had once been white.

"So that man was trying to break into the flat where you've been living," he commented as we descended to the ground floor. "I've seen you coming and going for the last couple of days. By heck I'd not fancy living there – did the agents not tell you that the last fella hanged himself in the living room?"

"The living room? I heard it was the kitchen," I told him.

"No, mate, the living room. He were dangling there like a sack of spuds, tongue stuck out, face all bloated-like and blue. I can still see the poor beggar, swinging to and fro, fair give me the willies for days. I tell you, I'd not fancy sleeping in that place. Have you moved in then?"

"Not exactly."

"What's that supposed to mean?"

"That's a good question."

"By heck, trust an Irishman to talk in bloody riddles!"

I cast my mind back to my trip down to Cornwall, ten days ago now. Had Molly been the one who'd persuaded me to try to wash away the stink of the family's dirty laundry?

Or had it been my own obtuse, stubborn curiosity that had made me jump into the quicksands that were about to close over my head?

I guess I'll never really know.

All I really found out was that once I got involved in the mystery, it was bigger than I could possibly have ever imagined, dating back almost a century. And that people much more powerful than myself, including government ministers and billionaires, had far too much to lose to let me win.

And that unless I got the right answers, I'd be coming home to Whitstable in a box. . .

*

Ten days earlier

Triplinghoes Estate, Mevagissey, Cornwall, England

I gripped the steering wheel and stamped on the brake.

But I still crashed into the unicorn.

I'd misjudged the hasty left turn, my old Land Rover veering onto the grass and giving the large stone ornament a terminal whack.

It wasn't an auspicious start to the meeting with my prospective client, Sir Martin Trefus. He'd invited me to his Cornish estate to discuss commissioning me to do a portrait, and since he'd said it was an urgent job, I had driven nonstop for hours and I was feeling bleary, weary and banjaxed. I got out of the car and knelt down to examine the damage, discovering the two halves of the unicorn lying sideways on the grass.

"Oh my Lord, what have you gone and done? That thing were two hundred years old!"

I looked up to see a tall young woman, who was

walking purposefully across the grass. I got the vague impression of a red mini dress, the longest brownest legs I'd ever seen and a Shetland-style pullover with a zigzag pattern stretched tight around lots of curves. I did a double-take when I looked at her lovely face with its big-eyed stare, peering out from the mane of blonde hair. In that first moment I was sure that I'd met her before, but for the life of me, I couldn't remember where.

Smashing a statue and some kind of weird déjà vu experience? What a start to a sunny Saturday.

"I'm sorry." I stared down at the broken sculpture as I got to my feet. "I really am so sorry."

Then, to my amazement, she began to laugh. "Well, I ain't sorry, mate! I been wanting to smash that horrid little fucker for years, I have! Blessed if I know why my husband insists on putting it on display here. Look." She came close to me, clutching my arm, enveloping me in a tidal wave of sweet perfume. "Let's you and me put the bugger back and no one'll even notice. I promise you," She leaned even closer. "Right good at secrets I am, and I won't tell anyone if you won't. Deal?"

This weird conspiracy with the intriguing mystery lady seemed like a crazy and exciting fantasy, especially with the tantalising déjà vu feeling when I'd seen her face, that crazy notion that we'd met before. Our strange, unspoken pact was sealed when we lifted the base section of the statue back up. It comprised of legs, bottom and mid-section on a square plinth. Then we picked up the top part, resting the chest, head and front limbs and lower stomach onto the base, where it sat neatly, its upper hooves held aloft, single horn challenging as if it was up for a fight.

"There, now, ain't he just as good as new, with his lovely little thrusting horn? What a rampant little rascal he is!" She laughed again, bent down and gathered some muddy soil in her hand and smoothed it along the crack, and around the rest of the sculpture, making the break virtually invisible. "Right, mate. I'm guessing you're Sean Delaney? And when you're not smashing up horrible old statues, you paint people's portraits?"

"That's me right enough."

"Good to meet you, Sean. I'm Molly. You park up, then I'll take you inside. My husband's fair spitting feathers to see you, been waiting all morning, you're late!"

From Miser's Lane, the tree-lined approach road, Triplinghoes Hall had been hidden from view until my ill-fated final sharp left turn. Suddenly the clouds gave way to a burst of bright sunshine and I could drink in the joy of the sight of the beautiful building's stone façade with its many windows that blazed and sparkled in the sunshine like outbreaks of dirty fire. There were castellations at roof level, with red ivy clinging to the walls, turrets and a central portico with grand stone pillars where the huge dark timber front door looked large enough to withstand a siege. If Sir Martin Trefus wanted me to paint his portrait, there was a good chance that he might want me to live here for a couple of weeks for the sittings, which was an enticing prospect. From the little I'd seen of it so far, this part of South Cornwall was a fine place right enough, even in winter. Clean beaches, clear blue sea and tiny villages with narrow streets, where seagulls squawk and strangers smile. At least that was what I was guessing, for I'd not seen the place before today.

Half an hour later, when I was sitting on the lumpy sofa in the large gloomy ground-floor drawing room, I was reminded of my old granny's mantra 'Nothing is ever as good as it seems'.

"We were told you were a talented portrait painter,"

The Bad Hail Mary

little Sir Martin Trefus began, leaning forward in the huge, floral chintz-covered armchair that seemed to bury him, and fixing me with his glacial stare. "And we would like to use you for a particularly sensitive project."

Use me? Oh sure, that put me in my place right enough from the start. But if there was a job on offer it wouldn't be the first time I'd had to put up with an uppity client who treated me like a lickspittle. I'd been told it was *of the utmost urgency*, so I'd dropped everything and left my home in Whitstable, Kent and travelled right across England to be here, slept in a motorway service station car park on the way and completed the journey overnight. I was shattered, with an aching back, muzzy headache and a mouth as parched as sandpaper. Yet there'd been no offer of tea, coffee or breakfast.

What's more, none of these shenanigans made sense.

After getting the phone call out of the blue, Googling 'Sir Martin Trefus' had revealed to me that he was the major shareholder of the famous art gallery and antiques auction house, Rackhams International, of London, New York and Italy, not to be confused with Rackham's, a well-known Yorkshire department store. He mixed in elite circles of the art world, and would be on familiar terms with most of the top-class portrait painters there were in England, indeed in Europe and America too.

So why would he want to employ a relatively unknown portraitist like me?

How had he even heard about me?

Despite my exhaustion I was beginning to get used to the musty smell of ancient furnishings, old timber and crackling logs in the open fireplace as I sat opposite him and Molly in the huge front room of ancient Triplinghoes Hall. Sure the old house was a contender for one of them 'most haunted' TV shows, where prune-faced investigators march around spouting shite into tape recorders and pretending to be scared. Triplinghoes was the real deal right enough, and its grand drawing room had one of the highest ceilings I'd ever seen, intricately patterned chinoiserie-style wallpaper and obviously valuable furniture, including what appeared to be a genuine Chippendale sideboard and chairs that were uncomfortable enough to be centuries old. I noticed that the thick once-cream carpet was frayed to threads in some areas, reminding me that most of the mega rich aristocrats I've known never throw anything away if it contains a shred of usefulness. It was a cold day in January, and despite the roaring log fire I couldn't stop shivering, wondering if I was heading for the flu.

And for sure, short, sixtyish Sir Martin was a sorry specimen of manhood, right enough. He had thinning silver hair, a lean wizened face that never cracked a smile and indeed he seemed to emanate an air of the deepest misery. His Pringle cashmere yellow jumper and brown jodhpurs and riding boots didn't match his sharp features and gimlet-eyed stare behind frameless spectacles, his face housing a set of nondescript features that seemed to melt into the soggy floral fabric of his horrible armchair. Assuming that he was commissioning me to paint his portrait I wondered how I'd be able to bring life to those dead cold eyes and presence to those wizened features. His dark wet flabby lips put me in mind of a slavering boxer dog.

Mind you, painting a portrait of Molly Trefus, or 'Lady Molly' to be more exact, would be grand sure enough. She was to my right, perched in another geriatric armchair, seemingly young enough to be his daughter. Molly was not only easy on the eye but tall and statuesque, several inches higher than her puny, stick-limbed husband, almost my own height of six foot one, and her tight red skirt allowed a view of muscular brown thigh, where her long red fingernails tapped restlessly. I supposed that wearing summer clothes all year round made sense if the heating bills were paid by a rich husband. Lady Molly Trefus sure had the kind of pizazz that can make a portrait zing. Firm but sensitive large mouth with an occasional uplift at the corners, deep-set blue eyes and flaxen hair, falling to her bare freckled shoulders. Boy oh boy, Molly Trefus certainly was something. . .

And even more troubling, her face was already a guest in my head. Why oh why was that?

Where the hell had I seen her before?

The memory was tantalisingly close, yet a million miles away.

"Well, I've got a lot of experience as a portrait painter," I answered gloomy Sir Martin, realising that however poorly I felt, now was no time for levity, or false modesty. "I can give you references of satisfied clients—"

"I don't need all that nonsense, you've already been recommended or you wouldn't have been invited here," he snapped. "I understand you're Irish?"

"So I am."

"Mm, well, never mind," he went on, as if I'd confessed to an addiction to hard drugs. "So, Mr Delaney, I'd like you to paint a portrait of my son, Darius. A large portrait to go on the wall, here, over the fireplace. It has to be something grand and striking – large, as I say, ideally his top half or maybe full figure, whatever you think best."

"Does he live here?"

"No."

"So where would I be expected to go for the sittings?"

"Bradford, in Yorkshire."

"No problem."

"Not true I'm afraid," Trefus replied, shaking his head. "There *is* a huge problem."

"Which is?"

"He's dead."

TWO

"Excuse me?"

I looked from one to the other, momentarily baffled.

"I told you it was a sensitive project." His face creased into a frown of irritation, as if I was being deliberately obtuse. "Listen, please, Mr Delaney, because I'll only say this once. My son Darius hung himself in his flat in Bradford three weeks ago, on Christmas Day in fact. You won't have read about it in the newspapers because I've got a certain measure of influence in high places, and was able to get a D-notice issued – that's an embargo on journalists, instructing them not to report on it."

Fuck it, does he think I was an ignorant Irish yokel?

His wet flabby lips trembled fractionally, as if he was on the verge of breaking down. "Darius's flat is still packed to the ceiling with his possessions, and I just can't bear to set foot in the damned place. The apartment has to be emptied and sorted out, but I can't use a house clearance company. I've heard that in addition to being a portrait painter who isn't exactly inundated with commissions, you are also a painter and decorator, and you're not averse to turning your hand to manual work."

"I earn a living where I can."

"Quite understandable. Well, the fact is, Molly and I have no really good likeness to remember him by," he went on. "Apart from a few photos of when he was a boy. Nothing recent, because we haven't kept in touch with him in the past few years because he's been living a strange kind of life, the kind of life we don't approve of. And he's been living with the girl who we hold responsible for wrecking his life and driving him to his death. We have no intention of having anything to do with her."

I nodded into the silence, using the interrogation technique I learned while I was in the police – wait and see, let the silence stretch for ever and a day, rather than jump in with a comment that breaks the flow.

"So, Mr Delaney, if you're agreeable, we'd like you to go to his flat in Bradford, search through his belongings and find all the recent photos and videos and pictures on his laptops that there might be. Darius was a filmmaker, and there are a number of his films with plenty of footage of him. I'd like you to use these items as you think fit, to paint a large head and shoulders, or even full body, portrait. Is that possible?"

"Well, obviously painting someone from life is best, but there are computer programmes to enhance good photos and I could extract stills from the videos he's made and do the same to those. It's not ideal, but it could be feasible."

"Good." He sniffed and frowned. "For various reasons I won't go into I – that is we—" he turned to Molly, who was staring at me, "—want the place emptied as soon as possible, so we'd like you to take all the images you might need to produce the portrait to your own studio to do the portrait there, and put everything else into storage and do the entire operation as quickly as you can. Any obvious rubbish, or sensitive material, please just get rid of it as you think fit – destroy it, shred it, burn it or whatever."

"Sensitive material?"

"For God's sake, don't keep interrupting me!" he snapped.

Keep your hair on, you old bastard.

"Okay."

"I realise this is a lot to ask, uprooting you from your life and commitments in Kent for a while, but we'll pay you well for your time and your expertise. I'm afraid you'll find things are pretty basic there, Darius and his wretched girlfriend, *Paula Swan* – [he pronounced the name in a sarcastic jeer] – appear to have lived there like pigs and everything is just as it was when he died, and the Swan creature went raving mad and ran away to God knows where, and it seems she's put herself out of touch, and I gather she was not even prepared to attend the funeral. Police took his body and cleaned away. . ." He paused, breaking down for a moment. ". . . all traces of what happened."

I nodded in relief, wondering why he always referred to the girlfriend by her first and second names, and why he seemed to hate her so much. "How much stuff is there?"

"It looked like a lot when I went there that one time, I'm afraid. Clothes, books, papers, goodness knows what, strewn all over the place, the two of them lived like farmyard animals. It's basically just the contents of the rooms in a two-bedroomed flat, that are spread around everywhere. Frankly it's utter chaos. Any furniture can be left. It's just we need someone we can trust to handle his papers and personal items, which I warn you might be somewhat, well shall we way, *unsavoury*. I gather that Paula Swan was into using all kinds of – er – *items* to spice up their sex life. You get the picture?"

"Uh-huh. Don't worry, Mr Trefus," I deliberately avoided saying 'Sir Martin', because it's particularly galling for an Irishman to crawl to English aristocracy. "Nothing shocks me."

"Really?" He stared at me as if I was mad. "Well, I can assure you that plenty still shocks me, I'm afraid. Anyway, the person who recommended you was a high-ranking police officer, who told me that you yourself were once a police officer, and that you can be trusted implicitly, and that while you're working there, you'll keep the premises extremely secure at all times." He coughed and looked at the floor. "Actually we have reason to believe there may be illegal substances there too, class-A drugs, and possibly even illegal items such as weapons, perhaps even large amounts of cash – so you'll understand why it has to be someone whose integrity is beyond question. So you see why we need to have someone who can be trusted implicitly not to sell stories to the press, and who'll also take security of the premises seriously. And if you find anything incriminating, we'd be grateful for your discretion. Of course we wouldn't ask you to break the law by handling anything illegal yourself, just to inform us so we can organise its disposal."

"And apart from that, there's another reason why we don't want a house clearance company to clear the flat," added the sexy Lady Molly, looking at me with an unflinching gaze as she slowly uncrossed her legs, succeeding in dragging my attention away from her troll of a husband.

"Another reason?"

Skinny Sir Martin looked as if he was going to be sick, his words escaping like prisoners reluctant to be released. "When he was younger, Darius went through a phase of what I believe is referred to as *gender confusion* or some such nonsense. He experimented with wearing women's

The Bad Hail Mary

clothing, posing partly naked as if he was a woman, dressing as a drag queen and I gather he performed in comedy clubs. I think there are a number of photos of him appearing like this. If the press got to see some of his costumes imagine the headlines: *Rackhams Director's Suicide Son dressed in drag, was he a man or woman? The heir to the Rackhams fortune doesn't know if he's Arthur or Martha?* I'd be grateful if you find any such photos if you'd destroy them."

"Okay. So let's get it nailed down. First of all you want me to go through his possessions to find photos and films and pictures to use for the portrait, put them separately to take home and use. Then box up everything else and put it into storage, apart from obvious non-compromising rubbish which I get rid of discreetly. Then, I take all the material to use for the portrait back to my studio and try to produce a life-sized portrait. Additionally, I tell you if I find firearms, drugs or anything else that's illegal, and you get it dealt with. Then I go ahead with the painting, at my own home. Plus I have to dispose of sex aids, clothes, obvious rubbish, and destroy completely any compromising material or pictures so as to make sure they don't fall into the wrong hands. And security is top of the agenda at all times."

He nodded, looking happier now. "Thank you, Mr Delaney. We were told that you catch on fast. I think we're very lucky to have found you. We've already had a locksmith fit a fully monitored alarm, cameras and state-of-the-art new locks, to make the place as secure as possible. But having someone trustworthy actually living there while there are still items in the place is the best security there can be."

"*Items?*" I asked him. "Precisely what items are we talking about, now?"

"I don't know for sure."

"Explosives? Poisons?"

"Good God no, of course not!"

"Lots of valuable jewellery or money then?"

"I doubt it."

"Yet you seem to be expecting someone to break in."

"No. It's a possibility, that's all."

"If there's nothing valuable, why would anyone want to break in?"

"That's not your concern." His voice was barely above a croak, and I noticed the twitch of his upper lip as he stifled back tears. Suddenly, he waved his hands in front of his eyes and blinked. I picked up on his emotion. The surge of strange warmth I felt towards him took me by surprise.

Maybe he wasn't as much of an arsehole as he'd first appeared to be?

As if he'd read my thoughts he went on, "Look here, Mr Delaney, can we start this meeting all over again?" His voice was breaking, he was almost in tears. "Please forgive me. Can I call you Sean? And you must call me Martin, *please.* I've behaved badly, I've no excuse apart from the fact that I'm at my wits' end with all this terrible business. I'm aware that I've been rude and condescending, and I'm very sorry, believe me I don't mean to offend you, I'm immensely grateful that you've travelled right across the country to help us at such short notice. And I'm also aware I might have sounded abrupt with you just now, you must make allowances, you see it's down to the stress I've been under this past month. Goodness." He gave a weak smile. "I planned to make a good impression on you, yet I've made a bog of it, because I'm upset and nervous. Cards on the table? The fact is that we've heard that you're a good, decent reliable guy, who we can trust implicitly. And if you'll help us we'll be eternally grateful, and you'll be doing us a big favour. Will you help us, Sean? I realise you're a busy man, it's a difficult project when there's no live model to work from, and packing items and putting them into store is a job that I'd not normally ask someone with your talents to get involved with, so feel free to employ trusted assistants if you want to help with the manual work. Staying in a place like a pigsty where someone's killed themselves isn't a pleasant prospect for anyone, but I hope you're not overly sensitive. And of course Bradford in January isn't exactly sunny Barbados. But please will you help us?" His voice cracked to a halt and he stopped speaking for a few moments while he swallowed and regained control. "We'll pay you whatever you want, money isn't an issue." His head dipped into his hands momentarily. "You see, it could all have been so different. Three years ago, Darius approached us, explaining that he'd gone through a difficult phase in his life, but that he wanted to set things straight. He was one of my two children, and Celia, my daughter, isn't exactly, er, well I won't go into all that, let's just say she is unsuitable to take over Rackhams as my successor, or indeed to take any kind of family responsibility. I was delighted when I realised that I could leave my business interests to him, perhaps even retire and let him take over in a few years if he shaped up. Rackhams International is a private company, not in public ownership with shareholders and so on. I own fifty-two per cent of the shares, so nominally I have full control and I am the CEO as well. Rackhams International has been in my family ever since 1946, when my father stepped in to rescue the 300-year-old firm from bankruptcy, effectively buying up the business and taking control. The war, you know, it ended lots of businesses like ours. Anyway, Darius had given up all that gender confusion nonsense, and finally he was on the right track. He'd been accepted as a mature student at

Brasenose College, Oxford, to read History of Art and Business Studies to prepare himself to enter Rackhams at the bottom, to learn the ropes and earn the respect of our people. A year ago we were over the moon, everything was going fine. Then, before the university term began, he went to Brighton and had the damn silly idea of getting a tattoo, and Paula Swan was the tattoo artist he used. And that was the beginning of the end.

"Once the fair Paula got her bloody claws into him she filled his head with nonsensical ideas, made him decide against further education and persuaded him that he had the talent to earn his living as a filmmaker, exposing scandals if you please, blazing a trail against government corruption around the world, publicising the efforts of the climate change activists, animal rights, anti-royalists, you name it. Paula belongs to a narrow political group who are dedicated to destroying the capitalist system and regards Rackhams as representing all the values she hates. She destroyed his prospects of any kind of proper future and now she's made him take his own life. Another condition of doing this job, Mr Delaney, is that you have no dealings with Paula Swan, should she come back to the flat for any reason. If she objects to you being there, refer her to me."

Should I have gone ahead, with all these warning lights blazing away? Of course not. But money was tight, and it sounded like what I call a 'cut and thrust' job. One of them projects where you go in, work hard, get out and get paid. *Beggars can't be choosers,* was another of Granny's sayings.

"And there's another thing," he went on, scowling like a man on death row. "This is an extremely sensitive time for my company. We're in talks with an American competitor, Apperline Webb, discussing a merger of our two companies. This is currently top secret, until all the I's are dotted and the T's crossed. But it's essentially a done deal, and when this merger goes through officially, in a few weeks hopefully, the value of Rackhams International, or RI, will go through the roof – as will Apperline Webb's monetary valuation. We'll be known as Rackhams Apperline Webb International, or RAW International, and we'll be indisputably the biggest art and antiques auction house in the world, coupled with our famous London art gallery, which attracts thousands of visitors. As I say, we're a private company, so I and the other directors will be making quite a killing in monetary terms. So this deal is in the balance – bad publicity would scupper it. So at this delicate stage, the last thing we need is newspaper headlines."

"I see."

"So, Mr Delaney." He shook his head and began to try a tentative smile that I'm guessing rarely came out of his closet. "Sorry, I mean, Sean. What do you say?"

"Doing a painting from photos alone doesn't always work well. What if I do the portrait and you're not satisfied?" I asked him.

"You're a talented portrait painter, aren't you?" he answered. "So it's hardly likely, is it?"

"Sorry, Martin, but without a live model I can't guarantee a good result. Sure, I've never even met him, have I?"

"Fair enough. If in the unlikely event we don't like your work, you'll still be paid. As I told you, money isn't an issue."

"*Please* do this for us, Mr Delaney." Molly pitched into the conversation, leaning forward in her seat, entreaty in her eyes. I couldn't help picturing this unlikely pair together, this skinny little midget and the big sexy amazon. It sure seemed like a cockeyed match.

"I've not said I won't," I told them. Then I turned towards her. "May I ask you something that's worrying me, Mrs – er, I mean, Lady Molly? Your face is familiar."

"Is it?"

"I'm sure I've seen you somewhere. Have you been on TV?"

"Not recently." She smiled again, another real 100-watt job, that caught me fast in her web. "But a long time ago you might have seen me splashed across the tabloids as *Molly the Maiden* because I sailed alone around the world in my yacht, the *Molly Maiden*. I was famous for about a week in 2001, my fifteen minutes of fame. You might remember me from that." She looked across at her puny, pinch-faced elderly husband. "But after all the fuss died down I was back to being grateful for a job in the corner shop in the little Cornish village where I grew up. Martin was a widower when I met him ten years ago. He rescued me from a dead-end job and a dead-end life."

"Excellent news," Martin Trefus said briskly, getting to his feet and rubbing his hands together, apparently keen to curtail my conversation with his wife. "Thank you very much indeed. We don't need to delay you any longer, I'll get my secretary to email you with all the details."

"Could I ask you something?" I began, staying put on the sofa, deliberately delaying my abrupt dismissal.

He gave a curt nod, hovering there, clearly hoping I'd leave.

"You say he was a filmmaker, he made films that were critical of institutions, highlighting criminality, that kind of thing."

"I believe so."

"Are the police certain that he killed himself? Could he have been murdered? If he was making films about exposing

The Bad Hail Mary

wrongdoing, he might have upset people who wanted him silenced."

"No, the police never suggested anything like that, nor do we consider it likely. Listen, Sean, please don't get the wrong impression and read too much into this situation. My son wasn't a trailblazing journalist, driven to expose the wrongs of society, willing to take on powerful enemies for the good of humanity. He certainly was not driven by any moral crusade, even if Paula was a dedicated iconoclast. He wasn't political in his soul. He was a pragmatic kind of person. He wasn't particularly clever, he wasn't stupid, he wasn't really special in any way, he was just *our Darius*. He always had certain emotional issues, had trouble making friends, he was bullied at school, not one of life's natural leaders, poor boy. He was just an easy-going lad who'd got himself into a mess, and had finally pulled himself together until that bitch destroyed him. He was bumbling through life quite happily until his world was turned upside down by an evil girl from the gutter, who had a shady past of her own, and encouraged all this filmmaking and political conscience nonsense. She encouraged him to take drugs that addled his brains, and which eventually drove him to talking his own life."

"You said there might be illegal substances in his flat, bundles of cash. If he was dealing in drugs he might have owed money to dangerous people," I went on. "Could drug dealers have been involved in his death?"

"Look, Sean." His voice had taken on an angry edge of irritation. "Rest assured, I have it on the highest authority that the police have gone into every possibility surrounding his death, and suicide is the only answer. I've spoken to the Chief Constable of the West Yorkshire Police Force, and as a favour to me, he hasn't searched the flat, which he would have been obliged to do if there had been any suspicion of foul play. He appreciated the fact that no good would be served if it was made public that my boy had taken drugs and broken the law. Don't get any ideas about investigating his death, the professionals have examined every conceivable scenario already, and the coroner has already recorded the death as suicide, which in the fullness of time, the inquest will no doubt concur with. We'd just like you to do as we ask. Nothing more, nothing less."

"Fair enough. . ."

Lady Molly, or just plain old Molly as I preferred to think of her, took my arm as she led me through Triplinghoes' entrance hall, the shadows made by the huge stained glass window on the landing at the top of the grand staircase flickering reds and greens across the burgundy coloured walls.

"We're right grateful, Sean," she whispered in my ear in her thick Cornish accent, before looking round to make sure her husband couldn't hear her words. "Don't mind old misery-guts, he ain't no good at showing his feelings, I reckon all them generations of stiff upper lips have a lot to answer for." She turned again, to check the old man wasn't behind her. Pitched her voice deep-down low. "How would you like it if I come and see you in Bradford?"

"Would your husband be cool with that?"

"Ice cool. In fact he's been ice cool for years now, if you get my gist. Besides, who's going to tell him?" She paused and licked her lips. "I can come up and help you sort through the photos and such of Darius, and I can tell you which are the most like him, which are the best ones for you to take and use. And when you start on the painting, I reckon I can give you tips on Darius's face, make sure you're capturing his looks properly and if it's a proper likeness. I'll come on my own. Martin's away in London a lot, so there's no reason for him to know nothing about it, is there?" She leaned closer, her perfume making me lightheaded. I could see the moistness of her lower lip as she talked, and the flick of her tongue against the small but enticing gap between her two front teeth, which seemed incredibly sexy. "I reckon we got something in common, Sean. Summat tells me you're good at keeping secrets, aren't you? I reckon we might have a right good few secrets to keep later on, you never know, do you? Just like that broken unicorn. *Our first shared secret.*" She touched my hand and gave it a gentle squeeze. "That's gonna be the first of many."

"I'm sure I've seen you before. Not on telly, but in person. I'm sure I know you."

Her face lit up. "That's 'cause you've seen me in your dreams."

As I drove away, out of Miser's Lane, and out into the much wider road, Fothergill Way, I pondered on the reality that I already had a girlfriend back home in Kent, and what's more flirting with a married woman was immoral and stupid. It wasn't even as if I really liked her, or could envisage falling in love, because I knew deep down that the attraction was purely sexual. No, Molly wasn't enticing, she was simply sexy, nothing more. While I was deep in thought I almost missed seeing the red Alfa Romeo sports car that suddenly appeared out of nowhere.

There was a screech of brakes as it tried to stop, but it was too late.

My body slammed forwards, jerking into the seat belt's stretch as the red car crashed into me, head on.

THREE

I sat there for a few seconds, shaken by the crash and jerk of the belt cutting into my chest.

But the windscreen still held, and my old Land Rover had been built long before safety air bags had been invented. The chunky green bonnet appeared to be undamaged, and I knew that the front bumper of my car had been designed to resist the odd bump and scrape, for it was solid unyielding steel.

I was looking at the driver of the red sports car, who was staring back at me, as stunned as I was: a dark-haired woman with sunglasses like saucers. She slowly opened the door, stepping into the road.

"I'm so sorry," she apologised. "It was my fault, I'll pay whatever you tell me it costs."

I got out and inspected the damage. Sure, the Landie was practically untouched, but her lovely Alfa Romeo seemed to have a dent in its radiator grille, just above the bumper.

"Forget about it," I told her, smiling in spite of myself, because the situation seemed almost comical. I knelt down to examine the front of her vehicle. "My car was built for off-roading, jungles and battle zones, but yours is more of a lounge lizard. I'm guessing you might need a new bumper."

The Bad Hail Mary

"It hardly matters, I don't care. Look I ran into you for a reason. Can we talk? Please?"

"Who are you?"

"Listen, I'll back off and reverse into the next layby on the left, and you park there too? Please? *I really need to talk to you.*"

"Do I have a choice?" I yelled back.

My day for lunatics, I guess.

She reversed much too fast, but with flair and panache, swerving into the passing place in the narrow lane. I parked in front of her car and found she was already on her feet, waiting to talk to me.

"Mr Delaney?" she asked breathlessly. "I know that's who you are, because I overheard them saying you were coming this morning, and I just missed you at the house."

"Sure, I'm Delaney. Who are you?" I got out and stood in front of her.

"I'm Celia Trefus, Darius's sister. Have you agreed to go to that filthy Bradford flat and sort things out there?"

"That's confidential."

She was everything that Molly was not. Where Molly was wild, untamed, rock-star flamboyant, with free-flowing clothes and who-the-hell-cares behaviour, Darius Trefus's sister was respectability on steroids. But nonetheless she was extremely attractive. Shortish, perfectly styled jet-black hair cut in a fringe, with faultless make-up and style with the kind of inherent breeding that money can't buy. She looked to be a few years older than me, around forty, with deep, interesting grooves around her mouth and the kind of face you can't forget, that made you long to see what the huge black sunglasses were hiding. The bright red expensive-looking fur-collared coat clung to her slim figure as if it had been tailor made, and it swung open to reveal tight black leather trousers, whose high-belted waist accentuated the curve of her hips.

"Look, Sean, you've travelled all this way at a moment's notice, so I'm guessing you're strapped for cash, and you really need this portrait commission. Am I on the money?"

I was aware of her appraisal, and remembered that my old black sweater had seen better days, as had my well-worn blue jeans, tatty leather jacket and scruffy old trainers. I had a three-day growth of beard and blearily tired eyes and my hair made a haystack look neat as ninepence.

"The thing is, Sean, I'm warning you, they're not telling you everything. This job…"

"This job?"

"It's a crock of shite."

I laughed. "I didn't know sophisticated ladies like you used language like that."

"Ladies like me can be hard as nails, Sean, as I'm guessing you know very well. Don't underestimate me, just because my father told you I'm inadequate, the profligate daughter he's ashamed of. Things are much more nuanced than that, there are all kinds of other reasons he doesn't like me. But I'm no idiot, I promise you that. I'm a successful architect with a thriving practice, and I've been a town councillor for three years now. I see the world for what it is and I don't suffer fools. Believe me, my father and that trollop he married want to use you to do their dirty work. Do you really want to be their paid skivvy?"

Use me. There was that patronising word again. It hurt the first time, and it hurt even more now. Hey, but maybe I'm just too sensitive?

"Sorry, Sean, I don't mean to sound arrogant or to denigrate your talents. But you must realise that the portrait commission is just a carrot to lure you in to doing the main job, which is clearing out that flat. No offence meant, but why else do you think they're asking you to do it, when they could get any number of famous portrait painters to paint Darius's portrait?"

"Listen, Celia. As you rightly say, at the minute I'm not exactly deluged with commissions and I've got bills to pay. So I've been offered a job that isn't going to be a breeze, but I'm going to grit my teeth and do it."

"Even if it lands you in a shedload of trouble?"

"Trouble? What sort of trouble?"

"I don't really know, that's the worst of it. You see, Darius was his own worst enemy. He had everything he could ever have wanted, then he screwed it all up. That's the story of his life. Poor darling Darius was up to all kinds of things, he was confused. Confused with his sexuality, with his career and mixed with all kinds of people who made use of him. Many of them not to be trusted, they regarded his good nature as idiocy. And believe me, Darius was no fool."

"What kind of people?"

"Dangerous people who will stop at nothing. They're not telling you everything. There are risks involved."

"Such as?"

"If I knew that I'd tell you, believe me. The thing is, I believe in karma. And luck. Darius had everything you could ever want in life, as I just told you. But he was unlucky. Surely you've known people like that? It seems as if God's given them everything they could have wished for: wealth, intelligence, decent parents, good health. But somehow whatever you try and do, things always come along and knock everything to crap. All his life he's been unlucky, he's always landed himself in messes. Do you think it's lucky to have to worry about the possibility of gender dysphoria?"

"Jeez, I couldn't even spell it."

"It's a very serious issue with some people, so please don't make fun of it. And now, finally, he's landed himself in the worst mess of all. The end of everything. I loved him, you see, I always tried to look after him, but he stopped listening to me and insisted on going his own way."

"When he met the devilish Paula Swan?"

"She's not the bitch they've told you she is. In fact, Paula was good for him in a way. I liked her actually. I like anyone who follows their own beliefs. And she loved Darius. She *really* loved him." She took off the sunglasses, and moved closer, something in her unblinking stare a bit disquieting, but those smile lines beside her mouth were definitely intriguing. "Listen, Sean, I'm going to take a big chance and be completely honest with you. You see I'm good with people. People are *my thing*, I can sense what they're like by just looking at them. And you seem nice. Kind – the sort of person who wants to help people. And if you'll forgive my saying so, you seem so nice you might be a bit naive, a bit too *trusting* if you know what I mean. The trouble with thinking the best of people is that they always let you down. Dad and Molly are using you. Darius got himself into serious trouble when he got himself involved with Paula, and settled into that squalid flat in Bradford. You know about his sexual difficulties, God knows what their personal relationship actually was. Was it even sexual? I have no idea. And that flat, it's chockfull of shitty rubbish and junk, it's awful, it smells, it has a horrible atmosphere, and, believe me, Sean, if you had any idea what it's like, you wouldn't want to go there. You should just go home now and forget you ever came here."

"Look, Celia, I appreciate the warning."

Her mouth wasn't a mean one, it was a big one, wide

and generous, with full red lips. But it was nothing like sexy Molly's mouth, with the gap between her front teeth that I couldn't quite forget.

"Look, Sean, if you insist on going ahead, for goodness sake don't swallow all that guff my dad said about friends in the police hushing things up for him, Father has no powerful friends, he's a law unto himself, he's a good man, he tries to do his best, but you can't believe anything he says. This proposed merger with Apperline Webb is all he really cares about right now, and he's desperate for it to go ahead, and daren't risk any scandals coming out that could piss off the Americans. The Apperline Webb directors are hard-line Christians from Tennessee, who regard even ordinary homosexuality as connected to the devil, and as for gender confusion, they'd think it was satanic nonsense. And for goodness' sake, don't trust Molly, whatever you do. She trapped Dad into marriage and she hates him almost as much as she hates me. Don't think you're the only one she flirts with either, though not many of her boyfriends are as drop-dead gorgeous as you are."

She came up to me, looked into my eyes and took the lapels of my ancient leather jacket in her hands.

"Believe me, Sean, Paula wasn't a bad influence. But Molly? Molly is poison with passion. She'll use anyone to get what she wants."

"And what does she want?"

"Goodness only knows." She dropped her hands and her gaze moved down to the ground for a few moments. "Generally she wants what's best for Molly, I'd say." Where Molly's perfume was raw and earthy, Celia's scent was pure class, something fine, fascinating, fragrant and rich, redolent of top class hotels and fancy drawing rooms. Everything about Celia spelt money, power and assurance.

She looked up into my eyes again. "Take my advice, Sean, please. You may have promised to do this job, but all you have to do is tell them you've had second thoughts, you don't even have to face them. Just go back to Kent and tell my father you've changed your mind. Honestly, Sean, I'm warning you, you don't want to get involved in my family secrets."

"Family secrets is it?" I smiled at her. "Look, as I say, Celia, I appreciate your concern, but I've been in a few tight spots before and I've always come out fine and dandy. Why are you making such a song and dance about this? Sure it's nothing but a glorified house clearance, with a portrait commission tacked on at the end, and there'll be a good bit of crack in it for me. That's all."

Caroline has various issues had been what Martin Trefus had said, and the tell-tale signs were there. The absurd way she'd waylaid me, the jerky frenetic way she had of talking, the swift mood changes, the ice-cold stare as she held my gaze without blinking. Yet I liked her. And something about her seemed deadly sincere.

"So you won't take any notice." She sighed heavily and replaced her sunglasses. "Well, call on me if you need my help." She handed me her card. "If you land yourself in trouble I doubt if there's much I can do, but I can try. I'm on your side."

"Thanks, Celia, but I don't understand. What's all this about *sides*? And if there are goodies and baddies, why do you figure I'm one of the good guys? You don't even know me."

"Oh, Sean." She stared into my eyes again. "You came to London at eighteen to train at the Slade School of Art, you tried to set up as a full-time artist, failed, got married, then joined the police to get a steady income. Your wife died and when you had to leave the force you decided to try and make a go of it as a portrait painter, and now you get commissions here and there and fill in the rest of the time as a painter and decorator."

"Why the hell have you been checking up on me?"

"Why do you think?"

Without another word, she swept into her car and drove away, leaving only the tail end of her scent, a whole barrage of questions and a big decision that was nudging me, just like the childhood memory of the rasping tickle of the tongue of my old lazy dog when he licked my face.

Her business card said: *Liberal Democrat Town Councillor, Celia Trefus, RIBA, LLS, award-winning Conservation Architect*. With an address in Sennet Cove, and her website and phone number.

Out of curiosity, I put her website address into my phone and was impressed at the results. Her past renovation projects included a grand moated manor in Somerset, and a huge Victorian church in Stoke-on-Trent, along with more modest extensions and after-fire renovation jobs on mainly big detached houses. Celia was a successful, clever and interesting woman, no doubt about it. How did that square with Sir Martin's dismissal of her as 'having various personal issues'? It didn't make sense.

Of course, now I know that I should have taken Celia's advice. I should have cut and run before the dangerous mystery sucked me under.

But I didn't.

Because everything about this job intrigued me, tugged me in like I was a nail slamming into a four-ton magnet. And wouldn't you just know it, by the time my car had edged back out onto Fothergill Lane, en route for the busy A-road that led to the motorway, I was well and truly hooked. Maybe it was sexy Lady Molly who, despite my misgivings, had exerted some kind of a hold over me, and the nagging obsession that I somehow already knew her.

Why is the forbidden thing you know you cannot do, the thing that is the most tantalising?

But I plunged straight into the maelstrom. As my granny used to say: 'The boy was born a fool. He always makes the wrong decisions'.

FOUR

Albany Court, Bradford, two weeks later, resumed from earlier

"You were there when they found Darius Trefus's body?" I asked the old man who'd saved my life just now, as we walked down the stairs to his flat after my fight with the would-be burglar.

"Oh aye. See I were watching telly and I heard his girlfriend, Paula, screaming like a ruddy banshee, so I rushed upstairs to see what were going off. Stumbled into the flat and there he was. Poor lass running around like a headless chicken, screaming her head off, woke up the entire block, I reckon. She flitted soon after that."

"Flitted?"

"Ran off for good, did a bunk. And I can't say as I blame her. You've taken over the flat then?"

"No."

"But you're living there?"

I stopped walking. "Not exactly. I'm Sean, by the way. Sean Delaney."

"Good to meet you, Sean. I'm Billy Furness. Hey, it looks like we're in luck!" he said, peering at the ground near my feet. "That bloke has left his calling card!"

Sure enough there were five or six business cards scattered on the lower stairs. I had a vague memory of ripping his jacket pocket as I'd dragged him away from fiddling with the lock on Darius's door in the seconds before he spun around and whacked me. I picked one up. It said *Gordon Dallorzo, Dallorzo Private Investigators Inc.* with a local address, here in Bradford.

Ten minutes later, I'd cleaned up my face in Billy's bathroom, noting that my split lip would be twice its normal size for a while, I'd be talking in a painful lisp for the foreseeable, and I'd not be winning any beauty competitions. My almost-beard dark stubble cloaked a face that, to my surprise, a fair few women had told me was attractive, but I always reckoned that the break in my nose and the scar on my chin from my bare-knuckle boxing days scotched any pretensions to handsome. But who knows what appeals to women? Sexy Molly and Crazy Celia appeared to like my looks, it seemed.

After sluicing my face with water and drying myself, I went back to Billy's comfortable living room, where beige monotony was the order of the day. Beige carpet, beige walls, beige doors and a comfy sofa and armchairs that wished they were beige, but were unaccountably sky blue. Now I'd swilled away the blood, and was holding a bag of frozen peas against my face, I felt a pleasant island of calmness and companionship in my world, that had been so lonely for the past few days. I was sipping Billy's lovely brandy cautiously, avoiding the injured part of my mouth, as the throbbing intensified. We were both bitching about the idle prick of a police operator, who had answered with more than the usual abundance of gloom and apathy: "We'll send someone if we can, but being Saturday night, we're a bit pushed. And you say they didn't gain access to your neighbour's flat, didn't even damage the door, so there's no point giving you a crime report number if you're not making an insurance claim. And even though he assaulted you, he'd probably say that you attacked him first." Their attitude had been so negative, it seemed hardly worth even telling them about the business cards we'd found. I made a mental note to sort it out on my own.

I decided to tell Billy everything. Maybe I was breaking a confidence, but I reckoned after his help, he deserved to know the truth.

*

"So did the lovely Molly come to see you?" Billy asked, after I'd filled him in on everything.

"I never said she was lovely."

"Nay, lad, you didn't need to say it – it were there in your face when you spoke about her."

"No, she never kept her promise," I told him sadly. "I'm guessing it was all for the best, you know? Look, Billy, how about coming upstairs with me? I want to show you what I've been doing."

Magnolia walls, dark grey carpet, vulgar leather three-piece suite that had once been white. The faint scent of stale urine, rotten food and old socks still knocked me sideways, even though I'd opened the windows wide on the first day and had had time to get used to it.

Darius had apparently been an aspiring filmmaker, but the bland reproduction prints on the wall were nothing but the junk posters on sale in IKEA. I'd made order out of chaos, and sorted items into piles, and rammed a lot of junk into black bags. On one wall was a corkboard, on which were pinned copies of newspaper articles that featured Darius and the girl I'd seen in photos and assumed was

Paula, plus various others in a crowd, holding banners. There were several bookcases, the books spilling over onto the floor. Plenty of newspapers and magazines and clothes in the bedroom that I hadn't got around to dealing with yet.

I recalled that going into the couple's bedroom had been a bit of an ordeal, and I had felt awful invading their privacy. The unmade bed, the tawdry gashed wallpaper, the discarded socks and underpants on the floor, the burgeoning clutter of female clothing bursting out of a half-open drawer, tights and an old pillowcase hung over the back of a chair, dangling there like a dirty shroud. In the kitchen there were several stinking half-eaten takeaway meals on paper plates that I'd thrown away on my first day, as well as a couple of saucers, overflowing with the remnants of spliffs, smoked down to half an inch. Saucers with traces of white powder. There was a lingering odour of racy perfume, stale food and body odour. It still had an air of seediness and decay that I hate to remember. Small wonder that for the two nights I'd been here I'd camped out in a sleeping bag on the living-room floor.

"It was a hell of a mess when I came here, the day before yesterday," I told him, recalling the floor-to-ceiling mess, stuff all over the floor, dirty clothes, books, newspapers and assorted detritus that I'd managed to get under control.

"And did you find anything incriminating here?"

"Didn't I just! Take a look at this." I took him across to the cheap chest of drawers and opened the top one. There, resting on a folded pillow case, was a large black automatic pistol, a Glock 9mm.

"Blimey, is it loaded?" asked Billy, staring at it.

"I don't know and I don't care," I told him. "I'm not touching the bloody thing or getting anywhere near it. Last thing I want is to put my fingerprints on the gun, when for all I know someone's been shot and killed with it, and if it's found to have been in my possession I could get a mandatory five-year prison term. I'm leaving it where it is, for Trefus to get rid of. Anyone asks, I've not seen the fucker."

"And the money?" Billy was staring at the rolled-up bundles of cash fastened by rubber bands that were beside the gun.

"Same as the gun. I put surgical gloves on to put the cash into that drawer and that's where it stays. I'm not handling it. Nor am I going to handle the plastic bags full of white powder, here," I opened the adjacent drawer to show him. "Trefus, with all his friendly police contacts, can break the law."

I took him to the bedroom, where the assembly of large black dildos, strange black plastic objects that I guessed were what are called *butt plugs* and pink coloured plastic penis-style vibrators were strewn around on the floor near the bed, alongside strange-looking items of frilly underwear, thigh-high shiny black leather boots and a vicious-looking whip. The discarded clothing, some of it unwashed, was going to be crammed into black bags as soon as I could get around to it. There was a huge pile of flat-pack Shurguard boxes from the eponymous storage facility, ready to be assembled to receive all the other items not destined for the council dump.

That was when I remembered the large white van that I'd noticed was often parked outside Albany Court, saying MAN WITH VAN on the side. Beside the mobile number below it was the name *Billy Furness*.

"Look, Billy," I asked him. "Is that your van outside?"
"Oh aye."

"Do you fancy earning a few quid? Helping me pack this lot up, and then giving me a hand transporting the boxes to the furniture store depot in town? You can charge what you like, Sir Martin Trefus is paying."

"Never turn down any work, me. You're lucky too, happens I'm in between jobs."

"At last things are finally going my way," I remarked, leaning back in the chair. "Tell me, Billy," I asked him, "Did you ever meet Darius?"

"Saw him a couple of times on the stairs, chatted to him once or twice. Seemed a nice enough bloke. Looked kind."

"Kind? Sure, I suppose he looked kind right enough," I observed, remembering the rather weak-chinned spectacled face I'd got to know after looking at the photos and videos I'd looked at over the past days, though to my regret there were precious few of them. He often sported an eager-to-please smile and struck me as an inoffensive, rather weedy-looking bloke, who looked as if he'd like to pat stray dogs and look after old ladies. I hadn't shown Billy the other photos of him I'd found, when he'd been wearing frilly knickers, full women's make-up, and very little else. He had been posing for the camera in what he thought were provocative poses.

"What about Paula Swan?" I asked Billy.

Billy's smile faded. "Hard. Sexy. Tattoos up to her arse and a smile like a rutting polecat. Summat a mite dangerous about her, I reckon. I'd not say she looked kind. Nay, nowt kind about our Paula."

Of the handful of pictures I'd managed to find, the majority were duos, Darius was standing side by side, or had his arms entwined with, a dark-haired girl whose tattoos spelt edgy, and whose moody glare spelt trouble. If there is such a thing as breeding or 'class' he had that indefinable upper crust style, whereas Paula had all the class of a mangy mongrel. Indeed they were an oddly matched couple: Darius, the slightly weak-chinned effete character who didn't look as if he had the gumption to knock the skin off a glass of hot milk. And Paula, with her coarse features, bulging tattooed biceps and thrusting breasts, looking several years older than he did, and about as delicately feminine as a charging bull. However, her face was pretty memorable. Indeed it was etched into my memory by now.

Paula had the face of all the prostitutes and strippers I'd ever seen.

"Now you mention it, he looked a bit of a Jesse in these photos, but he weren't that wet really," Billy went on. "Bit of a Paul O'Grady type, you might say. Looked a bit of a whoopsie, soft as shite. Until you knew him a mite better, then you got the feeling there were summat tough about him, summat *unyielding,* like. And to have a bird like Paula I reckon he couldn't have been as soft as he seemed. Happen he could probably stand his ground with the best of 'em if he had to."

"The trouble I've got is, there aren't many photos of Darius here," I confessed to Billy. "As far as I can see there are hardly any clips of him in the films either. I'm worried that with what I've been able to find, I just won't be able to do a decent portrait."

"Aye well, not down to you, is it?" Billy pointed out. "All you can do is your best. And if that's not good enough, it's too bad."

"But it's professional pride, don't you see? I'm a portrait painter, and if I fuck up a portrait, my reputation is down the pan."

"Old Yorkshire saying, Sean. You can't build a castle out of clay. You can only do what you can do with what you've got. Nowt more, nowt less."

We sat in silence for a few moments, while Billy looked around, staring at the piles of stuff.

"So all there is to do now is get rid of the rubbish and pack up everything else in the boxes and put it in store," said Billy, casting his eye around the room. "We'll have this done and dusted in no time, mate."

"That's grand."

I thought of the large detached house in Streatham Vale, South London, where I'd agreed to clear junk from the house and to decorate the main hallway for the son of an unpleasant character, Neville Peasgrove, a career criminal who had died recently, the house about to go on the market. It was a big job to do on my own, but it would pay pretty well, but before that, I planned to go home and see my girlfriend Julia, a sculptor, who had a teaching post at Canterbury School of Art, and lived close to my home in Whitstable.

"You're right, Billy," I told him. "But before I finish off here, I'm going to pay a visit to Gordon Dallorzo, the bastard who whacked me. No one hits me and gets away with it."

*

Bradford is the kind of town where tall grime-blackened red-brick Victorian buildings glower down at you like great dark cliffs, making you as miserable as the poor souls who slaved away in its grizzly woollen mills two hundred years ago must have been. Centenary Square, in the town centre, is where they've made efforts to stagger into the twenty-first century, and it looked like Bradford had taken a deep

The Bad Hail Mary

breath and smiled at its success. On one side of the square there's the grand grey stone City Hall, with its pretty lights shining out of the windows in the evenings, and it looks a bit like a grand old castle. Centenary Square's opposite side has a modernistic City Library, a Wetherspoons pub called Turls Green, and a range of eateries that lean out over the square's grey cobbles and concrete as if they're jeering. Last night I'd wandered around the town for a change of scenery, and ended up feeling even more depressed. If only I'd befriended Billy before now, as he'd said I could have had a few jars with him to pass the time, instead of mooning about alone, thinking about why my prospects were so desperate that I was prepared to do such a shite job, just because of the accompanying portrait commission. Which, because there weren't enough decent photos to work with, was likely to end in disaster.

Billy was right. I needed to be businesslike. Drive home, get this portrait done, deliver it to Sir Martin and Lady sex-on-legs Molly, then crack on with the house-decorating job I'd been offered in London.

However, in a lot of ways I liked Bradford. There was a fine square cathedral, the modern Broadway Shopping Centre, and ritzy glass-fronted shops that shouted 'look at me' to anyone passing. Now, in winter, there was a fine cold drizzle in the air and my breath formed clouds of smoke in the sky as I walked. However, in spite of its grimness, there was also something distinctly formidable about Bradford, and something likeable too, like an ugly troll with a kind heart. Maybe it was the square-ness of the buildings, the width of the pavements and roads and the gritty determination of the surroundings that tried to make you feel small, yet somehow failed. I headed towards the area of Bradford known locally as 'Little Germany', a nest of streets just east of the Broadway Shopping Centre, where in the 1800s German wool merchants built imposing warehouses. I walked down Church Bank and turned right along Peckover Street, searching for the place.

When I reached the address for *Dallorzo Detective Agency* there was no sign of it, until I eventually found a narrow door beside a fish-and-chip shop, bearing the handwritten notice with the name. A fat ginger cat paused to stop and stared at me, narrowiug his eyes as if he was smiling. Taking it as a good omen, I knelt down to stroke the puss, whose fur bristled appreciatively before he shook his back leg, peed on my shoe, and stalked off.

I rang the bell and waited. Just as I was about to give up, I heard a bad-tempered, "All right, all right, I can hear you! Come on up!" from the speaker at the same time as a buzzer sounded. The ill-fitting door shuddered as I had to push hard to get it open, and a steep uncarpeted wooden staircase yawned in my face as I trudged up to the first floor, the aroma of second-hand frying fish making me feel a wee bit nauseous. At the top, on the landing, there were cobwebs and dust on the windowsills, and in true Philip Marlowe style, *Dallorzo Detective Agency* was etched into the glazed top half of a dirty door with a brass handle that was so cold it froze my fingers as I turned it. Once through the door I saw an empty desk, overflowing with papers, with no one in sight.

When I felt the blow on the back of my head, I couldn't stop myself falling.

FIVE

The dirty carpet kissed my face.

But I was up and away from the stench of mud and dirty feet. I rounded on him, landing a pile-driver punch into his guts.

Dallorzo expelled a breath and spluttered, his face turning red as he rode the pain. Then he spat on the floor and staggered away, hobbling to the chair behind his desk.

I needn't have worried about fighting him again. His right arm was in a sling, and the black eye with its rings of redness made him look like a panda. My attempted ambush was clearly his last throw of the dice.

"Shit on a brick!" he grunted. "You!"

"Sure it's me. You left your calling card on the stairs," I told him. "Just after you made friends with the wine bottle."

"Fuck! Your mate's an arse-crazy lunatic! Still got a headache, haven't I? At the hospital they reckoned I was lucky not to have a skull fracture."

"Why were you breaking in?"

He glared at me, then sat down, indicating that I should take the client's seat opposite him. Gordon Dallorzo had a white dressing taped onto his bald forehead, and the eye that wasn't black was wickedly bloodshot. The unruly moustache fussed around his mouth, flowing like that of a Mexican bandit, apologising for his fat, red, veiny nose. The knuckles of his right hand were swathed in thick bandaging.

The office was painted a muddy grey and the floor had a threadbare brown carpet that had shrunk away from the skirting board in disgust. The room was as cold as it was outside, and the clutter of papers and two open laptops on his desk spelt a mind that thrived on chaos, or showed that I'd arrived in the middle of a crisis.

"Look, I'm sorry, but I've got this temper, see?" he muttered. "Like just now. Get carried away, don't I? Back then, when you hit me, I saw red, like. But I'm a daft bugger, I really shouldn't have hit you with that lump of timber. I'm glad you're not too badly hurt."

"Now I'm feeling like a spiteful shite, hoping you're hurting from here to next week!"

"Don't worry, I were lying, weren't I?" He managed a creaky smile. "I wish I'd bust your bollocks."

"One tip I learnt when I did the bare-knuckle boxing as a boy in Ireland," I went on. "The human skull is as hard as granite, and your knuckles are pretty sensitive fellas that can crumble like a bag of potato crips. If you're glove-less you should always wrap a cloth around your punching hand, unless you can aim for something a mite softer than bone, like I did."

"Aye well I squashed that fat lip of yours, didn't I, Paddy? You're lisping like a soppy five-year-old."

"And we've got a good video of you on the CCTV. Me and my new pal are thinking of giving it to the police. And I'm guessing that the last thing you want is to get on the wrong side of the law."

"Oh good God above. Fuck me sideways."

The Bad Hail Mary

"Love to, Gordon, but I'm busy right now."

He moaned, sliding back into his chair.

"I don't want to cause you any trouble, but I will if I have to. And my name's Sean, not Paddy."

"So what do you want, *Sean*?" He deliberately exaggerated my name, to accompany his nasty leer.

"I want to know why you were trying to break into Darius Trefus's flat." I took out my mobile and held it in my left hand, right hand poised to dial. "If you don't tell me I'm calling the coppers right now."

He looked doubtful for a few moments.

"I'm not as big a bastard as I seem," he mumbled. "I hit you because you surprised me, and I was nervous as fuck, keyed up to break in and them locks had me mazzled, no way could I tumble them, so it were useless anyway. Then you turned up out of the blue, and I just went crazy. Believe it or not, but I've never done owt like that before, I tell you, mate, it were an act of madness. This were a first and a last."

"So why did you do it?"

"Money of course. Business has been terrible these last months," he grunted, and moved aside his mound of papers so I could see his face properly. He put his chin into his one free hand, closing his eyes in misery. "Look, pal, fact is I'm desperate, that's God's honest truth. It's got so bad I don't know which way to turn. On Monday these fellas came to see me. Offered me five thousand quid if I broke into the flat and found them any mobiles, laptops, diaries, owt I could get hold of that might have information. They said no one were living there, there'd be no trouble, like, then you turn up out of the blue. Happen I took a big risk, but I'm up the swanny. God's honest truth as I'm sitting here. The wife's going to leave me because I can't afford the mortgage and they're on the verge of chucking us out on the street, This office rent's not been paid this month, they're repossessing my motor. It would have been a lifeline."

"Who were they?"

He shrugged. "Just a couple of ordinary-looking fellas."

"Age?"

"In their forties I'd say. One of them were a whoopsie – bit of a pansy way of talking, and he had an American accent."

"Their names?"

"Tom Cruise and John Travolta." He took his hand from his face, then used a smile that didn't match his ice-cold eyes. "Sometimes clients want to keep their identities secret. Not my business to pry, is it?"

"How were you supposed to contact them?"

"They gave me a mobile number. I was to do the job, then call them so they could come up here and collect the stuff. I've not even had the guts to call them yet, to tell them it's all gone tits up."

"This doesn't make sense," I told him. "The person who lived there is dead."

"All they told me was that there were no risks, the place was deserted, I just had to go in, grab what I could find and fuck off out of it."

"So if he's dead, why would anyone pay five grand to get his phones and laptops and papers?"

"How should I know? To me, it were just an address and a flat number, and nowt else." He shrugged. "Who was he then?"

"I'm not at liberty to say."

"Was he into summat illegal? Some murky business like prostitution or drugs?"

The Bad Hail Mary

"I really don't know."

"Well thanks to you, I've lost five grand and my hand's fucked." He blinked a few times, then looked at me seriously. "And just what has any of this got to do with you anyway? Just who the hell are you, and why were you hanging around the flat?"

"I'm a portrait painter. The tenant's parents have commissioned me to paint his portrait from videos, photos and anything I can find in the flat."

"So you've got keys to the place?" He smiled properly for the first time, a glint of hope flickering in his eyes. "Aye well, sounds like your lucky day. I reckon we could help each other out. You get me what they asked for and we'll go halves, eh?"

"Not a chance. And in case you've got any ideas of trying to break in again when I've gone, I've cleared out any phones or laptops I can find and removed them."

"Bollocks on an icicle."

"Tell you what I will do though."

"Yeah?" He was leaning forward enthusiastically.

"You can give me that mobile number for Messrs Cruise and Travolta."

"Can't do that, can I? Ethics."

"And in return I'll not give that video of you attacking me and Billy to the police."

He glowered at me and wrote the number on a pad and tore it off and gave it to me.

"I should have hit you harder."

"I wish you had, you might have smashed your knuckles even more."

"Wait a minute," he went on, staring at me. "I've just worked it out. You were being paid to clear everything out of the place, and guard it, to make sure nothing went missing. Did the parents reckon there might be a break-in?"

"I guess they must have done."

"They used you as a right mug, didn't they? Didn't even warn you. I call that a head fuck. A right dirty trick."

I shrugged, half agreeing with him.

"So what's so important about the dead guy's possessions?" He scratched his moustache with a grubby fingernail.

"Search me."

"You wanna watch yourself, mate. Take it from me, summat's not right here. Dodgy as fuck."

*

Summat's not right here.

As I sat in the Land Rover, Dallorzo's words ran through my mind like a slow-burning fuse, underpinning my mood of deep depression that had gone on for days now.

Next day I bought a pay-as-you-go phone with its own SIM card, and dialled the number that Dallorzo had given me. It rang for a long time, and I decided to play it by ear.

Until:

"Good morning, Rackhams International, Fine Art department, Graham speaking."

A warm, welcoming, plummy voice. I pictured a snazzy suit, an old-public-schoolboy tie, arrogance on a stick, entitlement to a wonderful lifestyle enunciated in every juicy, suck-my-cock-if-I-tell-you syllable.

"Morning. My name is Gordon Dallorzo. I've got the things you asked for."

Would my Irish accent give the game away, I

The Bad Hail Mary

wondered? I'm rubbish at accents, and mimicking Dallorzo's flat northern tones was beyond me.

"The things I asked for?" He paused. "Sorry, sir, I'm not with you. This is Meredith Gilliard's phone. It rang for such a long time I answered it for him. I think you need to talk to my colleague, Meredith. Can I take a message, or get him to call you back?"

"Yes, thank you." I wondered what to say, then decided to chuck in a big bad firework. "Can you ask him why he wants Darius Trefus's personal computers and phones? This is your Chief Executive Officer's dead son we're talking about. Sir Martin Trefus's boy."

"Sir Martin? Computers and phones?" A brief laugh of embarrassment. "I'm afraid you're not making any sense at all."

"Mr Gilliard paid me to steal them. I need to know why he wants them before I'm willing to let them go."

"Listen," he replied, rock-solid cool. "Look here, I don't know who you are, but all this has got nothing to do with me. I'll get Meredith to ring you back on this number."

The line went dead.

Fool, I thought to myself. I'd blown it. Should I warn Gordon that his friends would be coming calling?

No. Best to leave things be. Ten minutes later my phone rang.

"Hello? Mr Dallorzo?"

"Yes."

"This is Tom Cruise." This time the accent was American, lilting, a faint jeer at its frayed edges. "We need to talk."

"Why do you want Darius Trefus's phones and computers?"

"That's not your business. You get your money when I collect the goods. Can I come now?"

"No, not now. I'll call you in a few days."

"But—"

"Your name is Meredith Gilliard, you work for Rackhams International in the Fine Art Department, and your colleague wasn't surprised when I talked about you employing someone to break the law." I threw in the lie to rattle his cage. "I'd say your bosses at Rackhams would be mighty interested in that. I'll come and see you."

"Wait! *You can't do that!*"

"Why not, Mr Gilliard? Have you got something to hide?"

"Hide? Hey now, how dare you? Just what the freaking hell are you talking about? Do you know who I am?"

I hung up on him, then took the SIM card from the phone and threw both of them away in the rubbish bin.

Murkier and murkier.

Rackhams International Auctioneers? Why were people at Sir Martin Trefus's company interested in spying on his dead son? Who was Meredith Gilliard?

Curiosity killed the cat, and despite what my friends referred to as my inherent nosiness, whatever mess Darius Trefus was mixed up in, it was none of my business. It was time to draw a line under the whole mess, go home to Whitstable, do the best portrait as best as I could, deliver it to Sir Martin, grab the cash and put it all behind me.

I phoned Sir Martin's office number, got his PA, and explained about the break-in to her, telling her that Meredith Gilliard had authorised it. It was Trefus's company and Trefus's son, so it was up to him to sort things out with this character Gilliard. Maybe Gilliard knew about

The Bad Hail Mary

Darius's murky lifestyle, and wanted to blackmail his boss with evidence?

But before leaving Bradford, I decided to pay Gordon Dallorzo one more call.

The next morning was dull and dreary, and rocking up to Dallorzo's miserable office was something I did not relish, but I did feel that I ought to warn him about what I had done.

Outside, as I arrived, I was just in time to hear shouting.

Gordon Dallorzo was being dragged into the back seat of a white Datsun, and it looked like he was putting up quite a fight to get away.

"Hey!" I yelled, racing after the car as it picked up speed, but it was gone before I even got close. I recognised Dallorzo in the back seat, struggling to get away from his captors.

Panting for breath in the road, I took note of the car's number plate, aware that I had put the detective in danger.

The outer door was open, so I climbed the stairway that led to the upper floor and several offices, including his. As I had expected, there was no answer when I rang the bell to Dallorzo's dirty office. However, to my surprise, it looked as if the door was ajar. Cautiously, I opened the door, stepped inside and looked around.

"Who are you?"

The woman yelled from the open doorway. She was cowering away from me, the phone in her hand, backing up against the wall.

"Get out! I warn you I'm ringing the police right now!"

"Hi, I'm sorry, I have no right to be here." I stepped closer to her, holding my hands up in the air palms outwards, to indicate that I was no threat. "I came to see Mr Dallorzo and the door was open, so I came inside."

"I'm his wife!" she snapped at me. "I was with him just now and two men just burst through the door and told him to come with them. He protested, but they more or less frogmarched him away. I'm just about to call the police."

"I just saw a car leave here – your husband was in the back seat. Yes, Mrs Dallorzo, I agree, I think you ought to call the police. If he was going somewhere in a hurry, why wouldn't he tell you what was happening?"

"Yes, why? Oh goodness, he's been doing some very strange things recently, mixing with some dangerous people." She made the call.

We waited until a lone policemen arrived. He listened to what she'd said, but gave a bored response, telling her that she should contact them again if she didn't hear from him after forty-eight hours. When I told him about the car outside, and gave them the registration number, he wrote it down, but I could tell he wasn't really listening.

Mrs Dallorzo looked worried when I left her, and I felt a deep sense of guilt and dread, wondering if my interference in his affairs might have upset someone, and Dallorzo was paying the price.

Something was wrong.

Very wrong.

*

It was late and I was more tired than I can ever remember. But to my relief it looked as if, finally, the awful part of the Trefus job was pretty much done and dusted.

Two days ago, Billy and I had separated every last photo, memory stick, computer and video from the rest. Then we'd got rid of the obvious rubbish in black plastic bags and taken these to the local dump and then packed up everything else into the Shurguard boxes and taken them all

The Bad Hail Mary

to the Shurguard depot in the seamy side of town, home to industrial estates and wide roads and lots of traffic.

Along with the photos, phones and laptops, I'd gathered masses of papers, that might or might not have been of interest to his family, and taken a lot of them with me, along with the many controversial images of Darius dressed in drag, that I was going to burn in my back garden. There was one file of papers that particularly interested me, that I'd chanced upon. It was from Ancestry.co.uk, and had the details of Darius's DNA results, with several pages of suggested cousins.

The most curious thing I noticed was that it seemed that he was seventy per cent of West German ethnicity. And his most likely first cousin was also German, a man from Vienna, Austria.

This seemed crazy, as according to Wikipedia, Sir Martin's family appeared to come from a long line of English people, as did his mother. It seemed that Sir Martin's father, Walter Trefus, had been a rich businessman from the West Country, who in 1946, just after the war, had stepped in with a lot of cash and an art collection as a 'saviour' of Rackhams Auctioneers, a company which had been going for 300 years, but which had fallen on hard times and happened to be on the verge of bankruptcy after the vagaries of World War Two. I'd read about these top-drawer auctioneers, such as Sotheby's and Christie's. They apparently made their principle money out of the 'Three D' life events: death, destitution and divorce. Clearly, the only explanation was that Sir Martin's father Walter's first wife must have had a German boyfriend, or indeed Sir Martin had not been Darius's biological father. That was something that my miserable employer wasn't going to like, but luckily it wasn't up to me to tell him. He would find the Ancestry documents along with the other papers in the storage boxes he would have to dispose of.

I'd said goodbye to Billy and paid him in cash, then phoned Mrs Dallorzo. She was very worried, for Dallorzo had not been home last night and she hadn't heard a word from him. She had filed an official missing persons report with the police, and was phoning around all his friends and family, was even phoning all the hospitals in the area. Guilt gnawed away at me, for if he'd been silenced or worse, it could have been because of my phone call to Meredith Gilliard.

Driving from Cornwall to my home in Whitstable in Kent was one heck of a journey, even when it was broken by a night's sleep in a service station. As the motorway miles ticked away I realised that what I longed for most right now was to see my girlfriend Julia to discuss this weird project that was finally almost at an end, apart from the most difficult part: painting a portrait from a handful of lacklustre photos. I was in trouble, for there really were hardly any decent images of Darius to work on, about five at most. And I realised that my infatuation with Molly Trefus was utterly ridiculous, more like schoolboy behaviour. And on the spur of the moment I decided to call in on Julia, to bring myself back to reality.

Julia was a teacher of sculpture at the Canterbury School of Art, and I hadn't known her long, but so far the signs were good. Even though I hadn't warned her I was coming, I knew she wouldn't mind me dropping into her flat in Canterbury to stay the night as I'd done many times before, I'd even got my own key, as she had mine. I should have phoned her to check, but my mobile had run out of battery, and I couldn't be bothered to search for the charger

The Bad Hail Mary

lead. I'd take a chance – if Julia was out it didn't really matter, I could simply go on home.

After all the theatrics of the past weeks, it was reassuring to reflect that Celia Trefus's warnings of doom and disaster had been unfounded and quite soon I'd be able to get started on the portrait of Darius. But, sadly, I wasn't hopeful. Never having seen him in life, it wasn't going to be easy to bring him alive in a portrait with the few paltry images I'd got.

And the motorway miles were messing with my head. I was still seeing the red-brick edifice skyline of Bradford, the traffic jams of the city, grand Centenary Square and its wild rural outskirts, then the miles of road rolling under my wheels on the tedious journey south. I longed for the fresh clean air of seaside Kent, the smell of the ocean, the squawk of seagulls and the stretches of pebbles and sand and the lovely sunsets over the water. Julia's suburb of Canterbury was one of those areas of semi-detached thirties houses, and, tired out after my long drive, I found her house, no 64, when it was already dark and parked in the road opposite.

As I walked across the road I saw that her car was in the front drive, and I checked my watch to see that the time was 10pm. I knew she didn't go to bed early, and as I entered her front porch I thought I heard a noise from beyond the front door, as if it was coming from above, the upper floor.

What was it?
OOOOOH!
A scream.
Wild and shrill. Animal and scared, a woman screaming out in agony.

Someone was attacking her!

SIX

Fumbling with my bunch of keys for her Yale, I found it and jammed it into the slot, swung the door open and sprang into the hallway. Here, the screaming came again, wild and plaintive and terrifying. I heard a male voice mumbling something incoherent.

Taking the stairs three at a time, I made it to her bedroom where the noise was coming from, and charged through the half-open door, ready for anything.

I stopped short. There in front of me was Julia, naked, and strapped face downwards by the wrists and ankles onto the four corners of the bedposts, legs apart, her bottom thrust upwards in the air. Above her a large naked man held a black leather whip, and I could see the fresh red welts on her bare flanks.

The big bald hairy man turned towards me, shock and horror on his face, his tumescent penis wilting before my eyes.

"Mike, what the fuck is it?" yelled Julia angrily, squirming round to twist sideways, momentarily unable to see what was happening behind her. Peering out from her unkempt mane of black hair, her face was as bright red as her backside, her eyes clouded with orgiastic excitement, as she wriggled her bottom from side to side. "Why have you stopped? Fuck's sake, I told you it's enough, I'm as wet as Niagara, so why the hell don't you—"

Then at last she saw me. There was a long silence.

I couldn't have said another word even if I'd tried.

On my way out I shut the front door, trying and failing to block out the horrific memory. I thought I recognised the naked man with the whip – he looked like a guy she'd once introduced me to at a party, Mike Harbottle, or some ridiculous name like that. He was one of her fellow teachers at the college, whom she'd described to me as 'one of the idiots I have to work with'.

Emotion is a funny thing. I should have wanted to choke her to death, to scream and shout, to attack the hairy Mr Harbottle. Yet I did none of these things. As well as the fury and the pain I was feeling, there was a shred of *I told you so* in my subconscious. Julia had a regular income as a teacher, a burgeoning career as a successful sculptor, whereas I was struggling for every penny.

The idea of her having another lover was bad enough. But kinky sex and whips? Sadomasochism? How the hell had I known her all these months and had no idea she was into such appalling things? I knew that I never wanted to have anything to do with her ever again.

When I was a mile away, not far from my tiny waterfront home in Whitstable, I managed to lock my pain away, to concentrate on the work I had to do.

Get home. Try to find something to eat, and drink a few glasses of wine, then hope to be able to sleep.

Tossing and turning in bed I went through all the memories of the things she'd said to me, her declarations of undying love, how she couldn't stop thinking about me. Memories of happy days and nights together, as if we were meant for each other. Then I went through scenarios of what I'd say to her, how I longed to somehow pay her back for how she'd treated me.

Life is mostly about the varying stages of loneliness, I've found. When a friend dies, and you realise you never told them how you feel, when someone you're close to goes away and you know you'll never see them again. Or a girlfriend tells you she's found someone else. There's no sure-fire way to get over that kind of loss, the pain just seeps away gradually. The trick is always to keep busy and concentrate on work.

I decided that the coward's way out was the best. And, despite all my fancy ideas of terse, vicious words in emails, notes pushed through her door, or even a face-to-face confrontation, I knew I wasn't going to do any of those things. By 1am, I knew what I had to do. I found my phone, went to contacts and deleted her name and number.

*

The next few days?

Don't ask.

They were shit, I mean *really shit*, some of the most disappointing and depressing days of my life.

Breaking up with Julia was bad enough, but the portrait of Darius, that I really needed to finish, just wasn't working.

Never mind the fact that I'd never met him, from the pitifully few photos and stills from films I could find, I just couldn't get a real image of him in my mind. Maybe if someone had been with me to help, someone who'd known him, such as Molly, they might have been able to tell me what I was doing wrong, but as things stood it just seemed hopeless, as if I was groping in the dark.

I ran for several miles every morning, all along the coast

road from Whitstable to Tankerton Bay, the sea to my left and the buildings to my right. I ran and I tried to think, to clear my brain, to puzzle out some way of making my portrait better, but without enough photos it was just impossible. Afterwards, panting and exhausted, I rode the endorphins high, ameliorated by the aching legs and weariness.

My best friend, the local vicar Robin Villiers, was honest enough to agree with me when I showed him my effort.

"Well, maybe he was a weaselly looking bloke with a beaky nose," he tried to console me.

"I have no way of knowing what he looked like, not for sure," I complained. "That's the trouble. I was told there'd be plenty of photos of him, but there were only a handful."

"All you can do is show the father and hope for the best. You did warn him that painting a dead man is easier said than done. After all, you've never even met him, it's literally working in the dark."

"Yeah, but I had been hoping for more photos, more images to base it on. There are just these few, and in most of them he looks different, beard, moustache, different hairstyles. I even tried to use some of the ones where he's made up as a woman, but they're barely any better. As it is I'm guessing half the time."

"I thought you said he was a filmmaker. Aren't there any stills from his films?"

"No. All the content is of people he's interviewing, or things without including himself. Maybe he was shy or something. There was a factory where people were coming out on strike, a Greenpeace protest, all kinds of things. But there were hardly any bits of film with Darius on them, and those there were, were blurred and indistinct."

When I was on my own again, I reflected that there were plenty of images of Paula Swan. Paula going swimming, Paula talking to activists, Paula fighting police on a picket line. But none of Darius, doing anything at all.

So all I was left with were the photographs, some of them still as the old style transparencies (apparently he'd favoured a really old Leica), but the specialist lab I'd found had blown these up into six by ten prints and they weren't too bad. Plus there were a few digital shots on the three laptops I'd found, and on the memory card of one of the four big Canon cameras he'd owned.

The trouble was, Darius's appearance changed continually. Sometimes a beard, sometimes a 'tache. Sometimes long hair, sometimes no hair. Not to mention the ones where he'd been carefully made up to resemble a fairly attractive woman, which must have been in his 'gender confused' state. So in the end I only had about six reasonably good pictures to base my portrait on.

And, as I'd feared, while having photos of a model is an invaluable aid to a portrait painter, indeed many portraitists always have photographic back-up to a live model, a photograph is just no use as the only source for a portrait, at least the ones I had were not.

In the end I had gritted my teeth and done my best to create a passable likeness from the best photo I could find.

On the final day, when I was doing the finishing touches, I felt bitter and ashamed, knowing that it wasn't up to scratch. Oddly enough, in the time I'd spent trying to imagine the kind of man who Darius had been, I found myself liking him, feeling sorry for him. There was something strangely pathetic in his expression, a kind of desperation, and I really had the urge to help him. To find out why he had committed suicide, what terrible things had driven him to such an act. And if he'd been murdered, then I had the urge to find out who had done it, and wanted them punished. I don't know why, it was just that who else was going to help the poor bugger, now he was dead and gone?

There was nothing for it, but to take it to Sir Martin and Molly, and hope they might think it formed the basis of a portrait. On the journey I tried to comfort myself with the thought of possibly altering it under their instruction, if indeed they could tell me what was wrong. It was a truly horrible feeling to know that I'd failed.

And there was bad news from Agnes Dallorzo. Gordon appeared to have vanished into thin air, and the police hadn't the faintest idea what had happened to him. She had retained another private detective to search for him, and the man, who had been a professional colleague of her husband's, was doing the job for free, but was not at all hopeful.

I phoned the police, and finally got put through to the officer who was in charge of the case. I explained all that had happened, and how Meredith Gilliard and other people employed at Rackhams Fine Art Auctioneers had employed Gordon to break into Darius Trefus's flat after his death, and how I had contacted them, pretending to be Dallorzo, threatening to tell police what they'd asked me to do. And how a couple of days later, Dallorzo had disappeared, and I had seen him bundled into a car outside his office. All of which I had already reported to them, including the car's registration number. Did they want me to go in and make a statement? That wouldn't be necessary, the officer told me, anxious to get rid of me. I knew nothing would be done. Similarly, I gave the same details to Genevieve Dixon, Dallorzo's detective friend, but she wasn't hopeful either.

*

They say the light in Cornwall is like nowhere else in England, pure, crisp and clean so that colours appear more vivid and bright. That's why it's always been a mecca for artists, notably in the last century when Trewyn Studios was home to the artist Ben Nicholson and his equally famous wife, the sculptor Barbara Hepworth. She and Nicholson founded the Penwith Society for the Arts, which comprised Hepworth, Ben Nicholson and nineteen other notable artists, including Bernard Leach and Peter Lanyon. St Ives is still famous for its artistic community.

Now I was back in the West Country driving along, dreading the thought of confronting Sir Martin and the sexy Molly, I settled back to wondering why the character at Rackhams, this Meredith Gilliard bloke, had gone to the effort of employing a detective to nick Darius's electronic devices and papers. Oh well, it looked like it was going to be one of those mysteries you never solve. It was a puzzle that I'd been trying to figure out since it had happened.

When I'd told Sir Martin about the attempted break-in, he'd been very upset, until I'd reassured him that I'd thwarted the raid, and now the flat was completely empty, apart from the gun, the money and the drugs, which I was assuming he would take care of. The news that Meredith Gilliard had instigated the raid was something which, he said, he would look into and 'deal with'.

Had Darius discovered some racket that was going on at the firm, and was threatening to make it public? Had he been murdered to shut him up? And had Gordon Dallorzo been disposed of for the same reason? I had no way of knowing if he knew more than he had told me about, perhaps he knew some dangerous secrets.

And all of a sudden I thought about the film he'd made

about smuggling. One of the amateurish films I'd viewed was of Darius (out of shot practically all the time, therefore no use to me as a model) talking to the Rackhams agent in one of the Italian offices, discussing how he had an ancient Roman artefact that had belonged to his mother (presumably a lie), and that he knew it could be sold for more in England or America, and could they help him to do so? I knew that since 1984 Italy had introduced a law prohibiting the sale of artefacts found in their country from being sold anywhere else, because it was seen as depleting the 'natural stock of national treasures'. The trouble was that such items could command a much higher price in London or New York, giving rise to a thriving smuggling trade. All bona fide sales people and dealers, and especially auctioneers, are careful to steer clear of this illegal trade, and if it can be proved that they've transgressed the law, they can be fined or jailed for the practice. From the questions that Darius was asking the agent, it seemed that he was trying to trap the man on camera into admitting to being prepared to break the law in this way.

Had Darius discovered that particular people at Rackhams were engaged in this smuggling practice? Was he threatening to expose them to the police? If so, then it was possible that he'd been murdered, and his death made to look like suicide.

Sir Martin Trefus's estate, with its elegant mansion Triplinghoes Hall, was not far from Penzance, a bit further around the coast, near the fishing port of Newlyn and the marina where Molly had told me their yacht *Lively Lady* was berthed. I turned off the A road onto Fothergill Lane, noticing that the road was edged with trees until you reached the junction with the Devil's Dyke, that shot off to the left leading to Miser's Way. This curving swooping road led down into a valley until at the final turn, Triplinghoes came into view, the grand Georgian house that sprawled out across the sky ahead, greedily devouring the heavens, its turrets and battlements bearing testament to its main central section comprised of the shell of fourteenth-century Trewinnick Castle, that had burnt down in 1764, after which its core remained, to be bought by the famous local landowner Sebastian Grey, who had added the bulk of the building and rechristened the place.

The gravel's crunching echoed my raw and twisted nerves as my old Land Rover drew up in the shadow of a huge willow tree that stood opposite the main entrance. I looked at the statue of the unicorn, still there, despite the crack across its centre that I had caused. But luckily, although I could see the crack now, at least it was invisible from a distance.

Since the day I smashed it, so much seemed to have happened, pretty much all of it bad.

The stress of the past weeks had been tremendous, and I was delighted to think that this was going to be the end of it.

All I had to do now was face the music.

Ten minutes later there was a long silence in the living room, where I'd propped my portrait of Darius on the windowsill of the main picture window.

"I hope you don't expect me to pay for this," Sir Martin muttered quietly.

SEVEN

I swallowed twice. Licked my dry lips.

"After I'd gone through all the pictures there were precious few I could use," I explained. "I did my best."

Sir Martin snorted.

"I know it's not right. I wondered if you could give me some suggestions so that I could improve it."

"Improve it? What are you talking about, man? You're supposed to be a portrait painter, aren't you?"

"I told you it's not easy without a live model. I've never even met him, and it turned out that there were only a handful of photos for reference. I can't work miracles."

There was another long silence. Sir Martin looked as if he couldn't get rid of a bad smell in his nose.

"I don't reckon as how it's all that bad," Molly commented, staring at it. "It ain't too bad as a portrait, I mean." She went right up close to it and stared critically. "Only trouble is, it looks like someone else, not like Darius."

"Okay, it's a fucking disaster!" I snapped, getting up and striding across the room. "I warned you it might not work. I don't know what he looked like. I never met him." I didn't add that, *and you promised to pay me even if you weren't satisfied.*

"I'm sorry," I added.

"So am I. So are both of us." Sir Martin's face was a bully's flustered red. "You claim to be an expert portrait painter and you can't even—"

"I was told there'd be a number of good images to use. That was the understanding."

"No, Mr Delaney, the understanding was that you would produce a professional portrait and you've just brought us a dog's breakfast. We're very disappointed."

"So am I."

"It's not your son who's dead, is it?"

"By the way," I went on. "For what it's worth, one of those films he made, he seemed to be confronting a Rackhams agent about smuggling artefacts out of Italy, trying to trap him into admitting he'd be willing to break the law. If you've got crooks working for you, and they knew he was onto them, that might explain why they were keen to get hold of any incriminating materials from his flat. You told me there's a merger with the American company in the pipeline. Meredith Gilliard, who I told you arranged the break-in, and the other directors, wouldn't want that to be jeopardised."

"Don't talk wet," Sir Martin muttered. "Why on earth do you think that—"

"It also calls into question the manner of his death," I butted in. "If he was blackmailing someone at Rackhams they might have decided to shut him up permanently and make it look like suicide."

"I told you, the police have done exhaustive investigations, and they conclude suicide is the only answer," Martin snapped. "I've spoken to Mr Gilliard and he assures me that your story is nonsense, and he's never had anything to do with you, nor would he authorise a break-in at the flat. I've known Meredith for years, he's a good friend. I think I can trust his word rather more than yours!"

"Why would I lie?"

"Why would you pretend to be a competent portrait painter and produce this rubbish?"

"Christ, just listen, will you—"

"And, Mr Delaney, I told you that the manner of Darius's death has nothing to do with you. All we asked you to do was clear the flat and paint his portrait, which you've manifestly failed to do!"

I sucked in a breath that felt like it was laced with cyanide. In that moment I hated everything about this cursed job, the musty smell of Triplinghoes, the arrogant sneer on Sir Martin's face, even Molly's patronising smirk. I'd had it up to here.

"Well, Mr Delaney," Sir Martin said finally, turning away from the portrait to face me. "I think our business is concluded. I've already settled up for your efforts clearing the flat. At least you got that right."

"I've travelled all the way down here, twice."

"Here's a couple of hundred." The Rackhams director took out his wallet and counted out some notes, fanning them out in his palm before slapping them into my hand, as if I was a schoolboy who'd just cleaned his car. "That should cover your expenses."

"We agreed on two thousand for the portrait."

"Correction! We agreed on you doing a competent job and you've let me down. In the circumstances I think I've been more than—"

"We agreed on a price whether you were satisfied or not."

"But there was no written contract, was there?" he countered, smirking momentarily. "First rule of business,

Mr Delaney, always get things in writing. Perhaps you've been a trifle naïve."

"Go and fuck yourself."

I walked out without listening to his reply, remembering his daughter Celia's words to me: *Don't do it, you'll regret it if you do.* As I came out into the sunshine I tried to calm down, to mute my temper, but my hands were trembling with rage, and I had the urge to choke the little bastard to death.

Molly appeared, having run to follow me out.

"Don't take no notice of him," she said. "He gets upset, he says things he don't mean and he apologises afterwards. Bit like a spoilt child. Don't take no notice. Look, Sean, gimme a ride out to the marina. Don't leave like this. Let me show you my yacht."

Anger makes you do funny things. Was I really stupid and petty enough to want to get my revenge on him by seducing his wife? Molly was young, she was attractive, she fancied me and she was way out of my league.

Which made her doubly attractive.

And then there was that unfinished business. That nagging notion that wouldn't go away that I had met her before.

Today she was wearing bright blue jeans, a tight white teeshirt and a dazzling smile. She slid into the passenger seat, and I drove out of the narrow gate, not caring when I accidentally chipped some mortar from the left-side gate post.

"I was going to take the *Lively Lady* out this morning," she said, turning towards me. "How about joining me?"

"Thanks, but I'm no sailor."

"I bet you can ride a horse, can't you?"

I stared ahead at the road, the way the sunlight almost

was blinding me. "I rode a bit when I was growing up on our farm in Ireland."

"It's not so different. It's all a question of adjusting to the motion, of slipping into the rocking of the waves, as if they're a part of you, like when your horse rises up and down. Martin bought me the *Lively Lady* as a birthday present five years ago, and I go out on her whenever I can – she's berthed at the local marina down the road. Honestly, Sean, you've been cooped up in the car all this time, you're upset about the portrait and making a loss on all this business. You're angry, and I don't blame you. Going out on the sea is a tonic – the sea breeze is really refreshing, it's like nothing else on earth."

"Why not? I guess you can only drown once."

Half an hour later we'd driven to the marina and climbed aboard the *Lively Lady*, and I had to admit, I was excited. There's something special about going out on any kind of boat. But all I'd had experience of were huge car ferries, or tiny boats that were unstable, that buck around when you move. The *Lively Lady* was a top-end vessel, grand and dashing, her pure white fibreglass hull rocking on the water as she sat basking in the sun.

It was clear that Molly knew what she was doing, after she'd undone the mooring rope from the concrete post and jumped on board and I followed. She told me which ropes to untie, while she sprang around, doing all kinds of things to the sails and the rigging that I didn't understand.

Then once we'd launched, after a flawless blue-skied morning, the first problem of the day emerged. I noticed that a huge collection of black clouds were assembling in the distance, towards the horizon. There'd been no wind either until now, but I felt the breeze suddenly freshen drastically. The vessel was rocking on the waves, disturbingly fast.

"Do you think it's safe to go out?" I asked her. "That looks like a storm coming."

"Little blow-up, that's all," she poo-pooed me, giving my arm a squeeze. "You ain't gonna wimp out on me, are you, Sean?" she asked me, laughing. "Trust me, it ain't diddly squat, mate. Don't tell me nothing about storms — I've been round Cape Horn in storms like you can't even imagine. Even if there's a bit of a blow-up, this craft can handle it. Storms at sea are exciting! You really feel part of the elements. It's earthy, thrilling. Sexy."

She looked into my eyes.

I realised that I'd crossed the line. There was no going back now.

EIGHT

"Don't you get scared?" I asked her.

"Hmm, do you know summink, Sean?" She stopped what she was doing and stared at me, the wind whipping her blonde hair around her face, that sexy gap between her front teeth more and more enticing. "I've had a lifetime of people telling me not to do things because it's dangerous, to always be careful, to not take any risks. The people what tell you to be careful are lazy arseholes who are jealous that you've got some balls. I reckon that being scared is just an excuse for doing fuck-all. If you go around in your life being careful not to take any risks, you won't never do nothing and you end up as a boring fart. You just gotta jump into things and muddle through as best you can. I didn't have no advantages, no posh education or family money or nothing, and look at me now. With my own yacht, doing my own thing, and I ain't afraid of nothing or no one. I tell you, Sean, I'm no Lady Molly touch-me-not, swanning around in my big house, out of touch with reality. I do my bit to help. Do you know that there's lots of decent folk living around here who ain't got enough food to eat? Which I reckon is criminal. I help out at our local food banks, do what I can for the women's shelter, and at the hospital, on the wards where the poor old nurses struggle to get through the day. I don't just sit around on my arse all day spending money."

"What work did you do before you were married?" I asked her.

"Shop work, bit of bar work, helping mates here and there for cash. Anything I could get, basically. My philosophy is get what you can, when you can. I didn't marry Martin for his money, you know. At first he seemed so different from any man I'd ever known. I knew that if I married him I could share my life with someone who thought like me, who wanted to get things done, to help people in the world. Martin does a lot of charity work, in fact Rackhams Auctioneers has its own charity arm. That's how we met. I were working on the ward at St Luke's hospital, as a volunteer, and he came to see about organising a charity drive to get scanners and other medical equipment. We got talking, and that was it. In the early days our marriage was right perfect. Oh God, Sean, if you knew just how things have changed."

"By the way," I changed the subject. "I found some papers in Darius's flat. He'd had his DNA tested, to find out his ethnic origin. Was Martin's wife, his mother, German?"

"German?" She shook her head. "I don't think so. I never met her but I were told she were English through and through. Though funnily enough there was some scandal about Martin's mother, I think – she ran away or summink, disappeared, no one knew where she went. Right old family mystery, so they do say. Run away with some guy, I daresay, just upped and left the old man."

"It said in *Wikipedia* that Walter Trefus, Martin's father, came from Devon, and his mother disappeared when he was young. Sure, it's odd because according to the ethnicity test, Darius was seventy per cent of Western

Germanic origin. He had a first cousin who was German too."

"Cousins?" She frowned. "That don't make sense at all. As I said, Martin's dad came from Devon, I think, his mum from Yorkshire. No one ever mentioned any German connections."

"So could Martin's mum, or Martin's first wife, have had a German boyfriend? That's the only explanation that makes sense."

She laughed. "Who on earth knows. Too long ago for anyone to care now anyway, eh?"

She didn't talk much as we moved out of the harbour, under power from the outboard engine. Once we were at sea, she cut the engine and messed about with the sails and ropes so that the boat was moving fast, the wind in the sails, that were flapping constantly.

I was leaning against the forward rail beside the wheel, watching the foam on the waves, the coast fast receding into the distance. She came up to join me, hands on the wheel, staring at the horizon. I could smell the lovely shampoo in her hair, and the fine perfume scent I've never forgotten. Her hands made minute adjustments to the wheel, as she stared constantly ahead, a frown of concentration on her face.

"Are you glad you came, Sean?"

"Yes." I looked into the distance, where more clouds were gathering. "But I'd enjoy it more if there wasn't a storm brewing."

"Trust me." She turned towards me and smiled. Her hand suddenly went around my waist, seemingly a casual, friendly gesture, but I knew it was much more than that. I did the same, loving the feel of the warmth of her skin, knowing it was wrong, yet unable to stop myself. *She's married, she's just playing with you,* I kept thinking over and over.

"You like me, don't you, Sean?" she said, moving an inch closer to me, so that I could feel the warmth of her body against mine, before she turned back to stare into the distance.

"Of course I do." I tried to make light of it. "But you're married."

She nodded and smiled again. "And what about the portrait? Are you glad it's finished?"

"Sure I am. Even though it's a fuck-up."

"Clearing that flat must have been a right old bugger of a job. I meant to come and see you, but I just couldn't face it. That little flat, the squalid dump where Darius hung himself. Brrrr!" She shivered. "Bad fucking vibes, man. I admired you for having the guts to do it."

"I needed the money."

"Are you married, Sean? Do you have a partner?"

"My wife was murdered a while ago. But I've had girlfriends here and there since then."

"Is anyone *here and there* right now?"

"I had a girlfriend until a couple of weeks ago."

"What happened?"

I gave her an abridged version of events, of Julia and the horrible Harbottle.

When she started laughing, it was hard to resist laughing too, though the humour of the situation hadn't really registered with me up until now.

"Sorry, Sean, I shouldn't laugh," she apologised, serious once more. "Tell you what, the best thing about coming out onto the sea, is you can forget about everything else, and relax into your own little world," she went on. She turned the wheel to the right, altering course. Still staring at the sea, she spoke quietly. "All this malarkey about Darius, truth to tell I'm sick of it. Don't believe all that guff about Darius being Martin's great hope, the prodigal son who'd eventually come to his senses, and take over Rackhams and the Triplinghoes Estate, *Come home, Darius, all is forgiven*. Weren't like that at all. Darius wouldn't never have fitted into the mould Martin was making for him. Truth to tell, he was ashamed of his father, and Rackhams, the whole thing, he told me once that working for Rackhams would be like getting into his coffin. He were trapped, a bit like Prince Harry with the lovely Meghan Markle tempting him with the exciting freedoms of California. Darius wasn't bright enough to realise that he could only rebel against his inheritance if he had his own income, instead of relying on his trust fund and income from family shares to live on, as he did. Claimed he hated capitalism, while spending money like water."

"Why do you think he hung himself?" I asked her.

She shrugged. "No one knows. That gender whatchamacallit, it really was something that upset him deeply, although Martin reckoned it was all in the past, I don't reckon it was. For God's sake, it was a big deal, I mean, being a man or a woman is about the most important part of your life, ain't it? And if you've got any doubts it must eat away at you all the time. Paula, his girlfriend, she might know – she was the only one who was close to him at the time. Just before Christmas he'd had some kind of disagreement with Martin, and I can understand why." She moved even closer. "Since I've known him, Martin has changed. Or maybe I never really knew him. No one tells you that you can fall out of love, but you always do. Don't say nothing, just listen to me, Sean, because I mean it. I'm going to divorce him, soon as I can. Our marriage is over."

"Molly, I don't want to know."

"Yes you do."

It was getting too heavy. Despite my having an overwhelming sexual attraction to her, Molly wasn't for me, I didn't know her, and what I did know I didn't particularly like. But she was here. She was sexy. And she was driving me wild.

"This is none of my business."

"It could be your business, Sean."

"For goodness s—"

"Shut up, Sean! I mean it. Shut up or I swear I'll . . ."

And as we looked at each other something seemed to click. The boat was rocking and rolling with the waves, the wind even more powerful now, but I just didn't care. Resist it how I might, I didn't even care that I was contemplating having a sordid sexual affair with a married woman whom I didn't even particularly like.

"Believe me, Sean, It's over between Martin and me," she said breathlessly, holding on to my arms and looking into my eyes. "Our life together has just been a travesty for all these years. I want to divorce him, but he insisted on making me sign a prenuptial agreement when we got married. They say they're not enforceable in England like they are in America, but he's got right top-notch lawyers, and Martin always gets his way in the end. If I leave him I'll be back to being plain old Molly Snuff, who worked in the supermarket down St Kitts and went and got above herself. Martin needed a wife. . . And I needed money and security."

"I'm sorry."

"I ain't never been lucky in love, me. If only I'd met someone like you I wouldn't have cared nothing about money and property and such. Why on earth couldn't we have met before all this happened?"

The Bad Hail Mary

"Maybe we did? I know your face. I've seen you before, I swear I have, I just can't remember where."

"What do you mean, my lovely? In a dream or something? A naughty dream?"

The wind whipped up again, and suddenly the storm broke. The first flash of lightning filled the sky, then the crack of thunder came a second later. Suddenly, to the right, there was a giant wall of water that appeared before it crashed down, soaking us through. The *Lively Lady* caught the crest of the wave and the deck tilted abruptly, as we rode the crest.

"What do we do?" I asked her. Rain sheeted down, like a torrent, instantly soaking us both.

"Batten down the hatches and tie everything down, while I sheet the sails. No chance of getting back to shore now, we have to go below and sit it out."

Bent double against the wind and rain, I ran across deck, closing all the hatches and fastening them with the ropes and clips and so on, while she took down the large front sail, and the smaller one at the keel, the boat bucking and rolling all the time down and the wind drove us sideways.

And so while the wind whistled outside and the rain lashed down, it felt like an epiphany, as if the storm was finally breaking down our reserves.

"Come with me," she said as she grabbed my hand. "Hold on tight!"

We made it to the main hatchway leading to below deck, and just after the next wave crashed down over our heads, she unfastened it and I followed her down to the cabin, and closed the hatch over my head as the next wave crashed against it. We sat together on the cushioned seat behind the galley table. Through the port hole I could see the sky was black as night. And as the storm raged outside, I kissed her. And I knew in that moment how it must feel when you know you only have a few seconds to live. Not fear, not shock, not anything really, just a kind of acceptance that you're in the hands of fate.

Which I was.

Fate sure was my friend right then.

It was frantic, fevered, strange, but in that crazy moment, everything seemed to fit, everything seemed perfect, as if my joy could never end.

Eventually, just as suddenly as it had started, the storm eased, the wind dropped, and in a moment of elation, I realised we weren't going to drown.

We stood up and she led the way above deck and then she started the outboard motor, and we returned to the marina, without saying a word. As we climbed out onto the quay, I held her hand and knew I was high on adrenalin, fear, excitement and the thrill of the madness, that I did not want to end. I knew I wasn't falling in love with her, but right now I had second best, the thrilling excitement of illicit sex.

When we were back in my car, we sat in the front seats, soaking wet and exhausted, holding hands, still feeling the pulsing excitement of what was happening between us, any reserve there had been dissipated by the storm. As we kissed again, her hand flicked across my lap and I could sense that she was aware of the hot rigidness there. I drove off without speaking, and she told me where to go, which was along the main road and down a side track, leading apparently to nowhere. When we stopped the car, no other vehicles were in sight, we were on the edge of a field. After we'd got out of the car and climbed onto the bench backseat, I watched rainwater dripping off a branch onto the grass, as she snuggled closer.

"Why didn't you come and see me in Bradford?" I asked her abruptly. It had started to rain again, and the windscreen became a mass of water, and began to steam up with our breathing. "*The real reason.*"

"I wanted to." She bit her lip.

"So what stopped you?"

"Sean, shut up and listen, because this is important. Do you remember when we first met? You said you thought you'd met me before?"

"Yes. It's true, I did. I've been racking my brains where it was. Maybe it was a kind of déjà vu."

"Oh my good God no." She placed her hand on my lap again, pressing there as she smiled. As I felt her hand there my throat closed and my reasoning ended, and all I wanted was the ecstasy I knew was on my horizon.

"Think hard, Sean. I'll give you a clue. Think about fire. And death."

"Fire? Death? What are you talking about?"

"It was a long time ago. *Fire.* Think about it."

She looked into my eyes and licked her lips.

"*Heat. Flames. Smoke. Death. Running. Terror.*" She recited the words like a mantra, all the time staring into my eyes.

"I never forgot you, Sean," she whispered, arms around my neck, whispering in my ear. "Why do you think Martin approached you to do this job, when he could have asked any number of world-famous portraitists?"

"I have no idea."

"Because I persuaded him, that's why! I've followed your career ever since you left the police."

I stared at her in surprise, racking my brains. "Did I arrest you?"

"Arrest me? *Fucking no!* Remember that hot summer

night in Wolfreton Road in Hackney? The tiny newsagent's shop? I heard you was in hospital for quite a while after it happened. They reckoned you had amnesia."

Molly's face. Fire. Hell on earth. Terror. . Days of agony. . . The burn marks that still scarred my right arm.

NINE

Amnesia is a confusing term, because it's more often that you forget the moments immediately before and sometimes after an event, but not the event itself.

And with a horrible shock I recalled one of the most awful periods of my life, recuperating from an injury in hospital. And a mental scar, from which I never really recovered.

As Police Constable no. 462 Sean Delaney of the Metropolitan Police I had been patrolling along Cadogan Street in the East End of London, when I saw flames coming out of the upstairs window of a flat above a newsagent's shop nearby. I immediately called the fire brigade, who said they'd already been alerted and were on their way. Running closer, I saw a small crowd was milling around, and decided I should move them out of the way, thus allowing the brigade easy access.

But when I got there, a couple of men were pointing and shouting. "She's up there! I seen her go in before it started! And she ain't come out yet."

"She might have gone out the back way," said another. "No way can anyone go into that inferno."

As always happens, when you arrive at a scene like that

in uniform, the people look to you for directions, keen to comply with whatever you want them to do.

"You saw someone go in and not come out?" I asked the nearest man.

"Yes, mate, a young girl went in just before it went up."

"You haven't seen her come out?"

"No."

I ran along the tiny alley and surveyed the back of the houses. There didn't appear to be any fire escape or lower level roof, on which someone might have escaped.

So I kicked open the front door of the shop and ran inside. The seat of the fire appeared to be on the upper floor, from where most of the smoke was coming. I jumped over the counter into the back of the building, the heart of the inferno. I was in a narrow corridor, off which was a tiny kitchen, and stairs leading upwards, apparently nowhere else to go. Ducking into the kitchen, I found a towel and soaked it in water at the sink. Then threw it over my head, and ran out and up the stairs.

Visibility was virtually nil because of the smoke, and the heat was intense. Ignoring it, darting around like a hunchback, I opened each door in turn. Behind the second door was apparently the source of the fire, and I was beaten back by heat and smoke and closed it immediately, knowing that if she'd been inside there she'd be gone by now. But not before the flames had leapt out and spread across the landing, cutting off my retreat. I found her in the furthest room away from the stairs. Molly was lying motionless on the floor, and I ran across then scooped her up, throwing her over my shoulder in the well-known 'firemen's lift' which I promise you is harder to do than you might think.

Getting back to the top of the stairs is the part that's hard to recall easily, when I began to consider that it was

The Bad Hail Mary

hopeless. The top of the stairs was shrouded in flame and smoke. The only option was to go straight into the flames, trusting to avoid the worst of them. I prayed. Ducked. And ran as fast as I could.

I tripped halfway down the stairs, and we somehow landed at the bottom, where I must have lost consciousness.

My next memory was waking up in hospital, being told that I had burns to my legs and arms, but was otherwise fine and lucky to be alive. And that the girl I had rescued had recently recovered and returned home.

All in all I was a week off work, and when I got back had a long chat with my senior officer, who said that I was to be granted a commendation for bravery.

"And I read that a few years after that you accidentally shot an unarmed man when you worked with MS19, but were exonerated by the enquiry," Molly said, interrupting my reverie. "And later you left the police and set up as an artist."

"Yes," I told her, shaking my head, trying to assimilate this new crazy situation. "Let's get this straight. Years after it happened, you followed my career, and persuaded your husband to employ me on this project. Yet at the time it happened, you never even bothered to thank me."

"No," she apologised. "I couldn't do that."

"Why not?"

"For the same reason I gave the hospital a false name, and got away as quickly as I could. Didn't your colleagues in the police tell you what happened?"

"No one told me a thing, everyone thought it was best that I tried to forget everything that happened that night."

"The fire brigade investigators discovered that the fire had been deliberately started. The shop and the flat premises above them were heavily insured. The business was losing money, and the owners knew they'd not get much if they sold it. This way, not only could they make a claim for the repair of the building and the business, but also claim for thousands of pounds' worth of stock that wasn't there. I knew the son of the house, from when I met him on his holiday in Cornwall the previous year. They paid me to do it. I found out how to get the accelerant, looked up on the internet how to do it, but really I had no idea what I was doing. I started it off in the bedroom, then went to the room where you found me, to give it another go, because I couldn't get it going. But the first fire took hold real fast, and I weren't expecting that, was I? I ran towards the landing, but tripped and fell, where you found me. I must have inhaled more of the smoke than I realised, which was why I passed out. You've got no idea of the number of times I wanted to go and see you, to thank you, but how could I? I couldn't go nowhere near London for months. While the police were after me for arson I did the only thing I could do – get back to Cornwall and keep my head down."

"Why did you do it?"

She shrugged. "I needed the money. Dilip Patel, the boy I met who asked me to do it, said there'd be no risk, they just needed someone who was completely unconnected to the family to do it and make it look like an accident and get away. They were Asian, and there was an active right-wing group of thugs who'd been targeting the premises of Asian people in the area, so they reckoned that even if they suspected the fire had been deliberately started the racist gang would get the blame. They paid me half in advance, but I got no more than that because the insurance wouldn't pay out, and I daren't go nowhere near the family. They were prosecuted, but they didn't have enough

The Bad Hail Mary

evidence to convict them, and luckily they didn't grass me up. I were right lucky in them days."

"You could have killed other people."

She shook her head. "Weren't no one else in either side of the shop, and everyone else would have good warning, wouldn't they? And who was it harming? A hugely rich insurance company, that's all. Think of the millions they make, the vast majority of policies that they take fortunes for over many years and no one makes a claim. The greedy bastards deserve to lose money now and then."

"For God's sake, Molly! That's the excuse every tin-pot villain I've ever met comes up with."

"There were another reason why I needed money. My mum needed a hip replacement, and it were gonna be a wait of two years at least before they did it. Going private was the only other option, and it were up to me, weren't it? I got on and did what I had to do. Haven't you ever done summat that you're ashamed of?"

"I'm thinking we all have."

"So forgive me, Sean? Can't you forgive me?"

She moved closer. "Please, Sean? I need you to say you forgive me. You've got no idea of the times I longed to find you and thank you for what you did for me. And don't you see, I've paid you back? This was my way of thanking you. Ain't my fault if the job's all gone tits up, it ain't no one's fault. I thought it would all go lovely, that Martin would love the portrait and recommend you to other people. Sean, this was supposed to be my payback time to you – this could have made your career."

"Instead of which my career is in the shitter." I thought hard, trying to assimilate this new crazy information. "What if the arson case is still open?"

"No." She shook her head. "The case came to court

years ago. According to the Limitation Act 1980, what used to be the *Statute of Limitations*, a case like that can't be brought against me personally after six years. And since there was a court case a year after it happened, according to the double jeopardy limitations, the Patels' case was unproven – no one could prove that they employed me to start the fire, so there can't be another trial. I'm in the clear."

She grabbed my arms and pulled me close, staring into my eyes. "Why do you think I told you everything, Sean? Why do you think I set this all up, risking you recognising me, and now I've told you the truth?"

"How should I know?"

Her face was an inch from mine and I couldn't think of anything but my feelings for her. "Haven't you heard that old Chinese proverb, that if you save someone's life, you're responsible for them for ever? You see, Sean, ever since you saved my life, I never stopped thinking about you, dreaming about us meeting again and me telling you how I feel. I couldn't bear to have any secrets from you, that's why I confessed to doing that terrible crime. I took the risk of telling you that awful shameful thing about me, because I knew it were important that there were no secrets between us."

"Secrets between us? What are you talking about? Last time I looked you were a woman who was married to a very rich man."

"Listen to me!" She spoke frantically, as if she was scared of time running out. "I can't leave Martin today, or tomorrow or the next day, but as sure as eggs is eggs I'm leaving him soon. Mebbe this month, mebbe next month, but soon, I promise you. I set all this up, *everything,* because I was determined to see you again, and this was the only way."

"So why didn't you visit me in Bradford?"

Stupidly, I was falling into her trap. Betraying the fact that I was going along with her fantasy.

"I couldn't risk it. Not then. Someone might have found out and told Martin. Believe me, leaving him isn't going to be easy. You've met his mad-arse daughter Celia, haven't you? The bitch persuaded him to make me sign a prenup agreement before we married, and my lawyer says there might be a way around it, but not if I give him grounds for divorce. I can't go on living with Martin, and meeting you again has made me realise it all the more. But we have to be careful no one finds out yet. You do want to get to know me, don't you, Sean?"

"Look, this isn't right. You know I want you now, Molly, I'd give anything to take you right here and now. But we don't have a future. I'm not in love with you. I'm never going to be in love with you."

"Never is a long time, Sean. Never say never."

"This isn't fair on you."

"Don't matter about me, or my feelings! Let's not go wallowing in emotions, let's just do what comes natural! Can't you see I want it as much as you do?" she whispered urgently, once again pressing her hand against the heat at my groin. "I know you want me!"

The next kiss was hasty, snatched, sexy, exciting.

What the hell had got into me?

I put my arms around her and pulled her closer. Breaking apart and undoing our clothing in the confined space wasn't easy, but it was something which we'd both known was inevitable. When we were both naked below the waist, she undid the buttons of her shirt, put her hands behind her back and unfastened her bra, shrugging it away so that her breasts spilt forwards. As I held them in my hands I felt the tight pointed nipples, hardening in my hands.

She climbed across my body, facing me, and the joy as she eased downwards and my rigid flesh entered her was sublime and all consuming.

"Oh, Sean, *I love you, I love you I love you. . .*"

Time stopped.

Nothing mattered.

The revelation about Molly Trefus was shocking. After making love with her, I drove her back to the marina, where she assured me it would be best for her to take a taxi home. She told me that she understood how I felt, that maybe this was just a one-off, and she was cool with that.

"All them years ago, I was determined to get you, Sean, and I knew I'd get you in the end. Shhh, don't say nothing! I'll call you in a few days."

Now I was driving home, I knew that her face would now be forever associated with fire, danger and terror. But also with passion and longing, the longing for something I knew that I could never have. It had been stupid and ridiculous to have a thing with her, but it was more than obvious that I could never see her again, under any conceivable circumstances.

Did Martin know about his wife's past as an arsonist, I wondered? Committing arson is a serious crime, something that most people would baulk at. Did she have other lovers, as Celia had hinted, and I'd simply been the last notch on her bedpost? I simply had no idea.

I'd stop at nothing to get what I want. I played back her words in my mind.

Why hesitate? When you want something you just gotta shut up, grit your teeth and get it.

The Bad Hail Mary

I wondered just what lengths Molly would go to, to get what she wanted.

Could I believe anything Molly had said? Exactly what was the state of her marriage? Did she really never forget me, or was that just a line she was feeding me to get me to do anything she wanted?

I knew that getting further involved with Molly would be a big mistake.

But I would never have guessed that Molly would actually end up being arrested for murdering her husband.

TEN

The big detached house in Streatham, South London, had belonged to Neville Peasgrove, a rich, nasty money-grabbing gangster who had succumbed to a fatal heart attack whilst on a winning streak in a game of illegal poker – playing with a band of other professional criminals who regularly met in a backroom of a filthy café in Norbury to play cards for thousands of pounds, a venue referred to colloquially as a 'Spieler'.

I had been offered the job to repaint the entrance hallway and clear out the junk in his office courtesy of another gangster, Alf 'Slitguts' Waverly, who had been delighted with the portrait I had done of him for his family, and had recommended my decorating services to Gary and Anna Peasgrove, Neville's repugnant son and daughter-in-law. The pair had stripped the house of everything they wanted and were keen to put it on the market ASAP, reckoning that a smart-looking hall would impress buyers like nothing else. Gary and Anna struck me as a couple of ignorant, unpleasant twerps: mean-spirited, monosyllabic, grasping people, whose only interest in their father's demise was how much money he was leaving them.

Just like the Bradford job, it was a project that I wasn't keen to do, but it paid well. Another cut-and-thrust job: I could get it done quickly, take the money and get gone.

The Bad Hail Mary

It was as I was stripping the paper from the hallway wall that I discovered the secret cupboard, concealed by a thin panel of plywood. Underneath the panel was a door, which I opened, and found some papers and files.

Curiosity got the better of me, and I was absorbed in the first file, which listed a set of men's names on the left-hand side, against amounts of money and dates, all this year. Alister Heath McLacklen, £2,000 on the 7 January, Peter Paul Montgomery, £1,000 on 5 February. Each man was paying regularly hefty amounts. Then, in another file, I found copies of what appeared to be emails to the individuals. One read:

I have evidence and images that I will send to my friends in the media, and would cause you great embarrassment, both personally and professionally. Pay me £2,000 by the end of this week, or else I will go ahead and break my silence on these embarrassing matters . . .

There are very few crimes I find more abhorrent than blackmail, and it looked as if Neville Hamilton Peasgrove had been a professional blackmailer of the worst kind. Some of the names of the men indicated they were medical doctors, others lawyers, one was an MP. I had their email addresses, so without delay that afternoon, I set out a standard letter for each of them on my laptop:

Dear . . . .

You may have heard that Mr Neville Peasgrove died recently. I have discovered that he appeared to have been blackmailing you and a number of other people. I'm writing to reassure you that no one else knows about this regrettable business, that must have caused you terrible stress and worry, not to mention a lot of money.

This is to tell you that you have no need to worry any more. Fortunately, the people employing me to clear Mr

Peasgrove's house have asked me to dispose of all his remaining personal items, which includes several computers, memory sticks and papers and photographic images. I haven't examined any of these, and I am going to put all this material into weighted black bags, take them far out into the English Channel and drop them into deep waters, away from fishing lanes, thus ensuring that their contents are lost forever.

Blackmail is a disgusting crime and I'm delighted to take the burden of fear away from you. Whatever your secret(s) may be, they are nobody's business but your own.

Yours sincerely ….. ..

I sent the emails, then completed the job in a couple of days. I then transported all the computers and so on back home to Whitstable, went out with a fisherman friend of mine and, as I'd promised, dropped them all over the side into the ocean, watching the weighted black bags sink beneath the surface of the waves.

*

The massive chainsaw roared and screamed and bucked and swayed, sending showers of woodchips into the sky as the Rev. Robin Villiers gritted his teeth and tore the blades into the ancient timber beam.

The icy wind was cutting through our clothes as my friend Robin and I stood on the bare bones of the roof of the main nave of St Christopher's Church, in Abbotsford, near Whitstable. Robin's parish church had been built in 1680, the roof of its nave had been failing for years, and finally the money had come through for materials to repair it. Robin is a pretty unusual man of the cloth, because in his spare time he's a highly skilled woodworker, although his usual projects were those of a miniaturist, making perfect scale models of buildings in wood, MDF, metal and various other materials. Large-scale joinery like this, he assured me, was a lot easier and in many ways extremely rewarding. I do a fair bit of general carpentry myself, but I'm nowhere near Robin's brilliance at small-scale woodworking – he can even make dolls' house furniture, where tiny drawers go in and out of tiny sideboards! Repairing the roof ourselves meant that the church commissioners only had to pay for the cost of new slates and timber. It had taken us most of the day to strip off the broken slates and timber battening, and now he'd hacked out the rot in one of the massive oak beams and was assessing the damage to the timber skeleton beneath before the encroaching twilight meant we had to call it a day.

"Woodworm, but not deathwatch beetle, thank goodness," he told me, examining the little holes in a long section of beam he'd just cut out.

Ancient oak timber is literally as hard as rock, and the only way you can cut it is by using a chainsaw, that needs regular re-sharpening.

"Deathwatch is a nightmare," he went on, his boyish good looks marred by the sawdust clinging to his collar-length dark hair and clean-cut features. "Those worms stay deep inside the wood forever, whereas the longhorn surrey beetle, or woodworm, only fancies the top inch of juicy timber, then it gives up. Luckily the inside core is still solid in most of these supportive beams. So I can cut out the completely rotten sections, make matching pieces to scarf-joint them in, then we can renew all the battens, and finally do the re-slating."

It had been two weeks since I'd come back from Cornwall. My encounter with Molly was still fresh in my mind, but to my relief I had not heard from her. No-strings sex was pretty much anathema to me, but with Molly I'd somehow broken my own rules. I wasn't proud of myself, and I had to admit I still thought a lot about her. But having no contact was the best thing to happen, all things considered. Maybe I had treated her badly, but she had made all the running, hadn't she?

Why on earth had she picked me up from her past, I wondered? Was it just on a whim, was I just a plaything for a rich woman who already had everything? As for the idea of Molly leaving Sir Martin Trefus and his money, it was preposterous.

She had freely admitted that even though she apparently wanted to divorce him, she was afraid that the prenup agreement she'd signed would invalidate any possibility of keeping her lifestyle after the divorce, especially if he knew about her adultery. Lady Molly Trefus liked living in her stately home, enjoying the jet-setter lifestyle, her yacht and never having to worry about paying bills, and who could blame her? It wasn't exactly flattering that I was clearly just her latest cheap thrill.

Which was why on that cold windy rooftop, the call on my mobile took me by surprise.

"Sean?"

I immediately recognised Molly's Cornish accent, my heartbeat accelerating as I answered.

"Oh thank God, Sean, I've got you."

"Molly? What is it?"

"Help me, Sean, please, you've got to help me! I'm in terrible trouble and I don't know what to do."

I could hear her burst into hysterical tears.

"There's been an accident. The *Lively Lady* has sunk, and Martin's drowned and the police have been questioning me. They think I killed him, and I didn't! I swear I didn't! Even my solicitor doesn't believe I had nothing to do with it, but at least he's got me out on bail. I need your help, Sean, please! I'm really scared. I don't know what the hell to do. Please will you come down to Cornwall and see me now, so I can tell you all about it? If what happened between us means anything at all, please help me, Sean. I'm begging you! Please!"

ELEVEN

Twilight had changed to night by the time we'd climbed down from the roof and rushed in to the living room at the vicarage, to sit down and watch the TV news. It was the second item.

The female reporter was standing looking serious, her coat collar edges flickering around her ears against a strong wind, and you could just make out the movement of waves in the background. She was talking in that frenetic breathless way that young TV reporters have, but was clearly being careful with her words.

"Police Cornwall have put out a statement to say that Sir Martin Trefus, who was the major shareholder and Chief Executive Officer of Rackhams International Art and Antiques Auctioneers, is presumed to have drowned tonight, having been apparently trapped below decks in his family yacht, the *Lively Lady*, when it sank last night in the waters off Mevagissey in Cornwall. Police say that Mr Trefus's wife, Molly, has been helping them with their enquiries since she was released from hospital, after her unbelievable swim of nearly two miles to shore. Apparently the only reason she didn't succumb to hypothermia, the usual threat to life when people are swimming in the sea, is that the water was uncharacteristically warm for the time of

The Bad Hail Mary

year. It is believed that the yacht sank unexpectedly, but the cause is as yet unknown. Divers are expected to bring the remains of the *Lively Lady* to the surface tomorrow at first light, after which experts will assess why the apparently perfectly seaworthy vessel sank without warning. When asked to comment, Lady Molly Trefus claimed that the tragedy all happened in the blink of an eye, so fast that the boat sank before there was time to launch the emergency dinghy. She was fighting to stay above the water, and, although she searched frantically for her husband, she couldn't find him anywhere and so was unable to help him. According to the local lifeguard only an extremely strong swimmer could have managed to survive. According to the police, Sir Martin Trefus was an elderly man who couldn't possibly have managed to save himself, whereas his wife was an experienced sailor, who habitually swam for exercise, having been a champion yachtswoman in her youth."

"Wow," Rob said, shaking his head slowly. "So she obviously killed him."

"She's denied it. I don't think she's capable of murder," I answered, still reeling from the shock.

"Yet she's capable of committing arson for money and staying married to a rich old man whom she apparently hates whilst conducting adulterous affairs."

"You heard what the reporter said. Something happened which caused the yacht to go down fast, and she had no option but to save herself."

"Don't be such an idiot, Sean! Look at the facts. You told me that she claims to want to divorce him, but if she did she'd get nothing, because of the prenup agreement."

"She told me she was prepared to fight it."

"A long-drawn-out legal tussle costs a fortune, and he'd probably win in the end. If the police conclude that the shipwreck was accidental, assuming he's made his will in her favour, or indeed if he hasn't got around to changing his will since he married her, then she probably gets his entire estate, and she'll also inherit the controlling shares in Rackhams, which is a multi-million-pound enterprise. Not to mention any payout if his life was insured."

"But that's the first thing the police and the insurance people would assume. She's not stupid, so why would she imagine she could get away with faking an accident?"

"Who knows?" Robin went on. "But you've told me she's an expert swimmer and an experienced sailor. She'd be in a position to fake up some convincing fault on the yacht that allows fast entry of water, and looks as if it was caused accidentally. I've heard that you can have water pipes that perish, or get damaged seacocks that jam open. It's quite feasible that if a fault like that happened, it could be blamed on bad maintenance. Sounds as if the police have been questioning her, but haven't yet got enough evidence to charge her."

"Sure it does."

"So, Sean, what are you going to do?"

I felt an overwhelming surge of guilt and shame. I'd made love to Molly, and while I hadn't fallen in love with her, I'd formed a bond with her that I couldn't break. Plus I felt guilty that I'd had sex with her simply because of the temptation of the moment. And years ago I had saved her life. I felt as if it made me somehow responsible for her welfare. "She's asked for my help. The least I can do is go and see her."

"Well, first of all, pull yourself together and face facts. And for goodness sake, forget about when you made love to her."

"I never told you that."

"You didn't need to," Robin muttered. "After all these years, I know your moods by heart. The frame of mind you were in when you came back from Cornwall was just like you always are when you've got a new girlfriend, and I'm old and ugly enough to realise when you don't want me to ask awkward questions. But you, Sean, being you, you can't just have sex and leave it at that, you can't keep your emotions out of it, no matter how hard you think you are. Sex isn't just sex for you, it's an emotional rollercoaster. It's just the way you're made."

"Yeah, I guess you're right. After it happened I found myself thinking about her more and more, but when I didn't hear from her, I just decided the whole thing had been a mistake. But I can't just leave her in the lurch now. Besides it's not only that. There's this whole thing, the whole business, is rotten somehow, there's things going on that I don't understand. There's something wrong about Darius's apparent suicide, and the way I was dragged into this mess. There's something criminal going on at Rackhams International, and I want to find out what it is."

"It's none of your business."

"Look, I tidied up the flat, spent time there. The boy, Darius, died and I want to find out if he actually did kill himself or if he was murdered."

"Why?"

"I can't explain. It's as if he's died and no one is on his side. There's only me who can try to make some sense of what happened, and I feel as if I know him, as if I owe him something. And now his father is dead. I'm already involved whether I like it or not. The least I can do is go and talk to Molly, see what she has to say."

"No. The right thing to do is to cut her out of your life and leave this mess behind. Right now you've got to forget about your feelings and buckle up and face some cold hard facts. Are you familiar with the *Forfeiture Rule*, also called the *Slayer Rule* in America?"

"Not really."

"In essence it states that no person can gain financially from someone they murder, for obvious reasons."

I was still reeling from the shock, trying to assimilate the facts. "So if she's found guilty of murder, what happens to Trefus's estate?"

"The law treats the killer in exactly the same way as if she has actually predeceased the person she killed – meaning that any default beneficiary, usually the closest relatives, inherits everything instead."

"So Celia, Martin Trefus's daughter, would get the Rackhams shares and everything else?"

"Yes."

"Maybe Celia arranged the accident then? Intending to frame her stepmother. According to Molly, Martin hated her, so if he had only left her a token amount, it's the only way Celia would inherit anything from her father's estate."

"True. If it can be proved that Molly killed him, chances are that Celia gets the lot," Rob said. "Assuming that Celia is the default beneficiary, which I'd guess is most likely. If on the one hand, Molly is innocent and Martin's death was as a result of a sailing accident, or indeed if someone else was responsible for his death, then Molly hits the jackpot. Alternatively if she's found guilty she'll not get a penny and faces jail time, and Celia gets the lot . So listen hard, Sean."

"Do I have a choice?" My head was hurting and I didn't know what to think, or what I should do.

"She's already told you that she hates Martin and wants to leave him but knows she'd lose everything if she did.

The Bad Hail Mary

Darius, who I'd guess would have inherited a substantial share of the estate, is dead and it sounds as if Molly knows that Martin didn't rate Celia as being a suitable managing director of Rackhams, so he probably only left Celia a token amount, not a fortune, such as Darius, who Martin had been hoping would eventually get over his crazy way of life and take over as his successor, would have got. Supposing Molly somehow paid people to kill Darius first, to solve that problem, and now she's killed Martin as the second part of her plan? On the other hand it would have been a risky business. The boat suddenly sank, a long way from shore. According to the TV reports, she very nearly drowned swimming all that distance to the beach, and it only needed a strong current and she'd have been gone. What's more I've heard that most people can normally only swim up to three quarters of a mile before they get hypothermia. If she did deliberately stage an accident, would she really have risked having to take such a precarious swim to safety? Did the plan go wrong, so it sank further out than she intended it to? There's a lot to think about. From what you've told me, she's a gambler, prepared to be impulsive and take big chances. She might have calculated that it's hard to prove an accident has been staged, and that no one would dare risk such an arduous swim. She might have thought the risk was worth it."

"You could be right," I told him. "But let's assume the yacht didn't sink as a result of an accident. Supposing Martin was murdered by someone else? Rackhams are desperate to avoid any kind of scandal at the moment because of that merger deal with the American company they're all so keen to go through. If Darius had found out about some racket they've got going, such as using Rackhams' offices and facilities to illegally smuggle artefacts out of Italy or Peru, he could have been threatening to tell the authorities, and maybe Martin discovered the same thing, and was also posing a threat to them? One of Darius's films was an interview with a Rackhams agent in Italy, where he was trying to trap him into admitting he'd help arrange this kind of smuggling. Darius might have been blackmailing Rackhams' staff about a smuggling racket he could prove. Maybe they killed him to shut him up, and after I told Sir Martin about it, he looked into it and started asking questions? If Sir Martin was furious about this racket, even suspected that people from Rackhams might have killed his son, he might have decided to call in the police. They had to kill him to shut him up too."

"So why haven't they killed you too?"

"Maybe I'm next on the list."

Robin frowned and tugged at his lower lip. "If Rackhams were responsible for Darius's death, because of an incriminating film, why wouldn't they take the film when they killed him?"

I shrugged. "No time, no opportunity. You don't hang around after you've killed someone. And remember, they did plan to pay a detective to get his papers and computers afterwards."

"A man who has recently gone missing." Robin shook his head.

"But Darius's death. Making a hanging look like suicide isn't easy, I don't even know if it's possible. Remember, the police and the coroner are satisfied it was suicide."

"You can suppose all you like," Rob muttered. "But the police aren't fools, and they concluded Darius killed himself. And it's up to them to find out the precise cause of Martin's death. You have to keep out of it, otherwise you risk all kinds of things."

The Bad Hail Mary

"Such as?"

"For goodness sake, Sean, you know the law better than I do. Think. What if someone already knows you've been having an affair with Molly and has told the police? You met her at the marina, anyone could have seen you going off on the boat together. How do you know Martin wasn't having her watched, if he suspected she was going with other men? If you associate yourself with her right now, they might well conclude that she murdered him and you helped her in some way, even if it was just in the planning stage. As you know, colluding with a person to kill someone, even if you take no practical part in it, means you can be charged with murder too."

"Joint enterprise."

"Yes," he agreed. "Do you fancy serving a life sentence?"

"But I want to get justice for Darius, and his father. And Molly needs my help."

"Poor helpless little Molly needs your help. Right. And how long has she known you, a few months?"

"She knows I was in the police. I told you about how she never forgot that I saved her life, all those years ago."

"Wake up, Sean. Do you want to act like a prick all your life! Do you want to be a patsy all the way to a prison cell?"

"Fuck off, Robin."

"She's dangerous. She's treacherous. And think on this, mate. Where are her friends and allies?"

"What do you mean?"

"Don't you think it's odd that she should ask a casual acquaintance to help her out of a mess like this? She didn't even keep up contact with you after you had sex, did she? She'd had her kicks, she didn't need you then. If she's innocent, why hasn't she got closer friends to fight her corner?"

"I don't know. Maybe she asked me because I'm already involved, knowing about the break-in at Darius's flat, the film he made about smuggling that might have upset people at Rackhams. Maybe because she feels she can trust me."

"Or maybe because she knows you've got a thing for her, even if you don't realise it yourself. Think about it. Molly is a mystery. The only thing you know about her is that years ago she sailed a yacht around the world, dined out on it for a while, then married a rich old man for money. *Money,* Sean! Before that, she committed arson for payment, and you were the poor sod that nearly died saving her life, then she couldn't even thank you because she was too busy keeping herself out of jail. She didn't dig you out of her past for fun. She's been using you right from the start. She fancied you, and looked you up on a whim. You're a good-looking man, Sean. No one is surprised when a man goes after a woman purely because he wants her for sex. Why shouldn't it work the other way around?'"

"Come on, it's hardly likely."

"Face facts! She got paid money to start a fire to defraud an insurance company, a fire that could have killed innocent people. She's already admitted to having no scruples, and being ruthless about getting what she wants by whatever means are necessary. What's that old saying? That when someone tells you what they're like, believe them."

"Oh shit," I sighed. "I don't know what to think. You're right. She might well have murdered her husband. But there's no harm in just going to see her. At least I owe her that."

"You owe her precisely nothing. She's out on bail and

police are going to be watching all her movements, and they'll be watching you too if you go and see her."

"But—"

"Have you considered the possibility that she might be trying to drag you into a trap?" Robin went on. "She could even be setting you up, having sex with you and filming it or something, so she can tell the police that you're her jealous lover, and that you tampered with the boat because she won't leave her husband. That you wanted to kill Martin and her, for revenge? Have you got an alibi for the night he drowned?"

"Come on, mate, that's stretching things too far." I stood up and walked around, trying and failing to work out what to do. "It's stupid, but something keeps playing on my mind. She said that there's an old Chinese saying, that if you save someone's life then you become responsible for them forever, you have to watch over their lives."

"Sean, for goodness sake, grow up!" Robin shook his head sadly. "I've heard it too, and it certainly sounds impressive. Until you know it's complete nonsense, and that no Chinese philosopher ever said such a thing. I'm the philosopher here, remember, I studied theology and philosophy to degree level. And I happen to know that the concept of saving someone's life being an eternal responsibility is totally fictitious. Sounds good, but in fact it was invented for some TV drama, with the Chinese association thrown in for fun, to make it seem more authentic. Think about the ramifications if it was true. How many doctors on A&E wards would have to chase after the patients whose lives they saved, unable to let them out of their sight? How about if someone had saved the life of the Yorkshire Ripper, before he started his killing spree. Would that make his saviour responsible for the murders that the

Ripper went on to commit? I don't think so. It's crazy, illogical and ridiculous."

"I don't know what to think."

"Going to see Sir Martin and Molly and getting involved in doing the portrait of Darius has caused you nothing but trouble. It was a huge mistake, but you couldn't have known it at the time. Molly is dangerous, she's poison. What do they say? Everyone can make a mistake—"

"—But only a fool makes the same mistake twice."

I was thinking about the one woman who had never let me down.

It was time to talk to her. . .

TWELVE

Kate Doyle looked much the same as when I'd last seen her a while ago, when she'd helped me to penetrate an organisation who were forging paintings. The long chestnut hair with the green stripe along the middle seemed to match her colourful outfit of long bright green skirt and tightly-fitting green top, framing her firm, tight, neatly-shaped breasts. She had lovely white teeth, and a wide generous mouth, but her smile was always tempered by a wary look in her eyes. As a pioneering freelance journalist she'd received awards for her exposés of all kinds of nefarious affairs and earned a reputation for being a hard-hearted truth-monger, willing to do anything for a good scoop. She was ten times tougher than any man I've ever known, and if she'd been made of metal it would have been tungsten steel. I'd heard that she'd had a husband once, and if she actually had eaten him for breakfast she wouldn't have broken sweat.

The morbid dark South London Wetherspoons pub where she'd suggested we meet only had a handful of slovenly customers at this time of the morning, one of whom was standing at the bar, and making a meal of yawning and scratching his arse. The Spoons pub with the dirty carpet was called one of those Wetherspoons 'Moon' names: the *Moon and Compass*, the *Moon and Goat*, or *Moon on the Water*, or perhaps the *Brexity Moonshine*, I just can't remember now. Despite my long morning run along the dirty mean streets, I still felt bleary, weary and scared.

"I got a bit of background on Molly, and I pumped the Police Cornwall press office for anything else they'd give me, but as usual with an ongoing police investigation they were tighter than a duck's arsehole." She rattled away in her harsh cockney croak, that bore witness to nicotine-fuelled nights composing topical stories against a tight-as-tits deadline. She looked at her phone, scrolling with a finger that brandished half an inch of bright scarlet nail that had probably been used that morning to blind someone.

"Right, mate." She cocked a perfectly plucked eyebrow. "They've retrieved the yacht and brought her into harbour, and Sir Martin Trefus's body was found in the hold. The official line is that preliminary indications are that the outlet valve of the toilet's holding tank – called the joker valve – either broke or was deliberately smashed. This holding tank is fed when the toilet is flushed. The holding tank's toilet is designed to attach to a receiver tank pipe in harbour, so its contents can be pumped out, or alternatively the tank outlet can be opened up so it can discharge into the sea, via the seacock. Naturally the joker valve only allows water out, not in. And the joker valve is normally checked and checked again in standard maintenance. As a rule, if it's faulty it only allows in a small amount of water, leaving you plenty of time to get back to shore. If, however, the joker valve is deliberately smashed, it's normally below the water line, so seawater floods in, filling the holding tank, which spills over and floods the cabin in no time. Mind, if water enters the yacht due to any kind of leak, the bilge pump would automatically activate once it detects water on the floor, but it's mainly used for slow leaks. It has to be a high pressure leak to come in so fast that the bilge pump can't handle it, such as direct entry of seawater flooding in through a sizeable hole that would immediately flood the place below deck."

"So the joker valve broke."

"Or someone smashed it from the inside, by removing the cover panel. From outside the hull, a diver would have to use a tool to ram about ten inches through the pipe before it met the joker." Katie downed her neat whisky and frowned at her phone as if she hated it. She took a cigarette out of her pack and stuffed it between her lips, glaring at the waitress, who returned her stare, almost daring her to light up so she could be thrown out. The world-weary woman reconsidered and put it back in its box, smiling sweetly and curling a jeering lip at her new enemy. "But it seems that the more usual maintenance issue with holding tanks is that they jam up and clog, so that they won't let the shit and stuff out – the one-way valve rarely fails and lets water in the other way."

"Now for the goodies. Your mate Molly Trefus, née Snuff, is the daughter of Bert and Peggy Snuff, of Mousehole in Cornwall. Molly Snuff was a wild child – in trouble with the cops as a teenager – she fell in with a bad crowd apparently, and a group of them were arrested for making trouble at a nightclub. At fifteen years old, she was in a fight with another girl, who had half her ear bitten off. Before that she was cautioned for shoplifting several times. Finally brought before the Truro Crown Court when she was eighteen for possession of Class A drugs with intent to supply. But the case was discharged – not enough evidence to convict. When she was twenty-one she was competing in swimming competitions and had friends in the local sailing club, and she was crewing for them regularly. She had a gift for attracting publicity, and by the time she was twenty-three, she'd managed to get backing and funds for her bid to sail round the world alone, when she was christened *Molly the Mermaid* in the press. Before all that, at the time you saved her life in that arson attempt you told me about, her mother was fighting fit, winning dancing competitions, so the hip operation story was bullshit. Molly married old man Trefus five years ago, dropped into a fortune and out of the limelight."

"She said she sailed round the world."

"Yes, but our sexy Molly lied about that too. What she actually did was crowdfund an attempt to sail round the world, the idea being to get herself sponsored to raise money for charities. She got plenty of sponsors, local supermarkets and businesses, TV personalities. Lots of good-hearted folk all lined up to help raise money for a local hospice, and also a hospital for children and medical scanners for Truro Hospital. She got the yacht, chartered for free, from a big yacht company. And she set sail. But she only made it halfway and had to be picked up and rescued. It was a fucking disaster. And a financial mess. She got out of it without being charged because she claimed she had a serious mental breakdown, preventing her from continuing. The charities got nothing, and the sponsors lost a fortune. She was lucky not to be charged with fraud."

"Did she make any money?"

"No one knows for sure. Some people said she did the whole thing as an elaborate scam, and squirreled away some cash for herself. But it was impossible to prove."

"Thanks for doing all that."

"Don't thank me, Sean mate, you know me, I don't do nothing for nothing." She leaned closer, rubbing her thumb and fingertips together, in the age-old symbol for acquiring cash. "So tell me, what's in it for me? You gonna get me another big story I can sell to the dailies?"

"I doubt it. I was hoping you'd help me as a friend."

"Because you're making a tit of yourself over Lady Molly the murderer?"

"A tit of myself?"

"Like you often do, Sean, being nice and trusting people, when you should be like me – assume that everyone's a lying worthless arsehole until they've proved otherwise. Looking at the bare facts, here's what I reckon happened. Molly deliberately smashed the joker valve, and reckoned she done it in such a way as to make it look like a maintenance issue. She's a strong swimmer and knew she'd be able to make it back to shore. As you've explained just now, she wants to get rid of hubby, a divorce would only get her peanuts, unless she challenges the ruling, and risks losing even more, and failing in the end. If she can get away with it, she gets control of Rackhams, plus all his money, apart from some piss-poor little legacy he might have left to his surviving daughter, Celia, who you reckon Sir Martin disliked for some reason. Plus Molly would probably get a whacking big payout from any insurance, which he's likely to have."

"So there's three possibilities, and it has to be one of them," I reasoned. "Either she sabotaged the yacht, as you've just described, to kill her husband for his money. The boat's valve failed because of a maintenance problem. Or a third party smashed the valve, intending to kill both of them."

"And who would want both of them dead?" Kate bit her lip and frowned. "Celia?"

"It's possible. But unlikely. She might hate Molly

enough to kill her, but I got the impression she's on reasonably good terms with her father. And I think she's only due to inherit a nominal amount."

"There goes your trusting nature again, Sean! Grow up! If both Martin and Molly died together, you can bet your bollocks that she'd be the fall-back legatee, the *default beneficiary* as it's called, and she'd get everything he's got. After all, he's got no other relatives, has he? Molly's his wife, he's likely to have made her the principal beneficiary, but Celia has to be the default beneficiary for if they both die. Celia might hate Molly, maybe she reckons her father's betrayed her by marrying a second time. Hatred goes on festering and revenge can be sweeter than sex."

"Do you know that happened to Sir Martin's first wife? The mother of Darius and Celia?"

"Yeah." Kate Doyle flicked through her pad of notes. "She took an overdose. Known to have suffered from bipolar and drug and alcohol addiction for many years. When Darius killed himself it was reported that he'd probably inherited his mum's mental instability."

"If it was a murder attempt against both of them, it's more likely to be someone at Rackhams," I went on. "My guess is that Darius was blackmailing them about this smuggling racket they were operating, and they killed him to hush it up, so that this proposed merger with the American company isn't ruined."

"Yep." She flicked the papers with the scarlet nail and set her mouth in a hard line. "In some of the accounts of Darius's suicide they refer to his mum's similar death."

"So when Martin found out about this racket that Darius had exposed, presumably by watching the film I passed to him from the flat, perhaps he started stirring things up, so that they had to kill him too. And Molly was an innocent victim, who'd have been collateral damage. What about Sir Martin's mother? I heard she went missing a long time ago."

"Don't know nothing about that, mate, but I'll go on digging wherever I can. And I suppose I can't persuade you to keep out of it, and you'll go to Cornwall and comfort the Merry Widow," Kate said, flipping the cover back over her phone's screen. "Usual ground rules. If you get any fresh angles on the case, you tell me about them. On my side, I pass on anything I hear to you tout de suite, and I promise to get the go-ahead from you before I spill any stories." She narrowed her eyes, concentrating hard. "No one's so far dug up the angle about her wild younger days. She was a violent little cow as a kid, was also into supplying drugs, and you've told me she's admitted to being an arsonist. Which she got away with."

"For God's sake," I urged her. "She told me that in confidence."

"And I heard it in confidence. But, Sean, respecting confidences don't pay the bills, and if I can use that angle to sell this story, I have to use it, don't I?" Her smile was seemingly innocent and coy. "After all, I'm a struggling journalist trying to tell the truth and right wrongs."

"Please don't," I appealed to her, realising that I'd been a fool to trust her. "Please, *please,* Kate, I'm trusting you."

She leered, exposing the sharp white teeth that reminded me of a barracuda shark. "Only kidding, Sean. It's just I was fantasising about embellishing the whole thing, as a love story between the man who saved the life of an arsonist, only to find out that she was planning to murder her husband for money and set him up as the patsy who takes the blame. If it wasn't for the fact that I happen to love that patsy, that would get a load of traction, that would be a gift, a fucking gift."

"That's what worries me most. That the police might conclude that I conspired with Molly to murder her husband."

"Did you?" Molly stared back at me.

"For God's sake, Kate, you know me!" I told her, realising too late that she was pulling my leg. "Listen, I'll give you what I find out, as soon as it's safe. And I'm guessing it'll be worth your while."

"You'd better. Or else."

"How are things in your personal life, Kate?"

"That's personal." She smiled sweetly. "Whereas you, dear Sean, are an open book to me and you can't tell lies. But I'm a secretive fucker and I wouldn't tell you if I was fucking King Kong or the Prime Minister. That's the way I like it."

It was always the same. Kate Doyle was an attractive conundrum in nice clothes who probably pretended she was more dangerous and cynical than she actually was. I didn't know if she had a string of boyfriends or girlfriends, if she was rich or poor, or had sisters, brothers or parents, pet dogs or cats. I didn't even know her age, but guessed at anywhere between thirty-five and fifty.

But I did know one thing. She'd do literally anything on earth to get a good story, and she was fearless in her searches.

And I knew something else. I liked her, and she liked me.

And she had never let me down.

"But, Sean, you know you're fooling yourself, don't you, if you reckon she's innocent? Ask me, Molly obviously killed him."

THIRTEEN

Triplinghoes looked different at night. Floodlights blazed into life as my old Land Rover dipped and bucked over the stony ground and through the narrow gateway. To my shock, I realised that I'd knocked over the damned unicorn statue for a second time, and now it had fallen to the ground in two pieces, as it had done before. This time I didn't even bother to pick it up.

It was five days since Molly's frantic phone call. The day after it happened I'd helped Rob with the church roof repair, so that he only had to complete the rest of the tiling to make it waterproof.

From the moment I'd set eyes on Molly Trefus I'd known she was different from most people. She might indeed be a cold-blooded killer, who had somehow engineered Darius's disappearance or death, and/or the drowning of her husband.

The news put out by Police Cornwall's press office had altered slightly, and the official line was that the body of Sir Martin Trefus had been found below deck in the sunken yacht, *Lively Lady*. It hadn't been a fault with the joker valve as had been assumed at first, it seemed that the yacht had been deliberately scuppered by someone: One large hole had been drilled through the bottom of the hull – police had even found a heavy duty cordless drill with a two-inch-diameter 'tank cutter' drill (cylindrical tool with teeth around its circumference) still in its chuck – and the fibres of timber and fibreglass on its teeth matched those of the hole in the boat. The drilling device had a long shaft to allow it to cut through the ten-inch thickness of the hull, which was comprised of an outer shell of fibreglass, foam insulation and metal sheeting acting as the cabin floor. Police Cornwall's press office stated that: 'After the hole was drilled in the hull, water would enter the boat at such a speed that the yacht's submersion within minutes was inevitable. Someone who was on board the *Lively Lady* had deliberately drilled the hole'.

Someone.

There had only been two people on board at the time, Molly and Sir Martin. And Sir Martin, who couldn't swim, had no reason to scupper his own boat.

Or could it be more complicated than that? One of the morning's newspapers had picked up on the leaked news of the forthcoming proposed merger between Rackhams International and the American outfit, Apperline Webb. Any hint of impropriety, for instance if police started investigating unlawful activities at Rackhams, would most likely wreck the deal which stood to make all of the Rackhams directors very rich indeed – rich enough to retire and never work again. If Darius had been threatening to make public his film exposing Rackhams to police investigation, many people would be prepared to pay for his silence, or else silence him for good. Supposing his father had found such incriminating evidence in Darius's possessions, made subsequent enquiries and been murdered for the same reason?

As I stood at the entrance to the manor house and rang

The Bad Hail Mary

the bell, Molly opened the door to me, looking as if she'd aged ten years since we'd made love in the back of my car. It was chilling to think that I'd been on the *Lively Lady* with her, the same boat that had been her husband's coffin. A cigarette hung from her lips, and there were dark wrinkles under her eyes, her hair seemed straggly and unwashed, and the blue teeshirt and jeans looked creased and sweat-stained, as if she'd worn them for days. Oddly enough, the absence of make-up didn't detract from her looks as much as the haggard wariness behind her eyes. She looked scared. Deep down scared.

"Come in, Sean," she said quietly, taking the fag from her mouth. "You don't know how good it is to see you."

We went to the huge drawing room that I remembered from my last visit. A log fire was crackling in the grate, and the smell of wood smoke was pleasantly potent. The grand central chandelier cast muted yellow light all round, and I sat on the sofa, while Molly took the armchair opposite. Sparks shot up from the logs as she prodded the flames with a poker.

"I know what you're thinking," she told me as she turned towards me, holding my gaze unblinkingly. "You've heard that they know that the yacht was deliberately scuppered by someone on board while we were at sea. But it wasn't me. I'll swear on anything you like. I'd be lying if I told you I didn't fantasise about him dying and me inheriting all this, but I'd never have actually done it. For goodness's sake, Sean, I'm not a killer, I couldn't kill a fly! Yes, I hated him, and yes, I wanted him to die. But I didn't kill him. And if I had decided to kill him I wouldn't have been such a bloody idiot to do it like this, where I knew I'd come within a whisker of drowning myself and where I would be the chief suspect."

"So tell me what happened."

"God!" She closed her eyes and shook her head. "I've been though it with the police time and again." She sighed, licked her lips, and closed her eyes for a moment. For the first time I noticed the frown lines on her forehead, long deep furrows. "Okay, Sean, cards on the table. Things were right bad between us, we'd been rowing off and on for days. I reckoned like that if we went sailing it would be a bit of fun, he's been so wrapped up in work lately, this proposed merger at Rackhams is like being on a tightrope, his nerves were screwed up tight as a drum. He's been having a lot of meetings, and he wasn't happy with some of the conditions to do with the merger – the price or the number of shares, I dunno the details, summink like that. There's all sorts of other things going on at Rackhams, but will he talk about them? No, he just broods, keeping it all inside. But I've overheard him shouting on the phone. Seems like there's big trouble ahead, and it's all connected with them Yanks, bloody Apperline Webb."

"So Martin was against the merger?"

"Too right. He'd had rows with the other directors. He felt very strongly that the terms them Yanks were offering were too one-sided. He felt that it was all a big mistake. But all the other directors were mad keen to go ahead. However he had a fifty-one per cent holding, meaning that he could block the deal if he wanted to. The money they were willing to pay was out of this world, but still Martin thought they should stick out for more. Martin was adamant about how wrong it was, as I say, I heard him shouting on the phone.

"Anyway, Martin agreed to coming out on the *Lively Lady*. We drove to the marina and went out in the early evening. Everything was fine, we had a nice day, and it was beginning to get dark, so I altered course to go back home.

The Bad Hail Mary

Martin had gone down below deck for something, while I was top-side, checking the sails, sorting things out. Suddenly I sees another boat not far away, and it seemed to drop anchor. I only took all this in on the periphery of my vision, I were too busy rushing around getting things done. Then, out of the corner of my eye, I thought I saw someone in diving gear climbing on board at the stern. So I looked around and couldn't see no one, so I figured it was a trick of the light. Then I heard drilling sounds from below, so I went to the main hatchway and lifted it up to see what was going on. And this guy is down there, below deck, Martin nowhere to be seen. Without thinking, I bent down and picked up a hammer that were on the floor, from when we were doing some work the previous day. He's at the bottom in the hold, coming up the steps, and suddenly he launches himself at me to get past, and I lash out, don't I? I hit him in the face with the hammer, but he just falls back and then I sees something coming towards me, and I'm out like a light. I wakes up a little bit later and there's water up to my waist. It's all dark and I can see I'm below deck and the electrics have failed, there's no light. I calls out to Martin, but there ain't no reply and I can see that the water's gonna be up to my neck within minutes, and I know that if I don't get up on deck fast it'll be game over.

"We were sinking fast. I tried to get into the galley, to find Martin, but by then it was impossible to open the door. I only just managed to make it up on deck, by which time the water is over the planks and the yacht's going down before I can even reach round for a lifejacket. So I do the only thing I can do, because the water's up around my chest now, and I know that any moment she's going down, and if I don't shift fast I can get dragged down with her. So I kick off and swim like fuck, as fast as I can. And over my shoulder I can see the mast disappearing below the water. She's gone, faster than I'd have believed possible, and I'm all alone, swimming for all I'm worth, panting with the effort. I screams out to Martin, hoping he's managed to get out, but he ain't nowhere to be seen, and by now the boat's well under. By this time it's pitch dark and I'm alone and treading water to keep myself alive. Martin ain't nowhere around, and I know that there's nothing on God's earth I can do to help him, 'cos I can't hardly help myself. I could feel there was a right strong current. Then I panicked, 'cos there weren't no other vessels around – the one I'd seen before was in the distance, moving away fast. All I could do was swim away. It were beginning to get dark, and by a miracle I could just make out a few lights in the distance, so I realised that the shore had to be in that direction. So I swam for my life. I never thought I'd get there, just swam and swam using up all of my strength, getting colder, knowing that any moment hypothermia would kick in and I'd have had it. Sometimes I kept staring and the shore didn't seem no closer, and I panicked, reckoning I was going in the wrong direction, but there was one blessed point when I could see that the one light on the shore was getting brighter and brighter. I just fixed myself on that and went all out, fighting the water, struggling like hell, doing everything I could. Finally, after what seemed like years, I could see the beach and shingle. A couple of people had seen me and were running down to the sea and as I was about to give up I felt arms pulling at me, and the next thing I remember I was waking up in hospital."

"And after that the police took you in?"

"Questioned me for hours. They didn't charge me with nothing, but I could tell what they were thinking."

"What did they say about the boat you saw?"

"Wrote it all down, presumably made enquiries, I don't know, do I? But I don't think they believed me."

I thought long and hard without saying anything. "So you're saying that someone climbed on board and scuppered the boat, hoping to kill both of you?"

"They must have done."

"Did Martin have any enemies?"

She shrugged, shivering in the large room, unaware that the log fire had dwindled to a few half-hearted sparks. "Only the other directors at Rackhams, as far as I know, because of his opposition to the deal they were all intent on. I don't know if they felt strongly enough to kill him though."

"And does anyone hate you?"

She shot me a look of surprise. "Me?"

"You might have been the target of the attack, not Martin."

"I don't reckon so. I got no enemies, have I?"

"I'm just thinking about something. The people who paid the detective to break into Darius's flat worked for Rackhams. I'm wondering if the smuggling racket that Darius was investigating involved a lot of people at Rackhams, and he was threatening to make it public, so they killed him to shut him up. I told Martin about it, so maybe he tackled someone about what was going on, so to shut him up, the people at Rackhams, notably that guy Meredith Gilliard, had to kill him too. The proposed takeover would be wrecked if shady stuff came to light."

"Yes." She nodded. "That might make sense. But I got to know, Sean. Do you believe me?"

There was a long silence. "I want to believe you."

"But you think I might have killed him?"

"I don't know."

"For heaven's sake, Sean, what kind of monster do you think I am?" She was close to tears, her voice shaking. "And even if I had wanted to murder him, why would I be so stupid as to do it this way? It was a miracle that I managed to swim to shore, I came this fucking close to drowning." She held her hand up, finger and thumb pressed together. "I'd have been crazy to risk my life like that."

We went on talking for most of the night. And as dawn began to break I had no doubts any more. Much as I'd have liked to be certain that Molly wasn't capable of cold-blooded murder, I couldn't rule it out. But the facts were more reassuring.

If she'd planned to kill him and make it look like an accident there would have been much easier ways of doing it, ways which didn't involve her in swimming a greater distance than would normally have been possible to do before being dragged down by the current, or succumbing to hypothermia. In addition to that, with her obvious motive to kill him, if she'd done so she would have employed someone else, making sure she had an unbreakable alibi. Someone could have tampered with his car, there could have been a staged break-in and a firearm discharged, all manner of methods of murder by proxy were possible. And every one of them was more efficient than this one, and didn't involve her risking a watery death.

"So if you're right," she said at last, "and Martin was murdered because he was going to crack down on the smuggling at Rackhams, or if they killed him because he were standing in the way of the deal, they were prepared to kill me too as collateral damage."

"Yes," I agreed. "Or else they might have assumed that Martin told you what he was investigating, so they needed to kill you too."

The Bad Hail Mary

"Nice." She lit another cigarette, inhaled and blew out the smoke. "Which means I'm either going to be convicted of murder, or be the target of a contract killing in the near future."

"Sorry."

There wasn't much more I could say to comfort her.

"Who else knew you were going out in the boat that night?"

She frowned in thought. "He got a phone call just before we left. I think it was Meredith, Meredith Gilliard, that bloke you just mentioned. He told Meredith that we were going out sailing, and that he'd ring him back in the morning.

Meredith Gilliard. The man who had employed Gordon Dallorzo to break into Darius's flat.

As dawn was breaking, and we were both dozing on the sofa, all hell broke loose.

The noise of cars crunching on gravel and screeching brakes was deafening, and within seconds there was a loud crashing on the door.

"Police, open up, please!" yelled someone from outside.

FOURTEEN

"Sean," she gabbled quickly, shouting above the knocking on the door as we both leapt to our feet. "Will you help me?"

Despite my misgivings she'd talked me round. The least I could do was try to find out the truth. More crucially, I couldn't let her face this mess on her own.

"Yes," I promised her. "I'll do whatever I can."

"That's all I want." She came into my arms. "I know it all sounds crazy but I swear I'm telling you the truth, Sean. I'm not a murderer. Here's the number of my lawyer, will you call him and tell him what's happened?"

"Sure, I'll try him now. I'll do anything I can."

She walked out into the hallway and opened the door.

I watched, feeling like an intruder, while the three officers came into the hallway and read out the charges and her Miranda rights, before asking her to get her coat and personal items, then leading her away.

"I'll help you, Molly," I called out after her as we all trooped out of the doorway into the porch. She looked back at me.

"And I believe you," I gave her my parting shot. "I believe what you told me. I know you didn't kill him."

She nodded. The police let her turn around and lock the door behind us.

The Bad Hail Mary

"May I ask who you are, sir?" one of the police officers asked me as they took Molly away in one of the cars.

"Sean Delaney."

"Are you a relative?"

"No. I'm a friend of Mrs Trefus."

"A close friend?"

"Not really. I – er – I met her recently."

"Really?" He stared at me, frowning. "Let's get this straight, Mr Delaney. You're not a close friend, you only met her recently, and yet you're at her house, alone with her at 6 o'clock in the morning."

"She's in trouble. I want to help her."

He stepped back, still staring into my eyes. "Sir, you do realise that this is a murder investigation?"

"Of course."

He took down my name and address.

"Are you able to help us in our enquiries into this case, sir? For instance is there anything you know about this case you'd like to tell us?"

"I don't think so. But I'm happy to talk to anyone. I've got nothing to add. But I've also got nothing to hide."

"I'd advise you to take care, sir. Lady Molly Trefus is an extremely attractive woman. We may need to contact her friends, her business acquaintances." He paused. "And her boyfriends, if she had any."

"Of course. I was on the force myself. I realise you have to make a lot of background enquiries in such a serious matter."

"Hmm." He shook his head slowly. "We'll be in touch, sir. Thank you."

I watched the cavalcade drive away, and went back to my car. On my phone, I Googled the name of the lawyer's firm she'd told me, and called the office number, leaving a message for Ashley Drummond, the name she'd given me, telling them that Lady Molly Trefus had been arrested and charged with murder, asking him to call me back, or if he could, to go straight to the Trew Valley Police Station in Penzance where they told me they were taking her.

*

Agnes Dallorzo had phoned me early the following morning at the Travelodge where I was staying, explaining that her husband was still missing, and the police hadn't found any clues as to his whereabouts. I promised her that since I happened to be in Cornwall anyway, I would go to the station to try to find out what was happening.

Penzance seemed like an interesting town, and I found the police station in a turning off Market Jew Street, which was just beyond the large statue of Sir Humphrey Davy, the famous scientist who had invented the miner's safety lamp (known as 'The Davy Lamp'), in addition to discovering the chemical elements sodium and potassium. The illustrious Cornishman had died in 1829, and his statue was just in front of the Lloyds Bank building, with its dramatic frontage of grand stone pillars.

"As you surely know, I'm not allowed to comment on an ongoing investigation," said the policewoman who had come to the front desk at Trew Valley Police Station.

"Look, could we talk about this?" I asked her. The name on the lanyard round her neck said *PC Lucy Akehurst*. Quite frankly, for some reason I found I couldn't take my eyes off her. And, unless I was kidding myself, from the way she looked at me and hung on my every word, it was almost as if she felt the same way.

Sometimes you meet someone, and you just click.

"Obviously you can't tell me anything about Gordon

Dallorzo's disappearance, but I've got information you might need. The officer I met last night told me you might want to talk to me anyway, so I've come in to see you. What have you got to lose? After all, you're investigating a murder."

"You mean the death of Sir Martin Trefus? You think Mr Dallorzo's disappearance could be connected?"

"Yes."

"Well I'm not personally involved," she told me. "And even if I was I wouldn't be allowed to discuss the case with anyone, as I'm sure you understand."

"Naturally."

"Since it could be a murder case, the AMIT team have been assembled, and the SIO, the senior investigating officer, is a chief inspector from another force, using our team as back-up. Nor do we officially yet know if it is a murder or a case of accidental death. The coroner hasn't made a judgement, and nor have we. It's still early days."

"So why not listen to what I have to say?" I suggested.

"Okay, come through."

She led us behind the front desk and along a corridor and to an interview room.

"I'm Lucy, Constable Lucy Akehurst," she told me. "So first of all, Mr Delaney, what's your involvement in all this? What has it got to do with you?"

"I was commissioned to clear out a flat in Bradford, where a man called Darius Trefus, Sir Martin's son, had committed suicide. While I was there, an intruder tried to break in. That was Gordon Dallorzo, the husband of Agnes, the lady who's been in to see the police in Bradford about him."

"Reporting him as missing in strange circumstances," she replied. "She reported that two men took him away in a car, and he never came home."

"I saw them too. I gave the officer the registration number of their car."

"Uh-huh."

"I found out that Mr Dallorzo had been employed by Meredith Gilliard, a director of Rackhams International, to break into Darius's Bradford flat and steal computers, papers and cameras," I went on. "He failed to do so, and I phoned Rackhams, impersonating Mr Dallorzo, telling Gilliard that I had the items they wanted. The next day, Mr Dallorzo went missing, and since then, three weeks ago now, your West Yorkshire colleagues have been unable to find any traces of him. Then Sir Martin died onboard his yacht."

"Okay, Mr Delaney. That's one suicide, one disappearance, and one murder or accidental death."

"Yes. And all of them are connected to Rackhams International, which right now is in the process of negotiating a merger with a large American company that all the directors, apart from Sir Martin, are in favour of. But this American company would run a mile if there were any rumour of scandals involving Rackhams. I think that Darius was threatening to expose some racket that they wanted hushed up, so they killed him and tried to obtain and destroy any evidence he might have got of wrongdoing by the company. I myself found a film he made of a Rackhams representative in Italy offering to smuggle goods out of the country in contravention of international law. I think they were afraid that Gordon Dallorzo would tell people they'd employed him to break into Darius's flat so they killed him and got rid of the body. And I think that Sir Martin found this same evidence and was investigating it, so they had to silence him too."

"Hmm." Lucy Akehurst frowned. She had the kind of

The Bad Hail Mary

face you can't forget. A fringe of red hair. Hazel eyes, a retroussé nose and a mouth that lifted slightly at the corners, as if it was at home with smiles. She was lie-down-beside-me sexy, and I couldn't stop staring at her face, finding that her eyes couldn't quite tear themselves away from mine.

Unless I imagined it. Who knows, wishful thinking?

Her pale skin had freckles, and the crisp white shirt under her dark uniform served oddly to accentuate her femininity rather than make her look masculine. She couldn't be called beautiful, but there was something about her that was much better than beautiful and, frankly, it mesmerised me.

I really wanted to get to know her better, but now was hardly the time.

"Mr Delaney, I did a bit of checking up on you while you were waiting at the front desk. I see that you were in the job yourself. In the Met in London."

"Yes, some time ago now." I watched the corners of her mouth, the way they moved fractionally tilting upwards, and wondered how it would feel to kiss her.

"But, you're one of us. You know how it is. As a lowly constable, I'm at rock bottom of the pecking order. I've read novels and seen things on TV that are crazy: with a constable arguing with an inspector, or a PC yelling back at his sergeant. You know as well as I do what rubbish that is. You know the score: that if a sergeant bawls us out, we have to jump to it or we're in deep doo-doo. And an inspector is practically a god, someone you'd only normally speak to if he was giving you an order, or pulling you up on something, or at an interview board. If an inspector bollocks you, you'd not dare to answer back."

"I remember it well."

"So you also know that as a constable, what I say and what I think counts for nothing."

"Sure, I know that right enough."

"Liking you, and wanting to help you is a far cry from having any influence over what my bosses do, or what they'll even listen to. "

"Of course it is."

"But since you have first-hand involvement, I can't see any reason not to tell you how the land lies. Preliminary evidence of the drill found in the hold suggests that it was murder, not accidental death, so that's what we've got to run with, even if the coroner hasn't yet made an official decision. The CPS have been appraised of the evidence we've got against Lady Trefus, with a view to charging her, and they've not come back to us yet, and the general feeling is that there isn't going to be any actual evidence. If she is charged and subsequently goes down it's going to be on circumstantial evidence, and a jury will have to decide on probabilities, unless we come up with something else. As for Gordon Dallorzo, my contact in Yorkshire tells me that we've done all the usual checks and come up with nothing. His credit cards have gone missing, but they haven't been used. His bank account doesn't show any large recent withdrawals of cash, as might normally happen when someone goes on the run and doesn't want to be found. We've asked around and Gordon doesn't seem to be a ladies' man or seriously into gambling or drugs. CCTV in the vicinity of his home and office hasn't shown him walking anywhere, nor has his car been used, it's still parked at his home. We've checked on that car registration number you gave us, but it's a hire car, and the name given to the hire company turns out to be false. So the likelihood is that the last time he was seen was being taken away in that car, outside his office, by the men Mrs Dallorzo described."

"So what do you think might have happened to him?"

"My gut feeling is that he's dead and we'll find his body in a week or a year." She shrugged. "On the other hand he might have got out of that car he was taken away in, and for reasons of his own, joined the thousands of folks who walk out of their home one morning and never come home, and no one ever sees them again."

"The missing."

"Yes. So, Sean. You're convinced that our friend Molly is telling the truth."

"I am."

"How long have you known her?"

I told her all about rescuing her from the fire, and how she had re-established contact with me, persuading her husband to employ me to paint Darius's portrait. Of course I left out the fact that it had been her who had started the fire in the first place.

"Sean, I'm sorry to say so, but it strikes me that you're playing a very dangerous game."

"I know."

"You're stubborn, but then most of the men I come across are stubborn." She stood up and accompanied me along the corridor, back to the front reception area. "Thanks for coming in to see us," she told me. "I like you, Sean, I *really* like you. I honestly don't know why. It's funny, some people you meet and you just. . ."

"I like you too." She stopped walking and looked into my eyes and smiled, holding my hand in our goodbye shake a lot longer than necessary. "And because I like you I'm giving you some good advice. Something tells me this is a right nasty business that's going to get a lot nastier. Please,

Sean, just push off back to Kent and forget about all this. You can always phone me, anytime, and I can keep you up to date about what's happening. Maybe, if you're not in a hurry to go home we could meet up sometime. But as for this mess, you're best off out of it."

"Everyone tells me to mind my own business."

"Sean, I'm on your side, but I can see you'll not take any notice of what I say. But if all this blows up in your face – as I reckon it probably will – I'll help you if I can. Because, sure as sunshine, I'm certain that you're heading for trouble."

How right she was.

And in the moment she looked into my eyes, I realised that my feelings for Molly had never been anything like this. In another life, if she wasn't a policewoman involved in a case I was connected to, I'd have liked nothing better than to get to know her properly. Falling in love is a stupid description of something that's so nebulous, it's debatable if it ever happens. But I felt more than just a connection with Lucy, and I could sense that she felt the same way.

But right now, I had to tackle the mess that was in front of me. Little did I know that the trouble when it came was like nothing I could possibly have suspected. It was so wild and crazy it was almost unbelievable.

You see, the mystery was anything but simple, and my ideas were way off the mark by a million miles.

For the roots of this mystery went back to much deeper darker times, when thousands upon thousands of innocent people were murdered by monsters.

And it had all happened almost one hundred years ago.

. .

FIFTEEN

Where next, I wondered?

If I was going to help Molly, I had to get some answers, and every avenue seemed like a dead end. I could try to trace the Rackhams agent in Italy, who was in the film about the smuggling, but something told me that having any dealings with anyone at Rackhams would be a big mistake. After all, phoning Meredith Gilliard and impersonating Gordon Dallorzo might have got the poor bugger killed, and if they thought I knew they had anything to do with Darius or Sir Martin's death, they'd not hesitate to kill me too. The police enquiry into Martin's death was confidential and I had no hope of finding out what facts they were working with.

However, there was one person in this whole fiasco who I knew virtually nothing about: Darius's disappeared girlfriend, Paula Swan. Amongst Darius's possessions I had found her passport, driving licence, bank statements for her business and other private papers, so what could be more natural than trying to trace her in order to return them?

The day after Darius had died, the eight months pregnant Paula Swan had left immediately, apparently scared of staying in the flat alone, and refusing to give a forwarding address to anyone. Had she seen the murderers and was scared they would kill her too? Or did she know too much about the film Darius was making, exposing the criminals at Rackhams?

*

Bradford wasn't quite as cold and miserable as it had been last time I was here, back in January. The weather was slightly warmer, and the sun was shining on Centenary Square, twinkling in the stone mullioned windows of the oh-so-grey town hall.

When I rang Billy's bell at the Albany Court Apartment block, the little old man buzzed me in, and met me at the foot of the stairs.

"Hello, Sean mate," he said, shaking hands enthusiastically. "I heard all about the yacht accident and the lad's dad. Who'd have thought it, eh?"

We went for a drink together at the Twin Turls Wetherspoons pub off the Square. He tapped his pint glass thoughtfully as I asked him if he had any idea where to find Paula.

"As I told you she did a flit, she were that terrified," he said gloomily.

"What of?" I asked him.

"No idea, she'd not confided in me, I hardly knew her, did I? But I tell you what, lad," Billy went on, "practically a whole box of them papers we put into storage, had her name on 'em."

"Yeah, I thought so. As I explained, Molly, Sir Martin's wife, let me have the keys to Triplinghoes, in case she needed me to bring her anything, and I took the liberty of finding the keys to the Shurguard storage container and bringing them. Fancy coming with me, to pick out the papers connected to her, and helping me look through them?"

The Bad Hail Mary

"Why not?"

Next day, we found the box of papers that had mostly Paula's personal belongings in it.

In the hotel, I took out everything.

Driving licence. Passport. Amongst a lot of other bits and pieces, letters, forms, unopened mail and whatnot.

Paula had left all these vital papers, and obviously she would want them back. She had run away from her home without even taking these essential items, and the only reason she'd done so had to be that she was terrified. Had she seen Darius's killers, and could identify them? That's the only reason I could imagine why she'd be so scared for her life that she'd rush away, not even taking the time to collect her personal documents.

In the box, I also found a few flyers for a tattoo parlour in Brighton. Yes, I remembered now that Sir Martin had said that Paula was a tattoo artist, that was how she met Darius, when he went into her shop. She had worked there, or else had owned the place, so it was about the only lead I had.

Two days later I was in Brighton, bleary-eyed from lack of sleep and too much driving. I'd found a cheap hotel just outside town, and had driven into the city this morning, parking in the car park near the station and walking down Queens Road towards the city centre, then turning left along North Street.

Stung by Steel, the curiously named tattoo parlour where it seemed that Paula had worked was nearby, sandwiched between a shop called *The Sorcerer's Apprentice*, which appeared to sell books, candles, and beads – merchandise for witches, ghost hunters and warlocks, and *Erotonotto*, which seemed to be some kind of sex shop, catering for a variety of astounding needs. The antiques market called 'Snoopers' was nearby.

The bell rang as I opened the door into the darkness of the tattoo parlour, and the interior was so gloomy it was like entering a crypt, apart from occasional floodlighting to lend luminosity to the outsize posters of tattooed men and women, alongside strategically placed mirrors.

"Hello, mate." This was said by a huge man with a red beard that reached his chest. He was standing behind the counter at the end of the room. "What you looking for then, squire?"

"I'm trying to find the lady who I think used to work here. Paula."

"Oh yeah?" His previously friendly manner evaporated, and he looked angry. He ran from behind the counter, walked across to me and grabbed me by the collar, pinning me against the wall.

"You've got ten seconds to fuck off out of here, before I choke you to death."

SIXTEEN

I punched him in the guts, and he doubled over in pain, as I moved away.

"Listen, don't push me around! I'm not your enemy," I told him. "I know she's afraid of some dangerous people and they're probably after me too. I'm on her side!"

"How do I know that?" he groaned as he stood up, still in obvious pain.

"Look, please." I held my hands up placatingly. "Hear me out. I know Paula was living in Bradford and she had to get away quickly because she was scared and needed to protect herself because she was pregnant. I was paid to clear out that flat she shared with her boyfriend Darius, and I've found her driving licence, passport and other personal papers, and I want to give them back to her, but I've got no idea where to find her. If she's afraid of people at Rackhams, I understand. I'm afraid of them too. I want to find out what's going on."

The man leaned on the counter, his voice no longer a gasp of pain. "All I know is that Paula was in trouble, she was scared witless of something, some people. She told me there might be goons coming looking for her, so if you're one of them you can fuck right off!" He went behind the counter, bent down and produced a large baseball bat.

"Look." I showed him the passport and the driving licence that I took from my pocket, and held it up so he could see her name. "My name's Sean Delaney. I'm a portrait painter, and I do decorating and house clearances on the side." I took out my phone, and found my website and showed it to him. "I was employed to paint a portrait of Darius from photos for his father, Sir Martin Trefus, the man who's been all over the news because he was drowned off the coast of Cornwall. I believe that Trefus may have been murdered, and that Darius's death wasn't suicide, it was murder. I want to find out what's going on, and I'm hoping Paula can help me. And if I can find out who killed them, and why, maybe I can bring them to justice, and Paula can come in out of the cold, with no one threatening her."

The large man was staring at me.

"Here's my mobile number and my email." I wrote them on a piece of paper and handed them over. "If you're in touch with Paula, please pass them on, then if she'll agree to meet me at a place of her choosing, I can return all her things. No trouble. No pressure."

"Paula's had a lot of trouble in her life," he answered after a long pause. "She was going out with me before she met Darius. After she met him, she changed entirely."

"Did you hate him?"

"Yes, matter of fact I did," he went on. "He was a right little bastard, smarmy little shit. I ain't surprised he upset someone, he was one of them types, you know? Snarky, smirking, threatening, always had a *I know something you don't know* expression on his face and thought he was the bee's fucking knees. And look what's happened now? He's dead, but he's still ruining her life, and little Eleanor's life is fucked because she ain't got a dad, and her mum's living in hiding."

The Bad Hail Mary

"She had the baby?"

"Yeah. Eleanor is a few weeks old now, sweet little thing."

"And who are *they*?" I asked. "Who is she so scared of?"

He shrugged. "Never told me, did she?"

"Please will you help me?" I asked him. "I'm on her side. I want to do what's right. She can meet me in a public place – see me from a distance before she decides I'm not the enemy. Bring you with her, or other friends. Anything. Believe me, I just want to help."

"So what's your angle, mate? What's it got to do with you?"

"I've got involved with Martin Trefus's wife, and I believe she's innocent. I want to try and clear her name."

"And you reckon Paula can help you?"

"Maybe. Right now I've hit a dead end. She's my only lead."

I got the call that evening, just as I was wondering what on earth I could do next. Molly had phoned me earlier on, telling me that she was still being held in custody, but that her lawyer was trying to get her bail.

Paula sounded wary, monosyllabic and sad. She suggested that we could meet up in London, saying that she knew Wimbledon Common, which also happened to host a golf club. And could we meet there tomorrow, at 6pm?

*

Wimbledon Common is huge, and I remembered that it had been the place where a young woman, Rachel Nickell, had been murdered some years ago, and the police had initially arrested the wrong man, allowing the real killer, whose *own mother* had alerted the police to his likely guilt, to remain free for another two years. The wrong man, Colin

Stagg, had been in the police sights from the start, and their pig-headed tunnel vision had made some fool attempt to entrap him into admitting to a murder he didn't do. I knew all too well that once the police decide you're guilty they'll sometimes twist the facts to suit their case. Even some high-ranking officers could be so blinkered that they went after the wrong man, ruined people's lives and allowed killers to walk free more often than you might think.

The part of the huge park where I'd agreed to meet Paula was in Windmill Road, and signposted the Red Windmill Tea rooms and London Scottish Golf Club. The car park was large, and the adjacent tearooms were already closed, the white picket fencing surrounding the little café reminiscent of a sleepy village.

I'd got there early, and texted Sammy, the red-bearded tattoo parlour man, for him to text her in turn that I was sitting on a bench alone, just in front of the car park, and I was wearing a brown leather jacket and blue jeans. Eventually, a woman who looked like the photos I'd seen of Paula, arrived on foot. She had long black straggly hair and was wearing slashed-at-the-knee jeans, high black leather boots and a white teeshirt under a shapeless blue coat.

I waved to her, and she gave a tentative wave in return and moved towards me. From her anxious expression and the way she looked all around to see if I was alone, I could tell she was scared stiff.

"Sean?" she asked, comparing my website's photo on her phone with my face.

"Yes." I stood up to meet her. "I'm sorry for what's happened. I want to help."

"Let's walk. Do you think anyone's following you?"

"Haven't noticed anyone."

"If you're lying I'll kill you here and now!" She was in

front of me, about ten yards away now. She had produced a huge kitchen knife from inside her coat and held it out in front of her, moving forwards, as if she was about to stab me to death.

Then I was aware of someone behind me, and she froze, staring over my shoulder. She let out a yell, and ran towards me. . .

SEVENTEEN

Paula was within a few feet when she realised the person behind me was a harmless dog-walker, then she put the knife away.

"Follow me," she told me.

She led me across the park, to where the ground sloped sharply downwards and the dense trees made the day seem like night. We went on walking, down and down until we came to some kind of waterway, a shallow stream that extended as far as you could see. It was like a sleepy woodland dell in a fairy-tale, as if we were deep in the countryside, and the town and traffic were a million miles away. No one was nearby, and smells and sounds were muted a long way away, as if we were locked into our own private world.

She sat on the huge log, a felled tree. I sat beside her, purposely leaving a couple of feet of space between us. Paula was every bit as tough-looking as her photos had predicted, and, ironically, if I had been commissioned to paint her portrait I could have done it like a dream. Firm, hard features, eyes that could bore a hole into your soul and a ruggedly determined set to her chin. She had a small mole on the side of her nose, and I could even catch a glimpse of soft white down on her upper cheek, and the faintest of faint few dark hairs on her upper lip. In the photos she had looked aggressive and dangerous, every gangster's murderous moll. Whereas in person there was something more about her, strangely a sort of discernible kindness.

Paula put her hand into the large shoulder bag and took out the long sharp kitchen knife that she had threatened me with earlier on.

I stared down at it. "What are you going to do with that?"

"Depends. Depends on if you're on your own. Depends on if you are who you say you are."

"Fuck it, Paula. You've seen my picture on my website, your friend Sammy is satisfied I'm not dangerous. I'm on your side."

"Are you?"

"I've got all your stuff in my car," I told her. "If you're on foot I can give you a lift to wherever you're staying."

"Thanks, but I brought my camper van."

"I heard you've got a baby," I began.

"Yes, Eleanor. A mate is looking after her, I didn't want to risk bringing her with me in case I had to make a speedy exit."

"Why are you so afraid?"

She flinched as we both noticed the shadows from the tree branches that leapt and frolicked as they blew in the wind, flickering continually.

"Because they killed Darius. And if they can find me, they'll kill me too."

"Who?"

She stared into her lap and shook her head.

"And why?"

"You don't want to know. This is bigger than you can possibly imagine. You don't want to get involved, believe me."

"I'm already involved. Why the fuck else do you think I'm here?"

"Then you're a handsome Irish clown. Save that pretty face from getting ruined. Get out of it while you still can."

"Everyone keeps telling me that. And I tell you something, Paula. No one tells me what to do."

"Oh yeah, hard man, are you?"

"When I need to be."

"Is that often?"

"I avoid trouble whenever I can."

I stared at her watching the twitch of her eyelid, the fear etched into every feature as her neat, full-lipped mouth twitched and grimaced, as if she was wrestling with some internal pain. Was she deluded? Something about her clear-eyed stare told me she was no fool, not the kind to invent things and be scared of shadows. But the police had concluded that Darius had killed himself, yet she was convinced they were wrong.

Why?

"Okay," I tried again, shaking my head wearily. "You're ready to stab me to death because you think I'm some kind of enemy who lured you here. So let's do it this way. I'll tell you what I know and how I'm involved. I was employed to clear out your flat and to paint Darius's portrait from any photos or images I could find there. The job was a fuck-up right from the get-go. I couldn't find enough decent pictures, and Martin and Molly told me my portrait was bollocks, and refused to pay. Since I completed the flat clearance and the portrait, Sir Martin's died in mysterious circumstances, and his wife Molly has been arrested for his murder. I believe she's innocent and want to help her clear her name. I think people from Rackhams murdered Sir Martin. And I think those same people might have murdered Darius, as well as killing a detective who'd been employed by Rackhams to break into your flat, who's disappeared without trace after I contacted the company, pretending to be him and threatening to involve the police. I feel sorry for the detective's wife, she seems like a nice lady, and I want to help her get answers, because I feel as if I'm responsible for her husband's death. What I don't know is, if people at Rackhams did kill them all, why?"

I had her attention now. She was watching me like a hawk. She slowly replaced the knife in the bag.

"And if Darius was murdered, as you say, why does everyone believe he hanged himself?"

"People who are rich and powerful can do whatever they want if they know the right people. And the guys at Rackhams, the directors there. They're as rich and powerful as you can get. They look upon the likes of me and Eleanor, and you, as just so much shit on their shoe. We're expendable. Darius didn't kill himself, he had no reason to, he had every reason to live. For goodness sake, would he have killed himself when he was looking forward to the birth of his child? He was over the moon about being a father. He had everything to live for!"

"But the police must have considered all that. Is there any other reason why you are so sure that Darius was murdered?"

"Yes. I was there, wasn't I? Just after it happened."

She closed her eyes and flexed her fingers. The photos of her hadn't done her justice, portraying her as a hard, cynical, world weary sexpot. Close up, she wasn't like that at all. Above all, she had an interesting face: straight slightly blunt nose, firm mouth with character lines and a steely resolve in deep brown eyes that looked as if they could see clear through into your soul. She was sharp, hard, cynical and world-weary, as if she had seen way too much of life.

To my surprise I found myself liking her.

If only I had known what she was going to do to me later. And precisely how she was going to end up ruining my life, yet also saving my sanity.

"Did the killers see you?" I asked her. "Is that why you're terrified of them finding you?"

"I'm not sure. But yes, I think they might have done. I certainly saw one of them clearly enough to identify him. Even if they suspect I might have seen them, they could get rid of me in the blink of an eye. It's a horrid feeling, being in limbo." She shivered.

The twilight was on us now and, added to the virtual darkness of the dell of trees we were in, it seemed almost like night. The atmosphere was charged with a kind of strange power, and I had the feeling that what she said next was going to fundamentally change everything.

"Okay, Sean. I trust you. This is what happened." She looked at me, a direct truthful gaze that didn't believe in blinking. "Darius and I had a row that evening, quite a violent row as it happens. I went out for a walk, and to buy some booze and stuff from the all-night supermarket. When I came back, as I was about to enter Albany Court, three men in smart suits came out, walking fast and not talking. I only got a look at the face of one of them, but I looked up the Rackhams website afterwards, for their company personnel. The man I saw was Meredith Gilliard. Head of International Art Sales. But of course he wasn't urbane and smiling when I saw him, like in the picture. He was marching fast, eyes searching this way and that, looking like a cornered rat."

"And?"

"I went inside, a bit surprised that three well-dressed men would be in our building at that time of the evening. Went up to the flat, let myself in, and found Darius hanging there. I couldn't stop screaming, and that dear old guy downstairs, Billy, ran up and saw what had happened, cut him down and he called the police.

"I knew he was dead, it was obvious. And earlier that day, Darius had already told me that he had been talking to people at Rackhams. He was proud, boasting, admitting that he was blackmailing them, threatening them with what he knew, and he was certain they'd pay a fortune to keep his mouth shut, in fact they'd already paid something and he reckoned they'd have to go on paying him forever, or at least a big one-off payment to make sure the merger with the American people went through. That's what we'd been arguing about. I'd told him what a dangerous and ridiculous thing it was to do. Apart from that, for my own reasons, I believed that the truth should come out. It was obvious that they'd killed him to shut him up. If I'd waited around for the police, they'd have wanted me to give a description of Gilliard and those other men. And I knew that if I did that, they'd kill me too, to stop me telling anyone what it was all about – they have connections everywhere, even within the police. They'd kill me, which was bad enough. But the thought of my unborn baby never being born – it was worse than anything on earth. I've come up against people like that before in my life, and I know there's no stopping them. Darius left lots of money around, rolls of cash, so before even the police arrived, I grabbed all the money I could find, and also we'd been collecting photos for an album, so I also grabbed all the ones I could find, mostly of Darius, because I knew that was all I'd have to remember him by."

"So that explains why there were hardly any photos of him, then," I reasoned. "His parents commissioned me to paint his portrait and I couldn't do it properly because there weren't enough photos to use."

"Oh." She looked surprised. "Sorry about that. Anyway, after that I just ran to the station in a blind panic, hating myself for abandoning Darius, but knowing that if my baby was ever going to be born my only chance was to run fast and hide faster. I took a train to Edinburgh, where I've got a mate who put me up. She helped me, I stayed there for a few weeks, I had the baby there. I tell you I was so afraid that the shock of finding Darius's body would make me lose the baby, but luckily things went fine. After she was born, I bought a camper van with cash under a false name, so they can't find me, and I've been moving around since then. I'm in a hell of a mess, I'm running out of money, and I've just been living day to day, afraid that if I manage to get a job, they'll somehow hear about it. I just don't know what to do."

I let the silence stretch for a long time.

"So," at last I answered her. "What's it all about? What's this secret that Darius knew about? I saw the film that Darius made about Rackhams' foreign staff being involved in smuggling artefacts from prohibited countries. Is that it? Had he got evidence of Rackhams breaking international law, and was threatening to report them to the police?"

"That's all it could have been. Let me take you back to when Darius and I went on holiday to Italy, our last holiday as it turned out. Darius took me to see an archaeological dig on a historic site there. One of the archaeologists was telling us all about these local guys called *tombarolas*. They're locals who know where the ancient burial sites are, and sneak in when no one's looking and dig down and steal grave artefacts and sell them, to the outrage of the local people and the archaeologists who know that they're destroying archaeological sites, wrecking any chances of recording the history. You see in that part of Italy there are literally hundreds of graves, most of them have been ransacked over the years, but if you're young and strong, prepared to take risks and don't give a damn about destroying ancient irreplaceable artefacts you can make a reasonable living, despite the risks of being caught. Darius was asking about this and eventually he managed to make friends with one of these tombarolas, a man called Raul, who had a loyal band of friends who helped him. Darius managed to convince him that he wanted to take part in one of these raids, and they accepted money to let him come with them. They found a small stone carving, dating back I don't know, thousands of years I think he said. In the bar that night, Raul was drunk, and he introduced Darius to an older man called Geraldo, who he said was going to sell the item for us. There's a law in Italy to do with protecting Italy's cultural heritage that means it's illegal to export anything that can be considered 'objects with a cultural interest' without an export licence, which is unlikely to be granted. Yet the price of grave artefacts in London or New York is fifty times what anyone would pay in Italy, meaning that for some years now there's been a lot of smuggling. But Geraldo told us that he knew a man who was a town councillor who had a contact with Rackhams Auctioneers, who regularly organise for artefacts such as we had found to be smuggled out of Italy so they could be sold abroad. It was a big business, he said."

"So Darius tried to blackmail people at Rackhams about this practice?"

"That was his plan. First we had to try and get evidence, so Darius went to this guy, taking with him this ancient artefact he'd bought locally, and tried to trap him into admitting he could smuggle it out of Italy for a fee. He filmed the interview with him, to use it as evidence."

"What happened to the film?"

"I don't know. I don't care. All I know is that when we came back home, Darius phoned someone at Rackhams and went to see them, all excited, telling me he had them just where he wanted them, what's more, he would tell his father all about it – *wipe the smile off that self-righteous old bastard's face* was how he put it. He told me it had worked, they had paid him what he asked for."

"So they killed him to stop his blackmail and to shut him up," I answered.

"Yes." She looked down at the ground. "Mind you, there was one other thing that I wondered about."

"What?"

"The Austrian connection."

Which is when the whole mystery began to make sense.

But I could never have guessed the truth in a million years.

When I did find out the whole truth it blew my mind.

EIGHTEEN

"Darius went out to see someone in Austria. Let me explain," Paula continued. "Life was pretty tough for us all those weeks in Bradford. Rackhams had paid us some money, as I said, but the baby was due in days, and by then most of the money had run out. Before he tried to blackmail Rackhams, Darius had no work, and he'd been doing a bit of dealing – just a bit of weed, this and that, nothing too heavy, but he was getting in deeper, hence the rolls of cash in the flat, he even bought a gun, for goodness sake. I remember as clear as if it was yesterday, about this other thing. We were in that horrible flat in Bradford and tired out. One evening he got an anonymous call from a detective he'd been employing to try and dig up some extra information about the Rackhams smuggling, something he could use to put the squeeze on the company. He told him apparently that he had heard that there was a factory in Austria, set up by Rackhams employees, where this guy was making artefacts and passing them off as ancient grave items, and Rackhams were selling them, having created fictitious sellers in Germany and laundering the money somehow. The items had to be good, authentic enough to fool experts."

"Surely that's not possible?"

"Apparently it's easier than you might think. There was a man in England called Sean Greenhalgh who did it from his garden shed in Yorkshire during the '70s and '80s and he was mightily successful. He ended up going to jail, but for many years he was manufacturing 'ancient' relics in his garden shed, and he sold them to reputable auction houses and collectors. It's easier than you might think. You need a flair for art and sculpture and a knowledge of stone and metals and chemistry, but if you produce something realistic, people can be prepared to believe anything. Whereas with paintings there are a great many scientific tests for authenticity, for instance testing the age and type of canvas or wood background, and the composition of the paint itself, the pigments are a clue. It's not the same for old relics, because when you think about it, the piece of rock you're carving something from can itself be very old, so the only unknown is the actual date when the carving took place, which could be a thousand years or last week. Usually the big stumbling block for selling antiquities is the provenance, getting experts to put their reputations on the line by assessing a relic as genuine or a fake. This Austrian guy was supposed to be a highly skilled blacksmith and also a sculptor and an artist, but he taught himself to simulate all kinds of things: ancient Roman sculptures, grave goods, old vases, some of which are worth thousands. And he was able to fool many professional dealers and made himself a fortune."

"What kind of items would these be?"

"Anything that might have been put into an ancient grave. For instance the Assyrians and the Egyptians believed that the dead person needed all kinds of earthly items for the afterlife. Pots, vases, plates, serving dishes, jewellery, weapons of every kind, beads, trinkets like metallic jugs and pitchers, candlesticks, the list goes on and on. The component materials of something like a clay pot for instance, is local earth, and there's literally no way of knowing if that earth is two thousand years old, or dug from your garden a week ago. Since Rackhams were handling the sale, that fact alone, their reputation for honesty, meant that provenance wasn't necessary. Rackhams were in a position to invent fictitious clients who 'asked them to handle the sale', they sell it, authenticate its history, and funnel the money back into Rackhams, probably via a Swiss bank account. The detective said he'd found some evidence of this, but without going to Germany he couldn't say how big the operation was."

"Wow!" I said to her, looking out at the darkness.

"They killed him because he knew about Rackhams' shady practices, and was threatening them," she said without any hesitation. "Just like they'll kill you or me, if either of us tried to make this public. You've got no idea how rich these people are, how little we matter to anyone."

"But how do you fake a hanging?" I asked her.

"I guess you just overpower someone, fix the noose, make him stand on a chair, then kick the chair away."

"One thing interests me," I told her, trying to assimilate the information. "Did Darius make contact with this Austrian forger?"

"Yes. He did go to Austria in order to try and find out more about the man who was making forgeries of ancient artefacts. As I said there was this private detective out there who was helping him. When he came back, having talked to the detective, he seemed discontented, and he refused to tell me what he'd discovered, kept saying it was none of my business. He was in a foul mood, a really nasty temper and he wouldn't talk about it. He was changed after he came back: guarded, wary, it was almost as if he was scared of something, but I don't know what it was. He kept saying that he'd got the people at Rackhams where he wanted them, but also he had this kind of anger behind his eyes, I don't understand what it was all about. I assumed he'd got some hard evidence about the guy who was manufacturing these forgeries. But, despite the strange mood he was in, he was very excited about something. He kept saying 'I'm getting all my ducks in a row before I do anything drastic. I'll tell you all of it as soon as I can'. He came back from Austria on the Friday, and it was the Monday when they killed him."

"So you never knew what happened in Austria?"

"No."

It had started to rain, and the insistent pitter-patter was restful, soothing somehow.

"Come on, let's get back to the car park, and I can give you your stuff to take away. By the way, what's happening about Darius's estate? He must have had money, and presumably he left it to you."

"He should have done, he would have done, I'm sure. But the fact is, he didn't make a will at all. And we weren't married. Whatever he had goes to his next of kin. His parents, I suppose."

"But didn't Sir Martin offer you anything? After all there's Eleanor to consider."

"No. Sir Martin and Molly hated me. They thought I was a bad influence. They don't give a damn about their grandchild. Correction. Sir Martin said they would be prepared to consider making some kind of allowance for me, but only if I submitted her to a DNA test, to make sure that Darius was Eleanor's father. I was so disgusted I didn't reply. They blame me for Darius's death."

The Bad Hail Mary

"I'm sorry."

"Sean, listen." She looked at me, her gaze unblinking, direct. "As I told you, right now, I'm in a hell of a mess and I've done lots of things in the past I'm ashamed of. I'm alone, I'm scared to contact my old friends, because I don't know who I can trust. I can't work, because I'm afraid of giving employers my name, and Rackhams catching up with me. I believe that I've got powerful, dangerous enemies who killed Darius, and won't hesitate to kill me and my daughter. I'm afraid of staying in one place for too long. You're the only person I can trust. Will you stay in touch with me? I'll do anything I can to help if you're going to try and find out the truth of what happened to Darius, to get his murderers convicted. If you can expose this massive secret, whatever it is that the damned Rackhams bigwigs are scared of people knowing, presumably this Austrian factory, then I'll be able to come in from the cold and get on with my life. I'm not lazy. I'm a skilled tattoo artist, as you know. And I'm also an electrician."

"An electrician?"

"Yes, everyone thinks it's odd for a woman to do work like that, but it made sense for me. It's hard work physically, of course, but it's also very interesting, and it makes you think, there's a lot of theory and maths involved. I passed all the exams, if I could get my life back, I'm sure I could pick up jobs here and there. When the tattoo parlour was quiet, I'd do the odd rewiring job. I can make a good living, but with this hanging over me, I'm stuck, hiding away all the time. So, Sean, will you stay in touch with me?"

"Of course. I'll give you my mobile number, and you give me yours – I promise I won't pass it on to anyone, and I'll keep you informed of everything that happens. And there's one other thing. Amongst your things in the flat, all those personal papers, driving licence and so on, there was a big bundle of cash – a thousand, I counted it. I'm guessing it was your money, so I'm giving it to you."

"Thanks, but it wasn't mine. Darius had a lot of cash lying around."

"Well it was Darius's cash then. I'm sure he'd have wanted you to have it."

The answer was in Austria.

When I went there I found that I had opened up Pandora's Box.

Which was when I found out what it was like to stare into Hell.

NINETEEN

"Welcome to Steifflerstadt," the kind receptionist at the Hotel Internationale said, treating me to her most pleasant smile. "Mr Delaney?"

The village of Steifflerstadt, near Vienna, was covered in snow. The plane fare had cost a fortune, and my bank account was unpleasantly low, but this was something I felt I just had to do.

For the past few days I had been more or less at my wits' end.

Attempting to locate any information at all about this supposed 'Austrian manufacturer of Ancient Artefacts' was proving more or less impossible. Paula had told me that Darius had travelled to Austria last November, and in the papers I'd put into storage I had manged to find Darius's bank statements for the whole of that month, and there were items that had been paid for in Vienna, Austria. On the bank statement I found a name, Herr Tristan Neuberg, and on another note with his bank papers I had found Herr Neuberg's phone number and address and website. According to the website, Tristan Neuberg was a sculptor and blacksmith, with a thriving business, making castings in metal for other sculptors, taking commissions for one-off projects, as well as producing a range of custom-made railings and gates, plus items cast in various materials, and he welcomed commissions from anyone. I phoned him, and luckily he spoke English, and when I mentioned Darius Trefus, he agreed to meet me at his premises just outside Vienna.

Molly had phoned, telling me she had been charged with Sir Martin's murder and released on bail, but since I'd been travelling all around the country I hadn't yet had a chance to go back to Cornwall to see her. I wanted to give her some good news, but so far all I had was rumours and guesswork, nothing definite.

Sir Martin's murder was too hard for me to fathom, but I was working on the principle that if I could find out precisely how and why Darius had died, that would lead to an answer as to his father's murder. I was trying to piece together Darius's activities in the last weeks of his life, for these must have been what had caused someone to want to murder him, if Paula was to be believed. And it seemed that at a time when he was short of money and desperate to get information about Rackhams, he had seen fit to go to Vienna, and the only reason he could have had to go there, by the look of it, was to talk to this supposed manufacturer of fake ancient artefacts, in order to get evidence to blackmail the directors at Rackhams.

A taxi took me from the centre of Vienna to a hamlet just outside the town, and at the edges of the settlement was a scruffy barn-like timber-clad old building like a large shed, with a corrugated iron roof and apparently no entrance. Along the side I found a small doorway, and noticed it was slightly ajar.

Inside I was immediately aware of the pleasant plasticky aroma of glass-fibre resin. On the walls were large steel shelves, overloaded with white plaster and also grey and red clay models, mostly half-finished projects. The floor was covered in plaster dust, timber shavings and squashed red clay. A large man approached me.

"Mr Delaney? Sean?" he asked, smiling warmly. "Thank you for coming. Let's sit down."

Tristan Neuberg was like a large friendly giant, complete with a neatly trimmed black beard and lots of uncombed untamed hair. His bone-crushing handshake was warm and welcoming.

"Thanks, Mr Neuberg, it's good of you to meet me at short notice."

On one of the shelves on the left-hand wall were a number of plaster sculptures of faces. I was drawn to the one on the far right, which reminded me of Darius's face, that I had been trying to study from the paltry photographs for my failed portrait.

"Excuse me, Mr Neuberg, but those sculptures of faces over there. Is the one on the end of Darius?"

We walked across to the shelf, where he picked up the model of a face, made of white plaster.

"Yes," he replied. "This is what we call a death mask, Darius agreed to let me make it from his face. I gather that you are an artist, a portrait painter, yourself, Mr Delaney, so this might interest you."

"It certainly does."

He handed me the life-sized plaster face of the dead man, and I stared at it. "What's a death mask?"

"The wrong description really. It just refers to the method that used to be used to make models of people after death – in reality it doesn't work well then, because after death the muscles of the face relax quite soon, so it has to be done within a very short space of time. For a live model, you simply rub a kind of light, water-based skin grease –

you call it *Vaseline* – over the person's entire face, give them a straw to breathe through, then cover their face with plaster. When it sets hard, you remove it, so you have a ready-made mould. You then apply a release agent to the surface of this mould and pour in more plaster to recreate the face of your model. As you see, it works well. Darius was pleased, I promised to make a model of it in bronze, but he died before I got round to doing it."

"I'm sorry." I pondered on the frustrating possibility that if I had been able to borrow this item, my portrait might have been a success. What an irony!

"Come, Mr Delaney, let's sit down."

The long workbench where we walked to was host to several of Tristan's ongoing projects. On the end was a wire framework mounted on a wooden base, with a rough shape of clay applied to it. It was the nucleus of a model of a large bird of prey that looked as if it was waiting for another coating of clay to be applied to show the detail. Beside it was another, similar model, but this looked almost complete, the bird's beak feathers and eyes cleverly picked out in the red clay, the detail incredible.

"They're beautiful," I told him.

"You think so? Thank you, Sean." He picked up the completed bird model. "This will be cast in bronze. From this clay original, I make a mould, then it goes to the foundry, who pour in molten bronze. People like birds. They also like large figures for their gardens." He pointed across to the corner of the workshop, where a life-sized figure of a Grecian lady was mounted on a circular base. It was covered in the bluey-green patina of verdigris. "That one is three hundred years old. Unfortunately copper reacts to the atmosphere by producing a protective coating we call verdigris, that's the greenish colour. Some people like the look, others want it removed so that the original metal in all its beauty can shine out. That compound is a copper acetate, or else copper carbonate. Basically it's a protective salt that forms on base metals, typically copper, or a copper and brass combination that was used to make garden sculpture like this."

"What are you planning to do to that figure?"

"Clean it up, repair the broken fingers and the nose that's come off. But the green patina, no, that stays. It's practically impossible to remove it anyway. It is part of its history. Like the green moss and algae you find on garden statuary. Did you know that for modern statuary, they sometimes apply yoghurt to encourage the growth of mossy growths to make it look old? They call it a patina. Rather like people – as we all get older we all have our own personal patinas, defence mechanisms to protect us from others."

"Defence mechanisms?"

"Don't you think so?" He fingered his beard with a huge index finger. "Everywhere we are vulnerable, we can be attacked by others. We all build our own defences, in our own ways."

"Do you ever carve things in timber?"

"Not much nowadays," he went on, easing his large frame onto the stool, while I sat opposite him. "Blacksmithing was my original training, but I seem to do less and less of it these days. I used to work mainly with metal, but becoming a sculptor broadened my skills to cover a variety of fields. Carving timber, stone, using a mallet and chisel. For my own creations, I mostly use clay, using these kind of tools." He showed me a tray of wooden implements of various sizes, some pointed, some with flat ends, some with metallic blades, like dentist's implements. "People confuse sculpture with blacksmithing – working with metals, heating steel on a forge until it's soft enough to mould. They also confuse what I do with pottery, again, which is also working with clay. The difference is, a potter uses clay as the final material, it's fired in a kiln, whereas I use it as an intermediate modelling device. That is, I make an original model in clay, then make a mould, after which a material, either bronze powder mixed with fibreglass resin material is cast in the clay, or it's sent to a local foundry, who actually melt bronze itself and pour it into my mould."

I looked around this workshop. Assuming Herr Neuberg was the maker of forged antiquities, I couldn't see anything that looked like it came from an ancient Etruscan tomb, such as a large vase, urn, or Egyptian style model of an animal or a god. Perhaps the forgery of antiquities was only a small part of his work, and he relied on more mainstream projects for his income.

"Thank you for agreeing to meet me," I began.

"I'm only too glad to meet a friend of poor Cousin Darius," he said, in heavily accented English. "How dreadful that he killed himself, what utter hell he must have been going through. And I blame myself, I should never have told him."

Told him, I thought. *Told him what?*

"Just a minute, Herr Neuberg. Did you say *cousin*?"

"But I thought you knew. I thought that was why you were here."

"I don't understand," I told him. "Look, I traced you through Darius's bank account. It listed that he paid you some money. I thought you were involved in some kind of sculpture activity that he had found out about."

"Sculpture?" He blinked behind the thick lenses of his spectacles. "Why would I be doing sculpture work for Darius?"

The Bad Hail Mary

"Well, I'm sorry, Herr Neuberg, I don't mean to be rude, but I understood that you were a highly skilled sculptor, who was able to make fake antiquities – imitations of ancient grave ornaments, the kind of thing that they mine in Peru and Northern Italy from Etruscan tombs, and you've been manufacturing supposedly ancient artefacts, to sell in London. I want you to know that I'm not wanting to cause you any trouble, or report you to the police. My quarrel is with Rackhams International, not you."

"Oh dear me, Mr Delaney, this is not true at all. I have never broken the law in my life, nor would I ever want to. I don't know anything about Rackhams' operations. I had no connections at all with his father's company. Darius was my cousin. He wanted me to get various papers to do with our ancestry and I got them for him, and he paid me for the fees they cost me."

"Ancestry? Papers?"

"So tell me, Sean, how much do you know about my family?"

"Nothing."

"Phew." He stared at the workbench, shaking his head in shock. I noticed a speckle of plaster dust on his ear, a frown line on his forehead. He picked up a length of heavy-looking steel bar from the bench and balanced it in his hand, grimacing. "Okay, Sean. Let's start at the beginning." He shook his head and blew out his cheeks before continuing. "Darius did a DNA test with ancestry.co.uk. To his amazement, he discovered that he was ethnically 70 per cent of West German origin, and that I was his first cousin. I also was surprised that I had a cousin in England, whom no one had ever told me about. None of our relatives seemed to be related. It didn't make sense at all."

"Hmm." That was when I remembered the papers

from the family research company from the Bradford flat that I had glanced at, saying the same thing about Darius's ethnicity. "I understood that all his ancestors were English."

"So did he." Tristan nodded thoughtfully.

"Well," I went on. "As I understand it, his parents were English, so either his mother or his grandmother had a boyfriend that the husband didn't know about," I suggested. "That's the only answer."

He stared at me for a long time. "Oh no. Darius thought that too at first. Until he found out the truth. To be honest, Sean, I thought you knew about all this, and that was why you were here to discuss what's to be done."

"To be done? I'm not with you, Tristan."

"Come now, Sean. You surely know about his grandfather?"

I shook my head, mystified. "His grandfather?"

"Oh my goodness." He shook his head sadly. "*So you do not even know what we talked about?*"

I frowned. "I didn't even know why you met Darius. I've just come here as a last resort, clutching at straws, hoping to find something out about some secret information that Darius might have been using to blackmail the people at Rackhams."

"Tell me about his girlfriend, Paula. Darius told me all about her. He also told me all about his, how do you say, gender confusion, his belief that he may have been born in the wrong body. But falling in love with Paula had changed these thoughts. They were all behind him, his sexual confusion was no more. I think he was very much in love, he was very excited about becoming a father." Tristan held the steel bar in one hand, absentmindedly thwacking its length against his other hand. "Did she have the baby?"

The Bad Hail Mary

"Yes. A little girl."

"Good. I am so glad. So something of Darius lives on. That is good. In all of this terrible business, that is one good thing."

"Terrible business? The fact that Darius or Sir Martin had a biological father who was different to their legal father? Why on earth should it be a terrible business?"

"Oh my goodness. Sean, you don't know, do you? You don't have any idea?"

"About what?"

Tristan had gone pale as a ghost, and his face had changed, he seemed filled with utter misery.

"Sean, this is something which you will find pretty shocking. I am thinking that maybe it is better that you do not know. Indeed I honestly and sincerely wish that I did not know myself. Who was it said that the truth is like a caged bird? Once it comes out of its cage it flies free and will never come back. Go home, Sean, and forget about all this. That would be for the best."

"Tristan, I've travelled hundreds of miles to see you to find out what this is all about."

He sighed. "Well, this is something I don't really want to shout from the top of roofs, you understand? For my own reasons. If I tell you, I would rather keep myself right out of the picture. My own father changed his name so that no one would know about this."

"I understand. Whatever it is, I'll keep you out of it. I only want to know what you told Darius."

"Okay, Sean, but don't shoot the messenger, okay?"

"Please, my friend, will you just get on with it."

"Your friend?" His face was solemn, steady, patient, but tempered with something else, a secret shadow of shame. "Let's see if I'm still your friend at the end of our talk. I think there's a very good chance that very soon you will hate me so much that you will want to kill me."

TWENTY

"What are you—"

"Sean, please!" he shouted, and held up his hand theatrically. "Just shut up and let me do this my way. For me this is not easy. Not easy at all." He narrowed his eyes, looking beyond me into the distance, as if he was glancing back into a thousand years of misery. Still, he repeatedly hit his hand with the heavy steel rod, as if he was trying to beat something out of his soul.

For the first time I felt a shiver of fear, a kind of impending doom, as if I wasn't going to like what I was about to hear.

"First of all, Neuberg is not my name, I changed my original name."

"So?"

He shook his head and sighed. "My father died two years ago. On his deathbed he told me and my sister certain things. Certain things that I wish to God I had never heard. I made a recording of it. I almost wish I had not."

"Go on."

He closed his eyes, frowning. "Let's do it this way. Tell me, Sean, can you name some of the terrible calamitous evil things that have happened to the world in the past one hundred years?"

"Terrible calamities? Evil things? Sure I don't know. The Irish Famine, caused by the English? The atom bombs dropped on Japan at the end of World War Two?"

He nodded. "Go on."

"God, let's see."

Was he mad? Something about Tristan Neuberg seemed weird, unhinged, and I almost regretted coming. Indeed the way he was hitting the palm of his hand with the steel bar was disconcerting, surely a sign of madness.

"Go on! Keep going, Sean!"

"Shit, I don't know. The genocide in Cambodia, where all those thousands of people were massacred during the Vietnam War."

"Not that. But you're getting warmer."

"Is this some kind of fucking game?" I was getting angry with him, on the point of getting up and leaving. "Can't we get to the point?"

"Humour me."

"Okay, okay," I sighed. "Here's a hoolie. The Holocaust?"

"Yes, Sean, *the Holocaust*. Put that in your pipe and smoke it!"

Was he really as nice as he'd first seemed? In that instant I just got a hint of coldness and danger in his eyes, the feeling that all was not well. Did this mystery have something to do with politics? Antisemitism?

"Okay. Now I have a confession to make. Tell me, Sean, please try to put yourself in my position. How on earth would you feel if you knew that you were related to one of the most celebrated monsters in history? A man who was in charge of three death camps, and who had also spent time as the commandant at Auschwitz in the years when Jews were being gassed on an industrial scale." He was talking faster and faster, and I was convinced he was mad. "And that this man, this *vicious, disgusting murdering beast*, was not a cretinous moron who could lay any claim to ignorance to excuse his brutality. Indeed he was a highly educated man, a cultured man, a gifted musician and violinist, a historian who spoke perfect English, in fact who had been educated at one of England's public schools and Caius College, Oxford University. This was a man who had been educated in England before the war, spoke fluent English and French . He was an accomplished musician, who wrote poetry and had studied history and mixed with the upper echelons of society. His great interest was collecting works of art, paintings by the old masters. Herr Stephan Reinhardt Fleischmann was just such a man. Just like several of Hitler's cheerleaders, he was a mixture of the monster, the aesthete and the bon viveur."

"You are related to him?"

He wasn't listening, was off on his own personal rant, his eyes alive with a dangerous glitter. I was watching the heavy steel bar in his hand, rhythmically thumping his palm, aware he might hit me with it at any moment.

"Fleishmann was a high-ranking German SS Officer and police officer during the Nazi era." He closed his eyes. "He was one of the principal architects of the Holocaust. He served for a time as president of the International Criminal Police Commission – the ICPC, now known as Interpol – and was on the committee of the 1942 Wannsee Conference, which formalised plans for the so called 'Final Solution to the Jewish question', which was to be the deportation and genocide of all Jews in German-occupied Europe. He was on the hierarchy of the *Sicherheitsdienst* – the Security Services, called the SD – an intelligence organisation charged with seeking out and neutralising resistance to the Nazi party via arrests, deportations and murders. He helped to organise what was known as *Kristallnacht*, which was a series of coordinated attacks against Jews throughout Nazi Germany and parts of Austria, on the ninth to tenth of November 1938." His voice was almost a croak as he continued. "Fleischmann, along with his boss Reinhard Heydrich, was part of the *Einsatsgruppen*, the special task forces that travelled in the wake of German armies and murdered more than two million people by mass shooting and gassing, including 1.3 million Jews.

"As I told you, I knew nothing of this until two years ago when my father died. My father told me on his deathbed, that Stephan Reinhardt Fleischmann was my grandfather's brother. My *great-uncle.*" He leaned forwards, talking in an emotional whisper: "I am glad that he was not my grandfather, at least there is some slight degree of separation. I am deeply ashamed to say that my great-uncle Stephan was responsible for the deaths and privations of many thousands of Jewish men, women and children, apparently he was even proud of what he did for the Fatherland. It is a fact that I have had to live with ever since this burden was put on my shoulders by my father. He recorded all these details on an old cassette tape machine, and I gave the cassette tapes to Darius. It's something I cannot alter, much as I would like to, it is the reason my father changed our name and hoped that the secret would never come out, but when he was dying he knew that he owed it to me to tell me what kind of blood runs in my veins, in case, he said, God rest his soul, I decided I ever wanted to have my own children, so that this wicked line died out. It's something like a stone around my neck, a terrible obsession, a dreaded secret I never wanted to tell to a living soul. I wish I did not know this. I dread the fact of anyone finding out. And it is not my fault! Most of all, I dread the thought of my wife finding out. She is Jewish."

He looked worn out, pale and wan, on the verge of tears.

There was a long silence.

"I'm sorry for you, Tristan. And you're right. I cannot possibly imagine what it must feel like. But forgive a naïve observation. Just because your great-uncle was evil, there's no reason to believe it has anything to do with you. We all make our own decisions in life."

"Don't patronise me, Mr Irishman!"

He suddenly smashed the steel bar onto the bench, causing everything on its surface to rattle.

His eyes flashed danger, and I wondered if I should leave. Would he hit me with the steel bar? Was it possible that evil can be passed down through the generations? Who knows. But, unless I was imagining it, something of the monster seemed to lurk behind his eyes, and for some reason I had the urge to run away.

"You Irish were neutral in the war, were you not? The German navy made full use of your coastline to launch U-boat attacks on the allied forces."

"My grandfather joined the Irish Guards at the outbreak of the war to fight for the English, he was no friend of the Nazis. But you're right. We might have hated Hitler, but after the Irish Famine, when the English landowners watched us starve, we certainly were not in love with the English either."

"We Austrians welcomed Hitler as a liberator, did you know that? They called it the *Anschluss,* the wonderful alliance of our two great nations, Germany and Austria, historically linked as we were by blood and heritage. Indeed the Führer was Austrian himself, wasn't he? Hitler's forces entered our country and the people cheered and threw flowers. Austrian people were convinced that the German Nazi Party was just what we needed. Did you know that some of the most depraved and ghastly antisemitism was actually practised here, in Vienna? Have you heard of the famous Jewish obstetric surgeon at our leading hospital, who was forced to kneel down and scrub the pavements with a toothbrush? While he did it, the crowd watched him and laughed. And a woman came across the road, lifted up her dress, crouched over him and pissed on his head. My grandparents saw this happen, they remembered the piss dripping from this man's face, mixed with his tears as the soldiers prodded him in the back with their rifles and made him scrub the paving stones with the toothbrush even more. They spat at him, they kicked him, made him actually *lick the pavement*. Can you imagine that? Whatever anyone might tell you, we Austrians hated the Jews every bit as much as the Germans did, that's why they welcomed Hitler. The Jews in our land, because so many of them seemed to be rich, and they flaunted their wealth. Did we want to join Hitler's Germany in the war? I don't know about that, but we were part of the German Empire, the biggest empire in the world, that was going on to do great things. We knew that in time Germany would be masters of Europe."

There was a long silence.

"Is it true, what so many Germans and Austrians say, that they knew nothing about the horrors inflicted on the Jews?" I asked him.

"Maybe, maybe not. This is something I'd rather not discuss. Anyway, back to my great-uncle. I have had a long time now to get used to it. I have to believe that the sins of the father, or in my case, the sins of the great-uncle, should

The Bad Hail Mary

not be passed down through the generations. But nor should they ever be forgotten. Then again there are other people who think that all the progeny of such men should be blamed for what happened, so that the pernicious evil can be destroyed, root and branch. Do you think so, Sean? Do you think I should be killed, so that my genetic inheritance can never continue?"

"Of course not."

"I am a deeply religious man, Sean. Maybe, even though I didn't know it until recently, I knew subliminally that there was something wicked and depraved deep down in my soul. So perhaps subliminally on some level I chose to worship God as much as I could as a way to atone for my great-uncle's despicable life. Maybe on some deeper level I already knew. I don't know. It is a secret I wanted to take to my grave. I did the DNA test before my father had told me this dread secret, if I had known I would never have done such a thing. I am only telling you this because you tell me that Darius killed himself, and his father died recently, and this may have some bearing on their deaths. He told me he was prone to depression, so maybe the shame of finding out such a monstrous thing might have driven poor Darius to take his own life."

"Uh-uh. So you're saying that it was Darius's grandmother, the wife of Walter Trefus, who somehow had an affair with Fleischmann?"

"My older relatives have told me that after the war, most Germans claimed that they knew nothing about the Holocaust, that they were as repelled as the rest of Europe about what happened. But my own family couldn't possibly make this claim. My own father changed his name because he was so ashamed of the association with his uncle. And it seems that my great-uncle, Stephan Reinhardt Fleischmann, thankfully died in the closing stages of the war. Before he could be arrested and put on trial at Nuremberg, where he would undoubtedly, *deservedly* have been hanged."

"How did he die?"

"It was reported that he died in the Allied bombing in Dresden, the fire-bombing that is talked about so often. They say he was sheltering in a house during the raid, and the building was decimated, his body probably vaporised, the explosion and the subsequent fires did that to people, did you know? In such incredible heat a body can be so badly burned that it more or less vaporises so there's nothing left, not even bone. They say that sometimes bodies can be so badly obliterated by high explosives that all that remains is a red mist." He stared ahead, frowning at his demons, and I shut my mouth, aware he was on the precipice of lashing out. "So, Sean, fast-forward in my uneventful life. I fell for the TV adverts, where you can have your DNA analysed to discover your true ethnicity, so I thought what could be the harm? No huge surprises there, except that I did not realise that in addition to telling you your likely ethnicity percentages, they also send you a list of likely cousins you might have that you are unaware of. If I had known that, I would not have done it. I don't want to discover any cousins, not at all. But it was done, it was too late. And later, you can imagine my surprise when Darius Trefus emailed me from England last year, claiming that the company said that their DNA matching suggested that we were first cousins. I had seen his name on my cousins list, and I was surprised that I had an English cousin, but, frankly, I took it no further. He contacted me, then he insisted on coming to see me, excited and enthusiastic. I showed him my family tree, and he showed me his, and of course nothing made sense." He smiled. "Of course, we considered the possibility of Darius's grandmother having an affair with Fleischmann, but the dates don't stack up, for Darius's father Martin was born in 1948, and Fleischmann died in 1946."

"So?"

Fuck!

This wrecked everything. Nothing made sense anymore.

"I like reading English novels, Sean, particularly I am liking Sherlock Holmes. What did Herr Holmes always say to his sidekick Dr Watson?"

I shrugged, wishing he would get to the point.

"He said that when you rule out everything that is possible, what remains has to be the truth, even if at first it seems to be impossible."

He reached into his pocket and took out his phone and pressed some keys, then turned it towards me to see.

It was the Wikipedia entry for Stephan Reinhardt Fleischmann, with a good photograph of a severe-looking man at the top, in his uniform with its insignia.

Fleishmann was one of Hitler's 'inner circle' who actively believed in the righteousness of the cause of the Third Reich and the need to cleanse the world of their perceived 'inferior' races, notably the Jews, Gypsies, plus mentally deficient people including those with genetic physical disabilities, as well as homosexuals. He was known as 'The Unicorn' because the Führer used to refer to him as such at meetings, as a joke, because he had a strange protuberance on his forehead that looked like the beginnings of a horn. He was known to be a highly educated and cultured man with aristocratic connections. He was educated in England and before the war he studied European literature at Oxford and Hanover universities. He was a concert pianist with his own orchestra, and an accomplished violin virtuoso. His parents owned vineyards and were prosperous, their wine exported all over the world, and the family owned a number of large properties, including a castle on the banks of the Rhine. He had a particular interest in art and collected fine paintings and ancient antiquities and artefacts. . .

I held Fleischmann's picture up close and stared. Since I had slaved for hours, studying Darius's features, the similarity certainly was uncanny. Even down to the bump in his forehead, that both men possessed.

"So now, Sean, you know the truth. The DNA test proved that Darius and I were first cousins. All the evidence points to the obvious conclusion that Darius's grandfather was Stephan Reinhardt Fleischmann, one of just two brothers Fleischmann, the other being, of course, my grandfather Otto, and it seemed that none of Otto's descendants were connected to anyone in Darius's family. Darius's grandfather was a clever, cultured and highly sophisticated man, at ease with anyone. He was also undoubtedly one of the most wicked men of the twentieth century. He was a freak of nature, an aberration on the vile backside of the worst vestiges of the dustbin of humanity. If God had any sense of justice he should never have been born. His brother Otto, my grandfather, said that it was the greatest regret of his life that he had not strangled him when they were children."

I was stunned, still trying to make sense of it. "Tell me again, when did Fleischmann die in the raid on Dresden?"

"In April 1945."

"But he couldn't have done. Martin, Darius's father, was born in 1947. Even if Lillian, Martin's English mother, had somehow gone to Germany and had a liaison with Fleischmann, which is the only way it could have happened, according to you, the dates don't match. So Martin must have been born in 1946, and his birth year is wrong."

"Darius also was puzzling about all of these possibilities. But remember Herr Holmes, Sean. Our old friend the impossible, and the facts? I've checked and Martin Trefus, Darius's father, *was* born in 1947, and we can agree that the only possibility is that Fleischmann was his father, who died in 1945. So what are we left with?"

"Fleischmann didn't die."

TWENTY-ONE

"He couldn't have done. After the photo you have seen on Wikipedia was taken, he was indeed injured in a bombing, and his face was badly damaged, his features were horribly burnt, and he was unrecognisable as the man people knew as Fleischmann. Darius told me subsequently that he searched for his grandfather's identity, the man he knew to be Walter Trefus. The only Walter Trefus who was born on the day in question in the stated town in England died when he was three years old. Someone stole his identity in the same way as was done in the Frederick Forsythe novel, *The Day of the Jackal*. In those days, before the law was changed to stop the practice, once you'd got someone's birth certificate, you had an open sesame to all the other identity documents. In the tapes I gave Darius, are all the details. My father told me everything. Fleischmann was smuggled out of Germany, and he had a lot of help, from a senior politician, a high ranking MP who was in Clement Attlee's post-war cabinet. A man called Sir Clive Gaines, a very high-profile cabinet minister."

"But how would it be arranged?"

"Your British news was controlled and a great many difficult realities were concealed from the general public. As

The Bad Hail Mary

a result what not many people do not seem to realise is that before and certainly during World War Two there were a great many traitors amongst the English – you were *not* a united country in the face of the Nazis. Most of the Nazi sympathisers and active traitors at the lower end of the social scale were arrested and executed or imprisoned. But with virtually no exceptions, all of the high-born traitors, men who sold your country's secrets, and openly consorted with Nazi agents, and worked towards a successful German invasion of England, they *all* avoided justice, including even your abdicated king, Edward VIII, who longed for the Führer to invade and conquer the British Isles, then kill his brother George and reinstate him, Edward, as puppet king, with his consort Wallace Simpson as queen. It's now public knowledge that Edward Windsor, known to his friends by his real name David, was passing on secrets of British troop movements to the Swedish millionaire businessman and German spy, Axel Wenner-Gren while 'David' was the Commander of the Bahamas. Did you know that ex-King Edward wrote to the Führer asking him to bomb London more, as he was certain that more bombing would win the war for the Nazis? But your ex-King was not the only traitor. Before and during the war there was a huge network of British high-ranking people who had made advanced plans to stage a coup for the moment when Hitler invaded. There were many clandestine meetings to make strategic plans. Ben Greene, the brother of your famous novelist Graham Greene, was such a person. There was an organisation called the Right Club, started by Archibald Maud Ramsay MP, whose raison d'être was to obliterate and kill all Jews. Their motto was P.J. meaning *Perish Judah*, and they had a picture of an eagle killing a snake, meant to be the Jew. These closet Nazis prepared consistently for the day of the

Nazi invasion. They compiled long lists of important loyal British citizens, who would coordinate resistance via the Home Guard and other organisations, and these people were to be hanged from the lampposts the day after the Nazi invasion, as a warning to the English to accept their fate, and Hitler's conquest of the United Kingdom as a *fait accompli*. The common conception is that you British, you were all in it together. But I know that this was not the case. Because the British aristocracy always stick together, even if they are traitors and are hell-bent on conspiring with your sworn enemies. My cousin Darius did more of his own research, and asked his father Martin if he could go through boxes of old family letters, telling the old man he was keen to do family research. It seems that his grandfather, using the name of Walter Trefus, wrote a number of letters to a man called Sir Clive Gaines. Darius went on with his own research, and got information about Sir Clive and under the fifty-year rule, MI5 findings about the man had been released. He found out that during the 1940s, Clive Gaines had been found guilty of helping to organise a sophisticated ring of highly placed people, including Archibald Ramsay MP and General Fuller in the Right Club, that I mentioned earlier. During the 1930s, Osterley had been a close friend of Fleischmann when they were both studying at Caius College, Oxford, and prior to that they were both boarders at the English public school, Dulwich College. Did you know that the Duke of Windsor married Wallace Simpson when he was in his forties, but prior to that there were many rumours about his wild parties, his Bohemian friends, even his sexuality and the fact that he mixed with homosexuals, at a time when such people were shunned by mainstream society? During the 1930s, Clive Gaines and Fleischmann attended these parties, apparently as a couple. Bisexuality is not a recent phenomenon, despite what you might have heard."

"Fuck."

"I have a book for you," Tristan said, handing over a small paperback, entitled *Hitler's Special Friends*. "This gives you an insight into the man Fleischmann and his world, a chapter of the book is devoted to Fleischmann. Before the war, at the time of the *Anschluss*, the bloodless invasion of Hitler's forces into Austria, Fleischmann was made Commissioner of the district, with jurisdiction over the entire area of Vienna. Laws were introduced at that time, stating that Jews could not own or run businesses, and so the authorities, and also individuals, simply confiscated businesses and property, forcibly buying them for laughable prices to give a paper trail, so as to give the illusion that the sale was legal. As I told you, Fleischmann had a particular love of fine paintings and antiques, he knew a great deal about the great painters, he collected artworks. At that time there were a number of art galleries owned by Jewish families. So you see? Fleischmann had powerful friends within the British establishment who could arrange a new identity for him, but for a luxurious life, he would have needed plenty of money. In 1946, Rackhams International Auction House was on the verge of bankruptcy. Sir Clive was on the board of directors, and he just happened to know an Englishman who had been facially disfigured during the war. Indeed 'Walter Trefus' was so horribly disfigured that his face was quite a dreadful sight, despite the efforts of plastic surgeons, who had not got the techniques they use these days. 'Walter Trefus' came originally from Bruton in Somerset. He was apparently a man with an enigmatic past, with no ties, who had been a British soldier who'd taken part in a number of clandestine wartime missions in

Germany and been injured in the line of duty. A single man, cast back into his British pre-war life, he was fabulously wealthy, and happened to be prepared to stump up a great deal of money, in addition to offering a number of valuable paintings to establish a permanent public art gallery in London, and to virtually take over Rackhams International, so that in addition to the auctioneers' premises, they had the soon-to-be world famous Rackhams Art Gallery in London."

"So these commandants of towns in German-occupied towns could appropriate anything belonging to Jews, and then send the erstwhile owners to extermination camps, so that no one even knew what had been stolen?" I asked him.

"In many cases, yes. But, fortunately, a small number of Jewish people escaped the Nazis either before the war, or in the early stages, and managed to get to other European countries, or to the United States. And after the war, when the Axis Powers had the whip hand, Germany was ordered to make reparations, such as they could. In most cases this was of course impossible or impractical. But In New York an organisation was formed called the *World Jewish Congress*, whose aim was to recover property that had been appropriated by the Nazis, a process called of course *reparation*. The law was changed so that time limits for reclaiming reparations were abandoned, and descendants of the original property owners could claim the money off the descendants of those who had stolen it. There have been a number of successful prosecutions, meaning that even now, descendants of those Jewish folk who lost property and businesses can sue individuals and companies to get their property back, or money in lieu of it. Are you getting my drift, Sean?"

I nodded. "And, let's see, there'd be a monetary value

The Bad Hail Mary

set on what had been stolen all those years ago, and interest would be added over the years, yes?"

"You *are* getting my drift." He smiled. "Interest pertaining to the items themselves. And works of art have exploded in value over the eighty or so years since they were stolen. My estimation is that the amount of reparation monies due to the Jewish family members who are descended from this one family, the Weiners of Vienna, the family who Fleischmann stole from, would be many millions, possibly billions. Enough to bankrupt the company. In case you don't know, Rackhams International is still a private company, like Christie's and Sotheby's it's owned by shareholders, and its liabilities are not limited, as is the case with a 'public' limited company, whose losses in the event of bankruptcy are limited. So bankruptcy would involve personally impoverishing the directors. I happen to know that the Weiners, the family who owned the Weiners' Art Gallery in Vienna that was confiscated by Fleischmann, managed to escape to England in 1938. The family settled in Bath, Somerset, and now their descendants are prosperous people, this one child of the couple, Hans and his children and grandchildren who grew up in England, never knowing the nightmare of war or of what their family had lost. They are of course unaware that the man who stole their business that had been built up over five generations of Weiners, did not die. They have no idea that some of their family property may actually be on public view in an art gallery in London, the rest sold to realise millions of dollars. How could they possibly know?"

"So if all this could be proved, then the Weiners could approach the World Jewish Congress in New York and begin legal proceedings that would financially annihilate the directors of Rackhams?"

"Certainly. No doubt the legal process would take years, but think of all the bad publicity. Jewish people around the world have massive influence over many of the financial markets, including the art market. Rackhams would lose business in the meantime, the art world would turn their noses up in disgust when they found out that it had been financed by one of the most anti-Semitic disgusting abhorrent murdering monsters the world has ever known. I have been reading in the newspapers about the proposed takeover of Rackhams by the big American company, Apperline Webb. Any hint of something like this would destroy such a possibility of the riches to come when Rackhams becomes Rackhams Apperline Webb. After many years of litigation all the directors would lose every penny they had, their houses, their savings, *everything* and they would become personally bankrupt forever. Just before my father died he told me another thing. That there was a rumour that the British TV journalist, Jill Dando, found out about what happened, and that was why she was murdered."

"A rumour?"

"Yes. It may be nonsense, but with all this business, who knows what might be true? Ms Dando was murdered seemingly by a professional hitman, and he was never caught. Could that have been someone within the British establishment who was very keen to make sure this news never came out?"

TWENTY-TWO

I slept on the plane going home, mulling over all the ramifications of what I had learned. I Googled Sir Clive Gaines, and found a book on Amazon, published ten years ago, entitled *A Very British Nazi – the untold story of the English aristocrat who loved Nazis*. I downloaded the Kindle version. I skim-read the first chapter, discovering that according to recently declassified documents from MI5, there was reason to believe that Sir Clive Gaines had used his considerable wealth and contacts in the upper echelons of politics and the aristocracy, to create new identities for high-ranking Nazis after the war, arranging for them new lives in South America and Brazil. Gaines's activities had finally been discovered in 1951 and he had subsequently died in a car accident, the circumstances distinctly hazy, thought to be the work of the security services. Sir Clive had been a very close friend of Wallace Simpson, prior to the beginning of the Duke of Windsor's relationship with her, and there were rumours that the relationship continued throughout her marriage with the Duke. Gaines was also a known associate of the notable 'peace campaigner' Benjamin Greene, aforementioned brother of the writer Graham Greene. Gaines also sat on the Arts Council, and had many connections in the upper echelons of the international art world and was on the board of directors of Rackhams International during the post-war lean times. During the pre-war years he had become fabulously rich, and had acquired a great many works of art, at a time when Jewish art dealers in Germany were having their livelihoods taken away from them.

I pondered on what I already knew. Fleischmann, under his new identity of Walter Trefus, complete with his facial injuries that made him unrecognisable, had arrived in London in 1947 with a huge cash injection, enough to effectively take over the Rackhams International Auction House, which was on the verge of bankruptcy after its 300-year history. Because of the auction house's precarious financial position, no one apparently cared to question where Mr Trefus's money and collection of artworks had come from, nor did they question how he had come to acquire some of the priceless paintings that had formed the basis for the Rackhams Gallery, that he had established in Kensington. By opening a new art gallery, which allowed free access to the public, and rescuing historic Rackhams from oblivion, Walter Trefus had served to ingratiate himself into the elite world of British art collectors and connoisseurs. Fleischmann, aka Trefus, had met and married Lillian Grant, in London in 1947, and their son, Martin, was born the following year. Flora had disappeared in 1954 in mysterious circumstances, and despite a huge manhunt, no one ever found out what had happened to her. Fleischmann/Walter Trefus himself had died in 1956 from a heart attack, coincidentally during the same month that his close friend Gaines had died. Was there a connection? Had MI5 known about Fleischmann's monstrous double life, and decided that it was *in the national interest* for him and Gaines to be secretly murdered so that their secrets should die with him?

The Bad Hail Mary

The bedrock of money on which Rackhams had been reborn after the war, had been stolen from one Jewish family in Vienna, at the time quite legally by Hitler's commissioner in the district, Fleischmann. Possibly some of the paintings that were now hanging in the Rackhams Gallery in Kensington, might have once hung on the walls of Weiners Art Gallery in Vienna, prior to 1938. But would there be any kind of record of the contents of the Weiner Gallery? Hardly any records were likely to still be in existence after such a long time, and just after the war, provenance of ownership of paintings was nothing like it is today. Austria had been bombed during the war and many thousands of documents would have been lost. And of course no one was alive who could identify the paintings that had been purloined.

I Googled 'reparations' and discovered that, as Tristan Neuberg had told me, there was an organisation called the World Jewish Congress, based in New York. In 1992 this organisation established the World Jewish Restitution Organisation (WJRO), an umbrella body of Jewish bodies. Its purpose was to pursue the restitution of Jewish property in Europe outside Germany. Its mission was stated to: 'consult and negotiate with national and local governments to conclude agreements and ensure legislation concerning the restitution of property to the Jewish people who had been robbed'. Although most of the settlements were related to the descendants of Holocaust survivors, it seemed that if a person could prove that their property, or that of their ancestors, had been illegally annexed by the Nazi regime, or any individual belonging to that regime, then the WJRO had the authority to get the property or assets back and return it to its rightful original owner or their descendants. And also that in the case of stolen art works their value at the time of acquiring them would not be relevant, the reparation settlement would have to reflect how much the items were valued at today: in the case of artworks this would be a fortune, not to mention that the additional interest that had accrued over around eighty years would be an unimaginable sum.

If there were no surviving Jewish descendants of the families who were robbed by Fleischmann, there was no problem for Rackhams, because there'd be no one to stake a claim. But assuming that Rackhams were quite prepared to murder people to keep these facts secret it had to mean that there *were* surviving descendants of the Weiners who could be made aware of their lucrative options, if Darius chose to tell them what he knew.

I then Googled Rackhams, discovering that, as Tristan had already told me, they were a private company not a limited company. Meaning it was owned by the directors. Should the company go bankrupt, then not only would all the company assets go to the creditors, but also all the property owned by the directors, meaning that the wealthy directors of Rackhams stood to lose everything they had.

I closed my eyes and tried to sleep.

If ever there had been a good motive for murder it was here. If the directors of Rackhams wanted to keep the shirts on their backs, they had no option but to kill everyone who knew the secret.

What is more, if Rackhams were prepared to kill to keep it secret, it had to mean that they *knew* that there were living descendants of the Jewish art gallery owners who could start the legal process of prosecuting Rackhams for their money. Even if the claim went nowhere, which was a possibility, it was difficult to believe that the company could continue trading, with everyone aware that it had been taken over by one of the most notorious war criminals the world has ever known. As Tristan Neuberg had said: *it is appalling to think that the deceased couple, Mr and Mrs Weiner, had children and grandchildren who were now living and thriving as British citizens, but who were totally unaware that their lost family wealth was almost under their noses.*

But of course there was one huge snag. Apart from the cassette tapes recorded by Tristan's father, that I'd managed to find in storage in Barnsley, the only actual evidence that Darius Trefus was the grandson of Fleischmann was the DNA match that linked him to the Fleischmann family. And since Darius was dead, he couldn't give another DNA sample for testing, and the original sample had not been independently witnessed as belonging to him, so in law it had no validity. I had downloaded a book about DNA on my Kindle, and it seemed that for any kind of legal dispute where DNA evidence is considered, the DNA sample has to be taken in what's called a 'Chain of Command setting', in that independent witnesses have to observe the sample being taken from the person, and also witness it being sent to the laboratory, in addition to secure conditions at the laboratory, thus precluding any possibility of tampering with or altering the original sample (normally saliva) in any way.

Accordingly, the only possible way that Fleischmann could be linked to the Trefus family genetically was if the one surviving descendant of Walter Trefus/Fleischmann was prepared to give a saliva sample, with witnesses to testify that the sample came from her.

Celia. The woman who had warned me to keep out of her affairs. Or, of course Eleanor, Darius's daughter.

The other angle was to see if I could find out any more information about Sir Clive Gaines's actions. But after eighty years, it was hardly likely that there'd be anything that could prove what he did.

When I got back home, I phoned Paula and told her about all that I'd discovered.

"So do you realise what we have to do?" I asked her.

"Yeah. Nothing. Lie low and keep out of sight."

"Forever?"

"Yeah, mate, *forever!* Don't you see? This makes everything ten thousand fucking times worse! If it's all true, then these fuckers will kill anyone who knows. It's an eighty-year-old secret, and apart from us, and the Austrian guy you spoke to, who has his own reasons for wanting the past to stay in the past, no one is ever going to find out the truth. Even the bloody government will want this suppressed, won't they? How do you know the government are unaware of this anyway? Maybe they're in on the secret, and we've got fucking MI5 up our arses!"

"It's past the thirty-year rule. That's the time limit that's usually set for national secrets to stay secret. After that it's accepted that government secrets can be released under the Freedom of Information Act."

"Don't you believe it. Things like this stay secret. The top people set the deadlines. Some for thirty years, some for a hundred years. Some forever."

The line went quiet.

"Well, Sean? What do you suggest?"

"I suggest we go to town and tell everyone what happened eighty years ago and fuck the consequences. Fuck the lot of them," I told her quietly.

"How the hell do we do that?"

"We get whatever evidence we can find, check it out so it's fireproof, and then we blast this news everywhere, all at once, so it creates such an almighty firestorm all over the world, that it can't be killed."

"We can't," she replied. "Haven't you thought this through? The only evidence we've got that Stephan Fleischmann was the grandparent of Darius Trefus, and that his illegally obtained fortune underpins Rackhams, is the DNA test result, which will have long since disappeared, and which cannot be proved to have come from Darius. Martin, the father, is also dead, so his DNA is unobtainable."

"There is one member of the family who is still alive," I told her.

"Who?"

"The daughter, Celia. I don't know if she'll cooperate, but she's our only hope." I considered mentioning Paula's baby daughter Eleanor, but I kept the thought to myself.

"There's one thing you haven't thought of," she said quietly. "Molly."

"What about her? I'm doing this to clear her name, aren't I?"

"Haven't you realised, Sean? You started out on this quest to try and clear Molly of murdering her husband. But by making this business public, all you'll have done is show that the directors of Rackhams have a motive for killing Darius and Martin. But you've absolutely no evidence at all that they actually *acted* on that motive. You need solid evidence if you want to clear Molly of the charge of murdering her husband. The Catch 22 problem is, that in telling all this truth to clear her name, the fortune she stands to inherit if she's innocent will disappear. Don't you think she'd rather take her chances with the police? If all that you've found out comes out into the open, then she loses the big house, the money, every penny she's got in the world."

"She won't. Molly isn't like that," I told her. "She'll want to do what's right."

"Are you sure about that?" she said quietly. "Just how well do you know her?"

Little did I know then that, very soon, Molly was going to organise my murder. . .

TWENTY-THREE

"What are you doing here?" Celia asked me in surprise. I was standing at the doorstep of her home and she had swung the door open so fast I'd almost fallen into the hall.

In the weeks since I'd last met her I'd forgotten the clear-eyed stare, the partial frown, the way her eyebrows almost met in the middle. Her black hair brushed the shoulders of her scarlet floppy shirt, and the smoking cheroot between her lips waggled as she spoke. I'd also forgotten that for some unexplainable reason, I had kind of liked her.

"Celia, last time we spoke you told me I was a fool to get involved with the project of painting Darius Trefus. You were right, and I was wrong. I wish to God I'd never got involved."

"No wonder." She assessed me calmly, the cheroot smoke curling upwards before she took the black cylinder out of her mouth and slowly licked her lips. "I never thought Molly would kill him."

"I don't think she did it."

"The police do. That's why they've charged her."

"I don't believe she did it."

"Then you're a fool."

"Please, Celia, I'm in trouble, and I really need to talk to you. Can I come in?"

"How can I resist a sexy Irishman?" She stared at me some more and then smiled. "Don't you ever shave?"

"Not when I've been driving days and nights solid."

"Come in, Sean. Excuse the mess."

I'd driven non-stop to get to Celia's clifftop house, not far from Sennen Cove and Land's End, pretty much the most westerly part of Britain, a rural coastal area.

The drive up the cliff had been terrifying at times, the sheer drop to the right awful, so I was relieved when I finally reached the top. At first I'd not realised that the old stone structure was a private house, alone as it was on the rock promontory, with imposing grey stonework, stained glass windows and a sizeable front garden.

"How about coffee or tea? And toast?"

"Coffee and toast would be grand, thank you." I followed her along the dark flagstone-floored hallway, with its uneven white-painted rough plaster walls, the smell of old stone and timber sweetly overpowering, until she opened a door on the right. This was a huge contrast, for the large room was flooded with light, and there was a large worktable with several computers and a giant screen. Books and papers covered the rest of the surface, and the recently vacated leather chair looked as if it had been recently warmed by a swivelling body. I had looked Celia up on Google, discovering that she was what was termed a 'conservation architect', who specialised on repairs and alterations and extensions to churches and ancient buildings.

"This used to be a church, in case you're wondering," she told me, as she busied herself at the far end of the room, where there was a small kitchenette. "A small Methodist church that had long since fallen into disrepair, so I was able to buy it and sort out a conversion. That's the kind of thing that I mostly deal with for clients. Being a listed building means that you're not allowed to make too many changes, but certain things they're happy with, like, it's rare they allow extra windows, but fitting modern plumbing and electrics is usually fine. To make any type of change of use, or addition, any work has to be agreed both by the local authority Conservation Officer as well as the people from the Society for the Protection of Ancient Buildings, SPAB, or one of the other amenity societies if it's a more recent building. Nowadays before you even start on a request for renovation or change of use, you have to prepare a detailed report to show you understand the history of the building all as part of the original application. Clients can get a bit fed up with all the delays, but in the end they realise you can't shortcut the law. I'm a kind of part-time historian I suppose."

I sat on the stool beside the large pine table, leaning forwards, my head in my hands. "I didn't know that."

"But you're not here to talk about my work. You believe that Molly didn't murder my father, and for some reason you think I can help you clear her name."

"Yes."

"Why would I want to? I hate Molly. I hope she rots in jail."

"I know that. But you want the real killers caught, surely?"

"Come off it, Sean, the police think she did it, otherwise they wouldn't have charged her. They must have evidence for the CPS to have approved the charge. Why do you think the poisonous bitch is innocent? Did you know that they were talking about a divorce, but he'd made her sign a prenup agreement when they were married? If she hadn't killed him he'd have insisted on a divorce, and she'd have got nothing."

"Listen, Celia. During the course of investigating this whole mess I've found out some pretty shocking things."

"Such as? No don't tell me now, I'll get our coffee."

Ten minutes later she came back to the table with two mugs of coffee and sat down opposite me. I told her everything that had happened to me since talking to Paula Swan.

By the time I'd finished she'd smoked two more cheroots and made us another cup of coffee each.

"I can't get my head around this," she said at last, rubbing her hand across her face and frowning.

"I'm sorry."

"I should think you are sorry!" she snapped. "You come here and tell me that my grandfather was one of the most evil men who ever lived! A monster, who massacred thousands of Jews."

"I'm sorry."

"I should damned well hope so. Listen, Sean, if this is true, why on earth do you think I would want to know about it? And why the hell would I want anyone else to know about it?"

"Because it's true. And if a lie goes on down the generations I believe it's inevitable it'll come out in the end."

"It hasn't come out in eighty years."

"What's more, I believe that your brother Darius was murdered to hush things up. And that your father found out about it, was asking awkward questions, and that's why he was silenced too."

"But this is all guesswork, right?"

"The DNA test that showed Darius was a cousin to Tristan Neuberg wasn't guesswork. The testimony of the

Austrian guy, who was told all this by his dying father, wasn't guesswork either. Nor are the recordings of what he said that I'm hoping to get from the storage facility where I put Darius's things."

"But strictly speaking there's no evidence at all, because, as you've pointed out, the DNA wasn't collected from Darius under legally witnessed conditions, so no one can say for certain it came from him."

"That's why I came to you."

"Ah, I see. You want me to give a DNA sample in the hope it'll give Herr Neuberg as a match."

"Yes."

"Well I'd happily do that. But there isn't any point."

"Why not?"

"Sorry, Sean. But what you've just told me doesn't upset me as much as it might have done. Because Martin wasn't my father. Mum died when I was a toddler, but when I was sixteen, I got a letter from her solicitor, giving details about my real father, because she felt I needed to know. She had a wild affair with a man from the village. Which was why Martin has always hated me, why he's virtually cut me out of his will, apart from my being the default beneficiary – meaning that if both Molly and Martin died together I'd get the lot. Dad married Darius's mother much later, and she was much younger than he was, hence the age difference between Darius and me. Biologically, Darius and I aren't siblings at all."

"Fuck. That was my last hope."

Although, I thought, that wasn't strictly true. There was always Eleanor. But Paula would never allow her daughter's DNA to be tested.

We sat in silence for a long time.

"Listen, Sean, if you're right about all this, I really

would enjoy taking down the great institution that's Rackhams. All my life, the historic auction house has been at the centre of our lives, something we were supposed to be proud about. And I still remember, just before Dad married Molly, when we argued about it, he told me he never regarded me as being part of his family. And that the new will he was making after his marriage to Molly was going to only include a nominal legacy to me, just enough to satisfy the law, so that I had no grounds for contesting the will, that he'd even written an affidavit to the effect that I was not his biological daughter. Do you know, he even told me that he was so determined I'd get none of the family money that he'd had his will witnessed by two doctors, to make sure that no one could claim he was of unsound mind, which is apparently one of the very few reasons for having grounds to contest a will. His solicitor insisted that I should be the default beneficiary, for instance if he and Molly were killed together in a plane crash or something, but Dad wasn't happy about it. And, Sean, has it not occurred to you that I might want Molly to be found guilty of murdering my father? Because if so, as the default beneficiary I would get all his money if it's proved she killed him, under the Slayers Law, the Law of Forfeiture, whereby you cannot legally make any financial gain as a result of committing murder."

"You won't help me, but you can't help me anyway. So I'm fucked," I told her.

"I want to help you, Sean, I want to find out the truth. Wait a minute, I've got an idea." She turned to her computer and pressed a few keys, reading the screen for a few moments. "It says here that in addition to saliva from a living person, you can also collect DNA samples from the nail clippings and hair samples from a dead body, but it'll only work if you can get the sample within five to ten days

The Bad Hail Mary

after death. Dad died about a fortnight ago, but I think it's worth a try, don't you?"

"What?"

"Come on, Sean, the undertaker is just down in the town, about twenty minutes away. They're not going to refuse to let a woman have a last view of her father's body, are they?"

TWENTY-FOUR

Griswold & Son Undertakers was housed in the High Street of Penzance, on a corner, the premises fairly large and quite imposing, in that black-marble-and-silvery-letter style of décor that undertakers do so well. Celia had driven us there in the red Alfa Romeo sports car I remembered from before, and she drove with style and panache, drawing to a halt in their tiny car park at the rear.

Celia had blindsided me with her idea, but it did make sense to try to get a DNA sample from Sir Martin's corpse, even though the idea was pretty grim.

"Can I help you?" The dark-suited man with the white shirt and oh-so-black tie who was seated at the reception desk gave us a gracious smile, practised calm and courtesy woven into every fibre of his being. In front of him, his name was displayed on a plastic nameplate: Richard Griswold. The small room had a green carpet with such a deep pile it would make a fine enough mattress to sleep on, and the dark green furnishings, extreme tidiness, aroma of lilies-of-the-valley and the huge dark timber partners' desk made me feel weary. We sat in the comfortable armchairs opposite Richard, whose chubby red face made him look more like a jolly pub landlord than a man who arranged interments.

The Bad Hail Mary

"Yes. I'm Celia Trefus, and this is my friend Sean. We've come to view my father's body."

"Certainly, Ms Trefus, but I wonder if I could see some form of identification please? You understand it's the law, you see."

"Of course."

She handed over her driving licence, which he scrutinised, then looked up, his brow furrowed. "And this gentleman is, err?"

"This is Sean Delaney. He's a close friend."

"That's fine then, Ms Trefus. Your father is in our Chapel of Rest. If you would follow me."

We walked out of the back door of the building, and across a yard, to find a separate building, that looked a bit like a very large garden shed. Once through the double doors, we heard solemn organ music at low volume, and I noticed that the temperature was much colder than the office we'd just left, for obvious reasons. Mr Griswold led us across the room to where curtains were drawn around a bed-shaped object.

He opened the curtains in a dramatic flourish, and moved away, motioning for us to come forward.

"I'll leave you alone," he said quietly. "When you've paid your respects, just press the bell by the door and I'll come and fetch you."

"Thank you, Mr Griswold. You're very kind."

He nodded and walked away.

The only part of Martin Trefus that was visible was his head, his body covered by a white shroud up to the neck with some fancy stitching and a red cross at its centre, over his chest. His face looked somehow shrivelled, somewhat like a desiccated coconut, the skin waxy and yellowy, the features sunken, his lips practically colourless. I was reminded of the death masks I'd seen in Herr Neuberg's studio.

"Shit! I didn't expect this," Celia admitted. "We've got to get nail clippings and he's trussed up like a chicken."

"You keep watch," I told her.

"What are you going to do?"

"Just keep watch."

When she'd left, I closed the curtains behind me, took a breath and slipped out the Stanley knife I'd brought, gritted my teeth and bent down and slashed the shroud at the point where I guessed that his hands would be. I opened up a hole about six inches wide, then groped around, flinching as I managed to grab hold of his bony hand, which I pulled into view. Luckily, his nails had about a quarter-inch of growth, and I remembered that nails and hair always grew for a period after death. I took the nail clippers from my picket, and clipped as much as I could from the fingers, flinching when I caught the flesh by mistake. Of course, no blood flowed.

"Are you done?" Celia whispered through the curtains.

"Nearly."

I put the nail clippings into the envelope I'd brought with me, then took the scissors and cut several large hanks of hair from around the back of his head, and added them, sealed up the envelope and put it back in my pocket.

"Done," I told her, after I'd rearranged the shroud as neatly as I could, so that the cut material didn't show, and joined her.

When we got back to the main desk accompanied by Mr Griswold, a tall handsome man in a dark suit was waiting there to meet him.

"Hi there," he said to the undertaker, ignoring us completely. "My name is Meredith Gilliard, and I represent

The Bad Hail Mary

the company Rackhams International Auctioneers, whose director, Sir Martin Trefus, is in your care here. I'm here on behalf of Lady Molly Trefus, who cannot make it at this time, to have a personal word with you about her husband. There's likely to be a lot of press interest in his death, and we wanted to make sure that no one is allowed to take pictures of his body before the funeral next week."

Gilliard had an American accent and an air of arrogance, and the aroma of his aftershave drowned out the stench of the lilies.

"Good gracious, sir, we would never allow that," assured Mr Griswold. "We have a strict code of conduct."

"I'm sure glad to hear that."

"Obviously, sir, members of his family have the right to see their relative." He backed away slightly to indicate us with his hand. "I imagine you know Sir Martin's daughter, Ms Celia Trefus, who has just already paid her respects."

"I think we met once a couple of years ago at a works do," Gilliard said, smiling and shaking her hand.

He turned towards me, his attitude changing abruptly. "And who are you?" he demanded.

"This is Sean Delaney, my friend," Celia told him, taking my arm and walking us to the door.

"Delaney?" He stared at me, then his tone became dark and murderous. "Hey, just you wait there, fella. That name rings a bell. Martin was talking about you – you're the odd-job guy he employed to clear out his dead son's pigsty of a flat?"

"He also commissioned me to do a painting of his son Darius."

"Which you screwed up – he told me you were a crap painter. He was real disappointed that you screwed up the portrait so badly." He tried on a smile for size, coming closer. "But I'm glad we met. You put the boy's stuff into storage, so now that Martin's gone he would want me to take charge of all those things, so I guess you should hand over the keys to the storage facility."

"Nothing to do with me," I told him. "Talk to Mrs Trefus about it."

He glared at me. "You mean Lady Molly?"

"Titles impress Americans, don't they?" I scratched my bristly chin. "I'm Irish. We don't respect titles. We've had English aristocrats telling us how to live for hundreds of years."

"You strike me as the kind of fella that needs to learn his place."

"From you?" I returned his glare. "Keep your knickers on."

"Listen, Mr Delaney, I represent Rackhams International, and a lot of the material in Darius's flat was paperwork related to my company, so I have the right to take charge of it."

"You have no right to take charge of anything. Mr Trefus inherited everything that was in his son's flat when he died, and presumably this legacy was passed on to his wife, so, as I say, talk to Mrs Trefus."

"You will do as I say, fella!"

"And you're going to make me, are you?"

"Who the fuck are you?" he snarled. "What the heck business is this of yours anyway? Are you working for a newspaper or something?" He charged forward, grabbing me by the lapels. "I'm warning you—"

"And I'm warning you!" I knocked his hands away from me and pushed him, so he had to stagger backwards to avoid falling. "Touch me again and you'll feel my boot up your arse."

"I'll get the law onto you." He took out his phone. "I'm calling the cops. You got no right to be here." He turned his attention to his phone. "Police? Yeah. I want to make a report of aggravated assault. A man called Sean Delaney has just attacked me, and he's threatening to attack me again."

"Go and fuck yourself," I told him, shouting near his phone.

"Did you hear that?" Gilliard shouted down the phone. "He's making threats now. He's threatened to kill me. Yes, *to kill me!* I'm at Griswolds' undertakers in Penzance, just off of the High Street. Send someone down to talk to him. I want to press charges."

We left him and went out of the premises.

Celia and I didn't speak on the drive back to her house until she broke the silence. "Oh dear, I shouldn't have told them your name. He doesn't like you at all, does he? I hope I haven't got you in trouble."

"Forget it, Celia. Do you know something?"

"What?"

"I didn't like you when I first met you."

"And now?"

"Now I love you."

She smiled. "Has anyone told you you're charming?"

"Not recently. Mind, I get a nice line in insults."

"You're nice, Sean. Anyone can be nice if they make an effort. But you're nice naturally. You don't even have to try."

If only I'd realised that by giving my name to Meredith Gilliard, Celia had sealed my fate.

The next time I saw him he was dead.

TWENTY-FIVE

Walter Trefus was a quiet somewhat reclusive man who apparently served his country in a secret branch of the armed services, carrying out top secret operations in various theatres of war around the world. His face was horribly disfigured, and despite pioneering attempts by surgeons at the new hospital in East Grinstead that specialises in plastic reconstructive surgery, facial reconstruction had not been possible. This shy quiet war hero had his own personal fortune and before the war had been a keen collector of valuable paintings, and so in 1947 Rackhams International Auctioneers, who were on the point of bankruptcy after the war years, were rescued from the brink of oblivion by this man, who became effectively the CEO and major shareholder of the company, until his death, nine years later. . . .Indeed some said it was the unexplained disappearance of his beloved wife Lillian in 1953 that he never fully recovered from. Mrs Trefus walked out of the couple's manor house, Triplinghoes, Cornwall, one spring morning and never returned. . .

I was reading the book I'd bought *Rackhams International – 300 years of loving art*, a compendium of the company's history from the time when Westercott Rackham, a hat maker and amateur artist, opened his tiny art gallery in the Strand, London, in 1775, to its current

The Bad Hail Mary

status as one of the world's most influential art and antiques auction houses, which in addition owned a famous London art gallery, Rackhams Gallery, where paintings were on display on a year-round basis.

Tristan Neuberg had told me that Sir Clive Gaines had purloined the identity of Walter Trefus from a child who had died aged three years in 1910. Before I went any further I wanted to make sure that this was true. In neither the book I was reading, or in any references on the internet, could I find any more details about Walter Trefus or his life. The neat explanation for the paucity of information about his wartime years, that he had been engaged in top secret military operations, seemed unlikely. Surely, after the end of the war there was no further reason for secrecy? Other clandestine war heroes published their memoirs.

But if, as Tristan had said, a dead child's identity had been stolen, why hadn't someone in the child's family objected? If there was indeed some other Walter Trefus, who actually *had* fought for the British Army, then the entire premise of Fleischmann's illegal entry into British high society was flawed.

The village of Bruton in Somerset was quite beautiful in the spring sunshine. The buildings were mostly built of the local fine dark red stone. I had read about the village before coming, and apparently its chief claim to fame was a man called Sir Hugh Sexey, who was Auditor to the Exchequer to King James 1V until his death in 1619. There was a school and hospital named after this great man. I had booked into the local pub and found the church of St Mildred's, where I searched the small graveyard. It took a while, but I soon found the headstone, towards the back of the church grounds, sheltered by a large oak tree. The memorial on the tiny stone read:

Walter Trefus, died in 1910, aged three years old, gone to join the angels. . .

Okay, so far so good. In 1945 it was still possible to obtain a birth certificate for someone who had died, and then order other official documents using this, when of course since the film *The Day of the Jackal* highlighted this loophole in the law, the authorities made this practice illegal, ensuring that the death certificate triggered an automatic block for other required documents of living identity. But even forty years on, in 1947, there would surely be people who remembered the dead child, Walter, and would be aware that his identity was being used by someone else?

The local library was nearby, and the librarian, Mr O'Donnell, turned out to be a keen student of history, and happened to have an hour to spare to help me.

"Hmm," Mr O'Donnell said, when I outlined my request, that I wanted help to find out anything I could about the Trefus family, who, I told him, were related to a friend, for whom I was researching his family tree.

"Let's try local newspapers," the kindly Mr O'Donnell said, as we sat side by side in front of the computer. I had immediately liked this librarian, who was dressed in a worn tweed suit, was completely bald, and had such a cheery smile that you couldn't help but join in. "There's an excellent newspaper website where you just put in a word search and date parameters." He tapped some keys. "Yes, Mr Delaney, here we are. It says: 'Walter Trefus died aged three in 1910, due to infantile tuberculosis. His parents, Linda and Harry, say that they are devastated by the loss, as are poor Walter's two brothers and sister'."

"Can you check out some deaths of the other family members?" I asked him.

"Yes, we can go to the public records, but let's try the newspapers first."

"Can we try age parameters, 1944 to 1946?"

"Yes, certainly." He tapped some keys. "Aha! Now this is very strange. Read this." He turned the screen towards me.

Three siblings killed by mystery assailant, was the headline. The text went on in smaller type:

Peter, Constance and Herbert Trefus were all passengers in Peter Trefus's car, when a local boy, who has since been shot by police, opened fire on the three unfortunate adults with a submachine gun, killing them all instantly. This has led to a question in the House of Commons by one Member of Parliament to ask police forces to crack down on the terrible scourge of so many ex-wartime firearms being in open circulation, used by criminals, and being accessed by children, most often young boys.

I looked at the date that the incident occurred: 10 June 1946.

"Wait a minute, that name again, Walter Trefus! My word, it's come up in another search in another newspaper," said Mr O'Donnell. "Here we are."

He turned the screen towards me again. This was a piece in one of the national dailies, dated 4 August 1946:

THE SECRETIVE MR TREFUS

The man who has taken over Rackhams International Auction House is something of a mystery. Mr Walter Trefus is reputed to be a somewhat reclusive man, but rumours abound. I went to his place of birth, Bruton in Somerset, and no one had heard of him. Disfigured in wartime service, Mr Trefus seems to have taken personal privacy to a new level, in that his background and previous experience in the world of art and antiquities seems to be a complete mystery, and everyone is asking, who is he? Where has he come from? Your reporter has heard various rumours, from Mr Trefus being an eccentric American philanthropist, to a wartime secret agent, whose war work was so secret that no one is allowed to talk about it.

Oh well. Perhaps we'll just have to live with one more of life's little mysteries. . .

Later, after I'd left the library and thanked Mr O'Donnell, I put the name of Andrew Donaldson, the reporter who had written the story I'd just read, into Google. I found his obituary, which stated that he died suddenly and unexpectedly from natural causes on 10 August 1946.

According to the Rackhams book, Walter Trefus had officially taken charge of Rackhams International on 3 June 1946.

A week later, the only three people in the world who would know categorically that the man who'd become a national celebrity was not their long-deceased brother, had died in a mass shooting, whose perpetrator had also died. All three of them had died.

Shortly after that, a well-known national journalist had written an article, questioning the secrecy surrounding Walter Trefus's acquisition of Rackhams, and the apparent mystery of who he was and where he had come from. And a week later this journalist had died too.

And Mr Trefus's young wife, Lillian, had walked out of Triplinghoes on one fine spring morning in 1954 and was never heard of again, despite a large-scale operation to find her, or her body.

Coincidence?

It all pointed to the fact that the man calling himself Walter Trefus, who had bought Rackhams in 1946 was definitely *not* the Walter Trefus from Bruton, who had died as a child. I'd made copies of all the relevant newspaper

The Bad Hail Mary

articles and documents and emailed them to Kate Doyle, so she could add them to the dossier she was working on. I had found the tape recordings made by Tristan Neuberg's father, and also given these to Kate, so she could have them transcribed and translated from German into English.

It was time to look into the Sir Clive Gaines connection.

Meanwhile, Celia had promised to find a DNA company to whom she could send the hair and nail samples of the dead Sir Martin.

But I had the feeling that it was unlikely that these items would still be fresh enough to use.

*

"Gaines?" the man on the phone asked me. "Sir Clive Gaines? You want a source of information on that old bugger?"

The author of the book *British Fifth Column in the Second World War* was calling me back after the publishers had given me his agent's name and I'd left a message. Mervyn Rosen had a cheerful lively voice.

"Yes, I need to find out about him. Although he died so long ago it's a long shot."

"Not as long as you might think, old boy. For the book, I talked to his grandson, a very odd cove, called Rupert Vigo. He was prepared to talk to me, though he couldn't confirm very much. He kept bleating on about having the old man's papers and diaries that I could look at, hinting that he wanted to be paid a big chunk of change, which I refused to do. He seemed a loathsome bastard, and luckily I'd already got enough material on Gaines for the bit I was putting in about him. I'll give you Vigo's phone number. By the way, I don't want to pry, but are you a research scholar or something, writing a book maybe, something like that?"

"Not exactly. It's a long story."

"Well, old boy, I'll mind my own business, but a word to the wise. Prepare some story that'll impress him, make out you're some brainy researcher doing a TV show or something, who wants to whitewash his grandfather's reputation, then he'll be more likely to help. And you'll need to take a lot of money – in cash. He's a nasty, greedy little fucker. I wish you luck with Rupert. You'll need it."

"What do you mean?"

"You'll find out."

TWENTY-SIX

Rupert Vigo had agreed to meet me at his home, Landell's Manor, near Lamberhurst in Kent, which wasn't far away from my home in Whitstable.

It turned out to be not a 'manor' at all, but what used to be the gatehouse to a stately home, so that its grandiose external appearance gave the impression that it was just one part of a huge estate that lay behind, whereas the Landell's Manor House itself had been demolished, and modern town houses built on its site, leaving the small, insubstantial gatehouse behind like an afterthought.

"What do you think of my 'crib' as our West Indian friends say?" Rupert Vigo chirruped as he held up his fingers to represent quote marks, making a very fair impression of himself looking like a pretentious prick as he opened the door and led me inside. "I was lucky, the developers who were building the estate wanted this place too, but they couldn't buy it, your old pal Rupert was too clever for them." He tapped the side of his nose. He ordered me to follow him inside, using his hands to usher me forward in a proprietary way, as if I was a horse or a cow. "The owner of the estate wanted to sell this gatehouse as well as the main buildings to the developer. But we managed to get this place listed, just in time to spike his guns." Rupert gave a nasty smile.

"He hates me because he lost a packet, because since it's a listed building, it can never be pulled down, and in the end, he agreed to sell it to me, since no one else was prepared to take it on. I really screwed him down over the price!" His laugh was like a nail being dragged across a rusty sheet of steel….

Vigo had a strange body odour: stale sweat, pickled urine, and something behind it that I didn't want to think about.

I could see why no one wanted to buy his home. As a small gatehouse to a big manor it would have been just about adequate, but as any kind of home it was far too small, with only a couple of medium-sized rooms downstairs and up. I was shivering with cold on this freezing March day and there was ice on the ground outside, but inside where we were sitting, in the miserable kitchen, there was no heating at all. The room looked as if it had last been fitted out in the 1960s, judging by the lacklustre cupboards, chipped and brown-stained butler's sink and morbid green colour of the units. This colour was reminiscent of what your puke might look like after eating cabbage. The floor-covering was ancient brown lino, curling upwards at the edges. There was a slight smell of rancid milk and fag ash as we sat down on tiny stools at his grubby pine kitchen table that was festooned with variously chipped mugs, whose yellow tea-stained interiors yawned at me. I couldn't help noticing old-style plug sockets on the skirting boards, with multiple plugs leading from them, wires and cables everywhere underfoot. As I sat at the dirty pine table, I thought I heard a fizzing crackling sound from one of the multiple collections of plugs, from which wires and cables snaked out like an eternal conga line.

Suddenly the lights went out.

The Bad Hail Mary

"Bugger!" Vigo grunted. "Fused again, these bloody electrics!"

I watched him go to the cupboard in the corner of the room and open the door, and saw him kneel down and heard him rattling around. The lights came on again.

"I've still got the old ceramic fuses," he told me.

"Ceramic?"

"Yes, maybe you're too young to have seen them. Would you believe it, that in the 1930s, fuse boxes were made of wood, and inside were white ceramic fuses. When they blow, you have to pull out the fuse and replace the fuse wire inside. One of mine snapped in half, and of course they're unobtainable, so I thought what the hell and found an old hairgrip and pushed it across the terminals. Seems to work all right. At least the lights aren't constantly failing."

"Isn't it dangerous?"

"No! I know what I'm doing, I understand electrics. In this country too many people are mollycoddled, can't look after themselves, I never follow the herd, you see? For instance, it's cold outside but why should I put on the heating? I believe it does you good to put up with a bit of cold," Rupert Vigo said, smirking to expose yellow teeth.

He was a small, mostly bald, portly man of around sixty, in a shapeless muddy brown sweater, with an overgrown moustache that hovered over his mouth like a large hairy caterpillar. As he sat down, I noticed that he had a simian stature, with noticeably long arms with extremely large hair-covered hands, whose stubby fingers were stained nicotine-brown. "It's true of course that the electrics are a wee bit antiquated, but the estimates I've had to rewire the place would make your hair curl, or they would if I had any." He sniggered at his own joke and I managed to dredge up a smile that wished it had stayed at home.

He then proceeded to talk about his grandfather, Clive Gaines, or Sir Clive, as he preferred to say. His eyes were alight with enthusiasm as I heard occasional crackles and sparks from the plugs. I found it hard to concentrate, since I was shivering so much and I longed to get out of this filthy death-trap.

"Yessy, yes, yes," he went on, rubbing his hairy hands together. "In this country we're all a bit brainwashed, you know – ha now, Mr Delaney, don't deny it! We all know it's true! Brainwashed sheep. I have it on good authority that World War Two, let me tell you, matey, was a big mistake. *A big mistake.* I mean it! Did you know that our government throughout the 1930s were an absolute shambles? Neville Chamberlain was a useless lard-arse, bloody old idiot could barely tie his own shoelaces. Said he wanted peace, said he wanted to accommodate Hitler, and what did he do? Talked reasonably to the Führer in 1938, mad on the Munich Agreement, peace in our time, blah de bloody blah! Did you know that when he came back to Blighty, he was a hero! A hero! Everyone could still remember the last war, you see, no one wanted another bloody bloodbath, and quite right. Of course Churchill wasn't the hero they say he was, oh no, my granddad knew him, and had many a row with him. Obstinate bugger wouldn't negotiate with Hitler, wouldn't treat him reasonably, as Neville had tried to do and failed. Okay, Neville agreed to declare war because Hitler invaded Poland, when he said he wouldn't, but who doesn't lie in politics? My grandfather, Sir Clive, was a junior shadow minister, he had a lot of time for Lord Halifax and Sir John Simon, both of them keen to keep clear of war, but it all came to nothing. He fervently argued that we should have agreed to terms with Hitler right at the start and we could have avoided the conflict altogether. After all, Hitler never wanted to fight us, in fact he was astounded that we opposed him. 'We're both great nations,' Adolf said, 'we should unify the power of the British Empire with the German Reich, and together we would rule the world for a thousand years as partners!' And I say, old lad, what's wrong with that? We're Anglo Saxons, most of us, after all, and we've always hated the sodding French, and someone needed to crack down on those other races too. That's what Hitler said, but was anyone listening? He gave us a great opportunity, all those lives could have been saved, and we could have been part of the greatest civilisation in Europe that the world has ever known, the glory of the Aryan races discovering wonderful things in science, medicine, even space travel, we could have given the bloody Yanks a run for their money, instead of cringing and crawling to them as we've done for the last ruddy seventy years! The Germano-British Empire could have been a tremendous force for good in the world, indeed it could. Now it's fashionable to praise the Jews, but you tell me, why have the Jewish people been hated wherever they've settled, throughout history? Why, tell me why?"

Luckily he didn't wait for me to answer, and it's fortunate that I bit my tongue.

He droned on in the same vein for a long time, ranting and waving his arms about, and I knew what it must be like to volunteer as a prison visitor and regret it. But I had to remind myself that getting hold of some evidence of his grandfather's treachery was the only hope I had of getting Molly off a murder charge, so I had to endure it.

"Right," he finally said. "Mervyn told me you're keen to examine my granddad's papers for some kind of research you're doing."

"Yes," I mumbled. "I'm doing a paper for my master's

degree." In the ensuing silence I made the biggest mistake of my life. I still kick myself when I think about it. "I gather that your grandfather was a director of Rackhams International Auctioneers. I'm interested in how he managed to combine his career as a businessman in the arts world with his role in the government."

"Second jobs and all that?" He nodded. "Yes, even today the politicians are all at it, aren't they? Raking in the old spondulicks, as our Jewish friends say." Again he used the *apostrophe fingers* either side of his fat face. "Ha! You know I've never been one for books and studying, not me, I'm more a practical kind of feller. I should have gone through granddad's papers carefully, but I couldn't face it really. I'd rather leave it to scholarly chaps like you. When he died, I just put all his papers together in boxes and shuffled them away. You're welcome to look at them."

"Thank you."

"Of course there'll have to be a charge," he went on, licking his lips, which were already shiny with spittle. "I believe there's at least two years of his diaries in there somewhere – '45 and '46 and '47 I think, crucial years as I'm sure you'll agree. Granddad was in Mr Churchill's coalition government, but he hated the old man, then after the war, he was out, there was a labour government, with Atters – that's what they called Clement Atlee – and Granddad resented the fact his own talent was never fully recognised. He never got any promotion beyond junior cabinet minister."

"How much?" I got a word in finally.

"Sorry?"

"To read his papers. How much?"

"Hmm. Shall we say a thousand pounds?"

Fuck! I'd drawn out twelve hundred in cash, but I

The Bad Hail Mary

certainly hadn't planned on giving it all to this vile old shit.

"Nine hundred?" I offered.

"Sorry, old lad, no can do!" He offered another yellow-toothed smirk, and my urge to punch him in the face was mitigated by repulsion at the thought of making physical contact with him. "A thousand it is. Cheap at the price, I'm a fool to myself really."

"Okay."

I had no choice, did I?

I counted out the money on the table, and he nodded as he grabbed it, and folded it up and stuffed it away inside his old green corduroy trousers.

He handed me a printed form, asking me to sign. Scanning it quickly I saw it said that it gave me the right to examine the papers relating to Sir Clive Gaines, and to use them for academic purposes, in the interests of expanding historical knowledge of the period, and something about copyright which I didn't understand. I signed the two copies, keeping one for myself.

"Let me show you where they are. I didn't only buy the gatehouse, we listed the folly as well, and I got that too. Aren't I a clever lad?"

He led me out into the freezing morning, and across the grass to a very high, brick-built, circular tower. Following him inside, noticing his weird shambling gait, I traipsed after him up the seemingly interminable spiral staircase until we finally reached the top. The room he let me into was cramped, cold and cheerless, stuffed to the ceiling with cardboard boxes and papers. The window allowed a magnificent view across the countryside but I wasn't in any mood to enjoy it. In the confined space it was hard to keep my distance from him, but I managed.

"'Fraid it's a bit disorganised in here," he went on as I

became more aware of his rank and cheesy body odour. "As I told you, nothing's been organised or catalogued or anything. I offered to sell all these papers to Mervyn for ten grand, but he wouldn't agree, can't think why not. He could have written Granddad's biography using all this. Well." He looked at his watch. "*Tempus fugit* and all that, I'll leave you to get on. Sorry there's no heating or a desk or a chair or anything, but I'm sure you'll manage. Shifting all these boxes will warm you up no end. Knock on the door to the house when you're leaving. You're welcome to stay as long as you like, and to come back tomorrow if you need to, but if you do, I'll have to charge you another couple of hundred, I'm afraid, you know how it is?"

After he'd left me I saw something moving in the corner. A snaffling rattling sound.

Shortly afterwards I heard the gunshot.

TWENTY-SEVEN

"Rats," Rupert Vigo said, beaming as he returned to the room, holding a rodent by its tail. "So many around here, it's hard to keep the numbers down. Afraid there might be some around here. I hope you're not squeamish?"

When he'd left me alone, I looked out of the window at the most astonishing view out over the countryside. The nearest things were the new estate of attractive yellow brick houses, in neat symmetrical rows. In the distance you could see the slim blue line of the sea, beyond fields and trees and occasional houses. One of the nearest was a fine old oast house, its quirky slanting roof sparkling in the sunshine. . .

As he had said, keeping moving was the best way of staying warm, and I spent the next few hours ignoring my rumbling stomach, tipping the boxes of papers across the floor, and kneeling amongst them, searching for anything that looked hopeful.

There was nothing, and I realised that this was my one hope of getting somewhere, and if I blew it I was finished. Molly had got bail, but her case was due to come up in several months, and I really wanted to give her some good news.

Finding anything that made sense was hopeless, it seemed. All I could see was random typed sheets of paper, crazy notes of all kinds of things, relating to policy for a government that had long since been dead and gone. Looking through all these papers would take forever, and I only had a few hours or I'd have to pay the old shit more money.

I was there all morning and most of the afternoon, and it was getting dark by the time I was almost considering defeat. I had cleared a bare space on the floor in one corner, and was sifting through the massive pile of papers, and depositing the useless stuff onto the blank space that was rapidly filling up.

It was hopeless. There was nothing amongst these papers that was any use to me, and I realised the futility of wasting any more time here.

All in all I had failed in everything I had tried to achieve.

The only hope I had of proving that Meredith Gilliard and the other Rackhams directors had a motive for killing Martin and Darius Trefus rested with the possibility that Martin Trefus's DNA from his corpse might prove he was related to Stephan Fleischmann. It was touch and go whether the sample would be fresh enough. In desperation I had phoned Paula Swan to ask if she'd allow her daughter's saliva to be used, but she'd refused, meaning that was a dead end.

So everything rested on a knife edge.

During our last phone call, Molly had invited me to Triplinghoes in a few days' time, and I had really hoped to be able to give her better news. She was proud of what I was doing, but, just like I'd thought myself, all I was really doing was proving that the directors of Rackhams had a motive for killing Darius and also presumably Martin.

But so far I hadn't got a shred of evidence to prove they had acted on that motive, and actually killed Martin.

So, despite being out on bail, Molly would still soon have to face a trial for the murder of her husband.

*

Kate had got the cassette recorder tapes translated from German and told me that they pretty much matched up to what Tristan Neuberg had told me, and, if they could be authenticated, they would add to our dossier of information. I asked her what she thought about the supposed Jill Dando connection, but she shrugged, saying that it happened in 1999, there were tight restrictions on the enquiry and they had prosecuted and imprisoned one supposed killer, Barry George. But he was later found to be innocent and released with compensation, conveniently allowing public interest in the killer to wane during the years that had passed.

Kate had also managed to find the descendants of the Weiners, the family who had owned the Weiner Gallery in Vienna from 1925 to 1936, when it had been personally 'acquired' by Stephan Fleischmann, at that time the commander of the Abwher garrison of the German army, stationed in the town. She had found a lot of background information about the family.

Weiners' Gallery had been founded by the brothers Joseph and Lubec Weiner in 1888, and it had been a flourishing business, selling a range of valuable artwork to rich local people, as well as tourists. During 1936, when the company was run by the sons of Joseph, Jorst and Jacob, the company was 'bought' by Fleischmann, and the two brothers had suffered the indignity of being employed as porters in the business they had previously owned, until Jacob, the older of the two brothers, and his family were forcibly moved to one of the concentration camps, and none of them were ever heard of again. Jorst and Arabella Weiner and their three-year-old son Oscar were luckier. They took a huge chance and used all of their savings to pay an agent who was willing to smuggle them out of the country.

After a desperate journey of near misses and betrayal by the locals, the parents with their son Oscar eventually managed to get the last places on a flight out of Czechoslovakia bound for London, and landed safely at Croydon Airport, where they were arrested as aliens. After months of delay and obfuscation, the British government finally, and very reluctantly, granted them leave to remain, but only because that very week, war with Germany had been declared, and it was acknowledged that, as Jews, they would have been in danger if they had been forced to return to Austria. Having a well-to-do relative who lived in Kensington who vouched for them, and canvassed her MP on their behalf was helpful too.

Jorst and Arabella had struggled for many years in various forms of employment, until Jorst's interest in electrical appliances led him to experiment with various forms of electrical lighting. Up until that time all forms of electric lighting had been strictly utilitarian: single bulb 'Edison' lamps hung from the centre of the ceiling by an ugly strip of wire, with horrible shades that were reminiscent of the ladies' Victorian hooped dresses, complete with fringes at the edges.

Mr Weiner realised that in the early 1950s people were ready for more colourful, decorative and imaginative ways of lighting their homes. He remembered the wonderful Art Nouveau styles of art and antiques that he had grown up with, and was one of the first to produce a copy of a Tiffany electric lampshade, the iconic form of multi-coloured glass lampshade first produced by Louis Comfort Tiffany in 1893, and popular ever since. The original Tiffany shades were a starburst of different coloured stained glass, separated by lead caming. So, with genuine antique Tiffany lamps being extremely expensive, the Weiner collection of copies of these styles were relatively cheap to buy, and proved very popular. Success built on success, and Joseph commissioned a range of copies of other types of antique lamps and light fittings, ranging from the earliest gas-powered fittings and chandeliers to elegant modern styles that he designed himself, known in the trade as *Weinerlites*. By this time his two sons were also heavily involved in the business, and one of them, William, branched into lighting design, offering his services to architects and designers. The bedrock of their enterprise was the first Weiners' Lighting Emporium, a huge retail outlet in High Street, Bath. After that the father and son opened another outlet in South London, then Birmingham, and by the 1970s there were *Weiners Lighting Emporiums* in seven major English cities, and another was opening in Paris.

Now the third generation of Weiners was running the chain of lighting shops, and husband and wife Peter and Hannah were in charge. I phoned to make an appointment to see Peter and Hannah Weiner in their head office at the premises in Bath. For brevity I explained that I was interested in the history of his family company, and he told me he would be delighted to chat to me about how they had begun.

*

I was standing outside Weiners Lighting Emporium in Westgate Street in Bath, and looking at the fantastic window display before going in. I was a bit early for my meeting with Peter and Roger, when a large bearded man passed me and smiled.

"No need to stand and shiver on the pavement, my friend. Why not come in out of the cold, and take a closer look?" he invited me cheerfully.

"Thanks," I answered. "I've got a meeting with Mr Weiner, but I'm a bit early."

"Call me Peter." He shook my hand and we walked into the shop. "Everyone calls me Peter, Mr Weiner makes me think of Dad."

Peter was large in every way. Two inches or so taller than my own six feet, he had a barrel chest, a large handlebar moustache and flowing curly blond hair that reached his shoulders, making him look like a rock star of the 1970s. The smile lit up his eyes, and he put a friendly hand on my arm as he steered us through the shop.

"Let's go into my office. How about coffee? Or do you prefer tea? Or something stronger maybe?"

Thirty minutes later I was in his office, sitting across the desk from the two brothers, having given them a brief rundown of all the things that had happened to me. Roger was altogether smaller than his brother, a thin, ascetic kind of man with a lot of worry lines and thick spectacles. However, Roger had the same warmth in his eyes when he smiled.

"My goodness," Peter said at last. "I really can't take this in. Do you mind if I call my dad and my wife? I think this is a family occasion."

We were joined by Peter's father Theodore, a stooping man in his seventies, and Peter's wife Hannah. They both listened patiently while his sons explained the situation.

"This is all quite a shock, Sean," Theodore said at last. "I can't believe it."

The Bad Hail Mary

"Frankly, it might all come to nothing," I told them. "Before all this I assumed that the terrible criminalities that the Nazis did in the war were history and nothing could be done. But according to my friend, who's done a lot of research, the World Jewish Congress in New York has handled other reparation cases like this before, even though they're rare. It takes time, it's a bit of a legal minefield, but they usually get justice in the end."

"I would think," Peter answered, "that apart from the financial implications, an old established company like Rackhams would hate publicity of this kind too. And what about the British Government?"

"After eighty years, it's far too late for any government to take responsibility for one of its junior ministers committing a terrible crime like organising identity theft. Gaines, the minister who helped his close friend Fleischmann, died over twenty years ago, and his son died ten years ago. The grandson was the one who let me have the papers."

"He's not going to be very pleased," observed Theodore. "Dragging his grandfather's reputation through the mud. Does he know anything about what you've discovered?"

"No. And I'm not going to tell him either," I told him. "I can assure you that he's not the kind of person that you'd feel sorry for."

"And you, Sean," Peter asked me, laying a beefy hand on my arm. "May I ask why are you doing this? Why do you want to involve yourself in a mess like this after all this time? You don't know our family, you don't owe us any loyalty, and the people at Rackhams are going to hate you. What's more, the people who did these crimes are long dead. I'm sorry to sound suspicious, but I need to know. What's your interest in all this? What's in it for you?"

"As you say, Peter, none of it is any of my business. I stumbled into this mess by mistake, and I wish to goodness I hadn't. As I told you, Walter Trefus's grandson found out the truth and tried to blackmail the directors of Rackhams to keep it quiet. They killed him. Then, when his father found out, they killed him too. Now Molly Trefus, his wife, is under suspicion of his murder, and the only way I can clear her name is to prove that someone else had a motive to kill him. I also feel sorry for the boy, Darius, whom I believe was murdered. I think he deserves some justice."

"Even if he was a blackmailer?" Peter asked.

I nodded. "I don't know for certain that he was blackmailing them. Maybe he just wanted to do what was right. Perhaps he thought it was the only way he could try to atone for the terrible things his grandfather was responsible for?"

"Hmm," Peter muttered. "And maybe pigs will fly."

"The point is," I went on, "all I can do on my own, is prove that Stephan Fleischmann impersonated a dead man in order to evade being tried for war crimes at Nuremburg, where he would undoubtedly have been hanged. On my own, I can't possibly prove that Fleischmann stole your family's wealth and used it to finance his acquisition of Rackhams' shares, and possibly used the nucleus of the valuable paintings that were in the Weiner gallery to form the content of the permanent Rackhams Art Gallery in London. As far as I know there are unlikely to be records relating to Weiners' Art Gallery, with lists of stock. So the request for reparations has to come from you and your family. It has to be you who begins proceedings with the people in New York. It'll mean a lot of meetings with lawyers, court appearances, and so on and in the end it may not even be possible to prove you were robbed."

The Bad Hail Mary

"But you would like us to go ahead?" Peter asked.

"Yes. But frankly, it shouldn't be my decision. This happened eighty years ago, no one is now alive who was actively involved, so is it right to set things in motion that could destroy people's livelihoods? Honestly, it isn't my decision to take. On the other hand, several people have already died at the hands of these evil people who are desperate to keep everything secret, so maybe it's time for the truth to come out."

"Did you know that my other grandfather Oscar, who came as a child from Austria, is still alive?" Roger added. "He was six when they arrived here in England. He is the only one of us who has any memory of the old life in Austria, when his parents had the famous art gallery, and they had an important position in the town. He is in bad health and over ninety now. But do you know what? I think that this should be his decision. He's a very wise old man, and he's the only one of us left alive who has any memory of the old days."

"I agree," said Peter. "Oscar must be the one who makes the decision. But for the Nazis he would have had a very different life. What is more, he has charge of some old family papers, and I'm pretty sure he has an old sales catalogue for the Weiner Gallery, dated 1936. That would list some of the paintings that were stolen."

*

A week later, Peter and his wife Hannah and Peter's grandfather Oscar met me outside Rackhams Art Gallery, a stylish Georgian building in Kensington, London. Kate Doyle had come with us, and I could see by their appreciative stares and smiles that she had managed to charm them all. Oscar looked to be a cheery old man, ensconced as he was in his wheelchair that was pushed by Hannah. Kate, whose behaviour never failed to surprise me, was being particularly nice to him.

Inside the grand high-ceilinged building the lighting was subdued, spotlights highlighting the paintings that were high up on the walls. A friendly receptionist had sold us the entry tickets and assured us that the toilets were wheelchair friendly, there was a small café and to let her know if we needed anything.

For the first time in weeks I felt at ease in good company. The moment I'd met Peter I'd liked him, and his wife Hannah was equally charming. The old man, Oscar, was quiet and not so outgoing, but he seemed nice too.

The main gallery was a very large rectangular room, bright and white, with plenty of spotlighting, and the huge paintings resplendent high up on the walls. We stopped at each painting to study it. And then, towards the final part of the exhibition, Oscar did a double-take as he looked upwards at a triptych, three paintings of religious scenes, featuring the Holy Mother and infant Jesus.

"Oh my God," he said in astonishment, staring upwards. "The other paintings I did not recognise. Oh my goodness, it's the…"

"The what?" Peter asked him.

"It translates in English to *The Bad Hail Mary*."

TWENTY-EIGHT

Oscar continued, explaining about the painting that had caused him so much emotion.

"This was one of Raphael's lesser known works, similar to the famous *Sistine Madonna*, a Renaissance painting that was done around 1513. The actual artist was disputed, but it definitely fitted the period, because it was oil on canvas, the pigments used were malachite and orpiment. The *Sistine Madonna* showed Madonna holding the Christ Child and flanked by Saint Sixtus, and Saint Barbara, all of them standing on clouds. *The Bad Hail Mary* was similar in style, though experts dispute it was necessarily a work by Raphael, but my grandfather believed that it was. It's a similar theme, Madonna, the Blessed Virgin Mary, holding the baby Jesus, but heaven is depicted by stars in the sky. Its correct title, as I understand it, is *The Blessed Mary*. But the slang title, given we believe in the nineteenth century, meant that the Blessed Lady is flawed, her brow furrowed in pain, as if she knew the horrors that her blessed son was going to have to face in his lifetime. As you may know the venerated Catholic prayer *Hail Mary* comes from the gospel of Luke, the greeting by the Angel Gabriel to the Blessed Lady, originally written in Greek. We don't know the origins of the story, of the name change, and as I say we don't even know for certain if the painting is by Raphael, or even the School of Raphael, scholars are divided. But nevertheless, it is a very important, very valuable painting. And I loved it. Looking up at that huge painting on the wall of the gallery at home is one of my few earliest memories of my happy childhood, before the bad times. Oh yes, all the bad times."

And the old man began to cry, producing a large handkerchief to mop up the tears.

"What's the matter?" Hannah was kneeling beside him, holding his hand.

"This is my last memory of our home." His voice was barely above a whisper as he sobbed. "And it is part of my childhood, I had forgotten it all until now. And seeing this wonderful painting brings it all back, remember all those years ago, looking up at this painting, and my father telling me it was known as *The Bad Hail Mary*, and that he believed it had been painted by the great Raphael, and it once hung as an altarpiece in a Benedictine chapel in Piacenza, as somewhat less than beautiful, which in the Middle Ages was considered a sin. Raphael's patron at the time was furious and wouldn't pay for the finished piece, so it fell out of favour and for two hundred years it stayed in a studio until a descendant of Rembrandt came upon it and sold it to my several times great-grandfather, who fell in love with it immediately. He vowed that he would never sell it, and it was handed down through the generations until my father became owner of the gallery. As a child I couldn't take my eyes off it. Oh my God, seeing it brings back all those memories of the time in our old home that I had almost forgotten until now. A time when we were happy, before Hitler arrived, and all our neighbours began to hate us and all the dark days that changed everything forever. . . "

"Is everything all right?" asked a concerned-looking young man in a perfectly tailored dark suit who had joined us. "Can I do anything to help?"

"No, thank you," Peter answered him. "My grandfather just got a little bit upset about something."

"Well, look, the gentleman doesn't look at all well, why don't you all come into the back room and let me get you all some tea or something?" He looked with concern at Oscar. "Your friend looks as if he's had a shock."

So we all followed him to the back of the room, through an arch and into his large office, where he had a quick word with the receptionist who'd taken our money.

When we were all seated, he found a glass and a bottle of brandy and gave it to Oscar, who accepted gratefully. He asked if we were enjoying our visit.

"Very much," Peter told him.

"Yes, it's a wonderful gallery, isn't it?" the man enthused. "I was so lucky to get this job. Rackhams are such a wonderful place to work for."

"It has quite a history, I understand," I asked him.

"Oh yes, it certainly does. Did you know it was started by Francis Rackham in 1723? He was a hatter, would you believe. A hatter to the rich and famous, and his hobby was buying and selling paintings, mostly done by local artists."

The receptionist arrived with a tray of cups of coffee and biscuits that she offered to us all.

Then the Rackhams man walked across to the shelves in the corner and returned with some books.

"Here we are, *The History of Rackhams*, published just last year." He handed us a book each.

"How much?" asked Peter.

"Gracious, don't worry about that," he assured us. "I

think we can spare a few books." He looked at Oscar. "How are you feeling, sir?"

"Much better thank you," Oscar replied. "You are a very kind young man. Tell me, what do you know about Walter Trefus?"

"Ah, Mr Trefus." He smiled. "He rescued the firm from bankruptcy just after that last war, so they tell me. But an old fellow here once told me that his father also worked for Rackhams and he actually met him a few times. Funnily enough he said that Mr Trefus wasn't a very nice man. Apparently, there was some story about how his wife disappeared in strange circumstances, he married again, and then he died himself only a few years later, leaving poor Sir Martin, our late director, more or less as an orphan. Yes," he looked thoughtful, "It seems that Walter Trefus had quite a temper too, he once attacked a member of staff, and there was a lot of trouble about it – the victim was Jewish, and took him to court, so I understand. But I suppose it's the old story. Rich and famous people always will have enemies, won't they?"

"Young man, may I ask," Peter went on, "where you got hold of *The Bad Hail Mary* painting?"

"Ah now, *The Bad Hail Mary*, I believe there's quite a story about that. As far as I've been told, Mr Walter Trefus was something of a man of mystery, and no one actually knows very much about him. Some say that during the Second World War, Mr Trefus was working for the secret services on ultra-secret missions, and he was caught in an explosion and that's why his face was so disfigured. One story is that *The Bad Hail Mary* was acquired by him somehow in Germany while he was engaged in espionage, some kind of clandestine deal. Another rumour is that he was an international jet-setter, a wealthy socialite who dabbled in arms dealing, and sold weapons to both the British and the Germans, and that's how he came to be so fabulously rich, and able to acquire valuable paintings. Someone else once told me that he inherited a huge estate in Derbyshire, but decided to sell it secretly and the result is the huge amount of money and artworks that he had. The only thing anyone really seems to know about the mysterious Mr Trefus is that he was fabulously wealthy and very secretive about his past. Who knows? And now sadly his son, Sir Martin, has died too, so anything his father might have told him has gone forever."

*

We all went to the hotel where the Weiners were staying for lunch. Peter and Hannah wanted to go and look up a relative, and Oscar wanted to stay and talk to Kate and me in the large comfortable bar, which suited us fine. Oscar was settled in his wheelchair in the corner, while Kate and I sat opposite him on the comfortable leather sofa. The old man was drinking Glenlivet whisky which we had purchased from the bar, while Kate had some kind of cocktail and I made do with cola. I was working, and I wanted to concentrate. Apart from us, the bar was deserted, the lighting subdued.

After explaining all that had happened to his family, Oscar shook his head. "It is all so sad and so confusing," he went on. "I must confess, when Peter told me what you had found out, it all seemed too fantastic to be believable. But now that I've seen *The Bad Hail Mary* the truth has dawned on me. I'm still shaking from the horror of it all."

"So do you think you will want to approach the World Jewish Congress in New York and investigate what can be done regarding reparations for what your family have lost?"

I asked him. "It'll take a long time. There'll be a lot of legal wrangling, and it may not be successful in the end."

He stared at me, a tear forming in the corner of an eye. "*I have to do it. We have to do it.* Not so much for the money, but to put history right. To think of what that man did to us, and to all those millions of others, that he could then come to England as a hero! I owe it to my mother and father to get some revenge if we can. If there is an afterlife, I would love to think that they know about all this, that after eighty years we might finally have some justice, some restitution for the terrible things that happened to us."

"Tell me," Kate began gently, "did your parents tell you anything about how they got to England? It can't have been easy."

"I was told that it was a true miracle we made it. I was eight years old, and I remember only the train journeys, the smells, the clambering about in a boat, the silences, the fear in the air, the permanent feeling of danger. We travelled illegally, with other desperate people, who were also escaping the Nazis, whose soldiers and informants were everywhere. Some of our fellow passengers didn't make it. You have to understand that anyone escaping Nazi-occupied Europe who didn't have the requisite papers was committing an offence that wasn't just a matter of being arrested. It meant you were liable to be shot on sight. Many were."

"Go on, please," I encouraged him. "What actually happened?"

He drank some more whisky, shaking his head slowly.

"People. They think that us Jews that got out of Germany, or Austria, before the war, that we had it easy. I was just a little boy, but that journey stayed with me forever, a jumble of terrible experiences. Of course I don't remember in detail what happened, and my parents

The Bad Hail Mary

explained everything when I was older. All the deprivations and near misses we suffered.

"Before the nightmare overcame Europe there was the Anschluss. A referendum was held in Austria and Germany asking people to ratify the invasion of Austria by German forces. Those of Jewish and Roma origin were not allowed to vote. Everyone was required to vote for a poll that said: 'Do you agree with the reunification of Austria with the German Reich that was enacted on 13 April 1938 and do you vote for the party of our leader, Adolf Hitler?'

"It all happened, like a slow motion nightmare. I was too young to be aware of anything of course, but my father told me that you just carried on, as best you could, one day after another, getting on with your business if you could. Then one day, my father went to his art gallery as usual at 8am, and outside was a man in a long leather coat standing at the door, barring his way.

"'You will give me the keys,' the Nazi officer told him.

"'The keys?' my father repeated.

"My father was stunned.

"'You will complete some paperwork, listing all the items within this building, all the paintings on the walls, the sculptures on display, the money in the safe, and you will agree to sign a paper that says all the items within this building will be the property of the NSDAP,' the German officer told him. Of course, since the man had an armed guard by his side, my father had little option but to do as he was told. The art gallery that his grandfather had opened in 1880, that he had built into a wonderful business with a fine reputation, was now going to be taken over by this Nazi organisation, and he had no options in the matter. He spent the rest of the day in a daze, having gone into his office with the Nazi officer, who gave him a pile of papers that he had to sign. Before he signed, he asked what would happen if he refused.

"'That would be a very foolish thing to do, Mr Weiner. If you refuse to sign the papers, you will be taken outside into the backyard and shot. Your body will be removed and cremated, and your family will never know what happened to you. Indeed, we will pay a visit to your family and take them away to one of our new settlements for Jewish people, places that you may have heard about. They are called re-education camps, where there are classes for people to learn all kinds of things, there are swimming pools and cinemas, all manner of luxurious things for them to enjoy. We really should call them holiday camps, for they truly are wonderful places to stay in. Your family will be re-educated into the German way of life, to love and respect the Third Reich'.

"Of course my father had no option but to sign the papers, for he knew that if he cooperated with the man, who introduced himself as Commandant Fleischmann, he'd at least have a breathing space to find out if there was a way to get his family out of Vienna. To America, England, indeed anywhere at all that was a long way from the Nazi horrors, somewhere where you could be Jewish and still keep your dignity. For some weeks my family had witnessed friends and neighbours being hauled out of their homes, usually in the middle of the night, and taken to God knows where, never to be seen or heard of again. At that time we knew nothing about the concentration camps. It was a good thing we didn't know, for if we had, our last hope would have vanished."

"Good God," I said to him.

"A lot of people gave up a belief in Jehovah in those days. To see such terrible evil prosper and grow before your eyes has that most terrible effect. It makes you think that

The Bad Hail Mary

the evil is in *everyone*. Neighbours who we had thought had been friends were only too delighted to spit at us in the streets and to denounce us all as filthy Jews. It was as if they had always hated us, and the Nazis allowed them the freedom to do what they must have always wanted to do. Anyway, my father bided his time. He made contact with some friends in Germany, and found out that there was a small chance that for a hefty fee they might be able to arrange a chance to get away."

"You couldn't travel?" I asked him.

"Of course we couldn't travel!" Oscar glared at me as if I was stupid. "Travel was strictly illegal, especially travel to another country. Later on things tightened up considerably, but in those couple of months in 1938 there were still a very few people operating a smuggling system, involving false papers and travel documents. It turned out that the only possible route out of Austria was through Czechoslovakia, travelling partly by foot, partly by dangerous car journeys by men who had to be paid well, crossing rivers by unseaworthy boats, all to get to Prague Airport, where an aircraft might or might not be able to take you to England. We needed someone in England to sponsor us in order for the flight to take off, and we wrote to a distant cousin in London, hoping for a reply.

"But things came to a head," the old man went on. "My contact said things were hotting up, and we had to decide that day, to leave early the following morning, obviously telling no one. So at 5am on Wednesday 20 December 1938 my mother, father and I were collected in the arranged car – a battered old lorry that no one would think to stop on the road – that drove us to the station at Westbahnhoff. We boarded the train bound for Bernhardsthal, near the Czech border, and showed the guards the false papers that father carried for us. These did not have the 'J' stamped on them, as our own papers had.

"On the journey there was a brownshirt, that is a Nazi policeman, passing down the train, looking in all the compartments. He looked at us apparently. I have a very faint memory of that journey, of the large moon face of the guard looking down at me, and me staring up at him, looking into his eyes. Fortunately we could pass for non-Jewish in appearance, and the guard, as he gazed at me, broke out in a smile, and he winked at me – maybe he had a son of his own who I reminded him of. Anyway my parents looked upon it as a good omen, since he looked at our papers and raised no objections. But that good luck did not last.

"At the next stop, another guard came onto the train. He was asking everyone for their papers, and inspecting everything very carefully. At the time I wasn't aware of it of course, but Dad told me that he felt as if his heart was going to stop while the Stormtrooper was looking at our papers, and back at our faces. Then, after an eternity, he gave my father back the papers and went away, while I was blissfully unaware of how close we'd come to trouble.

"There was another tricky moment when we reached our destination, Bernhardsthal, which was a little old station with an old wooden building beyond the platform. A soldier was questioning everyone who got off the train, checking their papers. Again, things were scary for my parents, until he let us pass. The next thing I remember was us walking along a muddy track to an old inn, where we were given some food and allowed to rest for a bit. It was near a river, I remember the river, which was beyond a field at the back of the inn. After dinner, we walked out, and I remember walking and walking for hours alongside the river, and through a forested area, and the smell of damp

The Bad Hail Mary

and moss. Eventually we reached a broken-down old boathouse, which was the agreed rendezvous point. We waited there until night.

"Finally the boatman arrived. He told us that he could only travel on the darkest night – moonlight was deadly."

"So what would have happened if anyone had caught you?" I asked him.

"We would all have been shot. This was a time when many people were just done away with by soldiers who had free rein to murder, rape or steal from anyone. Our lives counted for less than dogs. Unauthorised travel was not allowed, and the Nazi soldiers had discretionary power to do virtually anything they wanted. The boatman explained that if all went to plan we would arrive on Moravian soil, just outside Lundenburg, before dawn. Luckily we had the small boat to ourselves, and the man, Bruno, rowed away from the bank. We were rowed in silence for what seemed like hours until Bruno pointed at some dots of light above the trees. 'See over there?' Bruno whispered. 'That's Pohansko Castle. We're in Moravia at last'.

"Bruno climbed out and tied the boat to a post onto a tree on the bank.

"We lost no time in walking to the station and made it to Prague, relieved and worn out.

"Luckily, our false papers and visas were not questioned, and they let us on a flight. We left Prague on 9 February 1939, flying into Croydon Airport via Amsterdam on a DC 3 twenty-one-passenger plane. They took us to the police station at Wallington and locked us up for the night, but after what we'd been through we didn't care. Eventually, we were released. That was the start of our new life in England, where my parents worked very hard and made a good life after many years of struggle. I knew nothing of their sacrifices at the time, or of the high life they had once enjoyed, until I was old enough to understand. Now we weren't an important, rich and privileged family. We were foreigners, Jews in a foreign land. Hated again, this time by people who didn't even speak our language. But we didn't care. We were used to being hated."

There was a long silence. Kate looked stunned.

"So, Mr Weiner, your son and daughter-in-law said it should be up to you – whether to make all this public, and whether they should approach the World Jewish Congress in New York. What's your decision to be?"

He glared at me, his eyes shining like stars. "Get them! Tell them everything. Let the world know all about what happened."

"We will do our best, sir," I told him. "I promise to do what I can, but I can't be sure of anything."

Little did I know that right around that time, someone was arranging my death.

TWENTY-NINE

Lady Molly Trefus

Rackhams International Boardroom, Kensington, London

"As you all know, I am Martin Trefus's widow, and my solicitor tells me that once probate is granted I will have inherited his shareholding in the company," I said to them all. "Whether you like it or not, I am in charge."

"Of course, Mrs Trefus, I mean, er, Lady Molly," replied Stuart Gutteridge, a small balding man whose silver designer stubble and dark designer suit made him look more like a tramp in costume than the cool character that his fatuous smirks and arrogant nods suggested he thought himself to be. "But since your personal circumstances are somewhat difficult at the moment, no one would mind if you decided to not attend meetings or take any decisions right now."

"Meaning, that you're embarrassed because I'm out on bail awaiting trial for the murder of my husband. And if the jury find me guilty whenever the trial is, under the Forfeiture Rule, I won't inherit my husband's shares and assets, and me attending these meetings will have been a waste of everyone's time?"

"Well, er, not to put too fine a point on it, yes."

"Thank you for your honesty." I looked at all the eager faces, with their simpering smiles and hesitant frowns. "And for your support at this difficult time."

There was a stunned silence. I looked around the room, hearing someone's stomach rumble and a stifled belch. Someone coughed. No one wanted to look at me.

"So I am making an official statement, that I'm releasing to the press later today," I went on. "While I have been charged with the murder of my husband I believe that I will not be found guilty when the case comes to trial, so until and unless I'm convicted, I am innocent. And according to my husband's will, I am to inherit a major shareholding in Rackhams, fifty-one per cent, I believe is the figure. Whilst, legally, I may have to wait until probate is granted before being allowed to take any active part in proceedings, my solicitor tells me that I have the right to attend meetings and make recommendations during this interim period, which is what I intend to do. I am telling you that in all honesty I did not have anything to do with my husband's death, and the police have no evidence to use against me, and I believe that truth will prevail and I will be exonerated."

This time the silence was longer.

"I hope we can all work together amicably."

*

Lady Molly Trefus, talking with Meredith Gilliard, in Mr Gilliard's private office

"So, Mr Gilliard," I began, after listening to the raft of mock sympathy the man had oozed out, his soft, slick American accent as oily as wet grease. He was anxiously giving me his assurances that everyone had faith in me, that the police were fools to have any suspicion that I'd killed Martin. We were sitting in his office, on the eighth floor of Rackhams House in Kensington. The traffic on the busy road below us inched along, the eternal jam almost mesmerising. The day was hot and I was feeling stressed, and I'd have given anything to be back home in Cornwall. But I had an odd feeling that now that Sean had supplied me with the motive for my husband's murder, I'd finally reached a turning point.

Yes. Hip hip hooray!

Things were finally going my way.

Meredith Gilliard had made a big deal of asking if I minded if he smoked, then had proceeded to light the biggest, most phallic-looking cigar I'd ever seen, puffing smoke into the air like a blimmin' bonfire. I had the urge to whip the fire extinguisher from the wall and spray his cadaverous smoke-puffing face with it. He was good-looking in an obvious way: tall, with neat silver hair, and killer features that could have landed him parts in Hollywood. But he was just a little too squeaky clean for my taste.

I like my men a sight more macho than that.

"Listen," I told him when he'd paused for breath. "You know as well as I do that I had nothing to do with Martin's murder."

"Sure I do, we all think—"

"Because you killed him, didn't you?"

THIRTY

"Excuse me?" He coughed and dropped the cigar on the desk, stubbing it out in the ashtray, his mouth opening and closing like a landed fish. He stood up, walked across and closed the door to his office. His face paled almost to the colour of his white designer suit. The black shirt and colourful silk tie and languid relaxed style had previously spelt money, power and style.

But the new frown spelt fear.

"You didn't do it personally of course, but you arranged it. Maybe you planned for us both to die, and I was lucky. More importantly, now I know why you *needed* him to die."

"Lady Molly, I can assure you that I don't know what you're talking about." Sweat broke out on his forehead, tiny droplets catching the glare of the beam of sunshine. I'd once seen a lorry load of pigs going to the slaughterhouse with that same desperate expression in their eyes. . .

"You know *exactly* what I'm talking about." I grabbed his arm and held tight, squeezing him, pulling him closer, so that his fancy aftershave and cigar smoke aroma nearly choked me. For such a conventional man, the tiny gold earring in his right earlobe seemed incongruous. "I should have realised before. Let me tell you a little story about my stepson, Darius. He spat into a little tube and submitted his DNA to ancestry.co.uk, and discovered he had a German cousin. After meetings and research, he discovered that one of Hitler's narrow band of close commanders in the Abwehr, Stephan Reinhardt Fleischmann, was his grandfather, not Walter Trefus, the man who had actually died as a child and whose identity he stole. And that Rackhams had appropriated the fortune in money and artworks that Fleischmann had illegally confiscated from the Weiner family, who had a successful and prosperous art gallery in Vienna during the 1930s. And that members of that Jewish family managed to get out of Austria, just weeks before the Anschluss and settled in England. The descendants of this Jewish family are living and prospering here, in England, and they are under the impression that Fleischmann had died at the end of the war, meaning they couldn't present a case to the World Jewish Congress in New York for getting all that money back, plus eighty years of interest. If the Weiners find out the truth, their case would stand and they could claim many millions in compensation, what's called reparations. This would bankrupt Rackhams, and leave a black hole that could only be filled by the directors personally having to stump up the money from their own personal wealth. I'm guessing that Darius approached you with this information and blackmailed you into keeping it quiet. You paid him initially, but soon you decided a permanent solution made much more sense. Didn't you?"

"Er..."

"And when Martin found out about it, and wanted to do the right thing, you couldn't let him live either, could you?"

"Really—"

"Shut up and listen, Mr Gilliard."

His tiny gimlet eyes didn't leave my face.

"Do you think I'm going to tell anyone?"

He didn't speak, just went on staring.

"Don't you see, Mr Gilliard?" I paused, watching him sweat. "We're on the same side. Me, I don't give a flying fuck about what you did or why you did it. You did me a favour, getting rid of the old sod I married. Except insofar as that you know categorically that I had nothing to do with my husband's murder. Just now in the meeting with the others, I was sounding more confident than I really am, because how do I know what the police are thinking? I'm the one with the motive to kill him, I suggested we go out in the yacht that night, and it's possible they might charge me on circumstantial evidence, and leave things for a jury to decide. But I promise you, Mr Gilliard, that if I do get charged with his murder, I will tell the authorities everything I know, and hand over all the information I have, because that will prove what a motive you had to kill him, and once they know you have a motive, believe me, they'll look for evidence, and I'm guessing they might easily find it. My motive is out in the open, that I killed him to get his money, that's why the police think I did it. However, as you know, if I am found not guilty, I inherit my husband's entire estate, including the controlling interest of Rackhams. So you see, right now, I have an impossible decision to make. I have to choose between risking going to jail for a murder I didn't commit, or telling the truth to prove I'm innocent and losing every penny I stand to inherit."

"Jesus—"

"Let me spell it out from your point of view. If I do get charged with murdering my husband, or indeed if I die for any reason, the friend who's helping me will immediately release all the information he's got about Hitler's great pal, *the Unicorn*, as he was called, Fleischmann. That will of course immediately wreck the upcoming takeover bid for Apperline Webb that we're all banking on, so there'll be no lucrative merger deal, no cash cow for us all, that we've all been hoping for all these many years. We're back in the uncertain waters of a dodgy economy, with competition like Christie's and Sotheby's stealing our business. And after a protracted court case, with masses of negative publicity that will probably bankrupt the company, in the end you'll lose everything you possess, plus you'll probably be charged with two murders. It's in your interest, and mine, for me to be cleared of any suspicion of Martin's murder, and to become the owner of Rackhams, and in a position to keep Rackhams' dirty secret forever more, and to destroy any evidence that's been found. And believe me, matey, I know exactly where it is. How many of the Rackhams directors know about the Unicorn?"

"Only me and a couple of the others." Gilliard was looking at me, frowning.

"So, Mr Gilliard, I'm offering you a deal. You arranged for my husband to be killed. You didn't do it personally, because I saw the man who actually sabotaged the boat and it wasn't you. If you can arrange something, perhaps even spill enough of the details of whoever you used, to get me off the hook, then we're all winners. Obviously you can't incriminate yourself, but I'm told by my friends that you have a reputation for solving any problem. I'm trusting to your creativity to come up with some ideas."

"You're blackmailing me?"

"On the contrary. We both have a problem, which only you can solve. I'm planning a future where we're all winners."

"How do you know about the Unicorn?"

"This is the other part of the deal. That friend I was telling you about, who managed to find out all this information, he's a pretty clever, resourceful guy, an artist called Sean Delaney, and I'm letting him believe that I'm the original damsel in distress. He'll do anything for me. Now you tell me what happened with Darius."

He moved closer to me and sat down, putting his face in his hands. "The little bastard came to me with all the details he'd found out. The cousin he'd discovered living in Austria. What he knew about their mutual ancestor, how he'd been killed in the war, except that Darius realised that because his own father was the old man's son, he couldn't have died at the end of the war, like everyone figured. Darius had found out how they'd done it all, God knows how, but he knew all the details. The Duke of Windsor's involvement in helping to fix the false identity of Walter Trefus, Sir Clive Gaines, who managed to do all the detailed arrangements, who at the time conveniently happened to be a minister in the Home Office, and also was a director of Rackhams. Darius had it all documented, and he said that he was demanding that his father was to be ousted as director of Rackhams, and he was to be put there in his place, saying that we had to put pressure on him to retire. He was also demanding a couple of million, a sum he was sure 'we could easily afford'. We paid him a bit of money, but we knew we had to get rid of him once and for all."

"I understand."

"But *do you*, Molly?"

"It's Lady Molly to you!"

"Fuck that, *lady!*" He grabbed my arm and looked into my eyes. "Do you really understand, sexy little sexpot from the Cornish village, who figures she can play with the big boys? I've worked in big corporations all of my life. If you let an employee cause you problems you always regret it. You have to take action, you have to lance the boil, get rid of the troublesome guy, *get him gone*. This was a little more extreme than that. Your darling stepson Darius had to go. Then Martin found out about it, he found some papers in Darius's possessions that we hadn't been able to get rid of. He started asking questions, he was determined to make everything public. That's why he had to go too. And it sounds like your friend is too honourable for his own good."

"Yes, Sean isn't motivated by money, he's just determined to make all this information available, because he has morals, and he's relentless. You stopped Darius, and you stopped Martin. You have to get rid of Sean Delaney."

He didn't answer for a very long time.

"Sean Delaney. Yeah, I know the guy. I met him." His eyes lit up with anger. "He's been prying and poking around in Bradford and in Cornwall. He was at the undertaker's with your sister-in-law Celia, where she was viewing her dad's body. Do you think Celia knows about any of this?"

"She might."

"And are you sure that Delaney knows everything?"

"How else do you think I know it? He's been working for me, trying to clear my name, and he's travelled to Austria and found out all these facts, because he wants to clear me of suspicion of my husband's murder. He's determined to publicise everything to clear my name, and to make recompense to the descendants of the Weiners' Art Gallery in Vienna for all that Fleischmann stole from their family."

"He's your lover?"

"Yes. He'll do anything for me." I held out my hand, fingers splayed, palm upwards, smiling sweetly. "I've got him right where I want him. Right here!" I snaked my fingers back together onto my palm, in a crushing motion.

"So why don't you persuade him to keep things quiet? Offer to pay him off."

"It might work temporarily, but it's not a permanent fix."

"Why not?"

"He's got integrity. He believes in doing the right thing."

"Oh shit, they're the worst. A good guy."

"Unfortunately for him."

Meredith Gilliard nodded. "Sean Delaney. Real good-looking man. Dark hair, go-to-bed eyes?"

"Do you fancy him yourself?"

He gave a burst of laughter. "How did you know my secret? As I told you, I met him recently, at the funeral home with Celia. Before that he contacted me after we'd arranged for Darius's flat to be robbed. He was angling for information. Delaney sounded like a loose cannon to me, so I had him checked out. He used to be in the Metropolitan Police, had a rep as a quick-tempered hothead, kind of guy who'd get into fights. Hey now, how about this?" A thread of colour came back to his cheeks as his eyes flashed alive and he drummed his fingertips against his bony knees. "Do you figure that the police might believe that Delaney is a man who's so much in love with you that he arranged for your husband to die in a boating accident?"

"Neat idea, Meredith, but it wouldn't work. If he gets arrested he's going to tell them everything, and all the facts can be verified. What's more they might think I'd planned it with him."

"But think about it, Molly. This truth is way more slippery than you think. We're safe, don't you see? The facts

The Bad Hail Mary

about the Unicorn *can't* be verified. Everything depends on Darius's DNA saliva sample. Legally, it would have to be proved that the saliva sample came from him, which is impossible. Martin's dead, and a dead man can't spit in a tube. Is he being cremated?"

"Yes."

"Good, then his bodily DNA will soon be gone forever, just like Darius's. Unless."

"What?"

"Shit! *Of course!* That's the reason that Delaney and Celia were at Martin's funeral home. I'll bet they were harvesting his DNA, to send off for tests."

"Is that possible?"

"I have no idea, but it may be possible, with hair or fingernails or something. *Shit!*"

"So we have no choice."

"This Delaney guy sounds as if he's relentless."

"He is." I tapped my foot angrily.

"What's more, that still leaves the lovely Celia. If Sean told her everything she'd agree to have her saliva tested, and do the tests with witnesses."

"No point," I smiled. "Martin isn't her father. That's why he cut her out of his will, except as the default beneficiary."

"So we need to get Martin fried quickly, before any other interfering bastard takes his DNA. As for Celia, we'll surely have to dispose of her at some stage, but right now another Trefus death might be hard to explain away." He went on, frowning, "How about if Delaney gets arrested, then released on bail and dies shortly afterwards? He gets the posthumous blame for Martin's murder and he's too dead to defend himself?"

"No." I shook my head. "Too complicated. Too much

of a risk. And as I said, I would still be implicated in the murder, wouldn't I? Joint enterprise."

"Hmm, holy fuck, I guess you would," he mumbled. "But he is in love with you?"

"Sex is every man's Achilles' heel."

"Is it?" He fingered his earring. "I never found that out myself."

"Trust me, Meredith. He'll do anything I say."

"Give me all the details. Sure, you're right, setting up Delaney as the killer doesn't work. But just go with me on this. I figure that we can make it public that Martin had a heap of enemies who wanted him dead. There were shady deals he knew about, that he was threatening to spill to the cops, I can give them chapter and verse on that. I've got some ideas that might tip suspicion their way, or at least that will get you off the hook. Now, let's get way down to the gritty gristle. You said you were face to face with the guy who sank the *Lively Lady*, didn't you?"

"Yes. I hit him with a boat hook, and I gave a description of him to the police, but they thought I was making it all up."

"Well, that's good, that's really good, I guess we can work with that. Meantime, I'll arrange for Mr Delaney to meet a discreet end."

"The sooner the better. As soon as he gets any proof, he wants to break the news about the Unicorn."

"But he's got no evidence, has he? Even if any DNA samples he got off of Martin can be used, DNA testing takes weeks, and what else has he got? The testimony of some crazy feller in Vienna, which amounts to jack shit. No news agency would touch a story like this without supporting evidence. It sounds way too fantastic."

"That's true. But he's no fool. There are other

possibilities. Paula Swan, Darius's girlfriend, she has a baby daughter. Maybe he could use her DNA."

"Again, the testing would take weeks. Time is on our side. And I'm the guy that solves problems. Trust me, Lady Molly."

"I've changed my mind. You can call me Molly." I put my arms around his waist and looked into his eyes, willing him to kiss me. "And who knows how grateful I'll be to you when I'm no longer a murder suspect?"

"Sorry, Molly." He smiled and slowly unhitched my hands from behind his back. "If you had a six-pack, broad shoulders and something kinda chunky between your legs I might be interested."

"No problem, Meredith. Funny, I never even suspected."

"Why should you? I don't flaunt it. Anyway, trust me, Molly. The police will lose interest in you. And. . ."

"And?"

He smiled. "Sean Delaney is a dead man. I'll get the Moggster onto it."

"The Moggster?"

"I shipped him in from the States once before for a tricky job – the private detective, Gordon Dallorzo, who went missing a while ago. The Moggster is a contract killer with a difference. He kills the mark, then he always disposes of the body so it's never found. He used to be a butcher in the States, knows how to slice a corpse into nice easy parts to dispose of, or he figures out all kinds of other ways to make a body disappear. He's famous for doing it this way, and it's a double-safe system. Because no one can be sure the mark is dead for quite a while, by which time the heat has cooled off, thus protecting himself and his employers."

"But if someone wants a person killed for gain, don't

they have to wait seven years to prove he's dead before they get the money?"

"True, so those kind of jobs go to other people – indeed, that's why we can't use him for the guy we paid to sink the *Lively Lady*, he needed to be seen. The Moggster simply eliminates people permanently, leaving no trace, and believe me, that suits a whole heap of people, he's always gotta a queue of clients. This way is ideal for us, because we just want to shut the Irishman's mouth and have a long delay before anyone asks questions."

*

A couple of days later, a police car arrived outside Triplinghoes. All ready to be hauled in for another awful interview, I was surprised that the detective who'd previously been talking to me, Brian Prothero, seemed to have a totally different attitude.

"Lady Molly, I'm pleased to tell you that the charges against you have been dropped. You'll be receiving a formal apology from the SIO in charge."

The pair of plainclothes officers asked me to come down to the county mortuary to 'help them with their inquiries' and I went there in their car.

"Have you ever seen this man before?" the kind detective sergeant said as he lifted the sheet from the dead man's face. "This man certainly matches your description of the driver that you say climbed aboard the *Lively Lady* on the night she sank. Do you recognise him as that man?"

"Yes." I looked closer, pointing at the corpse's face. "I hit him with the hammer. When I was up close I could see the huge scar running from his ear to his mouth, that you can see here, that I told you about. I'd recognise that scar anywhere. Who was he?"

The Bad Hail Mary

"Conrad Erikson. He used to run a boatbuilding company in Newlyn. He died in a car crash last night – he'd taken a lot of sedative drugs and alcohol and it seems he deliberately drove his car into a tree. When we took a look round his boat builder premises, we took away his computers for analysis. His emails showed that he agreed to scupper the *Lively Lady* for a fee. It seems we owe you an apology, madam. If you'd employed him, you'd hardly have given us such a good description, would you? In addition to that, you said you tussled with him, and when you were arrested, we took samples of scrapings from under your fingernails. If those match his DNA, then that's proof you weren't lying."

"Who do you think paid him to do it?"

"We're doing our best to find out, but it isn't going to be easy. The email address he used isn't in existence anymore, and no names were mentioned. We've been told that Mr Trefus had a number of enemies, business rivals mostly. Terrible to say it, I know, but from your point of view, and ours, it's very lucky that Mr Eriksen died in that car accident last night, he's cleared you of suspicion. Between you and me, you'll be hearing officially that we've dropped all charges against you in the matter of your husband's murder. I can only apologise for putting you in this terrible position for so long."

THIRTY-ONE

Sean Delaney, one week later

As I drove along fast, the car appeared in my rear-view mirror, very close at first, then it dropped back.

A small white Fiat. Suddenly, for some reason the death of Princess Diana came into my mind, the association of the mysterious white Fiat that had been seen near the Ponte de l'Alma tunnel in Paris, shortly before the terrible crash in which she sustained injuries resulting in her death. The white Fiat was the car that Diana's vehicle allegedly struck in the tunnel before the accident, and which disappeared afterwards, its owner mysteriously dying by suicide in that same car a few weeks later.

Spooky or what?

Why should that morbid episode in 1997 enter my mind at that point?

The truth was, in the last couple of days I'd had the feeling that something was wrong.

Very wrong.

A week ago, Molly had been as thrilled as I was to discover the 'Secret of the Unicorn', but she was keen to keep the information secret until we had proof that people at Rackhams had killed Martin, rather than going off half-cock. She'd made me promise to ask Kate Doyle to keep quiet about any of my findings until we'd thought everything through carefully.

And then, last night, she'd given me the exciting news that all the charges against her had been dropped by the police, and she was free, telling me that she'd go into details when we met up.

So what next?

Whatever way you looked at it, I was feeling like a fool.

Something was wrong.

Very wrong.

I had discovered this massive story, something so important that several people had been murdered to keep it secret, and now the likelihood was that Molly would want me to keep it quiet, in order to preserve the fortune she was going to inherit from her husband. I'd spent weeks of my time, risked my life and spent a lot of money and made enemies to get this far. And I had made friends with the Weiners, who seemed to be good people, and the old man, Oscar, had been heartbroken when he'd seen the painting *The Bad Hail Mary*, bringing back to him the memories of his early childhood happiness that had gone forever. I had made a promise to him to try to do what was right, even though I was far from convinced that blowing open the secret was the wisest course of action. Could you balance the happiness of one old man against the prospect of many people losing their jobs and being driven into bankruptcy? The monster, Fleischmann, and the other guilty parties had died years ago, so any prospect of revenge for his actions was nonsensical.

Now, of course, if the secret came out, Molly would lose the fortune she was due to inherit. So obviously she would want me to keep quiet.

Which put me in an impossible situation.

Should I go ahead and do what was right, correct a historic tragedy, and in the process ruin the lives of everyone involved with Rackhams International? The truth was, eighty years was a long time, and nobody really cared about what the corrupt MP, Sir Clive Gaines, had done all those years ago, or about how an evil Nazi war criminal had staked a claim in a British institution. Fleischmann had only lived for ten more years, so his association with Rackhams was blessedly brief.

Bottom line? The Weiners would probably gain some financial compensation, but only after many years and wearisome legal proceedings – I'd read that typical World Jewish Congress applications for reparation were by no means always successful, and were never quickly accomplished. The old man, dear old Oscar Weiner, definitely wanted me to do the right thing, but his family were not so certain.

And nor was I.

However, just as with everything in life, things weren't that simple.

I had to think of my own life and that of Paula Swan. While the secret stayed secret, neither of us could ever be free of danger. Meredith Gilliard, who appeared to be the principle 'bad actor' in this entire fiasco, was clearly a very dangerous character who, according to Paula, had personally taken part in Darius's murder. If Gilliard found out that I knew what Darius been threatening him with, the chances were that he'd try to shut me up in any way he could. He already suspected I was investigating Darius's death and had made it clear he wanted me to stop.

It had been Kate Doyle who'd first filled me in on the latest developments a week ago, shortly followed by an excitable phone call from Molly herself. Kate had contacts in Police Cornwall, who'd told her about the discovery of the 'man with the scar' who'd scuppered the *Lively Lady*, and that his description matched the one Molly had given them. It seemed the police had now cleared her of all suspicion of her husband's murder. What's more, it seemed that Martin had a number of other enemies who had motives to kill him, any one of whom might have employed this mystery boat builder and sabotager of *The Lively Lady*, Conrad Eriksen.

As I ate up the miles I thought back to my meeting with Kate in London's Regent's Park.

"Sean, I'm sorry, mate, but I think you're fucked." Kate had sucked on her cigarette, emitting clouds of smoke as she exhaled. Her tight purple sweatshirt had the words *Little Girl Lost* emblazoned in white across her front as she sat back on the bench. Her white mini skirt hovered above mid-thigh black boots, leaving a tantalising ribbon of white leg. "I hate to break it to you, but Molly Trefus is off the hook and she doesn't need you anymore."

"That's what's worrying me," I'd told her.

"Sean, for once don't be such a fucking idiot!" Kate snapped. "You don't have to be a gentleman, play things straight, and always do the right thing. Think about your darling Molly. Years ago, you saved her from a burning building, when she was the one who'd started the fire, because she was paid. She married that old man for his money, and she's been lucky enough to get rid of him without a divorce, meaning she'll get all his money, not just the paltry prenuptial agreement amount she'd have got if she'd divorced him. She is about to become a very rich widow, so why would she want you spoiling the party? The best thing you can do, is tell her nothing about the proof we've almost got. Cut her out of your life, tell her *nothing,* and let me go ahead and screw her and all the other directors of Rackhams."

"At least I should tell her what I'm going to do. I owe her that much at least."

"You owe her jack shit. If you go and see her, she'll try and persuade you to keep quiet. And this is something you *can't* keep quiet about, mate. If you do, you won't live long."

"You could be right."

But yesterday, to my amazement, Molly had phoned, and suggested I should come to Triplinghoes to see her, so we could discuss what to do for the best. I did at least owe it to her to be honest about what I had found out.

*

The journey to Triplinghoes was much the same as when I'd first come here all those months ago. The sun was setting on the horizon, the last fiery blazes of fire were shooting out across the sky, and I felt about as dead as the dying sun, wishing I'd never got involved in this crazy business. Now, having spent quite a while away from Molly, I was ashamed to admit to myself that my 'love affair' with Molly was as ephemeral as I'd suspected. Sex is like a powerful drug, but it's no substitute for love, and, as I remembered how it felt to stare into the eyes of PC Lucy Akehurst, I knew that feeling was a world away from the frenzied sexual coupling I'd had with Molly, however exciting it had been.

I thought about Lucy in odd moments, deciding that as soon as I could I would go into the police station in Penzance and ask her out. What did I have to lose?

I was dreading my forthcoming meeting with Molly,

and I had a bad feeling of inevitable forthcoming misery and heartache. All the way here I had this old cowboy song running through my mind.

As I was walking in the streets of Laredo, as I was walking in Laredo one day.

I spied a young cowboy, all wrapped in white linen.
Wrapped in white linen as cold as the clay.
There's gold in the mountain, gold in the valley, gold in the river and gold in the sea
Fortunes are waiting, for men to claim them
But only the heartaches are waiting for me. . .

On and on it ran through my mind as I thought about what was happening to me. Why was I picturing some kind of showdown, gunfights in Laredo, a dead cowboy? I knew the answer.

The dead cowboy was me.

THIRTY-TWO

It was the dead cowboy wrapped in white linen.
Even then, at that moment, I knew that *something, somehow* was very wrong about this whole situation.
Crazy.

Nothing dramatic was going to happen, I tried to reassure myself. I was just going to see Molly to tell her what I had to do, and suggest how she could try to ameliorate the financial implications for herself.

It was crazy. By some fluke I'd unravelled possibly the most appalling scandal of the twentieth century. One of the most bestial, most abominable monsters of the Gestapo, the Abwehr, the worst of the worst of Hitler's narrow band of 'chosen few' Nazis, had appropriated a fortune in artworks, faked his own death, and possibly with the help of the ex-king of England, the Duke of Windsor and fascist traitor Sir Clive Gaines, had stolen the identity of Cornishman Walter Trefus and virtually taken over the financially ailing Rackhams International Auction house, the injection of money transforming it, so that all these years later it was one of the most famous auction houses in Europe and America, soon to amalgamate with its nearest rival in the States and become the leading operator in the world. My friend Robin had been right, the best plan was to mind my own business ns and keep quiet about everything I'd discovered, especially now that it seemed as if Molly was in the clear.

But if I did that, Paula Swan would live forever in fear. And I could never be sure of my own safety either. What's more, I would be breaking my promise to old Oscar Weiner, who wanted revenge for the terrible wrongs that his parents and their family had endured.

As I was eating up the miles the phone call on my hands-free showed Robin's number.

"Sean? I've got some news. You're not going to like it."
"Go on."

"I've been looking into that fire where you saved Molly's life in 1994. I've got a mate who had an inner city parish in that same part of London. As you know, at the time of the fire there was a lot of racial tension, rumours that it was a far-right racist group that had targeted the Asian-owned shop, and although the fire investigation team proved it was arson, they never found the culprit. After it happened feelings were running high, and Jim McDonagh, the parish priest, was doing what he could with many others to ease tensions in the area, working with the local Imam, and the Rabbi, a kind of interfaith group, going around, talking to people, trying to defuse hatred and bad feelings, talking to community leaders, you know? Well it seems there were a few things that the general public never got to know, that the authorities tried to play down for political reasons."

"What?"

The road beneath my wheels was rolling by. A lorry overtook me, its air brakes honking like a ship's foghorn as another vehicle strayed into its path unexpectedly, and a dreadful crash was avoided by a gnat's whisker. I watched. I slowed.

My soul began to die.

"It seems that the shop and the flat over it were not empty, as Molly told you," Robin went on. "There was the father of the shop owner locked up in one of the bedrooms of the flat. He was elderly, almost blind and deaf, and he died in the fire."

The lorry drew up level with me. Then it sped ahead. A car behind me was angry, flashing its lights, trying to move into the middle lane.

"So there was another bedroom," I told Robin. "If only I'd checked it out I might have saved him."

"The door was locked, you'd have needed to smash it open, and as I understand it, you barely had time to save Molly."

"Yeah, true enough. Poor bugger."

"The point is, apparently there was some kind of dispute in the family, and it was the father of the family, the old man who died, who actually owned the shop. The couple who ran the shop stood to inherit it on his death, and of course, they were able to claim on the insurance too. What I hate to tell you is, the likelihood is, that when Molly was asked to burn down the shop she would have been aware that she was murdering the old man."

"You don't know that."

"No," he replied, slowly and deliberately. "I don't *know that*, but it's a fair assumption. Think of how it must have been. She starts the fire downstairs, goes upstairs to make sure of it and starts another fire. She must have heard the old man banging on his door, begging to be let out. And I know you won't take any notice of what I'm telling you about Molly, about how I really don't know her. But if you've got any sense you'll at least listen to the facts. After you told me her name, and my friend found out who she was

– remember, she ran away at the time, no one caught up with her. Well, he made enquiries about her, her early life in Cornwall. She was taken into care because of problems at home. At school she was placed into a special school because of behavioural difficulties – the psychiatrist summed her up as having sociopathic, bordering on psychopathic tendencies. She attacked another child – practically killed her."

"She was a child."

"She deliberately allowed a man to burn to death when she was an adult."

"God, Rob, what are you saying?"

"I've got a gut feeling about this, Sean. *Don't go and see her.* Turn back now. You've got the power to vaporise her inheritance, to ruin her life. You don't know what she's planning."

"I promised to go and see her. I have to tell her what I'm going to do."

"*No you fucking don't!* You're heading into trouble, Sean. Think about it. She phoned you when she was in jail and she needed your help. Apart from a few phone calls, you've been chasing your tail on her behalf and she hasn't even come to see you to thank you. Now, suddenly, when she doesn't even need you anymore, she's inviting you up to Triplinghoes. There's something wrong, can't you see it?" Rob was getting angry. "Look I know how you feel about her. I've been in love myself, I know what it's like to be blind to reality. But for God's sake listen to reason, Sean. This is a woman who's been diagnosed as psychopathic as a child. She admits she was paid to set fire to shop premises for money, and was quite happy to murder a defenceless old man in the process. She stands to gain a fortune from her husband's death. The police have been questioning her all this time, and they know all the facts. Maybe she did kill her husband, but they just haven't got enough evidence to charge her right now?"

"Shit, Rob, we don't know everything."

"*That's the fucking point!* Listen, if she did kill him, from what you tell me, it looks as if she's going to get away with it. So do you seriously think she wants you to go ahead, lift the lid on the Fleischmann scandal and be financially ruined in the process? She wanted to use you to get her off the hook, but now she's managed to get away with it, she doesn't need you. Why do you think she invited you to the big house today?"

"I don't know."

"Listen, Sean, you're heading for a trap. Several people now know that you know a dangerous truth that could ruin them financially. That makes you a target. They killed Darius, that detective Dallorzo disappeared. They might have killed Martin too."

"Christ, I don't know what to do."

"Phone her now. Tell her you want to drop the case. See what she says."

He was right.

Fuck.

I pulled into the next layby, and phoned Molly.

"I can't wait to see you, Sean."

"Listen, do you know something?" I told her, trying to divine her thoughts through the line. "Now the police have dropped the case against you, are you sure you want to lift the lid on this scandal? Why don't we just forget about it? Leave it in the past, where it belongs."

"Why?" she asked me. "Don't you think that the bastards that murdered Darius and Martin should get what they deserve?"

The Bad Hail Mary

"But you do realise that if this comes out, you stand to lose everything you've got? All Martin's money, even the Triplinghoes estate."

"I'm prepared for that. We've got to do the right thing."

"Okay, we'll discuss it soon. I'm about half an hour away."

"I can't wait to see you."

Rob was right. I'd been a fool.

Something didn't add up.

She was deadly calm.

Too calm.

I'd expected an argument, doubts, indecision maybe, like when we'd talked on the phone. A notional tug of conscience, followed by an agreement that this terrible thing happened eighty years ago, the Weiners were prosperous and happy, and what's the point of stirring up trouble, when it would involve losing her livelihood.

I remembered my old bare-knuckle boxing coach back home in Galway when I was thirteen. "Go slow, boy, go careful now," he'd always warned me. "Steam in fast at the right time. Don't go in too early…"

Rob was right.

It was a trap.

I'd just turned onto the Abercrombie Road, beside the huge roadside sign for Wheelomatic Tyres, absurdly reminding me of the huge hoarding picture of a giant pair of black-framed spectacles, in the film of *The Great Gatsby*, the image marking an important landmark in the highway on the way to the millionaire Gatsby's estate. There were weird similarities to the life of the novel's hero, Nick, the famous businessman Gatsby's impoverished friend, and myself. Fictional Nick and I were both pawns in game where it was other people who had all the money and the influence. And all the fine characters who Nick had admired so much had turned out to be disgusting shits who betrayed Nick and everyone else too.

And then, stupidly, it was while I was musing on the novel, that it happened.

The thing that changed my life.

THIRTY-THREE

A white car overtook me.

Something about it was familiar, but I didn't think about it too deeply. But because I was thinking about white cars, because of the mysterious white Fiat that presaged Princess Diana's fatal accident, I noticed this one.

What I really noticed was the number plate, which I won't mention.

A mental game I play is remembering number plates of cars, a habit I'd formed when I was in the police, a memory test to keep in mind on patrol, when we were told to look out for suspect vehicles.

As I kept a discreet distance from the car in front, my heart kicked up a beat as I followed the white car along the Macintyre Road, up the Swayley Hill and Fothergill Way, and then Miser's Lane, leading to the sharp left-hand turn-off for Triplinghoes.

The car turned into the turn-off for Triplinghoes and I followed at a distance. In the brooding skyline lurked the huge red-brick mansion that hovered there, like the backdrop to a stage set.

I pulled into the side of the gravelled road and waited. Watched the white car draw to a halt in the manor house's large circular front drive.

As it parked, I watched.

Then I remembered where I had seen that number plate before.

Outside the office of Gordon Dallorzo, the private detective in Bradford who had disappeared shortly after talking to me. That same white car – a newish Ford saloon – had been parked outside, and I had seen the hapless detective being bundled into it. I'd told the police but it seemed that they hadn't followed up on it.

My car was parked now, about a hundred yards away from the manor house's circular gravelled driveway. I opened my glove box and took out the field glasses I keep there. I held them up against my eyes, scanning across. The porch of Triplinghoes, the stone mullioned windows, the wing of the white car.

A shaft of the dying sunlight sparked a blaze on the shiny steel of a pump-action shotgun that poked its way out from the passenger side window.

It was pointing in my direction.

I gunned the clutch, slammed the Land Rover into reverse gear, let it tear into mesh.

Trod on the gas.

Ducked.

As my Landie slalomed backwards, spitting gravel, the gears screaming.

There was a loud boom as the windscreen shattered, the droplets of glass tumbling onto my face. I went on careering backwards. The car jerked like a bucking horse as I hit something.

The white car was moving towards me.

Fast as fuck.

Closing the distance between us.

A red blaze and another cannon-blast.

From my hunched position I could see the back of the seat where my head had been. Smoking like a campfire, and ripped to shreds.

Still accelerating backwards. I left-hand-downed, then fishtailed madly into a hedge at the side of the road. Glancing over the dash briefly, I saw the alley on the left, just behind me. Then did a spurt backwards, steering carefully, so I was scooted back up into the narrow turning. The killer's white Ford coasted past, screeching to a halt, sending a black plume of burnt tyre streaming into the sky. As it reversed, I gunned the gas to the floor, the engine bucking as it roared. Then I slammed the gear into first, deafened by the shrill screaming of gears mashing steel, clutching down and sliding up to second as I ducked down and accelerated like mad.

And smashed my car into the killer's passenger door.

The lighter car rocked sideways and tilted. And I could see the deep ditch on its other side.

I reversed fast again. Slammed to a stop. Did the same thing again. In time to see the passenger shooter's gun lined up, directed at my face. Before the blast I rammed the Ford so that it tipped over onto its side into the ditch. Simultaneously the shotgun erupted, and in the second before I backed away again, I saw smoke and fire.

Backing away again, I managed to scrape past the car's corpse, knocking it sideways, and fishtailed madly back onto the drive, then took the hard right into Miser's Lane, revving like a maniac. It was hard to think as I crashed the gear into third, accelerating to sixty, the rush of air from the windowless screen smashing into my face, choking me, flapping my cheeks like rubber.

Molly had arranged my assassination, it had all been planned.

But I was going to get revenge on them all.

I was going to break this story and destroy the bastards.

Because now I had no choice: I had to destroy them before they destroyed me.

It wasn't long before the blue lights in my rear-view mirror came closer and the police car's whine nearly deafened me.

THIRTY-FOUR

"We had a traffic report of a car driving erratically along the Carmel Road, with bits of glass falling off it over the road," said the police officer, who I was delighted to recognise as PC Lucy Akehurst, the sympathetic officer I'd spoken to a couple of weeks earlier, when I'd gone in to tell the police about what I'd discovered. I remembered her small, elfin face, short red hair and quick-fire expressions that set my pulse racing. She had made a big impression on me last time we'd met, and in any other circumstances I'd have been very pleased to have met her again.

I was sitting opposite her in the interview room at Penzance's Trew Valley Police Station.

I felt as if I'd aged ten years in the last hour. There were a couple of fairly deep cuts to my face from the windscreen's flying glass, and the police doctor had dressed them and cleaned them up. His painkillers were finally kicking in, and I had the feeling that a humdinger of a headache was on the way.

I had that strange euphoric feeling that nothing mattered anymore. Two cups of black coffee had strung me up tighter than a drum. I felt as if I was about to explode.

The other officer present at the table in the interview

room was a silver-haired uniformed sergeant, who looked to be a good few years older than me, and clearly wished that he was somewhere else.

"Are you arresting me?" I asked them.

PC Akehurst smiled for the first time, easing the tension in the tiny room. "We should. As you know it is certainly an offence to drive an un-roadworthy vehicle, and having a windscreen is mandatory, as is having fully functioning lights, not a set of shattered bulbs. But I've had a quick check of the CCTV of that stretch of road, and half an hour before that time, your car was driving along there in the other direction and was undamaged. What happened?"

"Someone used a pump-action shotgun to try and kill me," I explained. "Luckily I ducked in time."

"Who was it?" she asked.

"Search me. I've got their registration number and the vehicle make and model." I gave her the details. "But that's all I have."

"And this happened in the approach road to Triplinghoes Hall?"

"Yes. I crashed into their car, the gun went off. It looked like the driver might have been hit."

"Right, I'll put this out over the radio and get a team out to the manor," the older man joined in. "Meanwhile you need to make a full statement."

They left me alone for a while, and I wondered what to do next.

The people at Rackhams, with Molly's assistance, had tried to kill me, just as they'd killed Martin and Darius Trefus, and presumably also the hapless Conrad Eriksen and Gordon Dallorzo. With the dangerous knowledge I had, no doubt they'd try to kill me again at the earliest opportunity. Their plan would have been to kill me, dispose of my body,

The Bad Hail Mary

and have my car disposed of, leaving no trace. But with a police report into this failed attempt, there'd surely be a temporary respite, and during that period I could spread the truth about Rackhams far and wide, so that there'd then be no point in killing me.

That's what would happen in an ideal world. But as things stood I was well and truly stuffed, knowing the truth and thus being a danger to my enemies, yet having no evidence whatsoever to back up my claims. Even if the DNA samples Celia and I had taken from Martin's corpse were of any use, it would take weeks for any comparison results to emerge, time I just did not have.

Lucy Akehurst and the other officer, Sergeant Bone, returned.

"So, Sean, are you going to stick to your story, that you don't know who tried to kill you?" she asked me. "Or are you going tell us what this is all about?"

"I really want to," I told her. "But it's a long story, and I doubt if you'll believe it. It's hard for me to take in the enormity of it."

So I told them everything. An hour, and a few mugs of tea later, they had every detail.

The strange thing was, I had not been charged with driving an un-roadworthy vehicle, or with anything else, so I had not been cautioned. Also the interview was not being recorded or videoed, as would have been usual.

"I've never heard of DNA evidence being used in this particular way in a legal case," Lucy went on. "Although it's not unknown. The GSK killer in America was eventually caught using voluntarily donated DNA from numbers of families. It was in the States of course, and it was mired in all kinds of issues regarding privacy and data protection, but they found a legal way through it. But of course you're right. The saliva sample, what's called an *autosomal testing*, from Darius Trefus is obviously of no relevance, because no one can prove that the sample came from him, and now he's dead and cremated, so that's a non-starter."

*

They held me overnight, and I slept badly in the cramped cell, thoughts turning over and over in my mind.

In the morning, Lucy and Sergeant Bone came into my cell, after my meagre breakfast of cereal and tea.

"I think this conversation needs to be off the record," Bone began, closing the communication trap in the door, and joining Lucy sitting on my bunk. They had brought in a plastic chair for me to sit on, and I was opposite them. "First of all, Lucy and I have discussed your situation. We both agree that your life is in danger." He paused for a long time. "And we both agree. We think that you should die."

"What?"

Lucy joined in the conversation. "Listen, Sean. Pretty soon after we brought you in, we found the car your potential killer used, still in Miser's Lane, and arrested the person in the passenger seat. He was alone and unconscious. I'm guessing the driver ran away, so he couldn't have been badly injured when your car crashed into him. In the man's possession was a pump-action shotgun, as you described, that had been fired several times. It looked as if the passenger was knocked out cold when you crashed his car into the ditch. Before he woke up, we managed to find his passport and did some checking. He's an American. According to the man we contacted in the States, it seems that Rudolf Albert Mogg is suspected of being a highly successful contract killer, who normally operates in the States, though no one has yet been able to pin anything on him, one reason being

The Bad Hail Mary

that he has this astonishing ability to get rid of the corpses so they're never found. What we should have done is to charge him with attempted murder and possession of a firearm, which would land him with a custodial sentence. In cases like this, when a foreign national is a known felon in their own country, unofficial policy is to let them know we're onto them, and if they haven't yet committed a crime, encourage them to go home. Apart from having the gun, which no one knows about, and attempting to murder you, he hasn't officially committed any crime in the UK. Unless of course you want to press charges, and then we'll have no choice in the matter. But since he didn't actually do any criminal damage to anyone except you, we have discretion to take the case no further, provided you don't press charges and he agrees to leave the country immediately. It would save us having to do a lot of paperwork if that's what happens. So, trusting that you're in agreement, we made Mr Mogg an offer which he fortunately accepted, and took a chance that you'd not want to press charges."

"Which was?"

"For him to tell whoever had employed him to kill you, that he'd succeeded. Apparently, this guy, called the Moggster, offers a pretty unique service. He kills the person, but always guarantees to dispose of the body, thus giving him the chance of time to get away, and for his employers to get more clear blue water between them and the victim. Do you see, Sean? If your enemies think you're dead, that gets your killers off your back, and leaves you with the time to do what you can to bring this scandal out into the open, so that they then have no reason to kill you."

"Has he agreed to do it?"

"Yes. He'd have been crazy not to. He gets to avoid going to jail, plus he still gets paid for the hit and he goes back to the States, and nobody is any the wiser."

"But if I'm dead, what do I do in the meantime?" I asked.

She shrugged. "Keep a low profile and quietly work like mad to prove that what you're telling me is true. To be on the safe side, keep well away from these Rackhams people, don't go back home yet, and change your appearance to be on the safe side. You've already got half a beard, let it grow until you look like a member of ZZ Top. Wear spectacles, dye your hair blond or shave it all off. I'd suggest walking with a stick and maybe stoop a bit so you look like a much older man. The people at Rackhams who want to kill you aren't going to go searching for you anyway, are they, since they believe you're dead? Remember, too, that they don't have the authority to check your bank account, or view CCTV along anywhere you might be going. So as long as you don't put out anything on social media, and only contact people you trust 100 per cent, you'll be fine. All you have to do, is keep out of sight for a few weeks. As far as they've concerned you're six feet under. Their problem has been solved."

"However, you can't go back to your home, they might check there," Lucy added. "But there's no reason why you can't tell trusted friends you're alive, even stay with them for a bit. No one is going to report you missing, or think you're dead, so as far as we're concerned there's no missing person's case for us to investigate either, is there?"

On Lucy's advice, I waited around at the police station all day and evening, and when I left it was close to midnight, and my eyes were practically closing as I walked out of the police station into the night, wondering what to do now. Lucy had recommended a local pub within walking distance where I could stay the night, and she'd

The Bad Hail Mary

also told me of her friend who worked in a car repair place, who'd fit in the repairs to my car at short notice. Driving my car involved minimum risk, she said, it was hardly likely that people from Rackhams would even know my car's registration number, nor would they have the authority to view roadside CCTV footage.

"Listen," she said as I was leaving, and Sergeant Bone had already gone home. She passed across a tiny slip of paper. "This is my mobile number. I really shouldn't have suppressed these offences, especially the discharging and possession of a firearm. Do you realise I've gone out on a limb to help you and I'm risking losing my career if anyone finds out what I've done?"

"I really appreciate it. You're kind."

"I'm not that kind," she disparaged my remark. "I did it because. . ." She paused, looking embarrassed. ". . . Because I admire what you're trying to do. And I like you. I don't know why. Some people you meet, and you just . . ."

"Yeah, I know, Lucy. I feel the same."

"You like me too?"

"More than *like you*. Since I met you I can't stop thinking about you. I thought all this happening would mean I'd blown my chances forever." I put my hand on her neck, felt her move towards me, and longed to kiss her. "I don't know how I can ever repay you."

"Don't worry," she whispered, taking the initiative and kissing me quickly on the mouth and then speaking into my ear. "I'll think of something. Oh God, Sean, I feel so stupid."

"Why? What?"

She didn't reply, just kissed me again.

"Lucy, God, how I wish I could hold you in my arms properly."

"Later. There's no rush. In the meantime." She looked around to make sure no one was around, and kissed me again on the lips.

"Lucy, I'm in trouble, I don't want to drag you into danger."

"No one's dragging me. I make my own decisions. I've wanted to be in the police since I was ten years old, yet I've risked dismissal for you. Doesn't that tell you something?"

"I don't know what to say. I just—"

"Shut up, Sean. Call me. Soon. I'll be waiting. . ."

THIRTY-FIVE

Being dead was crazy. It was kind of strange, but it was also kind of neat.

I'd phoned Celia and Robin, to put them in the picture. Robin had a friend who had a holiday cottage down in Deal, to the south of Kent around the coast, and the plan was to lie low there until there was some kind of breakthrough, ideally a match of Martin's DNA. Unfortunately, that could take weeks, and due to the circumstances of how I collected it there had been no way to make it in a 'chain of command setting', the legal term meaning that its origin was legally verified, although I could hope that Celia's witness testimony would work.

But was it enough? What I really needed was hard documentary evidence, and I had no way of getting it.

I was getting used to my new appearance, but it still felt strange to see myself in mirrors. Another week had allowed my beard to completely cover my lower face and achieve a bit of density, I'd found some plain-lensed spectacles with heavy black plastic frames, and I'd applied peroxide to my hair and beard, so that now I was completely blond. I'd almost got used to walking more slowly, using a walking stick. From a distance, no one would recognise me, so I felt fairly safe. The weather was cold, so a shapeless green anorak made me look sufficiently anonymous to be unrecognisable, even to people who knew me. To be on the safe side, Robin had lent me his car, an ancient Audi, just in case my car's number plate was recognised by my enemies at Rackhams. I spent my days mostly painting scenes from the town and harbour, and wondered if anyone would ever buy them. People like seascapes on the whole, but views of towns aren't so popular. I soon fell into a routine of going out running in the early mornings (when no one was about hopefully), then setting up my easel around the town during the day to do painting, then evenings reading and watching TV.

I'd called Lucy a number of times and got to know her pretty well. She was based in Cornwall and I was in Deal, so she would need to take several days off to be able to come and see me, and it would be crazy for me to risk going to that part of Cornwall, where Molly or her friends might see me. I spent ages sending and reading messages and learning about her life. Lucy was divorced, thirty-four years old, had lived in Cornwall all her life, and had a sister and two nephews, whom she adored. She also had a cocker spaniel called, coincidentally, Sean. My nightly phone call to Lucy was the high point of my day.

I'd caught a small piece about Molly on the national news. She had given a brief interview to Maggie Fitzgibbon, of the BBC News. She looked very happy, commenting on how 'although I'm very upset about my husband's death, I have to go on with business, I know that's what he would have wanted me to do'. And she really did look happy, as if all her worries were over. As far as she was concerned, her contract killer had murdered me and got rid of my body, so her future was looking bright. To think that only a few weeks ago I had felt sorry for her, wanting to help her out of trouble, unable to see how utterly evil she was.

Now I could see everything clearly. Now I was determined to ruin her, and all the other low-life scum directors on the board.

Now it was personal.

I was going to destroy Molly, and I was going to destroy Rackhams as a company. It wasn't a battle I'd been looking for but now it had been thrust open me, I had no choice but to see it through to the end. The merger with Apperline Webb would not go ahead, and Rackhams would be driven into bankruptcy, its 300-year-old reputation would be tarnished forever and the directors' golden blessed lives would be ruined. Revenge was going to be sweet.

However, as things stood I had nothing.

It would be weeks before we would know if the DNA sample from Martin's body was usable. Even if it was, the only way to use the evidence to prove a link between 'Walter Trefus' and Fleischmann would be to involve Tristan Neuberg, whose name I had promised I would keep out of the business if I possibly could. What I needed was more relevant evidence, some kind of documentary proof, which I hadn't got and couldn't think of any way of getting. Kate Doyle was fully up to speed, and although she was getting the tapes recorded by Tristan Neuberg's father transcribed and translated from German, again there was no proof that Tristan's father had made the recordings.

So I was pretty depressed on the day I drove back to my house in Whitstable to collect a few bits and pieces, arriving after dark, and planning to leave as soon as I could.

How the hell long could I carry on like this, hoping for a breakthrough that wasn't likely to come anytime soon? What on earth was I going to do?

Not many times do I get depressed, but I was now. There was simply no way forward.

So I decided to stay for a bit. During the evening I drank a bottle of wine to try to take the edge off my misery. At 9pm I was in that pleasant sleepy fug of confusion when I hardly cared about anything.

I think that was one of the blackest moments of my life, when I simply could not see a way out of the coffin I'd boxed myself into.

The loud knock on the door broke me out of my drunken reverie.

They had come to kill me.

Instantly I was on the alert, heart hammering, scared to death that they'd come for me again.

I grabbed a heavy club hammer that I'd been using to fix the roof recently, and tiptoed to the doorway, back to the wall, keeping out of sight.

There was another loud knock.

I swung back the door, saw the tall man, and grabbed him by the collar, dragging him inside.

THIRTY-SIX

"Who are you?" I yelled into his face, pinning him up against the wall, hammer at the ready to beat his brains in.

"Steady on!" he shouted.

There was something familiar about him. Then I remembered that I'd seen him on television some time ago, in a discussion programme. A tall, skinny man who looked to be in his sixties: smart dark suit, red tie, grey hair, a face that was bright red and spluttering as I released him from my chokehold.

"I'm Michael Fontanello. The Member of Parliament for Withenshawe."

"Oh, I'm sorry." I let go of his lapels. "Please, I'm really very sorry. I'm drunk. I thought you'd come to kill me."

"Kill you?" He stared at me in surprise as he stood away from the wall and brushed himself down. "Look, you are Mr Delaney, are you?"

"Yes."

"Good, well I certainly don't want to kill you. In fact I was near here on business today, and I've taken the liberty of coming to see you to thank you."

"Thank me?"

"Yes. Don't you remember my name? A few weeks ago,

you were kind enough to write to me, telling me that you'd discovered that I had been being blackmailed by Neville Peasgrove, and that you were destroying all his computers and papers, and to reassure me that my secret was safe – that you didn't even know what it was, nor did you want to know. You'll never know how much I appreciated your help. I found your website, and it wasn't too hard to find your address from there."

I smiled, remembering a few weeks ago, when I'd discovered a cache of notes regarding a blackmailing operation carried out by a recently deceased criminal, whose house I had been employed to decorate. I'd written to all the blackmailer's 'customers', telling them that their worries were over, and that I was destroying all Mr Peasgrove's computers and papers.

"I can see you're one of those people who helps people out without making a big deal out of it. You've even forgotten how much you helped me, haven't you?"

"Yes, a lot has been going on in my life. Come through into the living room and sit down, Mr Fontanello."

Half an hour later we were into our second glasses of wine. He was relaxed on the sofa while I was in my armchair.

"Quite frankly, I'm not exaggerating to say it, Mr Delaney, I think that you probably saved my life," he told me. "Every time that bastard Peasgrove sent another demand for money, I considered killing myself. I may as well tell you that when I was a much younger man, for a very brief period I belonged to a club for people who indulge in what is called infantilism. It's completely harmless, it's not abusing other people in any way, it's not even about sex, and it doesn't harm anyone at all. We dress up as toddlers, and there are women who pretend to be our nannies. Obviously

The Bad Hail Mary

most people regard this harmless peccadillo as ridiculous. Mr Peasgrove had somehow got photographs of me dressed in a nappy, being spanked by a lady who was wearing nothing but high-heeled shoes. It would have ruined my career, of course, but it would also have ruined my life, my marriage, everything. Thanks to you, for the first time in years I can finally relax."

"Glad to have helped, Mr Fontanello. Blackmailers are lower than scum. I'd kill them all if I could."

He smiled. "I do believe you're drunk, Mr Delaney."

"Too right I am."

"Look here, Mr Delaney, I won't offer you money, because that would make light of what you did, and you might regard it as an insult. But I am an MP, and I know all kinds of fairly influential people. If there's anything at all I can do to help you, I would be only too honoured to do so."

"Thanks, but I'm in such a hell of a mess that no one can help me. As I told you, someone has been doing their best to kill me, and I'm at my wits' end. Are you in a hurry?"

"Not at all."

"Then let me tell you what's been happening to me. I'd appreciate your advice."

I told him everything, from start to finish. Mr Fontanello nodded and listened seriously as the minutes ticked by. At the end, I put my hand over my eyes and shook my head.

"So that's why I gave you that strange reception, ready to smash your head in," I concluded. "I need to find some proof of all that I've discovered. At the moment my enemies believe they've killed me, but I can't hide forever, nor can I do very much investigating while I'm trying to keep a low profile. I have to find proof of what happened, so that I can make this whole thing public knowledge. That's the only way I can save my skin, yet I've hit a brick wall."

"Hmm. One advantage of being a busy MP is that I've had a lot of experience of listening to disgruntled constituents at my surgeries, and grasping their problems quickly, so that I can address them if I can. Seems to me that you need a top-notch historian, someone with a bit of a reputation maybe, who will be willing to go with you to this guy Rupert Vigo's house and have another, more comprehensive search of his grandfather's papers."

"Yes. There are hundreds of papers, and I searched as much as I could last time, but I'm no historian, I hardly even know what I'm looking for. And if I go back on my own, he's going to think there's something funny going on, and might tell people."

"My friend, I think I can help. Parliament is a strange place, filled with all kinds of peculiar people. The general public don't know that we actually have our own historian, a guy who has a tiny office in the House."

"The House?"

"The Houses of Parliament. The Palace of Westminster. Johnny Barleycorn is on hand to any of us who have a silver badge – did you know that's the official item we're issued as an MP that allows you certain privileges? Johnny sorts out problems for us, he helps us with our research, he'll basically do anything he can. I'll phone Johnny and ask him to do all he can to help you."

"Do you think he would?"

Michael Fontanello smiled warmly again, stretching his Savile-Row-suited legs out in front of him. I noticed that his shiny black shoes looked to be handmade. "Johnny is one of the most resourceful and brilliant people I've ever known. He helps MPs find out their personal genealogical

The Bad Hail Mary

issues, he does little investigations if any of us land up in trouble, he is an expert at locating information." He nodded to himself. "What's more he happens to be one of the most likeable, decent fellows I've ever known in my life. He knows all kinds of secrets about everyone, and yet when you meet him socially he never lets anything slip, never even criticises anyone. He's just a one hundred per cent nice bloke."

"If he's a skilled researcher, he'll charge heavy fees, and I've got no spare money—"

Michael held up his hand. "Forget about money, Mr Delaney, you leave all that side of things to me. Honestly, my good friend, you gave me back my life, and frankly I'm delighted to try and do the same for you – what's more I believe what you're doing is in the public interest, the very idea of a surviving Nazi war criminal funding a historic British institution, is absolutely monstrous. I'll explain it all to Johnny, and I know he will want to help you in any way he can. Dear old Johnny is mad as a box of frogs, but everyone loves him. He has an office in Downing Street, that no one knows about. It's not in Number 10, of course, oh dear me no, but pretty close, a secret place only known to a few insiders. He's a top civil servant, and his primary job is searching into and digging around with parliamentary records, *Hansard*, that sort of thing, but he's also responsible for looking after all the historical records pertaining to government, amazingly enough going back to the Middle Ages. I've met a lot of very clever people in my life, but I would go so far as to say that Johnny is a genius. I'm proud to say that he's a friend of mine, and as I say, he's a really nice, genuine bloke. I'll give him a ring, tell him the gist of things and I know he'll help you,"

"What if he tells someone who's on the Rackhams board?"

"I'll tell him the score, so he won't. Johnny wouldn't last long in his job if he wasn't the soul of discretion. He knows all the secrets of dozens of leading politicians, both living and dead. If he decided to name names he could earn himself a fortune from journalists. Indeed he could probably end a lot of marriages, even start a few wars!"

THIRTY-SEVEN

When I first saw Johnny Barleycorn, he was kneeling down on the pavement with his face an inch away from Larry, the famous Downing Street cat. Larry evidently liked him, was rubbing his face against his nose, and Mr Barleycorn was making mewling noises and stroking him forcefully. He sat back on his haunches, and Larry walked away, tail in the air, with a jaunty air.

Johnny was a man of around thirty-five, with frizzy unkempt brown hair, piercing blue eyes and a long pointed nose above a mouth that looked like it spent most of its time smiling,

"Mr Delaney?" the man said, getting to his feet and offering me an outstretched hand to shake, as I stood up, having bent to stroke the departing Larry, who hardly deigned to stop. "Larry is my close friend, but he's always a bit wary of strangers, next time you meet him, he might let you have a stroke." He appeared to be several inches over six feet tall, skinny as a rake, with mismatched socks, tight blue trousers and a denim shirt with half the buttons undone. "Johnny Barleycorn, good to meet you. My old mate Mickey Fontanello had a long chat and explained everything. Let's hope I can help you."

"It's good of you to see me."

"Not at all, it's you doing me the favour. History is the love of my life, and there's nothing a historian likes better than delving into a bit of intrigue and mystery. And what a belter of a story this is. Just like the most astonishing true scandals it's almost unbelievable – which is exactly what makes it credible!"

Michael Fontanello had managed to arrange for me to have some kind of security pass that I showed to the policeman at the end of Downing Street, an area that's shut away from the public. We seemed to be about halfway along the road, and a few doors away I could see the famous guarded entrance to Number 10, as a couple of people nodded to the police guard and opened the door to go in. Johnny led me to another door that was also guarded by a policeman, who examined my pass and let us both into the building. Johnny Barleycorn led me through beyond the desk, up three flights of stairs and along a number of corridors. Just like the TV portrayals of the interior of 10 Downing Street, this house in the same street looked similarly archaic, splendid, cramped and fussy, and the carpet-cum-woodwork smell was pleasant.

"I'm hidden away at the back of the place," he explained. "Honestly, I spend quite a while along the way at Number 10 and the various parliament buildings. You wouldn't believe how little space there is in parliament. Most MPs have a cubby hole that they call an office, I'm lucky enough to have this tiny room all to myself. No room for the massive collection of records, of course, I have to hotfoot it to the special part of the library along the road to get anything I need and bring it back here, or of course nowadays things are done more and more online, but it all has to be done on our version of the 'dark web', accessible only to the chosen few with the special software, for obvious reasons. We call it the 'Downing Web', which I confess sounds like a 1920s aircraft. . ."

He took us into a truly tiny room that seemed to be set directly under the eaves. His desk was piled high with papers. There was just enough room for him to sit on the tiny chair behind the desk and for me to take the one opposite.

"Now, Sean, traitors in the Second World War. Hitler's nasty little band of British groupies. There's lots of names here you'll never see on Google or Wikipedia, this is strictly top secret stuff that I'm not allowed to show anyone. We've had a fair few traitors, not least during the years of the Second World War, I've dug up everything I can find on our friend Sir Clive Gaines. Hmm. Hmmm. Of course I really ought to get you to sign the Official Secrets Act before you see any of this, but, well, it's all long past the thirty-year rule, though I see that some of his file isn't meant to be disclosed until 2034."

"You have access to things like that?"

"Far more shocking things than that, old lad. Oh yes, I can see anything I want because I have the necessary security clearance, meaning that if I blabbed to anyone I'd be shot. Apart from me, and a very few others, it's interesting to note that only prime ministers and leaders of the opposition, and sometimes members of the Star Chamber and the Privy Council can see restricted papers like this. Goodness, if journalists were allowed to see even a fraction of what I've seen, heaven knows what might happen. The file on Harold Wilson, prime minister during the '60s and '70s, and those of some members of the Royal Family. . . . Oh, it makes me blush just to think of it. Anyway, Sir Clive Gaines. Anything I tell you is probably known in other quarters anyway, so you could probably have found out the same information from other people." He pushed a hand through his wild shock of frizzy hair, riffling through the papers in a file. "Here we are. Peter Clive Fitzalan Osterley Gaines was his complete name, until he was knighted in 1938. During his time as a young MP he was arrested a number of times for soliciting young men in public lavatories, but never charged. Gay sex was illegal in those days, of course, and interestingly enough, Gaines voted against the Homosexual Equalities Act in 1968, how's that for hypocrisy? His homosexual activities were known to the police, but hushed up by someone in the government – it's normally the job of the Chief Whip. Any peccadillos or scrapes that an MP gets himself into usually get sorted out and suppressed quietly by one of the whips, who calls in favours with the police. Then he keeps the information shut away on record to use as a way of threatening any such wayward MP who might be tempted to vote against the government. Otherwise, Gaines seems to have kept his nose clean enough apart from – *ah yes!*" He read on, frowning. "Yes. The MP Archibald Ramsay had a prominent role in an organisation called the Right Club, and in 1940 made a speech in parliament, calling for an end to the war and immediate negotiations with Hitler for peace terms. The Right Club believed that there was a worldwide hierarchy of Jews who ran everything, and Ramsay maintained that the Nazis simply wanted to free the world of the influence of the Jews. At one point in 1944 MI5 kept him under observation for several months, investigating the possibility that he was working as a Nazi spy. Ah now what's this? Hmm, yes. It seems that the Israeli Secret Service, Mossad, was also investigating him at one time too."

"You have details of foreign security services?"

"Not always, but occasionally we do, especially if their targets are high-profile politicians. Now, what you're interested in is 1946, isn't it? The year that this supposed character Walter Trefus stumped up a huge chunk of cash and effectively saved Rackhams from going bankrupt. This appears to have been orchestrated by Gaines, who happened to be a director of Rackhams himself, and he vouched for 'Trefus', who apparently was a personal friend of his. Aha!" He read further. "There were rumours that it was more than just a friendship, but not much credence was given to the rumour. Gaines seems to have led a quiet time after that, he married late in life to a much younger woman, nothing special about her. Had two sons. No, sorry, Sean, I don't think there's much here that can help us."

"No link to Fleischmann?"

"Well there couldn't be, could there? According to all the available records, Fleischmann was dead. Now, now, wait a minute, I've had an idea. Let me phone an old pal."

He spent the next ten minutes talking on the phone. When he hung up he was smiling,

"That was an old friend who has access to the records of Dulwich College, the alma mater of Sir Clive, or Peter Clive Fitzalan Osterley Gaines, as he was known then, and also where Fleischmann was a pupil too. Of course, during the war all records of Fleischmann's attendance at Dulwich were completely removed, so nobody looking through the records now would have any idea he'd ever attended the school. Another traitor, William Joyce, an American also known as 'Lord Haw-Haw', who gave Nazi broadcasts on the radio, was also reputed to be an Old Alleynian – that's what old boys of Dulwich College are called – but this was a myth, put about just because he lived in the area as a boy for a short time, but he never attended the school. Anyway, back to our chums, Fleischmann and Gaines, it seems that they were in the same boarding house at Dulwich College, Blew House, and there was some trouble. That kind of thing was quite common of course – bum chums are all very well, but this went a good bit beyond that, Gaines and Fleischmann were a bit too obvious as a couple, and the other boys noticed. Gaines was taken out of school by his father, who had heard about the scandal. He managed to get him a place at Harrow, through the old boy network, and ironically Harrow was where that other Nazi sympathising traitor, John Amery, attended briefly. It caused quite a stir at the time, but in the true English tradition, everything was hushed up and Gaines went up to Oxford the following year as expected, while Fleischmann went back to Germany."

"Then how come you know all this?"

"My pal has access to Dulwich's 'unofficial' school records that are known only to a very select few."

"But it doesn't help us, does it?" I asked him.

"No, but. . ." He sat up straight in the seat. "Now, Sean, your problem. I think I've exhausted every possibility I can think of here. But I tell you what I *will do*." He looked at his watch. "I'm free this afternoon, if you are. How about if we both go down and see Rupert Vigo, and we *both* take another look through those records?"

"Fine, I'd be really grateful if you would. The only problem is, the first time I saw him I had different coloured hair and no beard."

He laughed. "Tell the old sod you're an actor and you've changed your appearance for a part."

"Last time I told him I was an academic researcher."

"Then you'll be the first academic researcher who's an actor too. You research the parts you take, to add to the authenticity."

The Bad Hail Mary

"The other thing is that last time he charged me a thousand quid."

"Hmm, now that *is* a problem. Let's see how well we can bluff things out," he went on.

*

The second time I met Rupert Vigo he was all smiles as before, but these were reserved much more for my new friend Johnny than for me.

Apparently Johnny had appeared on a TV programme once in his official capacity as parliamentary historian and this had impressed Vigo to the point that I was virtually ignored.

The gatehouse of the old estate in Kent was much as I'd remembered it, and Johnny had managed to charm Vigo into letting us see his grandfather's records without a charge. Johnny had hinted that he was helping with a documentary that was being made on Channel 4 about forgotten politicians, and his grandfather, Sir Clive Gaines, was to be amongst those included.

"Well, yes of course Granddad did achieve a great deal in his life," Vigo waffled on. "At one time he was tipped to be prime minister, but unfortunately that old dodderer Attlee got the gig."

When Vigo produced the forms he wanted us to sign, I signed them without thinking, anxious to get started.

Once Johnny and I were alone at the top of the tower of the folly, I showed him the boxes of papers I had already gone through and we began the mammoth process of going through all the rest, and anything irrelevant, which meant most of it, we put on the rejection pile. But Johnny appeared to be adept at assimilating information on the written page, and to my surprise he was able to whittle down a stack of papers in no time, scan-reading at a frantic pace, so that as much as half the papers in the room had been searched through, box after box after box.

Four hours later I was about to admit defeat, when I saw amongst the yellowing papers in Johnny's pile, I noticed something black.

"Hey, look," I pointed out. "I think you've got a passport."

We picked it out. The name on it said Walter Trefus, and it was dated 5 June 1946.

"If there wasn't some link between Gaines and Fleischmann, why would the old sod have Fleischmann's passport?" Johnny asked. "This is a good start."

"And, here," I went on, noticing something red in the papers. "This looks like a diary."

"It looks like four small diaries," Johnny agreed, taking them out and putting them on the floor.

I tipped the contents of the sixth box of papers and riffled through the top, then, right near the bottom, I spied a notebook with a red cover. It was a desk diary, for the year 1945. I held my breath until I found a similar diary for 1946. This could be it.

Sitting cross-legged on the floor I leafed through every page of the 1945 diary, noting Gaines's crestfallen comments about the Allied victory, the various defeats of the Nazis, scathing comments he'd scrawled about the Americans.

It was when I got to April 1946 that it got interesting:

Henni has sent word that by some fluke he survived the bombing at Dresden, though he has terrible facial injuries and he's currently being treated in hospital, but he's managed to keep his identity secret and miraculously enough, he's on the missing list, so they'll assume he's dead. He tells me that he's managed to bribe the doctors to get him out of Germany, and an old friend is arranging transport for the money, gold bars and jewellery he managed to smuggle out, as well as some of his favourite artworks, notably the core of the collection of the Weiners' Art Gallery in Vienna, that he acquired when the gallery was forcibly taken over by him in 1938.

I skipped forward to June 1946, where I struck gold:

It's all been quite straightforward. I managed to get the birth certificate of a man called Walter Trefus, who died in 1910 when he was three. Having got this, it was easy enough to get all the other documents for Henni. Since he already speaks English like a native he'll blend in perfectly. I can't wait to see him.

Further on was the clincher:

Success! I've done it! At the board meeting of the directors of Rackhams, they've agreed to accept the offer of Henni's cash and his artworks, and he's virtually taking over the company, thanks to the cash he's bringing with him, as well as his comprehensive knowledge of the history of art, and of course his artworks. . .

Tucked into the diary was an article from the *Daily Mail*, dated June 1946.

Saviour for struggling auction house comes from out of the blue.

Rackhams International Auction House, the three-hundred-year-old British institution, has been on the verge of bankruptcy throughout the war years, but a white knight has come riding to the rescue. Walter Trefus appears to be a remarkably shy ex-serviceman who took part in a number of theatres of war, in a top-secret capacity, working for one of the secret service operations. Mr Trefus was severely injured during the war years, having been left with terrible facial injuries. Supplying a huge amount of cash for the failing auction house, in addition to some priceless works of art, that is slated to form the basis for a new permanent London-based art gallery, means that the enigmatic Walter Trefus is now stepping into his role as Managing Director of the company, promising to usher in a new era of success and fame.

I looked at Johnny. "So what do we do now?" I asked him.

"We take these with us."

"But Vigo doesn't want any papers to leave this place."

"Fuck Vigo. This is the only proof we've got, and right now, we need to get it into the hands of your journalist friend, who will no doubt know experts who can testify whether these documents are genuine and not forgeries. But the ink and paper certainly look genuine to me. I believe that this is the gold you wanted, Sean. This and the passport and the birth certificate. With this lot you don't need DNA evidence."

THIRTY-EIGHT

Meredith Gilliard's office at Rackhams International London premises

"Excuse me?" A pause. "Yes, this is Meredith Gilliard. Who are you?"

Meredith Gilliard had answered the phone just as he was due for an appointment, and couldn't keep the irritation out of his voice.

"Ah, Mr Gilliard, you don't know me, but, in fact, my esteemed grandfather was a director of your fine company a long time ago."

"What?"

"Yes, Sir Clive Gaines. He was also a Member of Parliament. Ring any bells? Hmm?"

"Forgive me, sir, we do have a company historian who might know about your grandfather's connections with Rackhams. I'll give you her name and you can—"

"No, no, no, old boy, it's you I want to speak to, I've been told you're one of the directors. My name is Rupert Vigo, and I just had a rather strange experience you might want to know about."

"A strange experience? Really, sir, I'm very busy just now—"

"A couple of weeks ago, this peculiar character came to

study some of my granddad's papers, saying that he was interested in his connections to your firm, that he was researching the history of Rackhams."

"He was *what?*"

"Researching the history of Rackhams, he said. Frankly, I didn't like the look of him, seemed a bit evasive, baulked at the modest fee I was charging him."

"What was his name?"

"He said it was David Fisher."

"What did he look like?"

"Mid-thirties, down-at-heel, scruffy beggar. Hadn't shaved for a while, scar along his chin. He claimed to be doing the work for his master's degree, but I'm not sure I believed him. Something about the fella that didn't ring true. Oh and he wasn't English. Had an Irish accent. I've never liked the Irish, treacherous beggars—"

"Hey, wait, did you say an Irish accent?"

"Yes, do you know David Fisher then?"

"*Shit*."

"Sorry?"

"Did you get an address for him? A phone number?"

"No, I didn't think I needed one. So, Mr Gilliard, my David Fisher is known to you? He's contacted your company historian already I suppose?"

"Sure, sure he has."

"Well, the really odd thing is, he came back again yesterday, in company with that genuine historian, Johnny Barleycorn, the fella who's been on TV. Only this time Mr Fisher was in some kind of disguise – dyed hair, a full beard, spectacles. This time he told me that in addition to being a mature student, he was an actor, who'd changed his appearance for a part, but I didn't believe him. All sounded a bit fishy to me."

The Bad Hail Mary

"Tell me again, exactly when was this?"

"Yesterday. And Fisher and the television historian fellow, Johnny Barleycorn, they left me without saying a word. I was quite miffed, I can tell you—"

"Mr Vigo, listen, I really appreciate you calling me about this. Can one of my guys come and talk to you?"

"Why certainly. If you would like to look at my grandfather's records you're more than welcome—"

"Sure, sure, we'll discuss all that. Gimme your address please, someone will come by later today. Would 6 o'clock be convenient?"

"Yes, perfectly convenient, Mr Gilliard. Erm, so it's a good thing I called, then?"

"See you later. Thank you very much, sir."

Meredith Gilliard looked as if he was about to be sick. He dialled another number.

"Listen, get me the Moggster on the phone, as soon as you can. I don't care if he's gone back to the States. Get him! I need to fucking talk to him now!"

Ten minutes later, Gilliard answered the phone again. "Moggster, is that you?"

"Mr Gilliard?" the contract killer replied.

"You fucking lied to me! You told me you'd got rid of Sean Delaney!"

There was a long pause.

"I'm sorry about that. I didn't have a lot of choice."

"What happened?"

"The police made me an offer I couldn't refuse. They could have charged me with attempted murder and possessing a firearm, which in your country carries a mandatory five-year prison sentence. In return for letting you think everything was hunky-dory, even listening in on my phone call to you, they let me leave the country, on the understanding that I wouldn't come back in a hurry. Tell me, what would you have done?"

"You could have told me when you got out of England."

"They said if I did that they'd list me as a wanted person, so I'd be charged if I ever came back to England. I don't know if they could have done that, but I figured I'd best err on the side of caution. How did you find out anyway?"

"Don't worry about that."

"The job is as good as done, isn't it? Jeez, the guy knows you want him dead. Believe me, he's not going to be any trouble to you now."

"I'd like to kill you." Gilliard grunted.

The Moggster laughed, a deep guttural drawl. "Sure you would, but is it worth coming all the way to Texas to try and do something many professional killers have tried to do already and failed?"

"You owe me a lot of money."

"You still want the guy iced, yeah? You still figure that he's a danger to you?"

"Of course I do!"

"Then quit threatening me and listen. I got a lead for you, because obviously Delaney is going to be lying low from now on. It was a police constable woman who did the deal with me, her name is Lucy Akehurst, based at the Cornish police station near the stately home I staged out for the hit. I got the impression that PC Akehurst knew Delaney pretty well, that was why she bent the law to help him. If you want to find him, try following her."

THIRTY-NINE

Sean Delaney in Deal

"So you've settled in well?" Lucy Akehurst said as she ducked to come into the tiny terraced cottage in Deal which was my new temporary home.

Robin's friend owned the old house, having inherited it from an aunt a few months ago and not got around to selling it yet. It had been built in the eighteenth century, and was reputed to be in the area of town colloquially known as 'Smugglers Row', because many of the original residents had a secondary income from taking delivery of brandy, spirits and the like from ships trading with the European continent, and avoiding the excise duty. Because of this, some of them had secret passages in their cellars linking them to the beach, to allow for night-time secret deliveries of all kinds of items.

All that had happened to me in the last few days was still a bit of a blur, but after my time with Lucy I had never forgotten the way her red hair shone in the light, or the freckles on her neck that, to me, for some reason looked incredibly sexy. Strangely enough, in repose she wasn't especially attractive, had ordinary unremarkable features that would pass in a crowd. But when she smiled her entire face lit up like the sun, and you realised that she was something special. Maybe it was the kindness in her eyes, maybe it was the way her mouth moved, I don't know. Just something about her that captivated me.

"I've settled in well, sure I have, but I'm wanting to be back in my own home," I told her. "I'm hoping this mess will be sorted in a few days." I explained how I'd handed all the documents to Kate Doyle, who right now was checking the veracity of everything, before contacting the Weiners, who in turn were going to approach the World Jewish Forum, and lodge a formal application for reparations. So far we had no idea if the reparations could only be claimed from the personal descendants of Fleischmann, or whether they might be payable by Rackhams as a company. Since Martin Trefus had owned half of Rackhams anyway, at least half of the company's finances would be affected, not to mention all the bad publicity that would ruin their operations.

The front door opened straight into the living room of the tiny old house, and I led her inside. Let me tell you, old houses might look quaint and cosy but they certainly aren't as comfortable and snug as they look in the magazines. I'd managed to get the log fire burning in the old rusty black iron grate, and the flames accentuated the shadows and awkward corners of the room, whose ceiling was so low I often had to duck. The walls were of yellow, craggy and uneven plasterwork, and the dark timber floor sloped alarmingly, the wood bouncing up and down as you walked in the corner. The freezing wind whistled through the gaps around the windows.

"I do like this place," Lucy told me, swirling around as she smiled. She took off her coat, revealing a red top and blue jeans, putting her shoulder bag on the floor. "Real cosy, ain't it?"

The Bad Hail Mary

"It's got a lot of history," I answered as she sat on the pink floral chintz-covered sofa and I sat beside her. "Thank you for coming all this way to see me."

"I had to see you, to make sure you're okay, and I was due to some leave anyway."

"Listen, I haven't been able to thank you properly," I told her. "You should have charged the man who tried to kill me, yet you went out on a limb to help me."

"And I ain't finished yet." She held my gaze, and somehow it was hard to look away. "Yeah, you've managed the peroxide blond okay, and your beard is looking more wild now, right enough. But the blond hair needs touching up a bit. Have you dyed your hair before?"

"Never," I admitted. "I just did what it said on the bottle. Probably missed bits out."

"Let me fix it for you. I've often done it for my mates and my sister. Reckon I'm a dab hand at hairdressing. And I've brought some specs with plain glass in them, and in the car I've got a walking stick you can use."

"Hey, Lucy, I do five-mile runs!"

"All the more reason to carry a stick and walk more slowly. After all, you're still in Kent, where people know you. It only needs one person to recognise you and for word to get back to the people at Rackhams that you're still alive, and they'll get you again."

"I guess you're right."

"Okay then, where's the bathroom?"

"No rush, Lucy, I haven't even offered you anything to eat or drink."

"We'll eat later. Let's get this sorted out first."

The bathroom was very small, having been adapted from one of the large rooms. She got me to take off my shirt, then made me bend over the sink, while she washed my hair and then put on the hair dye.

"I reckon you're gonna look better properly blond, I really do," she said quietly, as she leaned over me to look in the mirror. I felt her hands around my waist. I stood up and turned around.

"Oh God, Sean," she whispered. "Whenever you're near me feel my heart racing. I never met anyone like you before."

"How long have you been divorced?" I asked her.

"Years now. Graham was a nice guy, but he didn't understand police work schedules, couldn't accept that I had to be out there, on the street, taking my chances and doing all that overtime. He were always wanting me to leave the force, and I love it, the job is my life." She looked down. "Graham, he were nice, but he weren't like you. He didn't take my breath away, he couldn't make my heart race like you can. How about you, Sean?"

"My wife died a long time ago. There've been girls since."

"I bet there have."

"But no one special."

She giggled. "You're supposed to say until now."

"Until now." I pulled her close and the kiss was almost chaste, soft and teasing. I felt my body responding, the old cycle of excitement building that's like nothing else on earth.

But this was more. It wasn't just sex, one more intimate encounter. This was way more than that.

And Lucy knew it too.

That was when I realised that my tawdry affair with Molly had been nothing compared to this. It couldn't possibly compare to what was happening to me now.

"Lucy," I whispered as she broke away. "I'm in the biggest mess of my life and I should be concentrating on

The Bad Hail Mary

surviving, but now you're here I don't care about anything. Sure I don't know what's happening to me."

"Nor do I." She stared at me solemnly. Then she began to undo the buttons of her top, so that it fell open, then put her hands behind her back to unhitch her bra and take it off. Her breasts were small and firm, and rose and fell rhythmically as she breathed. "There!" She took my hand and held it against the centre of her chest, her gaze never breaking from mine. "Feel my heart beating! God, what is happening to me?" She undid the top button of her jeans, then the zip and pulled them down.

"And you?" she asked softly. "Are you gonna keep your clothes on?"

I undressed too. "Lucy, are you sure you want this?" I asked her when we were both naked, and she fell into my arms, her nipples pressing into my chest, my hardness thrust up against her thighs, a bead of clear fluid oozing from the single red eye. "Because for me this is something more than special. I've been in love a few times, but it's never been like this. I want you, but I want to go on wanting you. I'll happily wait for you if you want, I don't want to rush it and spoil things. I want everything to be perfect. I want—"

"Shut up!" She held a finger against my lips. "Don't you realise that it's going to be absolutely perfect? 'Cos I know it, Sean my darling. Trust me."

"But—"

"Shut up and let's lie down on the floor. No need to be gentle with me, Sean. I want you right now, *I can't wait to feel you inside me.*"

*

She stayed the night, and in the morning I walked with her

to her car, which was parked in the car park a few hundred yards away because the houses had no parking spaces.

It was cold, the sky overcast, and after we'd kissed and she'd got into the car, I longed for her to stay.

"Lucy, when this is all over, can I come and see you in Cornwall?" I asked her. "I want to go on seeing you. I don't care about the distance between us, I can even move to the West Country if you want. All I know is that I can't bear the thought of not getting to know you better."

"That's what I longed to hear you say," she whispered. "Call me tonight. Let me know everything that's happening. The day when your journalist friend makes everything public. After that you'll be free of the danger, we can meet up, we can make plans. . ."

I nodded, already hating the thought of being on my own when she left. "Talk to you later."

Walking back to the house, I was hardly aware of the car that was illegally parked at the end of the road.

I'd just got back inside when I heard the knock on the door.

Shit!

No one knew I was living here!

Who the fuck was it? I wondered.

I tiptoed upstairs, crawled across the bedroom floor and managed to sneak a glance into the street over the windowsill.

At my front door were three men. One of them was knocking, while another was swinging a heavy red metal door-opener two-handed. The crash was deafening. . .

FORTY

I was running downstairs when I heard the splintering front door smash open, ricocheting off the wall with a bang. Without thinking, I picked up one of the heavy engineering bricks on the landing, that I'd been using to brick up a window.

The first man through the door didn't see me. Until the second before I heaved the brick into his face.

An explosion of blood. I felt his nose crunch into mush. Kicked him in the balls and watched him fall.

The second man had dropped the heavy metal door-opener and was running towards me as I backed into the house.

"I'll fucking—"

His talking, the momentary hesitation, allowed me to get into the kitchen. Where I picked up the mini fire extinguisher. I ripped out the safety catch and aimed it at him as he charged, squirting a sea of white foam into his face.

Blinded by the foam, he groped his way forwards. It was easy to smash my fist into his jaw, deliver a knee to his guts, and a kick to his balls for luck, as he fell down.

Luckily I'd been prepared for a swift exit, had an emergency backpack waiting.

I managed to drag the big heavy fridge across the kitchen and barricade the door, just as the handle turned and it began to open.

Underneath where the fridge had been there was a heavy trapdoor in the floor. I lifted it up, and ran down the steps to the secret passage underneath, slamming the door over my head and sliding the bolt across, so opening it wouldn't be easy. My backpack was already at the bottom of the steps, and I hitched it onto my back and started stumbling along, bent double in the narrow tunnel.

The secret passage had been built under the house in Deal's heyday of smuggling. I'd been told that it led to the coast, where, in days gone by, carts delivered casks and caskets of contraband fresh off the boats, to be brought back to the house secretly, away from the prying eyes of the Revenue Men. The darkness was complete, and I was groping my way along like a blind man, hoping against hope the other end of the passage wasn't blocked.

Everywhere there was the smell of the sea and salt, and a muggy aroma of dampness. At first, the ground beneath my feet was bone dry, but the further I travelled it gradually got wetter and wetter, so that in the end I was splashing through an inch of water, that was deepening all the time. Ahead there was still only impenetrable darkness. . .

For a moment I panicked, imagining I could hear footsteps behind me, my pursuers getting closer.

Then I wondered if this was a highway to nowhere, and the passage would end in a wall of stone or under the sea.

Then, in the distance, I saw a faint pinprick of light.

Heard the harsh sharp squawk of a seagull. Eventually I could see a circular section of sky and part of the sea.

Finally, I made it out to where the passage opened up

into a cave. At the cave's mouth, the water was about six inches deep, and above me was a steep wall of cliffs.

I climbed up to the beach, and walked parallel with the sea until I could see the town of Deal far above me.

Deal is a small town, and it didn't take long to run to the station, where I caught a train to Dover, then took the ferry to Calais. Luckily I'd thought to draw out a thousand pounds in cash for just such an eventuality, along with my passport and credit cards.

Once I'd arrived in the French town, after going through customs, I found the campsite.

Luck was with me. As I walked through the entrance and went to the camping section, I happened to see a guy who was sitting beside a tiny tent, propping up a large notice, saying *tent for sale, going cheap*, followed by the same sentiment translated into French, and presumably something that looked like German. He looked up at me hopefully as I passed.

"*Combien?*" I asked him. "How much? I only have English pounds."

"Hey, man, pounds are fine with me, I'm planning on visiting England next!" He had an American accent, a waist-length black beard, a forest of hair, and eyes so bleary that they looked as if he'd already died.

"See, the cops are looking for me, and I got no cash at all. I have to vanish real fast," he told me. "My name's Clyde, pleased to meet you. I gotta sleeping bag you can have too."

Finally I had somewhere to stay where no one could find me.

As I lay down to sleep in the tiny tent that night, I wondered how on earth they had found me.

There was only one answer.

They must have followed Lucy.

FORTY-ONE

Clyde's tent in the campsite in Calais was tiny, but Kate Doyle didn't mind sharing it.

I'd told her where I was, and three days later she had arrived in France to tell me what she'd been doing. Now, sitting in the tent with her legs drawn up to her chin, she somehow still managed to retain her sense of style, with her bright red minidress and colourful top. Today the blue central band of hair shook as she balanced the notebook against her knees and spoke fifteen to the dozen, unable to keep the sense of glee from her voice.

"Turns out that my mate, who freelances for the national dailies, has been trying to do a piece on Rackhams for a couple of years now but no one will touch it, because they've got some VIPs on the board of directors who are pretty powerful people." Kate was getting into her stride, talking fast. "He was approached by an ex-employee, who claimed to have a lot of evidence that Rackhams are involved in the smuggling of ancient artefacts from Italy to London and New York, because these items get much better prices in America and England than locally. This has been illegal since the 1980s, when Italy passed the first laws prohibiting the removal of national treasures from their country. This code of laws was updated on 22 January 2004, when the Italian

Government passed the 'Code of the Cultural and Landscape Heritage', comprising 184 official articles and what's called 'Annex A', detailing precisely the kind of activity that's internationally illegal. He also told me that his contact had details about money laundering schemes they were operating. Auctions were fixed, with several bidders being primed to deliberately restrain from going over a certain price, which was below market value. The item would actually sell for a higher price, but only the buyer and Rackhams knew, because the difference was paid in crypto currency to Rackhams, so there was no official record of it. So Rackhams made their commission, plus this unofficial hefty fee, and the seller never knew, nor did the Inland Revenue. What's more, Rackhams specialise in the sale of ancient artefacts, and they had a couple of guys running a little factory in a tiny village in Greece, where they manufactured these things. Apparently when it's old carved stone items it's more or less impossible to tell them from genuine artefacts. There was an Englishman a few years ago, who did the same thing. He made all kinds of 'old' items and made a fortune, and all he needed was his old shed, a few tools and chemicals, and his own self-taught expertise."

"So aside from being financed by a war criminal, Rackhams is a corrupt organisation in lots of other ways?" I asked her.

"Apparently so. Every now and then a big scandal threatens to break, then it dies down. But once this news about Fleischmann comes out, every aspect of Rackhams' business is going to be under the spotlight and all these other rackets are going to come to light, because the VIPs who are protecting them will have been discredited themselves. So aside from possibly being made personally bankrupt, some of those high and mighty directors on the board or Rackhams might have to go to jail."

*

It was ten days since I'd given the incriminating diaries to Kate and she'd made good use of the time. She had approached handwriting and document experts, and professional historians who handled ancient documents regularly, and these people had declared the papers to be genuine, and not forged modern copies. The deal with Apperline Webb was going full steam ahead, and, as Ben Chatterton Seagrave their director said, "Ain't no one got within a spit of stopping us now!" Ben Chatterton Seagrave came from rural Tennessee, and was teased by his more cosmopolitan colleagues, who were all from cities such as New York and Boston, but no one doubted his business acumen and sheer raw intelligence. Apperline Webb were just as keen to sign the merger deal with Rackhams International as the Rackhams directors were, and tonight was the night.

Which was why Rackhams International had booked the Wilmington Palace Hotel just outside Bath for the party-cum-press conference to mark the occasion when the two historic companies signed the merger deal. The Wilmington Palace was a hotel and conference centre that had once been a magnificent stately home in the eighteenth century, set in three acres of beautifully landscaped grounds. Built in the local honey-coloured stone, the Wilmington spelt luxury on a much grander scale than most people had ever seen in their lives, and the black-tie event – a dinner, followed by the press conference, then the public signing of the deal that was going to be televised nationally – was going to be an occasion to remember.

The Bad Hail Mary

The grand central hall was a huge room, alive with flowers and beautiful decorations, the essence of luxury, all the guests had arrived and the affair was in full swing. On the podium Molly had never looked so good, resplendent in her bright red evening dress, which was an exclusive one-off, designed by a leading Parisian fashion designer who I had never heard of. Next to Molly was Meredith Gilliard and the other directors of Rackhams, along with the American contingent, including Mr Seagrave, all of them quaffing their champagne and exuding wealth and bonhomie.

Molly looked as if she was on top of the world, her woes having long been left far behind her.

No one had tried to kill me for a second time, presumably because I had well and truly gone to ground. When my enemies had failed to catch me at the Deal house, my guess was that they'd simply given up, assuming I was no threat anyway. After all, from their point of view they were home free. If Rupert Vigo had contacted them, which was probably how they'd found out I was still alive, he would have assured them that Johnny and I had not taken away any documents from his house. As for the DNA evidence it was valueless: Darius's sample was invalid because its origin couldn't be verified. And it had been a fortnight since Martin had died, so the DNA we'd harvested from him was very unlikely to be usable.

Gilliard and his henchmen were clearly convinced that they had got clean away with murdering three men in order to suppress the story of the century.

Little did they know that my friend Kate Doyle had been working hard, quietly and secretly, had all her ducks in a row and had just now pulled the firing pin from her grenade.

And that now they were completely, and royally fucked.

Firstly, to my surprise it turned out that the DNA we'd got from Martin's fingernails and hair *was* usable, and Celia had signed an affidavit to the effect that she had seen me taking the hair and fingernail cuttings from his corpse at the funeral home, thus validating what we already knew. Herr Neuberg, Darius's Austrian cousin in Vienna, on the understanding of strict anonymity, was prepared to state that his DNA connected him to the 'Trefus' family, and also to the descendants of Stephan Fleischmann. The DNA results had not yet come in, but they wouldn't even be needed now. Because the entries in Sir Clive Gaines's diaries had been scrutinised by several highly respected document experts, who were prepared to put their reputations on the line and affirm that the diaries were genuine, as to paper, ink and handwriting. A copy of the diary entries had also been put into the public domain and verified as genuine by two other independent document experts. Also we had documentary proof that the real Walter Trefus, whose birthdate and address corresponded with the Walter Trefus who had rocked up in London after the war, had died when he was three, and his close siblings had also died mysteriously in 1946, just one week before Stephan Fleischmann had stolen their sibling's identity and come back to England to take his place at the top of British society, as the saviour of the country's most prestigious art and antiques auction house, which, thanks to Fleischmann, was now going to establish a permanent 'Rackhams Art Gallery' in London. And ninety-year-old Oscar Weiner had also been able to find his parents' tatty ancient volume that they'd brought out of Austria, listing all the paintings that had been on display at Weiners' Art Gallery in 1937,

The Bad Hail Mary

amongst them being the oil painting known as *The Bad Hail Mary*, officially referred to as *The Sistine Madonna* and thought to be the work of Raphael. This was proof enough that at least one of the paintings on display in London had originally hung in Weiners' Art Gallery in Vienna, the establishment that had been forcibly acquired by Fleischmann in 1938, under the Nazi edict that no Jewish person was allowed to operate any business in Austria, and such businesses could be brought for nominal sums by the Nazi occupiers.

The evidence was utterly conclusive.

All proof of the above was, according to Kate Doyle, going to become public knowledge at 8 o'clock tonight, timed to be put out as a press release from all the major news agencies in the world, just before the signing of the deal between Rackhams and Apperline Webb. Kate had explained that the various 'gold standard' news agencies, such as Reuters, will never publish anything that hasn't undergone their rigorous checking and cross-checking procedures. So the fact that tonight Reuters, the BBC, plus CNN in America and Aljazeera and various others were putting this out as urgent breaking news was significant.

But crucially, no one from Rackhams yet knew what had been going on, and nor did anyone at Apperline Webb, and all was apparently well and good.

I was the loose end that should have been tidied away neatly.

Boy oh boy, as I entered the crowded waiting room I felt quite the underdog, even though the hired dinner jacket and black bowtie made me feel more clean and tidy than I had felt for weeks now. It had been a relief to remove the beard, and have the hair trimmed a bit, so that now, apart from having blond hair, I looked pretty much as I had looked before I'd been 'killed' by the Moggster. This was the first night I had dared to appear in public as myself, and not the hairy weirdo from Kent. I certainly felt lonely, indeed I didn't know any of the guests in the crowd, and I only really knew Kate, who was in the reporters' enclosure towards the end of the room. It was thanks to Kate that I'd got a pass to enter the private party, as her personal assistant.

So as the room quietened down, and chatter ended, I sat down at the end of a row of seats, away from the dining area, and below the dais, where the board members of Rackhams, and several members of the board of Apperline Webb were sitting at tables, smiling smugly. I sure felt wary when I saw Meredith Gilliard looking towards me, with a furious stare. Their attempt on my life had been made a couple of weeks ago, but it felt like yesterday. It was comforting to know that no one would dare try to kill me in front of hundreds of witnesses, and representatives of the world's press, who were here for the press conference.

It had been the idea of the Americans to do things with a bang, and the table where the contracts were to be signed was free and clear for the cameras to film what would be happening. The main area was filled with tables and chairs and guests and so far the party had gone well, the band had played a lot of good music and now there was that air of expectancy as we all waited for the official signing ceremony. Several TV channels were represented, and the band of hand-picked journalists, from the leading national newspapers, as well as the BBC, Sky News and some cable channels all had their star reporters sitting there, enjoying the hospitality. Gaston Fleeb, the fat silver-haired, middle-aged Conservative MP who was on the board of Rackhams looked particularly pleased with himself, basking in the glory of the occasion.

I had arrived at the last minute, after the main

celebrations, and just prior to the press conference-cum-signing ceremony was about to start. Kate had told me that she had already talked to Mona Shirreff, her friend from Sky News who was here tonight, and, sure enough, Mona was glued to her phone, ignoring the chatter going on around her. The atmosphere was one of relaxed contentment. However, one by one, each of the news correspondents had become absorbed in phone calls and texts, and all were now frowning seriously, making notes on their iPads, gulping and tapping their feet and looking excited and anxious. One young woman stood up abruptly and practically ran to the other end of the room, where she was frantically engaged on a call that she wanted to keep private.

My phone vibrated, and I sneaked a look at the new WhatsApp message, from Kate: *Open up Twitter.*

I opened up my phone on Twitter and saw that *#RackhamsNazi* was trending at number one. About three identical leading tweets timed at ten minutes ago were leading with the story that representatives from the World Jewish Congress had officially issued notice to Rackhams International that they were beginning proceedings against them for reparations due to their clients Peter and Hannah Weiner, whose great-grandfather's business had been acquired by the man calling himself Walter Trefus, in 1938. Next was the revelation that Stephan Fleischmann had not only survived the bombing of Dresden after World War Two, but had illegally entered England with the help of government minister Sir Clive Gaines, under the false name of Walter Trefus, and used his stolen wealth to buy a controlling interest in Rackhams International. There was a steady flurry of fresh tweets, stating much the same thing, flooding my timeline. I scanned the random tweets, noticing that the Home Secretary had put out a statement, as had the Prime Minister. It was the usual prevarication stating that *'The situation is ongoing, and all the facts must be assessed as they emerge, but these revelations are on the face of it, extremely troubling. . .'*

The press conference began, with Meredith beaming at the others on the podium.

FORTY-TWO

I became aware of Meredith Gilliard seeing me. His avuncular smile vanished for a split second, his vituperative stare firing hatred into my eyes. I stared back at him, willing him to look away. He maintained eye contact and did a 'throat cutting' gesture, that nobody else seemed to notice.

And I knew in a horrifying moment, that if this news wasn't even at this second travelling down the wires, I would probably have been a dead man the moment I stepped outside this room.

Yet when Meredith tore his gaze away from me, he looked anything but disturbed. His night was going perfectly, and this amalgamation with Apperline Webb was going to be the highlight of his illustrious career.

"Ladies and gentlemen," he began. "For hundreds of years, Apperline Webb and Rackhams International have been business rivals and business successes, each of us on opposite sides of the pond, but each with offices in our competitors' countries, spying on each other in an always friendly way." He gave way to a titter of laughter from the audience. "And for some years now, those of us who are looking towards the 2030s and the 2040s are wondering why. Why on earth are companies like ours continuing to be rivals? When we both espouse truth, honour and a love of the finest artistic endeavours of humanity, why oh why have we been rivals? You've no idea of the joy it gave me when Charles approached our board with his suggestion of his company acquiring ours. Rackhams as a name might be dying, but Rackhams as a force for good in the world will go on and on for another three hundred years, but now we'll be part of our dear friends in the States, and forever now we'll be known as Rackham Apperline Webb, or RAW for short. RAW will always be synonymous with. . ."

I stopped listening, because right around then I looked up to see that Molly had noticed me too. She was staring across to where I was keeping to the shadows at the back of the room. She had seen me, and she was staring at me, looking furiously, as if she wanted me dead. I stared back unsmilingly. Suddenly, while Meredith was still in the middle of his speech, three phones actually rang at once, and the three directors of Rackhams answered, their faces lined with irritation, which soon gave way to horror.

"Well I think I've said enough." Meredith, still unaware of the mood in the room, was glaring around at his colleagues, who weren't even looking at him. "Next time we have an important press conference, I suggest we leave our phones at the front desk. It is not helpful to hear the damned things while a speech is continuing. *What in hell is going on?*"

There was an embarrassed silence.

"Well, I guess let's begin the press conference before we sign the contract." Meredith resurrected his smile. He sat down and nodded towards the small band of journalists. "Mona, from Sky News. What's your question, Mona?"

"Mr Gilliard, we're receiving reports that the World Jewish Congress in New York have issued warrants and legal statements, alleging that the father of your deceased ex-managing director was not Walter Trefus, but actually was in reality the Nazi war criminal Stephan Reinhardt Fleischmann, who acquired a controlling interest in Rackhams in 1946 after successfully posing under an assumed name and bringing his stolen wealth into the country by illegal means, aided by a government minister, Sir Clive Gaines, who wrote a detailed accounts of this in his personal diaries, which have just come to light. We're also hearing widespread reports of illegal activities within Rackhams International, and the Metropolitan Police are launching a full and thorough investigation into these practices. Have you anything to say, sir?"

"I – er – I – er. . ." Meredith Gilliard opened and closed his mouth like a fish.

Pandemonium broke out, even though another Rackhams director, Siegfried Kresiellyer, tried to continue with the press conference. The journalists had left their seats, and the contingent of American company representatives of Apperline Webb had got to their feet and were walking to the doors.

"Is your takeover offer withdrawn, sir?" asked an eager journalist of the rotund Seagraves, who looked as if he was a bull charging out of the room. "Sir?"

"Let's just say we've narrowly avoided a disaster," he snapped, marching forwards. "The directors of Rackhams were about ready to do a deal with us, yet they knew that this tsunami was in the pipeline, but they never said a thing. Back home we call that behaviour *rattlesnake charm*. After tonight I doubt if Rackhams will still be trading this time next month."

Kate had joined in with the other media scrum, anxious to be in the thick of it, revelling in the knowledge that in the morning it was her exclusive report that would appear in the national newspaper who'd offered her the most money. All the others would lead with the story as their splash headline, but they'd be padding out their articles with guesswork and flimflam, whereas Kate could line her copy with a cold clear wonderland of cool hard facts.

Out of the corner of my eye I could see Molly glaring at me, pure unadulterated hatred in her eyes. She was getting out of her seat.

I had seen enough.

Kate had joined her press colleagues at the front of the room, and I just wanted out, since I had seen all I wanted to. Earlier on, I had envisaged vague ideas of confronting Molly and Meredith Gilliard, smiling in their faces when I knew I'd won. But was I smiling now? No, my feeling was nothing like that. Instead of joy at winning the game, I felt a deep and abiding sadness that a company that had been trading for three centuries should be wrecked in this way, when the guilty parties had all died years ago. No one had ever needed to know this secret, and not long ago I had been more than willing to let sleeping dogs lie. Until Molly had arranged to kill me, and releasing the news was the only way I could survive.

It was strange, the feeling of a sudden release of tension. When you've spent nearly weeks watching everyone around you, avoiding all unnecessary contact with others, and expecting to be murdered at a moment's notice, the stress is unbelievable. I ought to have felt delighted, relieved, absolved of all that worry and stress. But in fact I just felt sad, weary and kind of empty. And most of all tired out.

It was over.

I couldn't believe it.

All I wanted to do was phone Lucy to tell her how things had gone, then drive home to Whitstable and sleep for a year.

I slipped out of the room, sneaking out past the grand entrance, following the path around the building, then away into the grounds, and towards the car park. I could almost taste the road home, the freedom from Rackhams, from Molly, from Meredith Gilliard and everyone else.

And then, in the darkness of the big car park I heard footsteps from behind. I turned to see Meredith Gilliard walking towards me.

"Fancy your chances?" I asked him.

"You better be a good fighter, Delaney," he snarled, running towards me and aiming a fist at my face.

I parried it easily. His kick to my balls had me reeling, and this time his punch hit home, and I staggered backwards.

Head down, I charged back at him, and caught him with a right uppercut that had him stumbling. I followed it up with another right-hander into his face. Blood spattered everywhere as a couple of policemen ran up to us.

I was held from behind, hands twisted up behind my back, as was Gilliard, whose face was a mass of bleeding redness.

"This man attacked me!" Meredith Gilliard spluttered. "I want him charged with assault."

"Let's all calm down, shall we?" yelled the policeman behind me. "Are you going to behave, sir?" he asked me.

I gave a nod.

The police took our names and addresses. Now that the police were involved, Gilliard was less keen to go to the police station and make a statement in the hope of getting me locked up for the night, especially as there was likely to have been CCTV coverage of the fight, which would show that he had started it.

"So, I want you each to go on your way, now," the older officer said. "We've reported this incident officially. If you don't agree to go away in peace, we'll arrest both of you and you can spend the night in the cells."

"That won't be necessary, officer," Gilliard said, still glaring at me.

I walked off to my car, leaving them behind.

Once I was in the Land Rover, I took out my phone, pressed the fast dial for Lucy's mobile and held it to my ear.

"All gone fine," I told her.

"It's on Sky TV news now," she told me. "Mona Shirreff's question made headlines, and I guess they're explaining the report because of this bombshell. I think I saw you at the back of the room. How does it feel to be famous?"

"As far as I know, no one knows it was me that started it all. That's the way I want it to stay."

I leaned back in the seat and closed my eyes.

Which was why I didn't notice when the passenger door opened and Molly slipped onto the seat beside me, holding a pistol that she pressed into the side of my neck.

FORTY-THREE

The gun's muzzle was pressed so tightly into my neck it was hurting.

I'd been holding the phone to my right ear, out of her line of vision. I dropped it on the floor, hoping Molly wouldn't notice it.

Seeing her beside me now, I reflected that Molly looked even more beautiful than she ever had. Her perfume filled the car, and something more. She was so close I could smell the champagne on her breath, and the faintest trace of sweat. I managed to glance sideways and look into her face. Her eyes were intense. Perspiration covered her upper lip. I noticed a tiny thread of saliva leave her lip as she opened her mouth to speak. I had already seen her at her worst, at her best, at her most sexy and flirtatious. But never like this. She was like a wild savage dog. She smelt feral and deadly.

"So you did it," she said slowly. "You did it. I never thought you had the brains to get it all together. Or the balls to fuck us all."

"You underestimated me. You always have. Before your contract killer arrived at Triplinghoes to ice me, I told you on the phone that I was prepared to drop everything, to let it lie in the past dead and buried. Why should I care who killed your husband, or Darius for that matter? Or what the fuck happened eighty years ago? I was going to drop the whole thing. All you had to do was believe me, and call off the Moggster. If you'd done that none of this would have happened."

"It's my fault?"

"You know it is. I've given it a lot of thought. You judged me by your own standards, as someone who's so fucking venal that they'd probably resort to blackmail to keep a secret quiet, whereas in reality I'd never have done that. If you'd asked me to drop the whole thing I would have done it, and you'd never have heard a peep from me again. But because you misjudged me, at the end of it all you're the one who's finished."

"That's where you're wrong, Sean. I'll get out of this somehow. Your case with the World Jewish Congress will go on for an eternity and cost a fortune, and this proof you claim to have will fall apart. You know me, Sean, I'll never give up fighting. I've got Triplinghoes. I've got Rackhams. I'm made for life. This is just a little setback. You haven't got any proof."

"Have you looked at the news on the Reuters and the BBC websites? I've got evidence and proof."

"I don't believe you. Your half-arsed attempts will fizzle out. Especially when you're dead, and can't tell anyone the truth."

At least she had taken the gun away from my neck, was holding it a foot away from me, aimed at my eyes.

"Okay, you plan to kill me. So let's play the truth game." I broke the tense silence.

It's odd. When you think you're going to die, it's not necessarily as scary as you might think. It's just a cold, empty feeling of inevitable nothingness.

"Did you kill Martin?" I asked her.

She smiled, as if a spring was uncoiling in her mind. "What do you think? The secret of being a good liar is to tell as much of the truth as you can, and chuck in the lie at the end, so no one notices. Everything I told the police was true, I just didn't tell them *all* of the truth. What I didn't say was that after I hit the diver, he ran away without doing anything, got back into his boat, probably aware that I'd seen him, and might identify him later, and he didn't want to risk being caught. Then after he'd gone, Martin was calling up to me from the hold, asking what was happening. And in that moment, I thought how the fuck long do I have to wait for the old bastard to die? My life was slipping by, trapped in a marriage to a miserable old man. I deserved a life of my own, didn't I? And I thought why not? I'd already got a ready-made killer, I could describe him to the police, all I had to do was finish the job he'd started. Risking the long swim was just a calculated risk – and you know me, Sean, calculated risks are what I do best. I'm a winner, I always have been a winner."

"So you're going to kill me?" I went on.

She nodded. Her profile in the darkness was stark, dangerous, deadly as a spitting viper.

"You won't get away with another murder."

"Why not? No one knows I'm missing. This car park is too far away for anyone to hear the gunshot. Afterwards I'm going to wrap your hand around the gun, make it look like suicide. Then simply slip back in the darkness to the meeting. No one will even realise I've gone."

"What will you gain by killing me?"

"Peace of mind. What's more, Sean, you've done your best to destroy my life, and I'm going to destroy yours. I used to love you, Sean. Has anyone ever told you how close the emotions of love and hatred are? They'm split by a tiny whisker, that's all. *A tiny little whisker.* Besides, we're going to win this battle. But with you still alive, who knows what other facts you've got up your sleeve? There's a good reason to kill you."

"That's Darius's gun, isn't it? The one I found in his flat."

I recognised the weapon, from when it had been hidden beneath a pile of underpants in that filthy Bradford bedroom. A heavy automatic, a Glock by the look of it, probably 9mm. At this range I wouldn't have a hope of surviving.

"There were some bullets with it. I took it out to the *Lively Lady* for fun, intending to do some pot-shots, but I never got around to it. Ended up leaving it in the boot of the car, under an old blanket. Maybe I had a premonition that one day it would come in useful. Martin brought it back to Triplinghoes, intending to destroy it securely, but he never got round to it. Have you ever looked closely at it? There's what looks like a bloodstain on the barrel, and Darius's fingerprints are likely to be all over it. I know you rarely get usable fingerprinting on a gun, but if that blood contains Darius's DNA, then it can be traced back to his flat in Bradford, which you had full access to. As far as the police will know, you took it yourself, and you used it to blow your own brains out."

"Why would I kill myself?"

She shrugged in the darkness. "People kill themselves for all kinds of reasons. You've just almost been arrested for having a fist-fight with Meredith, which isn't exactly normal behaviour. There'll be people around in Kent who've seen you looking crazy with the long hair and unkempt beard, behaving strangely. You haven't had any portrait work for a long time. You were depressed. I mean, why are you here, anyway? An uninvited guest to this reception? That's weird behaviour. You're a nutcase, Sean, everyone's saying it. And nutcases often kill themselves."

"You're sitting on my left. You plan to shoot me from there. I'm right-handed, so if I was going to shoot myself I'd do it from the right-hand side, wouldn't I?"

A look of fury flashed across her face.

"Give it up, Molly. This won't work and you know it. You might be an evil manipulative bitch, but you're not a fool."

"It's a very funny thing, Sean, but ever since I met you, I had this weird premonition that it would come down to this – my life or yours. You see, you saved my life all those years ago, so I should be eternally grateful. But I never was grateful, do you know that? I don't know why, but I almost felt guilty that I owed you so much, and I could never repay you. Yes, I chased after you, persuaded Martin to use you for the portrait, because I knew you'd be grateful, and I'd be like a cat playing with a mouse. Knowing that I had all the power and you were at my beck and call. Then after we had sex I fell for you physically, I really wanted you. But that's me, Sean. That's your little Molly all in a nutshell. Gotta have it my way or I don't want it at all. All my life I've wanted to fall in love but I go so far with the physical side, but then it stops and I can't go no further. And now, as I told you, my love's changed. It's come out all twisted up and changed to hate. I'm sorry, Sean. There ain't but only one thing I can do. . ."

I lunged for the gun.

But I was too late.

Time slowed to a heartbeat.

I saw her breathing freeze.

Geoffrey David West

I saw her lower lip tremble.
I saw her trigger finger tense.
The last thing I heard was the explosion.

FORTY-FOUR

I was stone deaf. The world was smoke and greyness. There was a stench of cordite, and something else, something sinister and beyond awful, like sizzling meat on a barbecue.

Smoke filled the car. The windscreen and side window had been shattered, the car's roof headlining was on fire. Opening the car door, I leaned out into the night sky, vomited, took a gasp of air, and couldn't stop coughing. I rolled out, so that I was on all fours on the ground, watching the flames licking the car's interior, growing every second. I saw that the sleeve of my jacket had been ripped apart. I had a fleeting nightmare vision of the metal-shredded remains of the pistol in Molly's lap, her amputated hand still attached to the handle, her wrist, a few shreds of bone, blood and gristle. Her face, or what was left of it, was a mass of horrifying redness, and I had to look away. Even in the darkness I could see that half her head had been blown off. The front of the car was a nightmare of blood and smoke and gore and viciousness.

Then, as I crawled away, I worked it out. The pistol had been in the drawer of the flat in Bradford. Since possession of a gun had been made illegal, a number of people who'd previously legally owned guns, and were fond of their weapons, had the option of 'legally deactivating them', meaning that a gunsmith removed the firing pin or some other part of the mechanism, so that the weapon could no longer fire. A cruder method of deactivation, that could be performed by anyone who had the skills to do a bit of welding, involved melting, or brazing metal into the gun's barrel, so that it was blocked and couldn't fire any kind of projectile. It was the perfect choice for someone who didn't want to risk going to prison for five years, but needed to be able to threaten people with what looked like a functioning firearm during dangerous drug deals. But if such a deactivated gun was fired, the bullet couldn't escape, and the explosive force would be such that the gun itself would become like a miniature bomb, exploding and throwing bits of metal at anything in its path.

Someone appeared beside the car, staring as the flames were growing around the engine bay.

"What the fuck happened?" asked the man who was kneeling beside me.

"Call the police, would you please?" I tasted saltiness, and realised I had a gash on my face that was pouring with blood. "And an ambulance."

"What happened to her—" He looked into the car, where the cordite smoke was clearing. "—Oh fucking hell!"

FORTY-FIVE

After I'd made statements to the police and had my wounds treated in hospital, I went to the Travelodge where I was staying and slept until the following evening.

My car had been written off due to the fire, which had spread past the dash and caught hold of the petrol. I didn't like to think of how they had extricated Molly's body from the wreckage, and what it must have looked like.

Fortunately, Lucy had stayed on the line during my final conversation before Molly fired the gun, and she had recorded the conversation, so now it was all out in the open. Although I would be required to attend the inquest into Molly's death in due course, the police weren't charging me with any offence.

It would have been nice to have had a catch-up with Kate, to find out what had happened after I left the hall, but she'd had to rush back to London immediately after the event. So, the day after the disastrous press conference, I left Bath on the train, then went on to London, then to Whitstable and home, where I told Robin all about what had happened, and helped him do the last part of the church roof repair: erecting the guttering.

Everything in life was looking better. I'd had a couple

of enquiries for new commissions for portraits: a rich advertising executive and a celebrated consultant surgeon, whose portrait would eventually hang on a wall in the premises of the British Medical Association.

I spoke and WhatsApp messaged Lucy several times a day and she'd arranged a few days holiday in a week's time, and I was planning to go down and see her then, perhaps take her for a holiday. Things were moving fast between us, and for the first time in years, I felt that she was a girl who I wanted to settle down with, get married, have children, the whole thing.

Then, Celia phoned me, inviting me down to Triplinghoes, where she wanted me to paint several exterior views of the old house.

Since Molly had admitted killing her husband in the car before she died, and Lucy had given the recording of her phone call to the police, it meant that Molly could not inherit anything from Sir Martin's estate under the Forfeiture Rule. In that instance Celia, as the default legatee of her father's will, inherited his estate, even though in due course it was likely that the Weiners would also have a claim on Sir Martin's legacy, despite the fact that the legal process was likely to take years. Although strictly speaking Celia was supposed to wait for probate to come through officially before moving into the big house, she already had a key, and had just moved in anyway, taking the logical viewpoint that no one was likely to stop her.

Since I was still without a car – the insurance hadn't yet paid out on my beloved old Land Rover – and I was horribly short of money, I went down to Cornwall on the train, carrying my painting equipment in a rucksack.

It was odd to go through the main gates of Triplinghoes on foot, after always previously having driven through them. I noticed with satisfaction that the unicorn model had been taken away, which was a huge relief, as something about the horrible little thing had always offended me – all the more so as it was forever associated with 'the Unicorn', alias Stephan Fleischmann. As I approached the front door, I pondered on how many things had changed since I'd first arrived, only weeks ago. Martin Trefus had met a watery grave, and Molly had blown her own brains out. I had escaped death by a miracle, and I had been part of an exposé that had destroyed the credibility of an old established business, and brought to light one of the most horrifying scandals of the aftermath of World War Two.

"Hi, Sean," Celia said when she came to the door to greet me. She enveloped me in a hug.

"Sean, I'm so sorry about everything that's happened," she told me. "Thank you for coming down here, I do appreciate it."

Celia was wearing tight jeans and a white shirt adorned with colourful flowers. Her jet black hair was neat and tidy, as usual.

"By the way," she went on as we walked into the main front living room. "I know this business has made quite a hole in your life. You've been through hell."

"Sure I have."

"Do you need any money?"

"What do you mean?"

"Don't be proud, Sean. Look, I know that Martin didn't pay you properly for the portrait of his son. You've been travelling all around the country, using your time to do all these investigations, you've even travelled to Vienna. You must be down thousands by now. As I told you, I'm a successful architect. Now all these things have happened,

I've inherited this place – though of course the circumstances are regrettable, the fact remains that I'm much richer, thanks to all you've done. Even if the reparations organisation claim back the money it'll take time, so I might as well enjoy it while I can." She paused. "Let me give you a couple of thousand, at least. Call it a loan if you like."

"No, Celia, look, I'll charge you for doing these paintings," I told her. "I have lost a fortune, but it's not your fault, and taking your money wouldn't be right."

"Okay, I understand. But remember this. I like you, Sean, I always have, ever since I nearly ran you off the road when we first met. If I can ever help you, whatever it is, I'll do it. Just ask and I'll be there."

Little did I realise back then that very soon, Celia would get me out of one of the worst scrapes of my life.

I spent the night in one of the many spare bedrooms, and next day I made a start on the painting of my first exterior view of the manor house, seen from the edge of the front drive. I was reasonably happy with the result, showing the eastern façade with the sun shining on the windows, and the trees in the background. Celia had been out all morning, and in the afternoon, she came out to talk to me.

"Sean, something very strange has happened. Can you come and look?"

Inside in the large kitchen-cum-pantry was where Celia had spread out some drawings on the table. We sat on stools in front of it, and I saw that it was a large floor plan of the house.

"As you know I'm a conservation architect, buildings are my life, and the first thing I do when assessing a place is a complete and comprehensive survey of everything," she explained. "Out of interest really, but also because I thought I'd send the plans to your friend Robin, to see what he thought about making the scale model of the house, that we were discussing – remember, you told me that your friend made miniaturist models of houses?"

I nodded. "Yes, he'd love a job like this."

"Well I've measured all the rooms, and the exterior and interiors of the walls, everything, and it all matches up as it should. Apart from here." She pointed to a wall in the main downstairs living room. "I've checked and double-checked, and it seems that the external measurement from the front of the house to the back is much longer than the length inside."

"Yeah?"

"I'll show you."

We moved to one of the largest rooms on the ground floor, and she pointed to the far wall. "Yes. It means that this wall here is six feet in front of where it's supposed to be."

"A hidden room?"

"Must be. Except there's no access to it at all, so it's a complete mystery. I scraped away the wallpaper, and the plaster looks different to that of the rest of the room. I think this wall was added for some reason."

"To hide something?" I asked.

"That's what I'm guessing. I think I'll get my builders in and knock a hole in it and take a look."

"I'll do it," I offered. "Have you got a cold chisel, sledgehammer and a lump hammer?"

"Will you? That would be great. There are loads of tools in the garage."

I rooted around in the garage while Celia rolled the carpet back.

Knocking down a wall is easy, especially if it's only a thin one-brick-thick wall, as this one was. The only hard part is making the initial hole: once you've got a hole, you can whack away around the edges and the bricks or blocks can be knocked away without hardly a tap. After I'd chipped away the plaster at around waist height, exposing the brick, Celia looked closely.

"Yes, as I thought." She was staring at the craggy surfaces and scraping at the mortar with a screwdriver. "These look like London stock bricks, whereas the main walls are of local stone, some of it lovely Cornish granite. Triplinghoes was built before they'd invented cement, so the rest of the building is made using lime plaster, whereas this is cement mortar – lime mortar crumbles easily, whereas this is hard cement-based stuff. This wall has definitely been added relatively recently. I grew up here and I remember it always being here, so at least I know it must have been done before I was born."

After a lot of crashing, I'd managed to chip into the side of a brick, then smash through and make a hole. It was only a matter of time before the remaining half knocked through. I pushed a long cold chisel into the hole, and it met no resistance at all.

"It's only one brick thick," I told her. "As we both know, if it had been an external wall it would either have a cavity and another skin, or it would be two bricks thick."

"So I was right," Celia agreed.

She came beside me and took the lump hammer (shorter than a carpenter's hammer, with a blunt chunky iron head and short thick shaft), knocking free the bricks above, while I tapped at the gap below the hole with the sledgehammer.

Pretty soon we had a big enough hole for me to climb through.

The smell hit me first: vile, fetid and mouldy, as if an

animal had died in there. Celia went and fetched a couple of torches.

I climbed in first, Celia came in behind.

Using the torch beam to probe into the darkness, all I could see was dust motes, from the building materials I'd disturbed.

That was long before I saw the grinning skull.

FORTY-SIX

The smell was overpowering, sour and damp, and something indescribable, but cloying and awful. We were in what seemed to be a tiny compact room that was only about five feet in depth.

First of all I saw the blackened spiders' webs across the far wall, which was relatively smooth: clearly this had once been the plastered wall surface of the living room.

Then, when we moved further inside, on the floor was a large object covered by a blanket, looking like a piece of furniture. When I lifted the blanket aside I could see what appeared to be a stack of large framed paintings. The top one looked like a large oil painting with an elaborately crafted gilt frame, of a magnificent white horse with a rider, who had the looks of a sixteenth-century aristocrat.

"Oh fuck!" Celia screamed, backing away from the other wall, where she had been looking. "Oh shit!"

She held her hand to her face.

I looked across to see a human skull, above the rest of the skeleton, the remnants of what had been clothes still attached to the bones.

When we were back in the main room, I saw that Celia had gone as pale as a ghost. Instinctively I crossed myself, and she just stared. We stood in silent respect for a few moments, too shocked to speak. "I was born in this house, and that wall's been there ever since I can remember," Celia muttered. "Dad always told us that his mother went missing when he was nine years old – there was a massive police hunt, but she was never found."

"Hmm," I reasoned. "I wonder if she found out the true identity of her husband, that he wasn't Walter Trefus, and she had to be silenced."

"Makes sense," she agreed. "And it looks like this was a secret hoard of some of the paintings that Fleischmann stole from the Weiners' Gallery, but he couldn't risk showing to anyone, in case they incriminated him – perhaps his wife found them? Dad told me that his mum had been some kind of art historian, an expert on the Dutch Masters so he told me. Maybe she found Walter's secret hoard, made the connection, so he had to shut her up."

"If Walter – or Fleischmann, was a practical kind of person, he could have built this wall himself, no one else would have known."

"Shit, this means police tramping around the place," Celia said resignedly, reaching for her phone. "How bloody undignified for my poor old grandma – bunged up into a cubby hole like that for all these years. "Bloody hell, Grandma," she addressed the hole in the wall. "I'm *so, so* sorry. Why couldn't you have done a bit of haunting? We'd have found you years ago and could have given you a decent burial."

"And you'd have found all those paintings, which might have blown the secret wide open," I surmised.

The police were there for the rest of the evening, and they took statements from both of us. It was 10pm by the time they'd sealed off the room with police tape, and told us not to go inside, and that a team would be coming back in the morning. Absurdly enough an ambulance crew had even arrived, due to some mix-up when we'd called the emergency services.

Next morning I woke up with the worst headache I could ever remember. And I was shivering.

What a time to come down with flu!

"I'll go home," I told Celia, as I managed to eat some toast. "I'll have to come back to finish the paintings."

"Can you travel though?" Celia said. "It's a long way. I'd drive you back to Kent, but the police told me to stay in for when they come back this morning."

"I'll be okay," I told her, my throat on fire. "I'll sleep on the train."

"Sorry, Sean, hope you're better soon. Why not just go upstairs to bed?"

"Thanks, Celia, but I'll be okay if I just get away now."

Maybe it was the stress of all that I'd gone through in these last weeks that had tipped me over the edge and I got ill. Although I liked Celia's company, now I hated Triplinghoes and couldn't wait to leave. I had tried to arrange to meet up with Lucy before leaving Cornwall, but her shifts had been awkward, so I hadn't been able to see her until a few days' time, Friday, when she had a free day.

I got away from Triplinghoes as fast as I could, packing my stuff in a rush.

And, stupidly, I left my phone behind. But I didn't realise that until I was already on the train.

Little did I know it, but getting flu was going to be the least of my problems. . .

*

Somehow I made it home. Luckily I had plenty of food in

The Bad Hail Mary

the fridge and freezer but in the event I didn't want to eat much, and the shivering was getting worse.

I went to bed and slept.

And slept.

So that by the time I woke up properly, sometime in the early hours, two days later, I was ravenously hungry.

A bit later in the day, after a bath and eating properly, I began to feel myself again.

It was 8am, and I worked out the dates. It was Friday, and I suddenly remembered that I'd arranged to meet Lucy in Cornwall, at 8 o'clock that night.

Things were working out well. Time to set out in an hour or so and catch the train and make it in time.

Little did I know that in just a few hours, my whole life was going to be fucked.

FORTY-SEVEN

I was upstairs, on the edge of sleep, wondering whether to get up and find something to eat before starting out on my long journey.

Robin knocked on my door and gave me his phone, explaining that there was an urgent call for me. Just as Celia had done, Paula Swan, Darius's girlfriend, had managed to trace me through Robin: as the local vicar his number was publicly displayed on the parish website. The phone call woke me up fast.

In all the vicissitudes and comings and goings connected with this business, I had almost forgotten that it had all started when I had looked into the questionable death of Darius Trefus. And then much later it was meeting his partner, Paula, that had broken the mystery. Paula, with her tattoos and scowl, her bitterness and everlasting burning hatred and fear. I pictured how scared she was, her fear of everything that was happening around her, running away and hiding as she had been, looking after her child, the most precious thing in her life. Now that Darius's secret was out, I had hoped that she could stop running at last and come back to some sort of normal life.

"You told me we'd get revenge for Darius's murder," she said to me without preamble. Her voice, low and

The Bad Hail Mary

murderous, a dirty whisper of hatred. "You told me that his killers would pay!"

I closed my eyes, feeling more tired than I could ever remember. "I said that I'd try and get to the bottom of what happened," I argued. "And that's what I did. I was guessing that the people at Rackhams were responsible for Darius's death because he was trying to blackmail them, but I have no way of knowing for sure. Even if I knew who had actually killed him I couldn't possibly prove anything."

"And you're not even going to try?"

"There's no point trying. It's impossible! See here, Paula, I'm just about done with interfering with other people's business. As you know, right at the start I discussed Darius's death with the police and they told me that unless we can present them with copper-bottomed new evidence, there's no way they could even alter the verdict of suicide and open a murder case. Everything else followed on from that. There's absolutely nothing we can do."

"*Fuck you, Sean!* All this time I've waited patiently, hoping that you'd get some justice for Darius, I did all that I could to help you with this wretched business. I told you the name of Mr Neuberg in Vienna, without me you'd have been stuck, you'd never have got the breakthrough you needed! Remember what happened, Sean? They were trying to kill you, and thanks to me, you exposed the truth, and saved your own life. And all this publicity – don't tell me you're not enjoying that. And the Weiners must be very grateful to you. Have they given you any money?"

"No, they haven't. And I'm not enjoying the fucking publicity. Frankly, Paula, all this business has been a living hell for me, nearly got me killed and caused me nothing but trouble. I just want to put it all behind me. And I'm sorry. I wanted Meredith Gilliard punished too. But some things are possible, others aren't. We'll never know if Meredith Gilliard killed Darius."

"You may not know, but I do!"

"Look—"

"Shut up and listen to me, Sean! As I told you before, on the night he died, Darius and I had a huge argument, and I stormed out and left him. Do you know what we argued about?"

"Tell me."

"That he'd got evidence of the sharp practices going on at Rackhams and he was successfully blackmailing them, and how clever he was to have found out some big secret that they were paying him to keep quiet about – of course now we all know what it was. But I didn't know then, and I was disgusted with him, I'd had enough of his scheming, his secrecy, his petty blackmail. He couldn't tell me the real secret, of course, he daren't do that because he knew that my mum was Jewish, that she came originally from Poland, and her grandparents died at the hands of the fucking Nazis. God, I just went mad when he wouldn't talk to me about what he knew. I screamed and yelled at him, telling him that I couldn't bear to be in the same room as him anymore, that I *hated him*. And I just had to get out. Added to that I was heavily pregnant, tired out, hormonal and moody."

"So you left?"

"Yes. I went out and just walked on my own for an hour, trying to get my head around this crazy situation. When I came back, I ran into four men coming away from our block of flats. They didn't say anything, just walked fast, looking down. One of them was Meredith Gilliard, I recognised him from the TV. And after I found Darius, I was in a daze, called the police. I told them about the men

The Bad Hail Mary

I saw leaving, but they wouldn't listen to me. Just told me that Darius had committed suicide. But I knew they were wrong. And I can picture what happened after I left, I know it had to be that way. While I was gone, those bastards came to our flat, poured whisky down Darius's throat then they manhandled him into the living room, put the noose around his neck, perched him on a chair and dragged it out from under him. They must have watched him kicking and struggling for his life, gasping and choking, probably laughing. I keep thinking of it over and over again. I know for certain Meredith Gilliard was one of the guys who killed Darius."

"So go to the police and tell them that again."

"Don't you think I haven't done that already? I did that the day after he died, I described all the men I saw leaving, but *no one listened to me.* I went to the police station yesterday and told them I recognised Meredith Gilliard and that I saw him coming away from our flat on the night Darius died. They looked bored. They told there was nothing anyone could do."

"I'm sorry."

"*What's the point of sorry?*" she screamed down the phone line. "I've been treated like shit by everybody! Darius's family always hated me, and blamed me for everything they claimed Darius did wrong. You picked me up and used me when you needed to learn about what happened to Darius, then never even contacted me again. And after you've done all your investigations and told the authorities, all that's going to happen is that the directors of Rackhams might possibly lose all their money, and a rich family who already have a string of lighting emporiums up and down the country are going to get richer. Why should I care about that? I helped you, yet you forgot all about that, didn't you? I bet you've forgotten I even existed. You know they killed the detective too, don't you?"

"The detective?"

"Gordon Dallorzo – the fella who broke into the flat, who you had a fight with."

I remembered the car I saw outside Dallorzo's office, the car whose number plate I remembered, belonging to, or hired to, the Moggster.

"And I've been talking to Billy, our old neighbour at Albany Court. He still has a key to access the storage depot, where all the papers from the flat are still stored, and he let me in to look at them. We've found all the details about Rackhams, the private addresses of all the directors. I've got the London address of Mr Gilliard. I'm going to make him regret what he's done."

It all came back to me. Darius's sordid flat in Bradford, where I'd cleared away all his papers and possessions and put them into storage, then gathered together the photos and computers and images I could find to take back to my studio in Whitstable in order to paint Darius's portrait. Billy, the friendly guy who'd joined in my fight with the burglar, then helped me clear out the flat and get the stuff into storage.

"What do you want, Paula?"

"I want them dead. At the very least the one I know is guilty, that man Meredith Gilliard. Sean, don't you realise that *Gilliard has to die*. I can't forget that on that last night, the final thing I said to Darius was that I would always hate and despise him for being a gutless blackmailer. And then, when I went back, wanting to apologise, when it was too late, I saw him hanging from the ceiling. The only thing that's kept me going since then is having his baby, and now she's born, she's everything to me. They killed Darius. So I want him dead." There was a pause. "If you won't do it, I will. I'm going to kill him. Are you going to help me?"

"To murder Meredith Gilliard?"

"Yes."

"No, of course I'm not. I don't want to spend the rest of my life in jail, and nor do you. Who'll look after Eleanor if that happens?"

She wasn't listening.

"I talked to Agnes Dallorzo, Gordon's wife, she's on my side. She helped me to get a gun with a silencer. And she showed me how to use it."

Oh shit, she was serious!

"Paula, are you mad? Do you realise what you're saying?"

"Maybe I am. Maybe I'm mad because I can't get the picture out of my mind, of Mr Gilliard and those other fuckers standing around while Darius kicked and struggled and choked to death. You promised me that you'd get justice for Darius, that you'd destroy the people who killed him. I did my half of the bargain, Sean. I helped you. And you've let me down."

"No, listen to me . . . "

"No, Sean, *you listen to me!* I'm going to Meredith Gilliard's London house right now. The address is 41 Honeystack Gardens, Hampstead, and I'm going to kill him, then I'll come home, and no one will know I did it, because I know how to cover my tracks. If you want to help me, it's up to you. I should get there at about 8 o'clock. If you're there, you're there."

"Listen, Paula, stop, let me talk to you—"

The line went dead.

"I overheard most of that," Robin told me. "What are you going to do?"

"What can I do? I've got no choice but to get up to London and try to stop her."

"Supposing you're too late? What if you get there and she's already shot him? If you're on the scene then you'll be arrested. Remember, you had a public fight with Gilliard at that press conference in the West Country. It's on record that he claimed you'd threatened to kill him. If he's killed you'll be suspect number one."

Meredith Gilliard died later that day.

And I was arrested for his murder.

FORTY-EIGHT

I looked at my watch. Three days ago I'd promised Lucy that I'd be meeting her in Cornwall tonight, and I had time to get there on the train. I knew I ought to forget about Paula's call. After all, maybe she was bluffing.

But my conscience made going to Cornwall impossible. If I left now I could get from Whitstable to Hampstead in north London, to Gilliard's house, in about three hours. I could make it there before her, and hopefully try to head her off before she landed herself with a murder charge. With any luck, Gilliard wouldn't be at his home, and maybe I could just meet her, get rid of the gun, and force her to change her mind.

Robin's mobile rang again. It was Celia. I explained to her what had happened. I don't know why I did it, but I needed to share my worries with someone other than Robin, and in spite of being in a relationship with Lucy, I felt a weird close kinship with Celia. I wanted to tell Lucy everything, but I couldn't, because I knew she'd have tried to stop me doing what I had to do.

"I'm in a hell of a mess actually," I told Celia. "Paula Swan – Darius's partner – she's just phoned me, threatening to shoot Meredith Gilliard."

"But she's not serious, surely?"

"Who knows. I always thought she was a bit flaky, but she just might be mad enough to carry it out. She's got his address in London."

"Fuck."

"I'm on my way there now, to try and head her off."

"Anything I can do to help?"

"No, it's okay. This is something I've got to do on my own."

"Don't go, Sean. You threatened Gilliard when you were with me at the undertakers, and you had a fight with him at the press conference, and the police were called. They'll have it on record that you threatened to kill him."

"Which is why I have to try and save his life."

"Just make sure you have a good alibi, and stay clear."

"I can't do that. I've let Paula down once already, by not being able to prove those bastards at Rackhams killed Darius. So she's taking matters into her own hands. But I can't let her kill him, get arrested and imprisoned so that her baby grows up in care. I can't let her down for a second time."

"Okay. Okay. Let's think. London, right? That's where she's going to confront him."

"Yes."

"Listen, Sean. I know I can't stop you doing this, but if things go wrong, I'll give you an alibi. If this all goes to shit tell anyone who asks that you've been with me, at Triplinghoes for the last three days – meaning you never left here, and you've been here over a week, since Sunday. After all, your phone's here, isn't it? They can check on the signal. Have you talked to anyone in Kent since you got home?"

"Only Robin."

"And can you trust him?"

"With my life."

The Bad Hail Mary

"Okay, then remember, the same goes for me. I told you before, if I can help you I will. So after dealing with Paula in London this afternoon, whatever happens, come straight back to Triplinghoes, and don't use your car, and keep away from cameras. And if the police want to know where you've been, tell them you've been here ever since last Sunday. You've travelled on the train, so your car won't have been clocked by any CCTV. If the worst happens, I can testify that you couldn't have made it to London to kill him, you were too ill, with flu. After all, the police saw you here on Tuesday, when the body was found in the secret room. Your phone's been here and it's still here, tell me your password to get into your phone and I can even do some texts now to prove you're here right at this moment and for the next few hours."

"But why would I be staying with you for so long?"

"I'll tell them you got flu and couldn't leave. Or that we're having an affair."

"What?" I said in amazement.

"Why not? That's probably the safest thing to say actually. Nothing else sounds convincing. Say that, Sean, that's the most believable thing. Say we're having an affair. I'll back you up."

"Let's hope it won't come to that."

"I mean it, Sean. I promise I won't let you down."

No way could I explain what I was planning to Lucy. She was a serving police officer, so how could I put her in the position of knowing I knew about a threat to someone's life, and that I wasn't reporting it to the police, because I wanted to protect Paula?

The law was the law and as far as Lucy was concerned, and I could hardly expect her to risk her career to help me for a second time.

I also knew with astonishing clarity that I was walking into a shitstorm.

As I ran downstairs and packed a few things into my rucksack, I reflected that Paula had struck me as borderline insane. She was just about capable of anything. But I'd let her down before.

I couldn't let her down for a second time.

FORTY-NINE

Paula Swan.

Paula Swan, the sexy tattoo artist who lived life on the edge, but who had been the woman who had truly loved poor mixed-up Darius Trefus, who, by all accounts had given up her life as a successful businesswoman with a tattoo parlour in Brighton, to throw in her lot with gender-confused Darius. And the young confused heir to the Rackhams millions wasn't a monster either, just a deluded fool who thought he was clever enough to manipulate dangerous men, not realising that his life was expendable. It was true, as Paula had said, that she'd been treated like a nuisance and waste of time by all the snobs in the Trefus family, when the very least they could have done was try to be nice to her and her baby.

I put a few bits and pieces into my rucksack and jogged to the station, and was just in time to catch the train to London Victoria. Once there, I caught an Underground train on the Northern line to Hampstead, and completed my journey on foot, keeping with crowds as much as possible, in the hope of evading CCTV camera identification. I was wearing a baseball hat with a large brim, and a scarf covering my lower face, hoping that would also help to conceal my identity as much as possible.

On the journey I tried to make sense of what was happening and try to guess what Paula would do. It might be all bluff. I recalled that during our long phone calls she'd told me all about her mental problems, the psychiatrist she was seeing who had tried to help her with her eating disorders, the terrible depressions she suffered with, the self-harming issues. She was right, at the beginning of all this business I had hoped to find out who was responsible for Darius's death, even bring them to justice, and that had been my initial motivation for getting involved in examining the circumstances of her boyfriend's death, and it's true, I *had* promised her I would try to get to the bottom of how he'd died. It wasn't my fault that since then things had moved on, and all the problems had multiplied, and my focus had moved towards my own self-preservation to the exclusion of all else. In my stupidity I had thought I was maintaining some kind of rough justice, but was I?

Paula was convinced that she'd recognised Gilliard as being one of the men she'd seen coming out of her flat on the night Darius died. It was pretty clear that the American director of Rackhams was a lousy bastard and a murderer, who deserved to be punished. But life is about practicalities. In a way, Paula was right. After all my efforts, had justice really been done?

Looking at things rationally, the reality was that the Weiners' ancestors had been a lively prosperous family in 1930s Vienna, and their wealth had been stolen by Fleischmann. But at least Joseph and Arabella Weiner and their child Oscar had managed to escape with their lives, and go on to live well in England, allowing their descendants to prosper in their adopted country. The evil monster who'd inveigled his way into British society, posing as part of the artistic elite, had only lived for a few years after taking root

The Bad Hail Mary

in England, and his fascist friend, Sir Clive Gaines, plus all the other English aristocratic traitors such as Archibald Ramsay MP, who had schemed to help the Führer in his plans for world domination had never faced justice, their actions suppressed by the King and Winston Churchill, going on to lead lives of political success and respect. It was the old story: the rich look after their own, and the common people are used to fight wars and maintain a nation's wealth, to keep the privileged classes in luxury. The directors of Rackhams were likely to lose all their money, but it was all a long way into the future, and they would fight tooth and nail in the courts to rebuff the efforts of the World Jewish Congress to order reparations and the legal process might take years, during which time they'd probably find ways of sorting their money into other places. And who on earth knew if the legal case would be ultimately successful?

41 Honeystack Gardens was a large detached house in a tree-lined road leading off Haverstock Hill. I got there at about twenty past eight, having jogged the last few hundred metres from the Tube station. There were a million imponderables. The most likely thing was that Gilliard wouldn't be at home, and I'd just be able to encounter Paula, try to talk some sense into her, and take her home.

The house looked quiet and still, and indeed to my relief it seemed as if no one was at home. Cars were parked all along the road, and there was no front drive. I'd last seen Paula's ancient camper van at Wimbledon Park, but there was no sign of it around here. However there was an old blue minivan parked nearby, looking out of place amid the ranks of the shiny parked Mercedes, BMWs and Range Rovers.

I crossed the road and walked up the drive of number 41.

Everything seemed silent. I could hear my heartbeat in my ears.

Where the hell was she? I entered the porch, saw the partially open door.

Strained to listen for voices from inside.

Nothing.

And, as I got closer, I caught a whiff of something in the air, an unmistakeable scent that I remembered all too well from my days in the police firearms unit, MH19.

The hot hard stench of burnt cordite.

Somewhere in this house, a gun had been fired recently. I pulled on the surgical gloves I'd brought with me, and put on the special shoe coverings I'd packed, the ones I'd had since my police days. 'Every contact leaves a trace' was the doctrine that had been dinned into me by mates who were Scene of Crime Officers, and I knew that the tiniest thread of fabric could link a murderer to a death scene, and could ultimately convict me of murder, or else joint enterprise in a murder, which carried the same sentence.

Heart hammering fast, I was aware that something beyond the door was beckoning me on. Every instinct told me that I ought to run.

But like a fool, I knew I had to go ahead and see things through to the end.

Carefully, I shouldered the door open.

An empty hallway. Blue carpeted stairs to the right led to the upper floors. There were cosy framed prints of countryside scenes, at the foot of the stairs the likeness of a Victorian gentleman, all resplendent whiskers and haughty stares. And still the smell of gunfire pervaded the silence, sinister and deadly. Whatever was skulking there was as nasty as a wet snake slithering along the nave of a church.

The Bad Hail Mary

Instinct made me climb those stairs, the stairs that held the key to whether I was likely to be shot dead, or locked up for years for a crime I didn't do. Because some strange feeling was telling me that the cold hard stillness of this bright friendly house spelt death. Death in a big bad way. A violent death that was going to suck me into its mesmerising grip.

On the upstairs landing, one of the doors – apparently to a bedroom – was wide open.

Inside.

Silence.

A vignette from a nightmare.

Paula was sitting on the bed, holding a handgun two-handed, resting its snout on the duvet. It was a chunky weapon, that looked like a large calibre revolver, possibly a Smith & Wesson .45, with an absurdly long silencer.

And it was clear that she wasn't there.

Paula's eyes were lost, cold, vacant, as they stared at the floor. Her mouth was open, drool gathering at the edge of her lips, and I judged her to be in a state perhaps of catatonic trance. To all intents and purposes she was stoned out of her skull. On another planet.

Gilliard was spread out on the floor, more or less dead centre of a white rug, his mouth agape, a gobbet of blood having vomited from his mouth, his chest a mass of redness.

"Sean?"

Paula snapped out of it. She looked up. Blinked. Closed her mouth. Gave me a weak smile. Swallowed. She looked at the gun as if she'd seen it for the first time, then she dropped it on the floor.

"You didn't think I'd do it, did you?"

"Fuck!" I stared at the scene, my mind in overdrive. "Do you realise what you've done?"

"I've killed the man who ruined my life."

"No. You've fucked the rest of your life away. And your daughter's going to grow up in care."

"I had to do it. I told you, Sean, *I had no choice.* It was easier than I expected. I knocked on the door, he let me in. But when I started asking questions, he just smirked, threatening to call the police if I didn't leave at once. It was the smirk that did it. He had no idea I had the gun. I hid it in the Morrisons shopping bag. Agnes told me how to use it, it was really a breeze. I didn't think I'd be able to do it, you know? When I shot him it was kind of like I was someone else, watching myself do it. Have you ever had that sensation? As if you're not actually there, but you're up on high, watching yourself?"

"Shut up, Paula. *For Christ's sake shut up!*"

I was struggling to think.

She gave me a bright tight smile. "But you don't need to be here, Sean, just get lost now. I'll wait till it gets dark, then slip away. No one knows I've been here, they'll never catch me. But you go first, Sean. Just get gone, and leave me be."

I just stood there.

Working out what to do next.

FIFTY

"*Well go, why don't you?*" Paula yelled at me. "There's no point in us both risking being caught for this!" She began to cry. "You shouldn't have come here! Just get out of my sight! I'll be okay, they'll never get me."

That was what did it.

All my initial thoughts of doing exactly that, while I had the chance, melted like snow. And it wasn't just Paula. She had a child that would grow up without a mother, a child who'd be sent to a children's home, a child whose life would be wrecked before it had even started. She didn't have the first clue about how to get away with murder.

I clicked into professional mode, thinking hard, making mental lists.

"*What the fuck are you waiting for?*" she yelled, having stifled her sobs. "*Get out now, you idiot!*"

I strode across the room and took her phone away, switched it off, then slipped it into my pocket.

Think hard. Think as hard as fuck.

Paula had no doubt driven to this place, then walked here from the road. At least one CCTV camera was bound to have captured her car somewhere on the route. If the body stayed here she was a goner. His body had to be found somewhere else.

Where? What did I know about Meredith Gilliard? Gay. He was gay, wasn't he? I knew of a large pub where a lot of the clientele were gay. It was the kind of place where men made casual pick-ups, where all kinds of unexpected things might happen.

"Sean?" she asked weakly, all the fight gone out of her. "What the hell are you doing—"

"Shut up!" I snapped.

"Sean?" She started to repeat my name again and again, louder and louder.

I slapped her face to silence her. Leaned down and stared into her eyes. I shook her by the shoulders, determined to get her to pull herself together. "Listen, and do what I tell you now. You do *exactly* what I tell you. Don't ask questions. Don't waste time."

She nodded.

"Help me roll him up in this rug."

Together, we managed to lift one edge of the rug and roll the body up inside it. Fortunately, it was a good dense rug, and the blood hadn't penetrated through to the other side. Outside, to my relief, it was already dark, and we managed to carry the rug and its grisly contents out of the front door, and cram it into the back of the car that Paula had driven up in. By some miracle no one was passing.

"Get into the passenger seat," I told her. "Wait for me."

She nodded.

Back upstairs, I picked up the gun and put it back in the Morrisons shopping bag, and found Paula's shoulder bag. A quick scan of the room showed nothing there that Paula had brought in. I took out a cloth from my pocket, and wiped hard everything she might have touched already: light switch, door handles, items of furniture.

The Bad Hail Mary

Outside in the cold evening air, as I got into the car, a man passed on the other side, walking his dog. Neither the dog nor the man looked across at us, and I breathed a sigh of relief.

"I'm an ex-policeman, Paula. I know how a murder enquiry works, what they look for," I told her. "Just trust me."

She nodded, all the fight had gone out of her.

I got out again and took the can of spray from my rucksack. Someone had given it to me years ago. It was supposed to obscure car number plates when flashed by a speed camera. I had no idea if it worked for CCTV cameras or not, since I'd never used it, but knew that it caused a reflective glare when speed cameras flashed it, so your number was blurred. I sprayed the numberplates on Paula's car, front and rear, then climbed inside and got going, grateful that twilight was well on the way, the light fading fast.

I soon got used to the old mini's handling, and made my way southwards, towards the parts of London I was familiar with. I ended up in Atlantic Road, Brixton, then a few streets further on, in the direction of Camberwell, I found the area I recalled from my days in the Met. The Gun and Donkey was a large public house that was popular with local prostitutes, but it was its reputation as a venue for gay men wanting to make discreet hook-ups that had attracted me. As we turned into the car park, it was clear that the place was undergoing building work, and I managed to park right beside one of the overflowing builders' skips on the far side. While Paula kept watch to make sure no one could see what I was doing, in five minutes flat I managed to drag the rug out of the car, tip out its human contents, and quickly drag Gilliard's body behind one of the overflowing skips, so that it couldn't be seen. I took some bricks and some rope from the skip and threw them into the back seats and drove away.

Eventually we reached Putney, and I parked in the main road that leads to Putney Bridge, outside the Five Guys fast food outlet. I crammed the two bricks into the Morrisons carrier bag, with the gun, then added Paula's phone and sealed it up with some gaffer tape I found in her glove box.

Maybe the most dangerous part of the whole operation came next: trying to look casual as I walked to the centre of the pavement of Putney Bridge, and looked anxiously around. No one was near. I flipped the bag over the ledge, and watched the splash as it was eaten up by the waters of the Thames.

The rug! What the fuck could I do with the rug, I wondered?

The answer came quite easily, as I drove south towards Croydon. A skip was in the road, so after parking behind it, I quickly managed to get the rolled-up rug stuffed beneath the broken door that was holding the skip's contents in place, so that the rug was completely out of sight.

Benjy Allardice runs a car breakers' business in South Norwood. I parked outside his yard, just off Croxted Road South, a big sprawling emporium filled with dead and rusting cars, some of them piled four-deep.

I found him where he usually was, in the local pub. Luckily I happened to have a couple of hundred quid in cash to pay him, and he was happy to accompany me back to the car.

Paula removed her bag and some other items from the back seat and glove box, and handed over the keys.

"What will happen to it?" she asked me, watching sadly.

The Bad Hail Mary

"I've paid him to crush it," I told her. "In half an hour it'll simply be a cube of metal."

"But I only bought it a few days ago because my camper van's broken down. I haven't even registered it in my name yet—"

"Good, then it can't be traced back to you. Don't you realise? You drove right up to Gilliard's house, and the car's bound to have been caught on CCTV during the journey. It'll never be found, and hopefully no one will look for footage of it on CCTV around there. With any luck, when they find the body so far from his home, they won't realise where he actually died – even if they conclude he died somewhere else, no one will know where. Now, we go by bus to the nearest station, which is Norwood Junction, and take separate trains. When you get home, take off every item of clothing, including your shoes and underwear, and get rid of it – ideally in rubbish bins in bags a long way from home. Does anyone know you came to London?"

"Only my friend who's looking after Eleanor. I told her I was going to a gig in London."

"Good. With any luck they'll think he was killed in the car park of the pub."

"If it all goes wrong, and they arrest me, don't worry, Sean. I won't tell a soul that you helped me."

"Let's hope it won't come to that."

Perverting the course of justice is a serious charge, and when murder's involved it normally carries a custodial sentence. What's more, I'd been in the house shortly after Gilliard had been shot, so I could conceivably be charged with murder, or joint enterprise murder if they thought I'd been there at the time that Paula shot him. I had no way of proving that wasn't the case.

I could only hope I'd been able to think of everything and covered every angle.

Because now I was involved up to my neck.

If Paula went down, I'd go down with her.

FIFTY-ONE

It was next morning when I arrived at Celia's house on the cliffs above Sennen Cove, feeling as if I was a hundred years old, having taken a bus from the station, and walked the last couple of miles. Since the police were still clearing up the discovery of the body at Triplinghoes, she had moved back to her home.

Celia answered the door.

"Come inside."

"What happened?" she asked. "Did you get there in time to stop her?"

I was so weary I couldn't answer, just took her arm and led her into the house.

I sat at the kitchen table while she made coffee for both of us. When she was sitting opposite me, I looked beyond her, out of the window, at the three graves in the front garden, remembering that she'd told me that her house had once been a Methodist Chapel.

For some reason I trusted Celia, and in a world where everyone was betraying me, I knew that she was my friend. So I told her all that had happened yesterday. I told her everything, leaving nothing out. She listened, saying nothing, then at the end, she nodded seriously.

"You did the right thing," she told me. "It's not just

Paula to consider. There's her child, Eleanor. She'd have gone to prison, and the child would grow up in care. Besides, Meredith Gilliard deserved it."

"Of course he did," I agreed with her. "But getting myself involved is a bloody disaster. When they find the body they'll be knocking on my door first. As you reminded me, I had a run-in with him at the undertaker's first, and then at the party."

"Uh-huh. Well, Sean, are you a good liar?"

"No, I'm bloody useless, but I've got no choice. Even if I was to tell them the absolute truth, that I covered it up, and drop Paula in it, I'm still fucked. And perverting the course of justice in a murder investigation means jail time."

"But it won't come to that. It sounds like you've handled things properly. I wouldn't worry about the Met Police causing you problems, you've thought of everything. Christ, when you think about the police, and how they normally carry on. In 1983, the detective Daniel Morgan was murdered by an axeman in a pub car park, and he was working on police corruption, and the Commissioner admitted thirty years later that the investigation into his murder had been inept and corrupt. The Yorkshire Ripper was only caught because he was arrested for a totally unrelated traffic offence, and by chance they caught him trying to dispose of the hammer he used to kill all those women. And years later, a senior officer came on TV stating that the official conclusion of their investigation into the death of the spy who was found zipped and padlocked inside a large suitcase was that he had committed suicide. On the whole, the police are so utterly fucking useless, my guess is that you and Paula are home and dry."

*

The Bad Hail Mary

But she was wrong.

There was a loud knocking on the door. When I answered, there were two policemen in uniform, plus another man in a dark suit.

"Mr Delaney?" the man in the suit asked.

"Yes."

All three men had a wary look in their eyes, and I knew without them saying anything they were onto me, and knew about my connection with Meredith Gilliard's death.

"Mr Delaney, may I ask where you were yesterday afternoon?"

Before I could answer, Celia was behind me.

"Sean was with me, officer, here," she interrupted.

That's when I realised why they'd thought I'd be here – when the police came to the undertakers to investigate Gilliard's complaint they'd asked where I was staying and I had given Celia's address to the undertaker and he had passed it on.

"And I take it that you are Celia Trefus, madam?" he asked.

"Yes, I'm Celia Trefus." She walked in front of me. "I'm Councillor Trefus in fact. I sit on the Police Committee as it happens. And I'm Sean's girlfriend. He's been staying with me in Cornwall for the past week."

Fuck, she'd said she was my girlfriend. I could hardly contradict her, could I?

"Is that true, sir?" he turned to me.

"Yes. What is this all about, officer?"

"We'd like you to accompany us to the station, please, sir."

"Why?"

"We need to ask you some questions."

"About what?"

FIFTY-TWO

Detective Inspector Harold Chambers was a florid overweight character with a receding blond hairline, a raggedy beard, and sweat stains under the armpits of his crumpled white shirt. His sidekick, Detective Sergeant Lee-Anne Craddock, was a thirtyish blonde with sad serious eyes, and I didn't like the way those resentful eyes never left my face. She had an intriguing habit of sucking her pen and frowning, and occasionally taking off her heavy black spectacles and tapping them on her nose.

There was no doubt that clinging to Celia's fake alibi, and sticking to the story that she and I were an item, was the only chance I had of saving my bacon. And as luck would have it, everything fitted, neat and tidy. My phone had been in her house and earlier at Triplinghoes for the past five days, switched on all that time, so they could check with the nearby phone masts that it had been in range during the time I was accused of killing Meredith Gilliard in London – in fact Celia had texted a few people on my contacts list. I had no car, and had travelled everywhere by public transport, never taken a cab once. Station platforms are usually too crowded to pick out individual faces on the CCTV. And as far as I could remember, apart from Robin,

The Bad Hail Mary

I hadn't seen or talked to anyone in Whitstable during the time I was supposed to be in Cornwall because I was in bed alone, ill with flu. So far, my alibi appeared to be as solid as Cornish granite.

But even granite can split wide open. It only takes one lucky strike.

"Mr Delaney, it would be fair to say that you and Mr Gilliard had a bit of history, yeah?" Chambers asked me.

"History?"

"He called the police recently and reported you for threatening him in the undertakers premises, Griswold & Son in Penzance. And then, only three weeks ago, the two of you had a fist-fight at a stately home near Bath. You punched him in the face. He hated you, didn't he?"

"So?"

"Come off it, Sean. You were a copper, you know how it works. Meredith Gilliard was a respectable businessman who, as far as we know, didn't have any other enemies. You encountered him at Griswolds' funeral home, where he accused you of poking your nose into his business. At the party at the hotel in Bath, where the Rackhams press conference occurred, the two of you had a fight, because he blamed you for wrecking his company's future and their merger deal by exposing their dirty secret. He hated you then, and he wanted to kill you. Now he's dead. We don't have to be Sherlock to work it out, do we?"

"No comment."

"Somehow, he tricked you into coming to his flat, where he obviously planned to kill you. But you were able to turn the tables and got him instead. That's what happened isn't it?"

"No."

"Look, tell us the truth, *all the truth*. If he was indeed

intent on killing you, then maybe you killed him in self-defence? You should have told us right away, but even if you have got rid of the evidence, a good lawyer can probably keep you out of jail. That's what happened, isn't it? He tricked you into going to his flat, tried to kill you, but you got the better of him?"

"No. That didn't happen."

"All right, Mr Delaney, you say you were in Cornwall yesterday afternoon."

"I was."

"So when did you arrive there?"

I tried to work it out. "A week last Saturday, I think."

"And why did you come to Cornwall?"

"I've been going there on and off for a while now. I got to know Celia Trefus, who's now living at Triplinghoes. She's a friend."

"A very good friend?"

"I suppose so."

"So, this lady, Celia Trefus," he snapped. "This *friend*. She is the stepdaughter of Lady Molly Trefus, the woman who died when she tried to shoot you dead. Tell me about Lady Molly."

"What do you mean?"

"She died, didn't she? She tried to shoot you with a deactivated gun that blew up and ripped half her face off."

"So what do you want to know?"

"Why did she hate you so much?"

"Because she found out that evening that I'd wrecked her financially, because of the legal case against Rackhams that you know about."

DS Lee-Anne looked up and joined in. "You mean the discovery that Rackhams International had been bought out in 1946 by a Nazi killer and war criminal?"

I nodded. "She admitted killing her husband to get her hands on his money, and thought she was home and dry. My friend Lucy, one of your officers, handed her phone, with the recording of Molly's confession, to the SIO on the case. You can check up on all of that."

"Umm."

I could tell she didn't believe a word of what I was saying.

"And how long have you been having an affair with Celia Trefus?"

I felt myself blushing. "Not long. A few days."

"You were staying at her house?"

"Yes. I'm an artist. She was employing me to paint various views of her house, Triplinghoes. And, as you know, I helped her knock down a wall in one of the rooms, and we found a body."

"Tell me, when did your close friendship with Celia start, Mr Delaney?" Lee-Anne persevered. "While you were going out with PC Akehurst, or before?"

"That's my business."

"Come on, Sean!" she snapped. "Lucy Akehurst is one of our own, she works from a station near here, and I can tell you now that she's a very popular officer, and she's told her friends that you and her are close. Do you like making her look like a bloody idiot?"

I hung my head in shame. There was nothing I could say.

"Yet now you tell us you've been staying with the lady councillor in her big house out near Sennen Cove. Come on, Sean, tell us the truth! Celia Trefus is a very attractive woman and she clearly likes you. Have you been an item ever since you met her, when you first came to Cornwall to get the commission to paint the portrait of Darius Trefus? Or did the affair only start a few days ago, as you say?"

"I told you, I've been painting exterior views of the house." I paused. "In a short time, we – er – I guess we became close. Things just happened."

"*Just happened?*"

I nodded.

"Like they *just happened* with PC Akehurst?"

"Look, this is all very difficult. Celia and I were discussing work. My friend makes scale models of houses. She wants him to make a model of Triplinghoes, and she wanted to discuss it."

"So how come she discussed it with you, and not this model maker?"

"He was busy." I struggled to think of something convincing. "I said I'd take a few measurements, some photos for him to get an idea of the job."

"Got lots of money, have you, Sean?" DI Chambers took over the questioning.

"What do you mean?"

"Ordinary folks, like DS Craddock and me, we're working, we can't just suddenly swan across the country to chat and socialise for days on end. Yet it seems that you can afford to do so."

"I was working, I told you. I painted exterior views of the house. You can see them – they're at the house, ask Celia."

Lee-Anne leaned forward, once again removing her spectacles and tapping them on the pad of notes in front of her on the desk.

"We're not blind, Sean," she said. "You're a very good-looking man, and Celia has obviously got a thing for you. Maybe it's one-sided, yeah? Unrequited love that she's hoping will be requited soon? *Is she giving you an alibi because she's in love with you?*"

"No."

"You don't sound very convincing about that, Sean. *Why is she lying for you?*"

"She isn't."

"Come off it, Sean. Fair dos, mate, frankly, I think you played a right blinder. You killed Meredith Gilliard and you got rid of the body, covering your tracks, using everything you learnt in the police."

"I did not—"

"Shut up and listen!" Chambers went on. "All right, Sean, here's what we know. Forensics are certain that he *wasn't* killed in the pub car park. No one saw him in the pub prior to that time, he wasn't seen on the CCTV inside the bar at any time, and according to our sources, it seems that although he was a gay man, he never went in for casual contacts, agencies on the internet, that kind of thing. He was a rich guy with a prestigious job. He chose his friends very carefully and didn't go in for casual pickups at gay bars. So we know he was shot somewhere else and taken to the car park, most likely by someone who was banking on his lifestyle being that of a man used to casual encounters with guys, but didn't know him well enough to know that he was very choosy. See? His killer got that wrong, because Gilliard hand-picked the guys he fucked, he was very fussy where he dipped his wick. We've examined his flat in Hampstead. There are traces of gunshot residue on the bedclothes, and according to his cleaning lady, a rug is missing. I think you shot him there and took him to the Gun and Donkey pub. CCTV in the road outside the car park shows an unidentified Mini Cooper entering and leaving at around 9pm that evening, and it wasn't driven by any of the customers. The number plate is unrecognisable, probably having been treated with a reflective chemical. Whoever deposited his body there knew about police procedures, and covered all the angles."

"Anyone who watches enough TV knows about forensics."

"We'll get you, Sean," Chambers went on. "If we don't get you today, or tomorrow or next week, *we'll get you in the end*. Why did you do it, Sean? Did you know Mr Gilliard well? After the encounter with him at the undertakers, he claimed that you and he had had a sexual relationship. And when he broke it off, you weren't happy, you swore to get revenge."

"You've just accepted that I'm having an affair with Celia, yet now you're telling me you think I'm gay."

"Lots of people swing both ways. More than you might imagine. So how about it, Sean? Are you a swinger?"

There was a long silence.

But in the moment he thought he'd browbeat me into talking, I realised his weakness.

They had no evidence to use against me.

If they'd got incriminating CCTV footage of me walking along from near Gilliard's flat in Hampstead, they'd have shown it to me by now. I hadn't shot him, so they wouldn't find gunshot residue on my clothes. Thanks to the gloves and overshoes I'd worn, they wouldn't find any trace of my presence at Gilliard's home. So even if they applied to the CPS asking if they could charge me, I knew that the answer would be no.

There probably were traces of Paula's presence there, but as long as they had no inkling of her involvement, they had nothing to compare it with.

The Bad Hail Mary

The only chance they'd got was if I admitted anything, and I wasn't stupid enough to do so.

Much later, as I walked out of the police station, Lucy was waiting by the main entrance. She was out of uniform.

"Sean?" she said, staring at me. "We have to talk."

My heart sank.

FIFTY-THREE

How the hell was I going to explain things? Could I trust her and tell her the absolute truth, that Celia was giving me an alibi?

"Sean," she began. "Let's go to the pub."

When we were seated at the Dog and Duck, I had to think long and hard. Confessing to Lucy that I had perverted the course of justice in a murder enquiry meant that she would be obliged to tell the police, for she was a serving officer. If she did so, not only would I end up in jail, but so would Paula.

"So how long has it been going on?" she asked.

"What?"

She glared at me, cold burning hatred in her eyes. "Your affair with Celia Trefus."

"Look, Lucy—"

"Don't bother to deny it! You spoke to me on Monday evening, telling me you were going straight back to your studio in Whitstable, that you were going to come to Cornwall later in the week to see me on the Saturday evening. Then I didn't hear a word from you."

"I had flu. I was ill."

"So ill that you stayed with Celia at Triplinghoes and never came home?"

The Bad Hail Mary

"After I left you, I just felt ill, so I stayed in the Travelodge, I was too ill to drive."

"So when you were feeling at death's door, you went to visit Celia?"

"Yes."

"Why didn't you call me? I would have looked after you."

"God, I don't know."

"No, Sean, you don't know, do you? You've been lying to me all along."

"Lucy, this is difficult. I don't know what to say. Celia asked me to paint exterior views of the manor house, so that if it had to be sold she'd have something to remember it by. While I was there, she asked me to knock down that wall, we found the body. . ."

"But when she asked you to paint Triplinghoes, you immediately rushed down here to see her, didn't you? You knew that thanks to my testimony, what I heard on the phone conversation, Molly's inheritance would be null and void under the Forfeiture Rule, so Triplinghoes and the money would go to Celia, the default beneficiary. Even though that inheritance is in doubt because of the Fleischmann business, there'll be years of legal wrangling, and who knows if the Weiners will ever get all their money or not? Besides, Celia is already a successful wealthy architect with a thriving practice. And for the time being, Celia is going to be a very rich woman, a very rich, interesting and sexy woman."

"Lucy, please—"

"And you couldn't wait, could you? You came hotfoot down to Cornwall, fussing up to her, offering your sympathy, telling her all about how brave you've been righting the wrongs of the past, becoming a latter-day

Robin Hood, redistributing the worldly goods of the descendants of Fleischmann to worthy causes. And I just bet she fell for it, didn't she?"

"No, Lucy, you've got it all wrong."

"So tell me where I'm wrong, Sean. You lied to me about being in Whitstable, when you were actually in Cornwall, five minutes away from where I live, when I could have been with you at any time from Tuesday onwards, when I came back from the course. You were playing for time, pretending you weren't even in Cornwall, that you were hundreds of miles away, because you wanted to keep sexy Celia sweet."

"Please, Lucy—"

"Sean, answer me this. You were with Celia at Triplinghoes on Wednesday, all day, yeah?"

I nodded.

"So why did you lie to me, telling me you had to go back to Kent, and couldn't see me for a week or so?"

"I don't know."

"You don't know." She glared at me, hatred blazing in her eyes. "*You know very well, you bastard!* Not long ago you asked me to be with you, to marry you, to share my life with you."

"Yes I did. And I still want to."

She laughed, and her laughter was even more cruel than her words. "You wanted to marry me until you saw a much better prospect. An interesting, intelligent architect, a woman who lived in a stately home, who can keep you in luxury while you play around trying to be an artist instead of getting a proper job."

"Christ."

"Truth hurts, doesn't it, Sean? You, a portrait painter? You well and truly fucked up the portrait of Darius Trefus, didn't you?" Again, she gave that vicious, savage laugh. "You know very well that if you were going to make it as a professional portrait painter you'd have made it by now, without having to be a part-time painter and decorator, surviving from job to job, with barely enough money to keep a roof over your head. I don't blame you. You had a choice to share your life with a hard-working police officer, who lives on an average salary, who'd want you to pull yourself together and earn a decent income and give up this hopeless dream of earning enough to live on as an artist. And sharing your life with a woman who'd never let you have to worry about paying bills, who'd let you fanny about playing the dedicated artist forever. No contest really, is there?"

I choked back tears. "You're wrong, you don't know how wrong you are."

She was crying too. "The truth hurts doesn't it, Sean. It *fucking well hurts!* You might as well know that I loved you more than anyone I've ever met in my life before. Sure I fancied you the moment I saw you, but for me, it wasn't just a physical thing, it was the whole package, you know? The real joke is, I wanted to be with you forever. I thought you were my soulmate, Sean, more fool me. Before this I would have done anything on earth for you!"

"Please, Lucy, please listen—"

"*Fuck off, Sean!* I hate you now. I hate you now and I always will. Nothing you can say is ever going to change that."

*

I'd arranged to meet the Weiners at the hotel in town. They wanted to introduce me to other family members, and representatives of the World Jewish Congress, who'd travelled over from New York.

Old Oscar remembered me, and when I came up to him his face lit up.

"You have made me so happy," he told me, grasping my hand in both of his. "If only my mother and father could have known you and said thank you. The Weiner collection will once more be together again. Something I thought had gone forever is back home to stay."

I felt like crying. The £10,000 that the Weiners had given me was very welcome, but it could hardly make up for the anguish of the past weeks. I'd met the girl I would have liked to spend the rest of my life with, but now I knew that she would always hate me, and I could never explain the truth to her.

"*The Bad Hail Mary*," Old Oscar said to me. "She is home at last. And all the other paintings that were hidden at Triplinghoes, they are part of my parents' collection. We can prove it."

"I'm glad."

"But you are unhappy, Sean, yes?"

"I'm unhappy."

"In everyone's life many things go wrong, it is no one's fault. All we can do is what we think is right, and hope for the best. God knows the truth."

"Does He?"

"Oh yes. Sean, I am guessing that you've been struggling with this business, and now it's all over, you feel as if it's all been a waste of time."

I nodded. "What have I actually achieved? You and your family are already rich, you don't need more money. I've exposed a scandal that happened eighty years ago, so no one alive really cares anymore. Rackhams' reputation is trashed, meaning they'll lose business all the time that the legal case rumbles on, so lots of staff will lose their jobs. I

The Bad Hail Mary

feel as if there was a great big pool of water. I've thrown a brick into it, and lots of ripples are going to spread out across the surface, but eventually the pool will be still again, and nothing will have changed."

"Sean, remember this. You tried to do the right thing. And that is all that matters. *You tried to do the right thing.* Let me tell you one thing that my sons will not tell you. They may be rich, but they've diverted a great deal of their money to helping refugees who come to this country with nothing, just as their grandfather did. We try to do good with our money, we use it. If we get more money, we'll be able to use even more to help refugees. We don't talk about this work we do, we do it quietly, but we do it nevertheless. So, if nothing else, any extra money we get will be put to good use."

"Thank you."

So maybe there was some purpose in my efforts after all.

I looked at the sunset, the red clouds spread all over the sky, and I wondered. . .

*

Lucy had dumped me. And paradoxically, now that I'd lost her, I wondered if things could have worked out between us, and I wanted to find out more than ever.

Celia had come to see me, and of course I'd thanked her. If life was fair we'd have felt a mutual attraction and, indeed, embarked on a passionate affair. But some things are never to be. I liked her. She liked me. But that was as far as it went, at least as far as I was concerned.

Next morning I found out that I had another, much more pressing problem.

Rupert Vigo was going to bankrupt me.

FIFTY-FOUR

I couldn't have seen it coming if it had been travelling at a thousand miles an hour.

One morning I got a letter from Rupert Vigo's solicitors. After all the things that had happened I had almost forgotten about the loathsome little man who lived in filthy gatehouse at the arse end of Kent. With a heading of *Newton, Dunlop & Spears*, it read:

This is a formal notice to let you know that our client, Mr Rupert Vigo, has informed us that prior to being given permission to look at private family papers pertaining to the personal and professional life of his grandfather, Sir Clive Gaines, you signed an agreement that you would not show any of these private papers to anyone without permission, nor would you take any documents without permission, nor would you publish any of them in the media.

It is apparent that you have broken this agreement by showing the contents of private diaries to national newspapers, and also that you have stolen these items, and this theft has been reported to the police. Consequently, we have been instructed to sue you for damages caused by divulging the contents of these private papers, in contravention of the agreement you signed, and will inform you of court proceedings in due course. Our client is seeking to sue you for the maximum amount, which is likely to be in the region of £8 million. . .

Accompanying the letter were various papers that I didn't understand.

My own solicitor had already partly reassured me, asserting that Vigo's grandfather was a criminal and a traitor was perfectly acceptable in law, because you cannot libel anyone who is dead, nor can their descendants sue you. However, the intellectual content of Sir Clive's personal papers, owned by Vigo, remained the property of Vigo, and these documents were private. I had signed the agreement in my haste to see the papers, but I should have read the contract, which stipulated that the documents could only be shared with the express permission of Vigo, and this had not been given. Since I had broken the contract, Vigo was within his rights to sue me not only for breaking the contract I had signed, but also for causing him stress and suffering and personal attacks, as a result of the accusations against his grandfather. Vigo apparently did have a case in law, and while his claim for damages of eight million was unrealistic, a court might well decide to award him part of that sum, in addition to considerable court costs.

Whatever happened, there was the distinct possibility, indeed likelihood, that Mr Vigo could bankrupt me.

To be fair to Rupert Vigo, there had been some horrible repercussions for him. His grandfather's grave had been vandalised, the headstone spray painted NAZI and I WAS UP HITLER'S ARSE, and someone had even made a half-hearted attempt to dig it up. That was nothing compared to what had happened to the grave of 'Walter Trefus', aka Fleischmann, in Newlyn churchyard. After the news came out, the headstone was immediately removed, but not before it was scrawled over with horrific graffiti, and someone had actually dug up the coffin, ripped it open and scattered the bones across the graveyard, even taking the trouble to pulverise the skull into pieces.

I had phoned Johnny Barleycorn about Rupert Vigo's litigation, and he listened and sympathised.

"Oh bugger, Sean. Tell you what, email over to me the document you signed. I've got a pal who's a barrister, and he'll give you some advice on the house. Too bad you signed that thing, but knowing that little bastard, he probably pressured you into it. Don't worry. When it comes to it these types normally settle out of court for a much lesser sum."

"But I haven't got even a much lesser sum."

"Well, old boy, you know the golden rule in situations like this?"

"No. What is it?"

"Say nothing to them, write nothing to them, no contact, no phone calls, no visits, no emails. Get legal advice before you do or say anything at all. Preferably get your lawyer to talk to his lawyer. Anything you might say if you contact him could be used against you."

But it was all very well for Johnny to talk. He wasn't fighting for his life and struggling to get out of a mess.

I phoned Paula Swan, asking if she would come with me and talk to Vigo and explain things from her point of view: that she had been living in hiding for fear of her life, and the only way she'd been able to come in out of the cold was by me making the scandal public. And, of course the same applied to me. I thought that by appealing to his humanity, he might just see good sense and do the decent thing and stop the litigation.

We arrived at his Lamberhurst home unannounced at about seven in the evening on a dark rainy night, gambling that if he'd been forewarned, he would refuse to see us.

The Bad Hail Mary

The gloomy front door of the old gatehouse reminded me of the awful times I had spent at this place, and how I had hoped never to have to come to this hateful hovel again.

"You!" he shouted when he opened the door. "My solicitor has told me that I shouldn't talk to you."

"Please," I asked him. "Look, this is Paula, she can tell you her story. I think if you hear why I did what I did you might relent. Apart from anything else, I haven't got a bean, so suing me for eight million quid isn't going to benefit you one bit. You can't get blood out of a stone."

"Umm," he muttered, keeping the door open only a couple of inches. Then he caught sight of Paula behind me, and opened it fully, his beady eyes as round as saucers. "Come in then."

Paula was dressed in a short denim skirt with a loose-fitting sweater that served to accentuate her larger-than-average breasts. The tattoos on her forearms were visible, as were those on her legs. Perhaps she hadn't deliberately tried to look sexy, or maybe Rupert Vigo had a thing for tattooed women. Whatever, his face lit up when he saw her, and his eyes glinted with lust.

Paula and I followed him into the filthy living room that I remembered from last time. We sat together on the sofa, and Vigo sat opposite us on his large armchair. The place looked just as it had done before: grim, dark, dreary and dirty. There was the same cheesy rancid smell of bad food, and the dim unshaded bulb hung over our heads like a beacon of doom.

"So what have you come for?" Vigo asked me. He couldn't stop himself ogling Paula's legs, her skirt barely reaching mid-thigh, part of a tattoo in handwriting saying *SEE YOU SOON IN S* was tantalizingly terminated at *S* by the blue denim.

"To accept my apology for what I've done," I told him. "To return your documents. And to ask you to withdraw your legal action against me." I handed over the carrier bag with his grandfather's diaries in it.

"Got you worried, haven't I, old lad?" He gave a short of nervous laughter.

"Yes, of course you have. I thought if you realised how high the stakes were at the time, you might understand why I did what I did."

"And that was why you trashed my grandfather's reputation?" he jeered.

"The people at Rackhams were determined to keep the secret about Walter Trefus. We can't prove it, but I believe that they murdered Darius Trefus and also planned to kill his father too, in order to keep the secret, and they tried to murder me as well. That's why I came to see you the second time in a disguise, because I wanted them to believe their contracted killing had been a success. To save my own life I had no choice but to expose your grandfather's treachery."

"Hmm," he muttered, then turned towards Paula. "And where do you fit into this mess?"

"I was Darius's girlfriend, or rather his fiancée. We were going to get married. I'm the mother of his child, Eleanor. I witnessed those men coming away from our flat after they'd murdered Darius. They saw me. I knew I had to get away fast, or they'd have killed me too. Sean has told the world about Rackhams so at last I'm safe. If he hadn't done what he did I'd still be living like a fugitive, hand-to-mouth, unable to work or rent a flat or live openly, for fear of being murdered. These people were all-powerful. Sean came to my defence. He saved my life."

"I see." Vigo pursed his lips. "Well that puts matters into a different light."

The Bad Hail Mary

"Good," I answered.

And waited.

"Well, Sean and Paula, I think I've got a solution to our problem."

"Yes?" Paula asked.

"I'll call off the lawsuit if you give me one hundred thousand pounds."

I breathed a sigh of frustration. "I told you, Mr Vigo, I haven't got one hundred thousand pounds. I haven't got any savings at all!"

"Come now, Sean. An up-and-coming portrait painter like you? How is your credit? Do you own a house or a flat? If you do, and it's on a mortgage, you could extend the mortgage, couldn't you?"

"And struggle in fucking penury for years?"

"Well, surely that's better than being sued for an amount you haven't got, then losing the case and being awarded court costs on top? I'm told that barristers charge astronomical sums, and you would have to pay my costs as well as your own. As well as the settlement for eight million. Sure you haven't got eight million, but if you owed it, you would have to pay me anything you earnt above a minimum amount, perhaps for the rest of your life. For me, that would be a nice little earner."

"But you wouldn't get eight million because I haven't got it!"

"Then we would have to see what the court has to say. I imagine the court could seize everything you possess and you'd be an undischarged bankrupt for the rest of your life."

"How would that benefit you?"

"Oh, it would be fine for me, I assure you, Sean. I'd get a little bit extra every month. And as I told you, I don't like the Irish. Did you know, I've had death threats since you broke that story! My family's reputation is in tatters thanks to you."

"Please, Mr Vigo, won't you do it for me?" Paula asked. "Show some mercy, can't you?"

His eyes lit up as he looked at Paula, and his hand unconsciously strayed towards his crotch as drool gathered on the edge of his blubbery lips.

"So, Miss Swan, if I called off the legal proceedings, what would you do for me? Eh? Would you be very grateful to me?"

"Yes."

"How grateful? Enough to come here every now and then and offer me a bit of comfort? I'm a lonely man, Miss Swan, it's a long time since I made love to a woman."

She gulped, looking across at this sad, chubby, repulsive little man, whose eyes were alight with excitement.

"By the way," Vigo continued, "you might like to know that I took the liberty of switching on a video camera when you first came in here. I shall show the footage to my lawyer tomorrow, I've got a feeling what you've admitted will help my case in court."

It was night time. Just then there was a crack and a flash and the lights went out.

In the pitch darkness, Paula took out her phone and used the torch function.

"Wretched electrics," he muttered. "I'll have to do the fuse again."

"I'll hold my phone so you can see," Paula offered.

He went to the side of the room where the stairs were, and opened the cupboard underneath them as he knelt down. Paula and I followed him.

I should have noticed that Paula had picked up an

open bottle of beer that she'd found on the table, and held it in her other hand.

While Vigo was opening the wooden fuse box, I caught sight of Paula tipping the beer around the dirty carpet, where he was kneeling. He was so intent on what he was doing he didn't even notice a damp knee.

I watched as he pulled out the large black knob on the back of the white ceramic rectangle, until it came out of its housing about an inch. It came out with a loud clicking sound, and I realised that this was the mains power switch, cutting off the current into the house, thus enabling him to handle the fuses safely.

In another wooden box beside the switch, was one large white porcelain handle that looked like it was designed to be pulled. I realised that this was one of a pair of fuses. The space beside it was an ugly gap, where a piece of wire was crudely pushed into two holes about two inches apart, to bridge the gap. Clearly there had once been a proper fuse here, but in its place, someone had jammed a piece of bent wire into the metallic grips at top and bottom to bridge the gap. The thin wire had a black mark on the white porcelain at its centre, where it had been burnt in half. Mr Vigo had found another shaped piece of stiff wire, and bent its ends in the same way so that he could replace the burnt wire.

As he pushed the new home-made fuse into the sockets I heard the loud click. And saw Paula's tattooed hand pressing the end of the beer bottle against the black knob on the mains power switch.

There was a loud bang and a crack.

Rupert Vigo's hand was thrown up into the air. In the light from Paula's mobile phone, I saw her grab a wooden broom and ram it against Vigo's claw-like hand, forcing it back onto the live metal. There was a second spark and a bang, plus a pungent smell of burning flesh and burning metal. Vigo keeled over sideways.

FIFTY-FIVE

I knelt down, felt at his neck for the carotid artery, but there was nothing.

"The beer helped to connect him to earth," Paula explained calmly. "Alternating current pushes you away, that's why I had to push him back for a second time. A live current will go to earth the quickest way. If it passes through your chest, down your body, through to the earth, it can stop your heart. Water or another kind of fluid facilities current flow. That's why any electrical controls aren't allowed in bathrooms. I told you, I'm a professional electrician."

"He's dead. You killed him."

"Good."

I could still smell the scorched flesh of his hand, could still remember the two times there was a giant spark and flash as the current arced. The rictus leer of his lips as he greeted death with a snarl.

"We'll be okay, Sean," Paula told me calmly, her hand on my shoulder. "I never thanked you properly for what you did for me. So it was my turn to take charge of things. When I came in, I noticed that the electrics in this house are obviously a death-trap, with those sparking plug sockets. No one saw us arrive, we just have to make sure no one sees us leave. The old fucker was messing about with a live fuse box, half drunk, having spilt his beer on the floor. What did he expect to happen?"

With the help of both our phone's torches we successfully found the video camera on the table in the corner of the room and picked it up and took it away.

*

Molly's funeral was more sparsely attended than I had expected. Strange how the similarities between this nightmare and *The Great Gatsby* novel abounded. Gatsby had been a rich famous man who held huge lavish parties. But hardly anyone came to his funeral because hardly anyone actually knew him.

Just like Molly.

It seemed that she had hardly any family left, or only her mum had bothered to come, and it looked like none of the Rackhams directors had attended either.

I was clinging on to the forlorn hope that Lucy might arrive, but the row we'd had had been fairly seismic. She wouldn't believe that I wasn't having an affair with Celia. She thought my alibi was true, that I had spent all that time in Cornwall, with Celia, and hadn't told her, that I'd been two-timing her – which of course was what I had told the police in my sworn statement. And if I told her the truth, I couldn't trust her not to tell her colleagues in the police, which would land me and Paula in jail, and Eleanor without a mother.

I was going to lose the chance of finding my life partner because of a ridiculous twist of fate. . .

There were several people around that I'd seen before, but I didn't know their names. Celia had told me she wasn't coming, for Molly had always been her sworn enemy, and she was no hypocrite.

The Bad Hail Mary

I thought back to all those years ago when I'd run into the burning building and saved Molly's life. It was hard to reconcile the beautiful innocent girl I remembered with the scheming evil tyrant who had done her best to grab all her husband's family money and get rid of him. And then, after I had done my best to help her, when I had suddenly become an inconvenience, she had tried to kill me too and almost succeeded.

After the brief ceremony, I stood at the graveside in the tiny little churchyard in the tiny Cornish village. It was a coastal settlement with the church on a hill overlooking the sea, and the screech of seagulls no respecter of the dead. There was a gap in the stout fence. I moved closer, and saw that it wasn't exactly a sheer drop to the rocky beach below, but to get down to the beach would be quite a dangerous scramble.

One of the Rackhams directors, Ralph Winterhouse, had turned up. He was a thick-set man in a dark suit with receding red hair, and kept on turning and looking round at me during the service. He seemed to be alone, none of the other Rackhams directors had come.

The committal at the graveside was as grim as I might have expected, the wind whipping up the vicar's surplice as he hurriedly read the service from a book, a tight handful of mourners, a blend of black misery blotching the landscape on the high clifftop against the cloud-ridden ugly sky, everyone wishing they were somewhere else. I didn't know anyone who was there, and no one talked to me. The wizened old lady who couldn't stop crying appeared to be Molly's mother, Mrs Snuff, the mother Molly had told me had never approved of her, and whom she hadn't talked to in years.

Afterwards in the graveyard, bulky Ralph Winterhouse

hung around after everyone else had gone. He came closer, watching me from across the gravestones, and the way he was staring at me, I could see how much he hated me.

"So you're the fucking bastard who ruined my life," he called across. "Aren't you?"

"I'm sorry?" I answered him, pausing in my stroll towards the broken clifftop fence.

He came closer. "I'm fifty-five years old and I've been working for Rackhams for the last forty years, progressed up the ranks, successfully being promoted time and again, and I've been given shares in lieu of bonuses, so that now I'm one of the major shareholders."

"So?"

"The deal with Apperline Webb that would have taken us from a private company into part of a much bigger, truly multi-national public company would have made me a multi-millionaire, and I was going to retire and live in luxury for the rest of my life. If only this secret had come out after the merger, don't you realise that being part of a limited company would have limited our liabilities, so the directors wouldn't have been personally ruined as we're now going to be? I worked hard for what I've got, slaved away all the hours when I was young, in the hope that something like this might come along, and it had. I tell you, Mr Delaney, I wasn't handed everything on a plate, not like some of them. Even if we hadn't been in line for a juicy takeover, Rackhams would have kept me in lucrative employment until I retired and then paid me a massive pension. I was safe."

A flock of birds were swooping across the sky and they distracted me from the sour-faced man in front of me.

"And now, because of you, Rackhams are going to go bankrupt and I'll be losing my house, my savings and my

The Bad Hail Mary

job, and who's going to employ me now? I'll have to take my teenage children out of their public schools and tell my wife she can say goodbye to her social life on the parish council and charity circuits, because we'll no longer be supporting any charities. We'll have to move to a small house, and we'll probably be customers at the fucking food bank where she used to volunteer to help!"

"I'm sorry."

"Easy for you to say. Was it worth it, Mr Delaney? Okay, this scandal was diabolical, no one doubts it, but it happened eighty years ago! Literally no one alive can even remember it! But to you, getting some publicity, selling a story to newspapers makes it all worthwhile, doesn't it?" He grabbed me by the lapels, pushed me towards the gap in the fence and I felt as if he was going to push me. "Well I'd like to push you over the edge of this fucking cliff."

"I didn't want to get involved in any of this," I snapped, knocking his hands away, noticing the glint of tears of desperation in his eyes. "I was in the wrong place at the wrong time. Yes, sure, you're right, I stirred up this shitstorm, because I thought Molly was going down for a murder she didn't commit, and back then it was the only way I could see to save her. When the police dropped the charges I went to see her and told her the best thing was to drop the whole thing and forget about it, for the sake of you and everyone else. But do you know what she said? She said we had to do what was right. And, stupid bastard I was, I believed her. I believed, that for once she had some integrity. So I went to meet her, and found out it was a trap to lure me into a killing zone. That was when I knew that no one was going to believe I'd keep my mouth shut. But, honestly, I wanted to drop the whole thing there and then. But if I wanted to stay alive, and if Paula Swan and her child wanted to stay alive, we had to get the truth out into the public domain come hell or high water. I did it to save my own life and the life of a young woman and her child. Not for money, or fame or anything else. Truth is, I've got fuck-all out of this mess except scars, near-death experiences and a heap of fucking misery."

"I hope you die soon and rot in hell."

He stared at me for a long time, then turned and walked away.

When he'd gone I walked around the cemetery for a bit longer, still hoping against hope that Lucy would arrive, but I knew in my heart that she wouldn't.

And then, just when I'd decided to give up and go home, I saw a lone figure in the distance, walking towards me. Coming closer.

And yes.

It was her.

FIFTY-SIX

I felt as if I was rooted to the spot, standing over by the broken fence where I'd been looking out to sea, and wondering how far it was to fall from here. I watched as Lucy came closer, her face set hard as stone.

"You came," I said at last.

She nodded. Her face was soft, and the lack of make-up made her look soft and vulnerable, her eyes red-rimmed with black shadows under them, as if she'd been crying for a long time.

"I had to see you one last time," she said at last. "And to ask you why."

"Why?"

"Why did you ask me to marry you, when you were having an affair with Celia?"

"Lucy, look I—"

"*Just answer the fucking question!*" she yelled. "You wanted to marry me, until sexy Celia inherited the money and the fancy estate. I've had a lot of time to think about it. Even if the World Jewish Congress successfully gets lots of the Trefus family money, they'll probably still be plenty left, won't there? Or maybe if Celia gets probate in time, she can work out a way to extricate herself from Rackhams, and keep the lot? Is that what changed your mind about me?"

"I swear, Lucy, I never changed my mind about you."

"You swear, do you? But you had an affair with Celia, Sean. *You've just made a sworn statement to the police that you were fucking her!*"

"I had to."

"Had to what? *Had to fuck her? Someone forced you to fuck her?*"

"Shit, Lucy. I just don't know what to say."

"No, you don't, do you? You *really don't*." She stared at me with barely disguised loathing.

"I wish I could tell you the whole truth."

"Yeah?" Her eyes narrowed and she stared as if she could see into my soul. "We were going to get married, Sean, so you don't need to lie to me. Were you lying, Sean?"

I couldn't reply. Just looked down at the ground.

"Are you lying about Celia to give yourself an alibi? Did you kill Meredith Gilliard?"

I shook my head.

"So are you trying to protect someone?"

And in that moment, I longed to trust her and tell her the whole truth, and hang the consequences. But I couldn't.

Because it wasn't my truth to tell.

If I told her God's total truth, that my alibi was false, she would have to report my lie to the police. No alibi would mean that, again, I'd be a suspect for the murder, and if they put a lot of man-hours into investigating my movements on the day, who knows what mistakes I might have made, so that they might find out and end up by proving my guilt? If they found out what had actually happened: that I'd moved the body. I would either have to pretend I'd killed him too, and accept a lengthy jail sentence, or tell them the entire truth and incriminate Paula so that she was imprisoned, and her daughter would grow up in care. Not only that, I would also risk being charged with, at the very least, perverting the course of justice, or at worst, of murder as 'joint enterprise' along with Paula.

"Was it Paula?" she asked me. "Is it Paula Swan who you're protecting?"

I couldn't answer. Closed my eyes. Tried to shut out the world.

"If you are protecting Paula, just think about this, Sean. Dear sweet little Paula has killed before. Paula Swan was on trial for stabbing her boyfriend to death, ten years ago. She claimed she killed him in self-defence."

I looked up in surprise. It was the first I'd heard of it. I remembered that Martin Trefus had grumbled about her being 'strange' and 'unsuitable' as a partner for his son, but he'd never said she'd done anything like that.

"She was cleared in the end. But that was because she had a very good defence barrister. See, Sean, I think it was a miscarriage of justice, and that Paula Swan is a danger to society." Lucy went on, "She was passionately in love with Darius, and has made no secret of the fact that she hates the man she thinks was responsible for killing him, Meredith Gilliard. She's been pestering the police to reclassify Darius's death as murder not suicide, and she's told us repeatedly that she's convinced that Meredith Gilliard killed him."

"She's killed before?"

"Didn't you know? Oh, Sean, you idiot, you must have known! It was in the papers at the time."

I thought of how I had seen her execute Rupert Vigo. The cold-hearted way she'd electrocuted him. To my shame I had been delighted that she had solved all my problems for me, but I'd never stopped to think how odd it was that she'd been so quick to make a decision to kill.

"Think on this, Sean. Paula Swan is a killer, and sure

as eggs is eggs she'll bloody well kill again. If you know anything you have to say so. Even if it lands you in trouble."

"Shit."

Everything was out of my control. Even if I did betray my principles and tell Lucy everything, Paula had killed Rupert Vigo, the man who would undoubtedly have ruined my life. I owed her everything, just for that alone.

"She killed her former boyfriend, Sean, claiming it was self-defence. It was a difficult case, could have gone either way. I think Paula Swan is a hard, dangerous, callous murderer. She killed Duncan Allardine. No witnesses. It was all down to a fancy barrister with a cut-glass accent, a pretty face and a talent for showing off in court, portraying the shy little tattoo artist as a poor helpless victim, which the jury believed."

Lucy stared at me. "I'm betting you fell for her little-girl-lost story, Sean, and when you went to Meredith Gilliard's house and found that she'd killed him, you felt sorry for her, because she probably told you she had to do it, that he was attacking her and things got out of hand. I think you broke every law under the sun to help her get away with it." She moved closer, glaring at me. "Didn't you?"

"Look, Lucy." I moved towards her, touched her arm. She flinched away from me.

"Just tell me the truth, Sean. If you and Celia *aren't* having an affair, and your statement is bollocks, and you don't have an alibi, I don't care, see? I love you that much. I'll do my best to help you if you do the right thing – I can get you a good lawyer, we can go and see him right now, go to the police and make a fresh statement, and I'll stand by you. See, Paula has killed once, and now I think she's killed again. God knows how many people she might have attacked in the past, but if she gets away with this you know there'll be a next time, don't you? And it'll be your fault."

She walked away for a couple of steps. Kicked a stone along the ground.

I said nothing, wondering what to do.

She turned back to face me. "If you tell me now, everything that happened that night, what are you looking at? Conspiracy to pervert the course of justice? That's serious, but it's not necessarily a custodial sentence, especially if you confess to everything. If you did that I'd respect you, Sean, we could have a future together. . ."

"And if I don't?"

"You said you loved me. That you'd do anything for me. And there's a little part of me that wants to believe that you and Celia weren't having an affair, that you're not the shit everyone thinks you are. This is how you can prove that you mean what you say. I mean it, Sean, I'll stick by you, if you just tell me the truth." She grabbed me by the arms and kissed me. For a moment I was lost, prepared to do anything for her. "I mean it, Sean. *Tell me the truth!* Were you having an affair with Celia, and your alibi is genuine? Or were you lying to protect Paula? Which is it? For fuck's sake! *Tell me!*"

Then I realised the truth of my life. Every relationship seemed to end for one reason or another, and this was no exception.

There was nothing I could say.

She waited and stared at the ground. When she looked up, she shook her head sadly. "So, Sean, that's your decision, is it? Your statement is true, and you're telling me that you and Celia have been having an affair behind my back?"

I nodded, too choked to say anything.

"Can't you forgive me?"
"How fucking dare you?"

So saying, she slapped my face so hard that I fell backwards, tripping over a gravestone. I landed on my back, getting a distorted snail's eye view of Lucy crying as she walked away.

I got to my feet and walked across the graveyard, past all the uneven stones, stumbling over uneven earth, ending up slumping down on the ground and staring out to sea through the gap in the fence.

And sat there for a long time.

When I looked around finally, the man seemed to come out of nowhere.

A big man.

I saw him standing beside a rotted old tomb. *Thomas Angel, Fell Asleep on 18 June 1897,* one of those large grizzly affairs with a dirty black headstone and a set of tumbledown rusty railings surrounding an oblong of horrible raised earth. The man was busy wrenching one of the rusty metal rods from the railing, pulling it free, stabbing its pointed end at the sky.

I recognised him as he came closer to me. Ralph Winterhouse, the Rackhams director I had argued with earlier. Now he smelt of dead whisky, and his face was flushed with rage and too much booze. There was hatred in his eyes, and I could see that nothing less than killing me was going to satisfy him.

He swung the iron railing at my head, but I parried the blow with my left arm. Managed a right hook into his eye that sent him reeling.

But back he came, this time, the rod swinging two-handed, smacking me in the guts and winding me so much that I bent over and vomited into the grass. I was in mid-retch, when he grabbed me by the shoulders and swung my body round, aiming my head at a crumbling grey headstone. Just before my skull was smashed, I managed to reach out, so that my palms struck the craggy surface. I grabbed the edge of the stone, used it to wrench myself out of Winterhouse's grasp. The old headstone snapped near its base, and I held it in front of me, using it as a shield as he swung the rod at me again. I swung the heavy stone block at his head, careless of consequences, perfectly prepared to splatter his brains into pulp. Then I dropped the heavy stone, exhausted and panting. He came at me again, swaying, almost in a stupor. I got a right-hander into his face, splitting his lip, sending out a torrent of blood that burst out like juice squirting out of a squashed plum. I slammed a kick into his balls, then another whack to his head, hard on his ear, splitting my knuckles on his cold hard bone.

He came onwards, a heavy fist like a pile driver, smashing into my jaw, driving me down. I stumbled back, sailing out past the gap in the fence. Over the edge. Falling backwards down the cliff.

I remember tumbling down and down, scrambling for my life, trying to grip on to scree and shingle, ripping flesh on jagged rocks, rolling and falling. Until at last I hit the sand at the bottom.

That was the last thing I remembered.

But I do remember the dream that followed.

It was all those years ago, a time when I was young and free and my life was all before me. I was in the fire where Molly and I nearly died. The dream that I've had so many times now, but this time things were different. This time I was running through the flames holding Molly in my arms when we reached a wall of flame, and I was getting hotter and hotter. I looked at her in my arms and in front of my eyes, her features melted and swam, and her face became the ruined mess I remembered just after the gun had blown up in her hand in the car, and her mouth and nose and eyes were an unrecognisable mass of ghastly redness, blood and bone. I knew, in that moment, that it was the crossroads of my life. I had to go on, into the flames, with the dying Molly, and that going on meant that we'd both have to die. I felt wet hot blood splattering my face.

I knew I was going to die.

Mercifully that was the moment when I woke up.

I felt rain on my face, not blood. Tasted the water on my lips, sure enough tainted with the blood that was flowing freely from my nose. Saw a gunmetal grey sky, felt sand under my fingers. And a sharp pain in the back of my head. Cuts and scratches came alive with a crescendo of agony that rose and fell like the waves beside me. It was cold as ice, and I was suddenly shivering violently, felt my teeth chattering in the cold.

"Dear me, me poor old love, are you all right there? Shall I call an ambulance?"

I felt the friendly wet nose of a fox terrier dog, touching my cheek. His owner, an elderly man in a large cowboy hat, was leaning forward, looking down at me sympathetically. I had the strangest view of an upside-down face, clear blue eyes, a flowing white moustache and a nose as big as an elephant's trunk.

"I'm okay. Thanks." I managed to sit upright, leaning against the cliff face. "I fell from the churchyard up there, must have hit my head on the way down. I've been out cold. Is it morning?"

"Oh aye, nigh on seven."

"Jeez! I must have been here all night."

"You ain't from these parts, are you?"

"No, sure enough. I'm a visitor."

"And where do you call home, son?"

"Whitstable, in Kent, Near Canterbury."

"Ah Canterbury, I've heard of that place, I have right enough." The old man chewed the end of his long moustache while his dog lifted its leg and peed against the cliff. "I had some friends who moved to Canterbury, name of Carver, have you heard of them by any chance?"

"Canterbury is a mighty large town, sir, and I'm afraid I don't know anyone called Carver."

"My pal Ken Carver, you'd know him all right if you'd seed him. Great big chin and sticky-out ears, he has. Teeth like tombstones."

"I'll keep a lookout for Ken."

"Let me help you get up on your feet, m'dear. I live just down the road, we'll get you indoors and my wife can clean you up a bit, reckon you've got a whole wallop of cuts and scritch-scratches."

For a second I saw a woman in the distance walking towards us along the beach. She had Lucy's exact hair, the same coat, the same way of walking. I felt the surge of emotion, tears sprang to my eyes, I suddenly felt an aching desperate surge of yearning. . .

And then, as if she'd read my mind, the woman turned and smiled at me.

But of course.

It wasn't Lucy.

"Friend of yours, that young lass?" inquired my new friend, watching my stricken expression and the tears that had started and wouldn't stop.

"I thought she was." Disappointment stripped me bare of pretence, of anything, stabbed me through like a knife and left me raw and dead. I gulped and swallowed, fought for control. "But I was mistaken."

"Your girlfriend?"

"Once upon a time."

The dog licked my face. I tickled his ears.

And in that moment I knew that I would never see Lucy again.

END

Printed in Great Britain
by Amazon